Margaret Dickinson

Pauper's Gold

PAN BOOKS

First published 2006 by Macmillan

This edition published 2014 by Pan Books
an imprint of Pan Macmillan
20 New Wharf Road, London N1 9RR
Associated companies throughout the world
www.panmacmillan.com

ISBN 978-1-4472-4537-7

3 5 7 9 8 6 4

A CIP catalogue record for this book is available from the British Library.

Typeset by SetSystems Ltd, Cambridge CB22 3GN
Printed and bound by CPI Group (UK) Ltd, Croydon, CR0 4YY

Visit www.panmacmillan.com to read more about all our books
and to buy them. You will also find features, author interviews and
news of any author events, and you can sign up for e-newsletters
so that you're always first to hear about our new releases.

For David and Una Dickinson,
my brother and sister-in-law

Acknowledgements

I am very grateful to David and Mavis Holmes for their kind permission for me to use Cressbrook Mill in Derbyshire as the inspiration for part of this story. The former cotton mill has now been beautifully transformed by them into apartments – a far cry from the conditions in which spinners, weavers and apprentices once worked.

Because I never use real people as the basis for the characters in my novels, I always change the names of small towns and villages deliberately. But with larger towns and cities like Macclesfield, a town with a fascinating social history, I like to keep its rightful name. Although I mention the workhouse there, I must stress that the characters and story are entirely fictitious and have no relation whatsoever to any real inmates or staff. Similarly, I have named actual streets and buildings, but have peopled them with my own imaginary characters.

My grateful thanks to Professor Chris Wrigley of the School of History at Nottingham University, who recommended that I should read *The Hungry Mills* by Norman Longmate (Maurice Temple Smith, 1978). This story of the Lancashire cotton famine, 1861–5, was indeed inspirational. I also consulted several other books and papers in my research, the most noteworthy of which were *A History of Macclesfield* edited by C. Stella Davies (E. J. Morten, 1976) and *Life & Labour in Victorian Macclesfield* by George Longden (Neil Richardson, 1986).

Very special thanks to members of my family Helen and

Acknowledgements

Mike Lawton, Carole and Paul Cairns and David and Una Dickinson, who gave generously of their time and knowledge, supplied books, maps and photos, and took me on tours of Macclesfield. Thank you too to the staff of Macclesfield Library, the Silk Industry Museum and West Park Museum for their interest, practical guidance and help. And not forgetting other members of my family and friends who have also read and commented on the script: Robena and Fred Hill, Pauline Griggs and Linda and Terry Allaway. The help and encouragement of all of you means more to me than you can ever know.

One

'We'll get rid of her. That girl's been nothing but trouble since she came in here.' Cedric Goodbody belied his name for there was nothing 'good' about the man. He was thin and wiry with a rat-like face. His grey eyes, sharp and piercing, missed nothing. His frown deepened. 'If I'd known what I know now, I'd never have admitted her. Her or her mother. The woman had the gall to refuse to pick oakum, on the grounds that she's a silk worker and the rough work might injure her hands.'

He drummed his fingers impatiently on the desk in front of him. The room around him was cluttered with files and ledgers. Papers were strewn over the surface of his desk and piled in untidy heaps on the floor. He was sitting in the only chair in the room. Any visitor – even his wife, Matilda – was obliged to stand. Hands folded in front of her, she was facing him now across his desk. She was no better than her husband. Thin and gaunt with a waspish tongue, she took a malicious delight in the misfortunes of others. Together – as master and matron – they ran the Macclesfield work-house just within the rules laid down by the Board of Guardians, and outside them if they were sure they would not be found out.

1

'The girl's got spirit,' Matilda admitted grudgingly. 'I'll give her that. Nothing seems to depress her for long.'

'Can't you try punishing her? I'm sure you can find a reason,' Cedric growled. 'She's too pretty for her own good. That long, blonde hair and those bright blue eyes —'

'My word, Cedric, I've never known you to be so observant.' Matilda pursed her mouth.

Cedric ignored her sarcasm. 'But it's her singing all the time that gets on my nerves. I can't abide cheerful inmates. In all my years running workhouses, I've never known an inmate to *sing*!'

Matilda shrugged. 'There's no stopping her even when she's locked in the punishment room on bread and water.'

Cedric smiled cruelly. 'Well, I've an idea that'll put a stop to it. Critchlow's sent word he wants four more paupers. She can be one of them.'

Matilda raised her eyebrows. 'Is he *still* managing to keep that system going? I thought all the cotton mills'd given up having pauper apprentices.'

'Most of them have. With all the new laws about the employment of children, it was becoming uneconomic. But not for the Critchlows. Tucked away in that Derbyshire dale, they don't get many visits from the authorities. They just ignore any law that doesn't suit them. I'm just thankful they have carried it on. They've always been fair in their dealings with me.' He cast her a shrewd glance. He'd never actually told his wife about the money he received from the Critchlows in exchange for a steady supply of strong, healthy orphans to work long hours in their cotton mill. But he was sure she had guessed.

2

It seemed she had, for, 'You want to mind the Board don't find out,' was her tart reply.

'They won't as long as you don't tell 'em.' His eyes narrowed. 'There's only you 'n' me know about it. So watch that tongue of yours, woman.'

'But I thought Nathaniel Critchlow—'

'Oh, Nathaniel!' Cedric was scathing. 'I don't deal with him any more. He's getting past it. Going soft in his old age. No, it's Edmund – his son – I need to keep in with.'

'Well, you'll be sending him a barrel of trouble with that girl. Besides, I don't reckon the mother'll let you send young Hannah all the way into Derbyshire.' Matilda smirked. 'Whatever fine tales you tell her about how wonderfully her daughter will be looked after and taught a trade that'll be the making of her.'

'The mother'll have nothing to do with it. If I say the girl goes . . .' Cedric banged his clenched fist on the desk and papers fluttered to the floor, 'then she goes. She's young and strong. Just the sort Critchlow wants.' He ran his tongue around his thin lips, greedily anticipating another generous payment.

'Maybe,' Matilda murmured. 'But she's not biddable. She's a mite too much to say for herself.'

'Edmund Critchlow's got his methods of taming the wilful ones. He's got a punishment room just like us.'

Matilda sniffed. 'Well then, young Hannah will likely be spending most of her time there.'

The subject of their conversation was at that moment working in the laundry. Little light penetrated the filthy windows, and the huge room was filled with steam and the sharp smell of disinfectant. Three other girls and two older women besides Hannah toiled over the wash tubs. Their hands were wrinkled from the hot water, their faces red and their clothes drenched with sweat. Hannah was hanging dripping clothes onto the slats of a wooden rack, which she then hoisted to the ceiling for the clothes to dry. Above the noise of the sloshing water, Hannah's voice trilled pure and clear. 'How sweet the name of Jesus sounds . . .'

'Ah, bless 'er,' one of the women at the tubs murmured. 'That was me mother's favourite. Eh, but it brings back the memories.'

Rebecca, Hannah's mother, looked up worriedly. 'I'm sorry if it upsets you. I'll tell her to stop—'

'Don't you dare. You let your little girl sing,' Alice answered. 'I might shed a tear or two, but me memories're happy ones. I'll tell you summat, Rebecca. She brightens our days with her sunny smile and her merry singing. Come on,' she raised her voice. 'Let's all sing. Let's show 'em . . .' And in a raucous, tuneless voice she joined in the words of the hymn.

Rebecca shook her head in wonderment and smiled softly, marvelling at the way her twelve-year-old daughter could spread even the smallest spark of joy in this cheerless place. There were few occasions in the workhouse when the inmates felt like smiling – some had almost forgotten how. But since Rebecca and her daughter had arrived, there'd been more smiles and fond shaking of heads than ever before, as they heard Hannah's piping voice echoing through the vast building. She led the other youngsters in games in the women's exercise yard and, for a few minutes each day, she made them forget the drudgery and misery of their lives. With her blue eyes full of mischief and daring, the young girl had become the darling of all the inmates. For, though the men and boys were strictly segregated from the women and girls, they could still hear her over the wall from their yard, could hear the sound of playful laughter.

The women in the laundry room were startled into silence by a loud banging and only Hannah was left singing at the top of her voice.

'That's enough, girl,' the matron snapped, grasping Hannah's arm in a painful grip. 'The master wants to see you.'

'Why?' Hannah ceased her singing and dropped the rough blanket she was washing back into the tub. It splashed soapy suds onto the matron's pristine apron. Matilda shook the girl roughly. 'Now look what you've done. My word, I'll be glad to see the back of you.'

Hannah's eyes shone. 'We're leaving? Mam,' she called, 'we're getting out. We—'

'Not your mother, just you.'

Hannah's eyes widened. 'Oh no, I'm not going without me mam.'

'You'll do as you're told.'

Drying her hands on a piece of rough cloth, Rebecca came towards them. 'What is it, Matron?' she asked in her soft, gentle voice.

Before Matilda could reply, Hannah said, 'She says the master wants to see me. I'm leaving. Just me, not you. But I'm not going without you, Mam, I—'

The matron gave an exasperated sigh. 'You'd better both come along to his office. He can deal with the pair of you.'

Moments later, mother and daughter stood before the master's desk, but it was the young girl who fired the questions. 'Has someone come for us? Is it me Uncle Bill?'

Cedric smiled cynically. 'And which uncle might

5

that be?' He leered at Rebecca, standing quietly beside her daughter. 'I expect you had a lot of them, didn't you?'

The older woman blushed and hung her head, but Hannah's clear, innocent gaze darted between them. 'No,' she retorted. 'I've only one uncle. He's not me real uncle—'

'I bet he isn't,' Cedric muttered.

'He lived next door to us. He and me Auntie Bessie—'

'Hush, Hannah dear,' Rebecca said softly, touching the girl's arm. 'Let the master tell us.'

Hannah pressed her lips together, but her blue eyes still sparkled with indignation.

Cedric shuffled some papers in front of him. 'I've found the girl a position working in a cotton mill in Derbyshire. A lot of the youngsters go from here.' He stared hard at Rebecca, daring her to argue. 'She'll be well looked after, I assure you.'

Hannah spoke up again. 'What about me mam? Is she coming an' all?'

'No, there's no place for an older woman. At least, not ones with no experience.' He glanced at Rebecca again. 'You haven't worked in a mill before, have you?'

'Only in a silk mill here.'

'That'd be near enough, wouldn't it?' Hannah put in before the master could answer.

Cedric glowered. 'No, it wouldn't. Not the same thing at all.'

She opened her mouth to retort but Cedric held up his hand. 'I don't want to hear another word from you, girl. And if you take my advice, you'll learn to curb that runaway tongue of yours. It'll get you into a lot of trouble where you're going, if you're not careful.'

For once, Rebecca dared to question the master. 'I thought you said she'd be well treated?'

'She will – if she behaves herself. Mr Critchlow, the owner of the mill, is a good master, but he expects loyalty and obedience from *all* his workers.'

Rebecca bit her lip. 'I don't want her to go. She's too young to go all that way.'

'You have no say in the matter.' Cedric's lip curled. 'If you and your – er – offspring . . .' he laid insulting emphasis on the word, implying so much more, 'allow yourselves to become a burden on the parish, you have to pay the price. You're no longer free to decide your own future. You'll do what the Board of Guardians tells you. And they always take my recommendations.'

Again, Rebecca hung her head.

Cedric turned to Hannah. 'You're to be ready to leave tomorrow morning. You'll be going on the carrier's cart as far as Buxton and then he'll arrange for you and the others to be taken on to Wyedale Mill.'

It was an arrangement that had worked well for Cedric in the past. For a few coins the carrier would take the orphans part of the way and then pay a local carter to take them the few extra miles.

'Others?' Hannah piped up again. 'Who else is going?'

Cedric stood up, dismissing them curtly. 'You'll see in the morning. Just you mind you're ready and waiting.'

7

Two

It irritated Cedric Goodbody that he knew little more about Rebecca Francis and her daughter than he had on the day they'd knocked on the door of the workhouse and begged admittance. Rebecca was a quiet, reserved young woman, well liked by the other inmates and staff yet not forthcoming about her life before that day.

It was shame that stilled Rebecca's tongue. The humiliation of entering the workhouse lay heavily on her. Once, she too had laughed and sung – just like her lively, innocent daughter did now – but then she'd made the mistake of falling in love and everything had changed.

Rebecca had been born in a street of garret houses, three storeys high, occupied by weavers. Her father, Matthew, had his workroom in the top storey, its long window giving him light to carry on the trade of his father before him. Her mother, Grace, had worked in a silk mill. Though the family – like every other family around them – had suffered the ups and downs of the silk trade, Rebecca's young life had been a happy one. When her parents had married they'd lived with Matthew's widowed mother, and when Rebecca was born one year later Grandma Francis had looked after the infant whilst Grace returned to work in the mill.

At ten years old, Rebecca went to work eight hours a day in the mill.

'Hello there, young 'un,' James Gregory, the man who was the supervisor over the workforce of women and children, had greeted her. 'Going to be as good a worker as your mother, are yer?'

Rebecca, with her shy, brown eyes, her soft dark hair hidden beneath her bonnet, had nodded, gazing up at him in awe. James had bent down and touched her cheek. 'Don't be afraid of me, young 'un.' Gently he'd traced his finger round the outline of her face. 'You're far too pretty to be afraid of anyone.'

From that moment, Rebecca had been James Gregory's willing slave. She idolized him. Through the years as she grew, the other women teased her. 'Mr Gregory's little sweetheart, ain'tcha? But just remember, girl, he's got a wife at home and there's a little 'un on the way.'

By the time Rebecca was fifteen she had the shape and demeanour of a woman. Working alongside adults all day long – women who talked and laughed and joked, and who didn't trouble to curb their raucous tongues before the youngsters in their midst – Rebecca could not be ignorant of the facts of life. She knew full well that it was wrong to meet James Gregory in secret, knew it was dangerous to give herself to him.

But Rebecca was hopelessly, helplessly in love with James's blond, curling hair and merry blue eyes. He was tall and broad shouldered, with slim hips, and he carried himself proudly as if he truly believed he was destined for better things. Rebecca was utterly, selflessly loyal to him and when, inevitably, she found herself carrying his child, she refused to name him as the father. Gossip was rife through the mill, but Rebecca stubbornly refused to blame anyone but herself. When her daughter, Hannah, screamed her arrival into the cramped bedroom of the terraced house, there was no loving father present to welcome her, only a reluctant grandmother. Even the grandfather had disappeared to the nearest pub to be with his cronies and to try to blot out all thought of his daughter's shame. Tactfully, his friends asked no questions. What was going on in Matthew's home at that moment was women's business.

Overcrowded and at times a hotbed of gossip though the houses in their street might be, there was nevertheless a deep sense of neighbourliness, of protecting their own. As news of her arrival spread quickly, there was soon a constant stream of visitors at the door. Some bore gifts, others came just to see the child and the young mother, yet more with an excuse to wet the baby's head.

'She's a bonny 'un,' was the unanimous verdict. But, tactfully, they made no comment on the child's wispy blonde hair and bright blue eyes. Only amongst themselves, they nodded their heads and said, 'No mistaking whose kid she is.'

Kept in ignorance, Hannah's early life was happy. She lived in the close-knit community, was protected by it, too young to remember when her grandfather, Matthew, died only three years after her birth. Rebecca's wage now supported them, with a little help from the work Grace was able to do at home. Their landlord rented out Matthew's garret workroom to another weaver. For a while, Grace and Rebecca were terrified they would be turned out of their home. Thankfully, the weaver lived elsewhere and was happy to walk the couple of streets to his new workroom.

Of Hannah's father not a word was ever spoken.

Not until she was old enough to play in the street with the other children did she begin to understand the circumstances of her birth. Slowly, it dawned on her why her surname was the same as her mother's and her grandmother's. Cruel names were hurled at her and sometimes she found herself excluded from the other children's games. Hannah would toss her bright curls and smile at those taunting her. And beneath her breath she would sing to comfort herself. Little by little, she won them over and when the day came that her mother and grandmother insisted she should attend school, it was now the children from her own street who defended her against curious strangers.

The first really harsh blow to disturb her childhood came when Hannah was eight years old. Her grandmother, Grace, was taken ill with distressing sickness and diarrhoea and terrible leg cramps. Rebecca stayed at home from work to nurse her mother but after only three days Grace died. After a simple funeral attended by their neighbours, Rebecca and Hannah returned to the home that now seemed empty and soulless without the old lady who had been its centre.

'I'll have to go back to work,' Rebecca said in her soft voice. 'I'll see if Auntie Bessie next door will take care of you.'

'I can take care of meself, Mam,' Hannah had declared stoutly, but Rebecca had shaken her head. 'No, no, I won't have you left alone. Bessie won't mind.' Rebecca had smiled gently. 'She'll never notice another one amongst her brood.'

So Hannah had become a daily visitor to the overcrowded house next door where Bill and Bessie Morgan, their three sons and two daughters lived. The Morgan children were all older than Hannah but they took the lonely child in and treated her as if she were another sister. Peggy, the youngest at twelve, was the closest in age, but even she was already working at the mill. Bill and two of his sons worked in the top floor garret of the house and Bessie had her hands full caring for them all.

''Course she can come to us. She can 'elp me with me washing,' Bessie had said at once when Rebecca tentatively broached the subject. It was from Bessie Morgan, who sang all day long in her loud, tuneless voice, that Hannah, amongst the soap suds and steam of the back yard wash house, was to learn the words of all the hymns.

'We'll mind her,' Bessie had promised. 'You get back to your work, Rebecca, while you've still got a job to go to.' She had cast a knowing look at Rebecca, and the younger woman had felt the flush of embarrassment creep up her neck.

In the uncertain silk industry, Rebecca had kept her place at the mill even through hard times when many had been laid off. She was well aware it was whispered that it was only because she was James Gregory's mistress that she had kept her job. And, in a way, Rebecca had to admit that it was true. Whilst he'd never openly admitted to being the father of her child – and Rebecca maintained her steadfast silence – James Gregory had always made sure she'd a job at the mill. And though she was no longer his mistress – hadn't been from the day he'd learned she was pregnant – he still favoured her, much to the irritation of the other workers. If she was feeling tired or unwell, he'd find her easier work. He allowed her time off – with no questions asked – if Hannah was ill. The other women grumbled, but there was little they could do about it other than to ostracize Rebecca. It was a lonely time for the young woman but she stuck it out. She'd no choice – hers was the only income her family had.

Hannah's time with the Morgan family was short lived. Life swiftly dealt Rebecca another harsh blow. In less than a year, James Gregory had left the mill. She had heard the news from the gossip that rippled amongst the mill workers.

''Ave you 'eard, 'ee's got himself another fancy piece. Daughter of a mill owner, no less. And her father's made him manager of one of his mills.'

'What about his wife and family? Gregory's married, ain't he?'

'Oh, didn't you know? His wife and kiddie died with the cholera last year. So he's fancy-free.'

'Is 'ee, by God! So, he's not marrying that girl – what's 'er name?'

'Rebecca Francis. Oh no. 'Ee's set his sights higher than 'er. And let me tell you something else. Once 'ee's gone from here, that little madam 'ad better watch out.'

And soon after James's departure, Rebecca was told that her 'services were no longer required at the mill'.

For a few months, she managed to pay the rent, though she grew thinner from worry and tramping the streets in search of work. By the January of 1851 there was no food in the house, no fuel to keep them warm, their winter clothes had been pawned, and she was hiding when the rent man called. Two months later, Rebecca and her young daughter were evicted from their home.

The workhouse was the only place they could go.

Three

'Now, have you got everything? How generous Mr Goodbody has been.' Rebecca fingered the clothes lying spread out on Hannah's bed. The garments – two shifts, two frocks, two aprons and two pairs of stockings – were not new, but Rebecca had washed and lovingly ironed and mended them. It was the final motherly act she was to be allowed to do for her daughter. 'And you must take care of this money. Two whole guineas,' Rebecca told her, handing her a cloth purse. 'Tie it round your neck for the journey, but you'll have to give it to . . . to whoever's in charge of you . . .' Her voice threatened to break, but she smiled bravely and added, 'Mind you're a good girl, won't you? Do as you're told and—'

Hannah's blue eyes brimmed with tears. She flung her arms around her mother's slim waist and hugged her tightly. 'I don't want to go. Don't let them send me away. I – I might never see you again.'

Though Rebecca embraced her fiercely in return and her voice trembled, she tried valiantly to make the words cheerful and hopeful. 'Of course you'll see me again. Once you've got settled in, you ask around. There might be a job for me there. I'm sure my experience in the silk mill will count for something, whatever Mr Goodbody says. You just

14

mind you tell them about me. Don't forget, now will you?'

'Oh no, Mam. 'Course I won't.'

The cart pulled to a halt at the top of a steep hill.

'Right, out you get.' The old driver dropped the reins and climbed stiffly down from his seat. He walked to the back of the cart. 'Come on,' he said roughly. 'I ain't got all night.'

Three of the four children riding in the back scrambled out. Only Hannah made no move to obey him. 'You're not leaving us here. There's no sign of the mill and you were paid to take us all the way.'

The old man coughed juicily and wiped the back of his hand across his mouth. 'Well, this is as far as I'm going, missy. I'm on me way back to Buxton now. You do as you please. This is as far as I can take you. My old girl wouldn't make it back up this 'ere hill if I teks 'er down. You'll have to walk rest of the way. It's down there.' He pointed to the road, disappearing steeply down into the dale below them. 'Just follow that road. Mill's at far end. You can't miss it.'

As Hannah climbed down, she looked about her and, suddenly, she smiled. The sun was setting behind the hills, casting a golden glow over the slopes and glinting on the trees. Even the rough road on which they were standing was bathed in golden light.

'It's a pretty place,' Hannah murmured.

The man climbed back onto the front of his cart and picked up the reins. 'Aye, missy, take a good look at the sunshine. Pauper's gold, they call it. I reckon that's the only gold you'll ever see. And you won't be seeing much of that either – not in Critchlow's dismal

15

mill, you won't.' He laughed loudly at his own joke and flapped the reins. The horse, as if knowing it was homeward bound, moved forward with an eager jerk. Within moments the cart was rattling back the way it had come, leaving the four youngsters standing forlornly in the road. Far below them a river wound its way through the deep valley between hills that seem to fold in on each other. They could see houses dotted here and there, and sheep in a line following a track along the hillside, making for home. But there was no sign of a building large enough to be a mill.

'Should we ask the way?' Luke jerked his thumb over his shoulder towards the Wyedale Arms behind them. Hannah glanced at it, but the door was shut and there seemed no sign of life. She was the eldest of the four – and the boldest – and the others were looking to her to take the lead. She felt a tiny, cold hand creep into hers and looked down into the small, white face of the youngest. Jane was only ten and small for her age. She had been born to a young widow in the workhouse who had died at her birth. She was truly an orphan. She looked exhausted by the day's travelling, her eyes huge in her pale, gaunt face. Tears were close. 'Are we lost?'

Hannah gave the child's hand a comforting squeeze. 'No, 'course we're not.' She glanced round at the two boys – twin brothers, Luke and Daniel Hammond – trying to instil confidence into her voice. 'Come on, you lot. It's down this hill, the man said. We'd best get going if we're to find it before dark.'

With more purpose in her step than she was feeling inside, and still holding Jane's hand, Hannah strode down the hill, the other two falling in behind them.

'Lead us, heavenly Father, lead us . . .' she began to sing.

She'd sung the hymn through once and was about to start again, when Luke said, 'How much further is it?'

'Dunno,' Hannah said cheerfully. 'Maybe we'll see it round the next bend.'

They walked on beneath the canopy of trees overhanging the lane as the shadows lengthened and the sun dipped out of sight. Dusk settled into the dale.

'I'm tired and me leg hurts,' Jane murmured.

'I'm hungry,' Daniel moaned.

Luke and Daniel had been left at the workhouse door five years earlier when their mother had died and their father couldn't cope with the lively six-year-olds. They hadn't seen him from that day to this and had given up hope of him ever coming back for them. Now, coming up to twelve years old, they were excited at the prospect of a real job. They were small and thin like most of the children in the workhouse, but they were fit and healthy with the same mop of unruly light brown hair, hazel eyes and cheeky grins. Their teeth were surprisingly good, white and even. Just the sort of boys that Mr Critchlow was looking for, Cedric Goodbody had assured them.

But now, they too were tired, their excitement waning.

'It can't be much further,' Hannah said, almost dragging the weary little girl alongside her.

The shape of a house loomed up on the left-hand side of the road.

'Is that it?' Jane pointed. 'Is that the mill?'

Hannah eyed it doubtfully. 'I don't think so. It's not

17

big enough.' She paused and added, 'Is it?' She wasn't exactly sure just how big a cotton mill was, but she imagined it must be at least the size of the silk mill where her mother had worked.

'That's a farm,' Luke said scathingly and his twin nodded. 'It smells like one.'

Hannah glanced at them. She'd only known town streets with no trees or fields. The only animals she'd seen had been scrawny dogs and cats and most of them had been strays. So, she didn't argue, aware that the boys had known six years of life before coming into the workhouse. Who was she to say that they hadn't seen a farm?

As if answering her unspoken question, Luke said, 'Our dad worked on the land, but he moved about from job to job.'

Daniel nodded. 'Every Lady Day, we'd be packing up and moving to a new farm.'

She saw the two boys glance at each other and knew they were remembering happier times.

'Come on, then. Best walk a bit further,' Hannah said briskly, trying to inject some encouragement into her tone. But they'd gone only a few yards further when they came to a crossroads. The lane to the left led to the farm, but they'd no idea which of the other two roads they should take.

'Which way now?' Luke asked

'I don't know.' Perplexed, Hannah glanced this way and that.

'Let's ask at the farm,' Luke suggested. 'They'll know where the mill is.'

Hannah pulled a face, reluctant to knock on a stranger's door, unsure of the welcome that four work-house brats would receive. 'All right then,' she agreed

18

diffidently, aware of how tired they all were. They were hungry and thirsty too. She turned and frowned at the two boys behind her. 'But just you two mind you behave yourselves.'

They grinned up at her with identical saucy expressions. 'Yes, miss,' they chorused.

The four of them trooped through the gate, the boys closing it carefully behind them. 'You always have to shut gates on a farm,' Luke said.

'Oh – yes – right,' Hannah nodded. She wasn't sure why it was necessary. There was no one about in the yard but, again, she didn't argue.

As they neared the back door, there was a scuffle, and a black and white collie appeared out of a kennel set to one side of the back door and began to bark.

Jane gave a terrified scream and clutched at Hannah's skirt, hiding behind her. Even the two boys took a couple of steps backwards. Hannah too jumped, but she pulled in a deep breath and held out her hand. 'Here, boy. Good dog. Nice dog.'

'He might not be as nice as you think,' Luke muttered. 'He's a sheepdog. A working dog.'

'And a guard dog,' Daniel added.

But the animal ceased its barking, whined, wagged its tail and licked Hannah's outstretched hand.

'Well, would you look at that!' Luke grinned at her. 'Charm the birds off the trees, you could.'

In the workhouse, males, females, girls and boys had been strictly separated, but on the few occasions they had glimpsed one another, Hannah and Luke had liked what they'd seen. And now here they were, having travelled together all day, standing outside the back door of a farmhouse seeking help.

'Go on then,' Luke encouraged. 'Get on with it.'

19

Hannah glanced at the other three as she raised her hand to knock, seeing a mixture of trepidation and hope on their weary, pinched faces. It was exactly how she felt as she turned to face whoever should open the door.

They heard heavy footsteps and then the door was pulled open. A tall, well-built, red-faced woman wearing a white bib apron stood looking down at them.

'Come away in.' She smiled and held the door wider open.

It seemed they were expected, yet Hannah still hesitated. 'Is this the mill?'

'Lord bless you, no. This is Rushwater Farm. The mill's further on . . .' She jerked her thumb over her shoulder. 'Along this road.' Her smile broadened so that her round cheeks almost made her eyes close. 'I guessed that's where you're heading. I'm used to youngsters coming to my door. Eh, dear me—' She shook her head and her smile faded. 'If I'd a pound for every child who's knocked at my door to be fed, I'd be a wealthy woman.'

'Oh, we . . . we only wanted to ask the way. We weren't sure, you see, which road—' Hannah began.

'Come along in, all of you,' the woman stood back and beckoned. A mouth-watering smell wafted from her kitchen and the two boys, forgetting their promise to Hannah, pushed forward.

Drawn by her own hunger and encouraged by the woman's kindly, beaming face, Hannah stepped over the threshold. Jane, still clutching Hannah's hand, followed.

'Sit down, sit down. You've had a long journey, I'll be bound, sitting in Bert Oldfield's draughty cart.'

The four children gaped at her. 'How . . . how did

you know ... ?' Hannah began, but the woman chuckled. 'You're from Macclesfield workhouse, aren't you? You've come on the carrier's cart to Buxton and then Bert's brought you to the top of the hill. But the wily old bird won't bring you all the way down in case his scrawny horse can't get back up again. Am I right?'

The children glanced at each other and then smiled.

'How d'you know all that?' Luke asked.

'Because it happens every year, that's why. When Mr Critchlow wants more children to work in his mill, he sends word to the master of the workhouse and along you all come. Bin happening for years.'

'Why ... why does he need so many?' Hannah asked. A sudden shiver ran through her. She wasn't sure she should have asked the question. She might not like the answer.

'Ah well, now,' the woman turned away, busying herself over a huge pan of stew sitting on the hob of the kitchen range, 'I wouldn't know about that.'

Hannah stared at her stooping back. She had the feeling that the woman knew only too well, but didn't want to tell them. She sighed, but as a plate of stew and dumplings was set before her, she forgot about her worries and concentrated on filling her empty belly.

The farmer's wife sat down opposite. She let them eat their fill before she asked, 'Now, tell me your names. Mine's Mrs Grundy.'

'This is Jane Pickering and these two are twins.'

Mrs Grundy nodded. 'Aye, I can see that. Like as two peas in a pod, aren't you?'

'Luke and Daniel Hammond and I'm Hannah. Hannah Francis.'

The woman smiled at them and nodded, 'I'm pleased

21

to meet you all. And don't forget, if you want to visit me any time – any time at all – there'll always be a welcome for you at Rushwater Farm. You'll not meet my husband today. He's busy with the evening milking now, but he'll be pleased to see you an' all. He loves children too.'

Hannah rose from her chair. 'You've been very kind, Mrs Grundy,' she said politely, 'and we'd love to stay longer, but perhaps we'd best be going. Could you please tell us which road we should take to the mill?'

''Course I can,' the woman said, heaving herself up from her chair and leading them to the back door. She walked out of the yard to the road and then pointed. 'Take the road on the left here and just keep on. You'll soon see it. Mind you,' she went on, 'you'd be best to go straight to the apprentice house. Go up the steep slope at the side of the mill to the row of houses directly behind it. It's the third building along. A white house. Ask for Mr or Mrs Bramwell. They're the superintendents. Now, off you go. They'll be expecting you and it'll be dark soon.'

She stood watching the children walk along the lane until they were out of sight.

'God be with you, my dears,' she murmured, thankful that the youngsters couldn't see the tears in her eyes.

22

Four

'Is . . . is that it? Is that the mill?' Luke's voice was suddenly scared. 'It's awfully big, isn't it?'

The four children stood in the pillared gateway and looked at the place where they'd come to live and work. There were three huge buildings. The biggest was rectangular and set with its back against a steep hill, its rows of numerous small-paned windows facing down the dale. Set at right angles to that was another oblong shape, and the third, a square building, stood at the end of the second one.

'Look at those houses built on the hill behind it,' Luke murmured. 'You'd think they'd fall off, wouldn't you?'

'I can hear water,' Daniel murmured.

Luke turned suddenly and darted across the road. 'There's a big pond here and a stream that goes under the road.' He re-crossed the lane. 'And it comes out here. Then it goes in front of the mill.' He pointed to the bubbling brook. 'And joins the river over there. On the far side of the mill. See?'

They were all silent, staring about them. Jane, white-faced, cowered behind Hannah.

'Come on,' Hannah said briskly at last. 'We'd better go and find this Mrs Bramwell.' She smiled down at the younger girl and gave her cold hand a comforting squeeze. Jane dragged her feet, and glanced apprehensively over her shoulder. 'I don't like it,' she whispered. 'It's so big. I want to go home. I want to go back to the workhouse.'

'We can't,' Hannah said. 'There's no one to take us back. Besides, we've been sent here. At least let's give it a try. It might be better than the workhouse.'

'Anything's got to be better—' Luke began.

'Than the workhouse,' Daniel finished.

They climbed the steep hill to the first row of houses perched just above the mill.

'This end one looks like a school,' Luke said excitedly. He grasped hold of the high window ledge and hauled himself up to peer in the window. 'There's boys and girls sitting at desks.'

'At this time of night?' Hannah stood on tiptoe, trying to see in, but she was too low down, and she had no intention of scrambling up the side of the rough wall and tearing her clean dress.

'It'll be after they've worked at the mill,' Luke said. 'There's a boy asleep at his desk. Oh!'

Suddenly, he let himself drop to the ground.

'What? What is it?'

Luke was laughing. 'The master saw him sleeping and cracked his cane on the desk. The lad didn't half jump. He thought he'd been shot.'

'Do you think we'll go to school?' Jane asked quietly.

'I don't know,' Hannah said. 'Maybe for a few hours a week.' She sighed. 'But what I do know is – we've been sent here to work.'

They moved on, dragging their feet now that they had seen the other children. Suddenly, however strict school life might be under a cane-wielding teacher, they yearned to join those children instead of entering a new and frightening world. At least a classroom – even a different classroom with strange children – was a familiar world to them. There had been a school-room at the workhouse with a master for the boys and a school-marm for the girls. Of the four of them, only Jane couldn't read or write. She'd been a sickly child, and her schooling, even in the workhouse, had been spasmodic.

They knocked on the door of the white house, next door but one to the school, and waited. A girl, not much older than they were, opened it.

'Come in, the missis is waiting for you.'

They trooped after her, through the large kitchen and a hallway, and were shown into a small, stuffy room where a woman was sitting at a desk going through some papers.

The girl bobbed a curtsy. 'The new ones have arrived, Mrs Bramwell.'

'Thank you, Mary.'

The girl left the room, closing the door quietly behind her, leaving the four new arrivals standing nervously just inside the door. The woman didn't even look up but continued to write notes at the edge of one of the sheets of paper. They waited for what seemed an age, until Jane tugged at Hannah's hand and whispered urgently, 'I need the privy, Hannah. I need it now.'

'Hush,' Hannah whispered. 'You'll have to wait.'

'I can't.' Jane's voice rose in a wail. 'I'll do it. Oh – oh, I am . . .'

The woman looked up. 'Take her out this minute. It's out the back.'

Hannah pulled open the door, dragging Jane with her. She rushed back the way they had come, startling the young girl, Mary, as they hurried through the kitchen. Hannah paused briefly. 'Where is it? Where's the privy?'

Mary pointed. 'Out the door and down the path to the left. It's the—'

Hannah waited to hear no more but hustled the unfortunate Jane out of the door and along the path. 'There it is. Hurry up.'

Moments later, Jane emerged from the wooden hut. She was calmer now, but tears ran down her cheeks. 'I'm sorry, Hannah.'

'Yes, well, you should've said you wanted to go before we went in.'

Jane sniffed loudly. 'Sorry.'

Hannah took her hand and smiled down at her. The little girl was obviously weary from the journey and fearful of the strange place and people. They all were. 'Come on, we'll have to go back.'

Mrs Bramwell was a tall, thin woman. In her early forties, she nevertheless looked old to the young children. She had a long, straight nose and grey eyes. Her mouth was small, with thin lips that rarely smiled. She was wearing a black dress with a white apron, and her hair was hidden beneath a white cotton bonnet tied beneath her chin, its white frill framing her face.

When they entered the room once more, Hannah saw the telltale puddle on the polished wooden floor. Mrs Bramwell rose from her desk, and, standing before them with her hands folded in front of her, she scrutinized them slowly.

'Well now, so you're the four urchins Mr Goodbody's chosen to send us this time.' Her gaze rested upon Luke and Daniel and she sniffed. 'Hmm. Boys, eh? And twins by the look of you. Mr Critchlow prefers girls. So much less trouble.'

Luke dared to laugh out loud. 'Her won't be.' He jerked his thumb towards Hannah. 'Her's as bad as any boy. Worse.'

Mrs Bramwell's glance swivelled to Hannah.

'Well, we'll see about that, young lady, won't we?'

Hannah bobbed a curtsy as she had seen this woman's maid do. 'I'll be as good as gold here, ma'am. I promise.'

Mrs Bramwell nodded. 'You certainly will,' she said firmly. Her words had an ominous ring. 'Now,' she went on briskly. 'I expect you're hungry after your journey.' She paused and there was the briefest flicker of amusement as she added drily, 'Or has the good Mrs Grundy been feeding you her stew and dumplings?'

The four youngsters glanced at each other.

Hannah's honest gaze met the woman's eyes. 'Yes, ma'am. We stopped – just to ask the way – and she was very kind . . .' Her voice trailed away. Had they done wrong? Were they all in trouble already?

But the stern-faced woman was nodding. 'It does you credit, girl, that you haven't lied to me. For that, you'll all still be given supper.' She sniffed. 'I doubt that skinflint Goodbody ever fed you properly. You'll find Mr Critchlow – Mr Nathaniel Critchlow, that is – a fair man, a caring man, but in return he demands hard work and utter loyalty from all his employees, *especially* from his young apprentices.'

The four youngsters stared at her, and then murmured in chorus, 'Yes, ma'am.'

'Very well then. Come along and I'll show you where you're to sleep.'

As the four children began to troop out of the room, Mrs Bramwell pointed down at the floor. 'You!' She prodded Jane with a sharp finger. 'When I've shown you the dormitory, you can fetch a bucket of water and a cloth from Mary and wash this floor.'

'I'll do it, ma'am,' Hannah began. 'Jane's only little and she's tired. She—'

'Did I ask you to do it, girl?'

'No, ma'am, but—'

'Then you'll oblige me by holding your tongue.'

Jane began to cry, and Hannah faced the superintendent, her mouth a determined line. She was about to protest further, but she felt Luke tug on her arm and hiss, 'Leave it, Hannah.'

Mrs Bramwell led the way up the stairs, keys jangling from a chain around her waist. First she took them to the boys' dormitory, where Luke and Daniel were shown the square wooden box-like bed, set on legs, with a straw palliasse and one blanket.

'You sleep two to a bed. Clean clothes every Sunday and clean sheets once a month. You wear your best clothes for chapel service on Sunday morning, after which you come back here for your dinner. We haven't got a chapel in the village, but a preacher comes to the schoolroom. In the afternoon, I teach the girls to sew, and the boys have more schooling. Unless, of course, there's work to be done in the mill, cleaning machinery and such, that can only be done on a Sunday.'

Hannah was scandalized. 'Don't we get any free time?'

'The devil finds work for idle hands. That's Mr Critchlow's motto. We live by it.' A note of bitterness crept into the woman's tone as she added, 'We all do. Now, you girls follow me.'

She led the way to a door, unlocked it, ushered the girls through it and then re-locked it.

'Boys and girls are separated.'

'Nothing new there, then,' Hannah muttered.

'What?' Mrs Bramwell snapped.

'Nothing, ma'am,' Hannah said brightly.

'Hm!' Mrs Bramwell frowned doubtfully. She was going to have to watch this one, she was thinking. A mite too much to say for herself had Hannah Francis.

'Here we are – this is your dormitory.' They entered a long room containing beds, just like the boys' room, but there were even more here. On each side of the long room was a row of ten truckle beds, set side by side, with scarcely an inch of space between them. There was even a row of five beds set end to end in the centre of the room. Twenty-five beds, Hannah counted. There was only one girl there, sitting on a bed at the far end of the room. She looked up apprehensively, and when she saw Mrs Bramwell she bit her lip.

'What are you doing here, Hudson?'

The girl ran her tongue nervously around her lips. 'I didn't feel well, ma'am. Mr – Mr Edmund said I could come home early.'

Colour suffused Mrs Bramwell's neck and crept up into her face. 'I – see,' she said tightly. She hesitated for a moment, then she moved towards the girl, leaving Hannah and Jane standing near the door.

Mrs Bramwell spoke to her in tones so low that Hannah couldn't hear what was said. Then she saw the girl shake her head, her eyes lowered.

'Very well, then,' Mrs Bramwell said on a sigh as she came back to Hannah and Jane. 'Hudson will tell you anything you need to know.' Drily, she added,

29

'Since she's here, she can make herself useful.' She walked towards the door leading to the stairs, turning back only to point at Jane. 'And don't forget to mop my floor.'

Jane gave a tearful hiccup.

When the superintendent had left the room, Hudson came bouncing towards them, her hazel eyes sparkling, her wide mouth smiling a welcome. Her hair, a mousy colour, was none the less curly and shining with cleanliness. She was a pretty girl, Hannah decided, and probably two or three years older than they were, for already she had a womanly body that was still evident beneath the long skirt and shapeless white cotton smock. But she didn't look ill, Hannah thought fleetingly, and couldn't resist saying, 'Are you feeling better?'

The girl threw back her head and laughed aloud. 'I wasn't ill. Mr Edmund sent for me and then let me leave work early.'

Hannah was curious. 'Why did he do that?'

Hudson stared at her for a moment and then grinned. 'You ask too many questions for a young 'un. Don't worry, he'll not bother with you. Not for a few years, anyway. Mind you,' the girl murmured thoughtfully, 'you're just the type Mr Edmund likes. You'll be a beauty one day, an' no mistake. Then you'll have to watch out. Know what I mean?'

Twelve-year-old Hannah wasn't sure that she did. So far, her mother and grandmother had sheltered her, protected her. With the strict segregation of the sexes in the workhouse, the longest time she'd ever spent in the company of boys had been on the journey here with Luke and Daniel. But, not wishing to appear ignorant, she smiled and nodded.

30

Briskly, Hudson changed the subject. 'You can sleep over here,' she went on, leading them to a bed next to hers. 'You have to share. We all do.' She paused and eyed them up and down.

Nettled by the girl's scrutiny, Hannah lifted her chin. 'Will we do, then?'

For a moment the girl looked startled. She put her head on one side and said offhandedly, 'Yeah. You look all right.' Then suddenly she grinned, and to Hannah's surprise flung her arms around each of them in turn. ''Course you'll do. We all get on well together.' She pulled a wry face. 'Most of the time, anyway. Case of having to, really, when we're living and working so close. Still, we're pretty well treated here – if we behave ourselves,' she added with a note of caution. 'What's your names? Mine's Nell. Nell Hudson. Put your things over there and we'd best go down for supper. The others'll be coming from school in a minute.'

Hannah introduced them both and then added, 'Jane's had a bit of an accident. Where can she rinse her underclothes out?'

Nell pulled a face. 'She can't. She'll have wear them until we get our clean clothes on Sunday.' She smiled down at the little girl. 'Don't worry. They'll soon dry. Come on, let's get down to supper. I'm starving. Mind you, I'm always starving.'

Jane tugged at Hannah's arm and whispered, 'What about her floor?'

'Yes, yes, we'll see Mary when we get downstairs.'

'You'll come with me, won't you, Hannah?' the little girl begged.

Hannah sighed. It would likely get her into trouble, but she said, 'Yes, 'course I will.'

When Jane knocked timidly on the door of Mrs Bramwell's room, with Hannah close on her heels carrying a bucket and floor cloth, there was no answer.

'Go on,' Hannah whispered. 'Open it. Maybe she's not there.'

The girl opened the door and peeped inside. 'No, she isn't.'

'Come on, quick then. Let's do it before she comes back.'

Jane opened the door wider and they crept into the room. Hannah dropped to her knees and began to mop the floor, wringing out the cloth in the bucket of hot water.

'Do hurry,' Jane urged, hopping from one foot to the other. 'She might come back in a minute.'

'There, that's all done,' Hannah said, throwing the cloth into the bucket. 'Come on, let's—'

She was in the act of scrambling up when the door opened, and Hannah saw a pair of feet – surprisingly dainty feet in button boots – then the hem of a long black skirt. Up and up to the trim waist and gently rounded bosom. Then she was looking into Mrs Bramwell's severe face.

'So – you disobeyed me.' Ethel Bramwell sighed. She and her husband were strict in their running of the apprentice house – they had to be – but they always tried to be just and fair. She didn't want to punish this new girl so soon. She liked to give all the youngsters time to settle in, time to learn the rules. But this girl had deliberately flouted her direct instruction, and couldn't be allowed to get away with it. If Ethel Bramwell or her husband Arthur relaxed their authority even for a moment, these unruly little tykes would take advantage, and mayhem would result.

'You, child,' she pointed at Jane. 'Take that bucket back to Mary and get your supper.'

Jane picked up the bucket and scuttled out of the room. As Hannah made to follow her, the superintendent put a heavy hand on her shoulder. 'Not you. You and I, girl, need to have a little chat.'

She shut the door and propelled Hannah to stand in the centre of the room. Then she sat down on a couch, spread her skirt, folded her hands in her lap and looked up at the girl.

'What am I to do with you, miss?'

Hannah smiled, her blue eyes sparkling with mischief. 'Well, if I was still at the workhouse, I'd be given no supper.'

Mrs Bramwell fought to keep a straight face. 'Full of Mrs Grundy's excellent stew, that would be no hardship, would it?'

Hannah wrinkled her brow, giving the matter serious thought. 'No, I don't suppose it would. In that case, then, I'd be sent to the punishment room. D'you have one here?'

'Indeed we do, miss. So, is that where you think I should send you?'

Hannah gave an exaggerated sigh. 'I suppose so, ma'am.'

'Then you'll spend the next hour in the punishment room whilst everyone else has their supper. It'll give you a taste of what to expect in the future, should you choose to disobey me again.'

'Yes, ma'am,' Hannah said meekly.

Mrs Bramwell rose from the couch, her keys jangling. For a moment she stood looking down at the girl. 'Why did you do it, Francis?'

As in the workhouse, Hannah realized that they would

all be addressed by their surname. But, just as she always had, she refused to refer to her friends in such a way.

'Jane's ten, ma'am, but she's small for her age an' very shy and frightened. I was just trying to look after 'er. She's got no mother or father.'

'So, why does that make her different? You're all orphans.'

Hannah shook her head. 'I'm not. I've got a mother. She—'

Mrs Bramwell's mouth dropped open. 'You – you've got a mother?' Hannah blinked. The superintendent made it sound as if it were another crime. 'But – but you're all supposed to be orphans. From the workhouse. Paupers.'

Hannah smiled. 'Oh, we're from the workhouse, and we're certainly paupers. But my mam's still there.'

'Is she indeed?' Mrs Bramwell murmured.

'Yes, ma'am, and . . .' Hannah took the plunge. 'And I was wondering if there was any work here for her. She's worked in a silk mill, but I'm sure—'

Hannah got no further. Mrs Bramwell shook her head vehemently. 'Oh no. We can't have any relatives of the apprentices here. It'd lead to all kinds of trouble. Oh no, it's out of the question, and if you take my advice, you'll keep it very quiet that you've got a mother. Mr Edmund wouldn't like that at all. Goodbody's only supposed to send orphans.'

'Why?' Hannah asked candidly.

Ethel gasped. 'You've got some cheek, girl. You'd better learn to watch your tongue, else you'll find yourself spending more time in the punishment room than out of it.'

'But why should he only send orphans?' Hannah persisted.

Mrs Bramwell gripped her arm. 'Never you mind that, girl. Just learn to do as you're told and not ask so many questions.'

The superintendent marched the girl up the stairs to a little room at the end of the attic storeroom. She opened the door with a key on her bunch and thrust Hannah inside. 'We'll see if an hour or so in there'll teach you a lesson.'

The door slammed, the key turned in the lock, and Hannah was alone. The whitewashed room was completely bare except for a rough blanket thrown in one corner on the cold, bare floor. Hannah went to the window and looked out. Night had fallen in the dale. There was no pauper's gold illuminating the hillside now and sparkling on the river. The blackness was complete.

She pressed her forehead against the cold pane and began to sing softly. 'Abide with me; fast falls the eventide . . .'

About to turn away, Ethel Bramwell paused in astonishment and stood still. 'Bless me,' she murmured. 'The child is singing.'

Never, in all her born days, as she would tell her husband later, had she ever heard any child sing when locked in the punishment room. Cry, scream, rage, bang on the door to be let out, but never, ever, had she heard them sing!

Five

Hannah was let out in time to go straight to bed. When she entered the dormitory, Jane ran straight to her, arms stretched wide, tears running down her face. 'Oh, Hannah, I'm so sorry, it was all my fault.'

Hannah hugged the girl. 'Don't worry,' she said, kissing the top of Jane's head and stroking her long brown hair, now released from its plait for the night. 'It's not as bad in there as the room at the workhouse. At least there's a window. I 'spect it's quite a nice view in the daytime.'

'But aren't you hungry?' Jane's mouth still trembled. 'You missed supper.'

Hannah laughed and rubbed her stomach. 'What, with all that stew Mrs Grundy gave us? No, I'm fine. Now, let's get you into bed. Dry your tears and we'll snuggle down together.'

As they began to undress down to their shifts, some of the other girls clustered around them, staring at the newcomers. Nell shouldered her way through and began the introductions, reeling off names so fast that after a moment Hannah laughed. 'Oh, stop, stop. I'll never remember.'

'You'll get to know us all soon.' Nell laughed good-naturedly. 'You'll be sick of the sight of us all in a bit 'cos we never get away from each other.'

Again Hannah nodded, but silently she was thinking, *Well, I will. I'll get out of here sometimes. Walk down the lane to see that nice Mrs Grundy. Climb the hills and . . .*

'Come on, we'd best get into bed,' Nell shooed the others away. 'She'll be up in a minute.'

The 'she' was Mrs Bramwell, who walked through both the girls' and the boys' dormitories to make sure they were all in bed, to make sure they were all still there.

The only segregation between the boys and the girls in the apprentice house was in the sleeping arrangements. Everywhere else they mingled freely. It was still dark when the door of the dormitory was flung open and a tall, broad-shouldered man with a stick walked between the beds, banging the end of each one to wake them.

'Time to get up.'

Dragging themselves out of bed and shivering in the cold, the girls dressed hurriedly.

'Quick as you can,' Nell whispered, 'else you'll not get a turn in the privy before we have to leave for the mill.'

'What about breakfast?' Hannah asked.

'They bring it to the mill at eight o'clock. We can't stop working, you just have to snatch it when you can.'

Summoned by the bell in the tower on the roof of the main building, they hurried down the steep hill towards the mill, following the clatter of the other children's clogs.

Hannah greeted Luke and Daniel. 'You all right? Sleep all right?'

'Not really,' Luke yawned. 'There was a boy in the next bed to us. Joe, I think his name is. Well, he —'

'Snored,' Daniel added.

'How about you?' Luke asked.

'Slept like a log. We were both tired.'

Luke grinned. 'Is it true you were sent to the punishment room last night?'

Hannah laughed wryly. 'Yeah. Made a good start, didn't I?'

'Whatever did you do? You've only been here five minutes. I'd've thought even you could've kept your nose clean for that long.'

Hannah pulled a face and murmured, 'I'll tell you sometime.' With her eyes, she gestured towards Jane running alongside her.

Luke glanced from one to the other. 'Ah, right.'

Jane said nothing. She was still clinging to Hannah's hand as if she would never let it go.

'Don't we get breakfast before we start work?' Daniel grumbled as they passed through the gate into the mill yard.

Hannah repeated what Nell had told them, and Luke murmured, 'You know, I reckon this could be worse than the workhouse.'

For once, Hannah said nothing. She had a feeling that he could well be right.

A man was standing by the door into the nearest building. At the sight of him, the children behind them began to run forward, passing the four newcomers until they were left at the back, the last to arrive before him. He was more smartly dressed than the workmen hurrying into the mill from all directions. He wore black trousers, a waistcoat and jacket, with a crisp, white shirt and red necktie. Whereas all the workmen wore caps, this man wore a black top hat.

'Ah, you're the new ones. How do?' As he stroked his drooping moustache and long sideburns, Hannah noticed that the third and fourth fingers on his left hand were missing. His voice was gruff and his face pock-marked, but she thought his brown eyes were kindly.

The four youngsters stared up at him wordlessly, until Hannah shook herself, cleared her throat, and said politely, 'Good morning, Mr Critchlow.'

The man stared a moment and then threw back his head. His laughter echoed through the morning mist shrouding the hilltops. 'Lord bless you, I'm not Mr Critchlow. I'm his overlooker, Ernest Scarsfield. I work for him just the same as you're going to.'

Hannah's gaze travelled upwards to marvel at the grand hat he was wearing.

Reading her thoughts, he laughed again. 'Ah, now you're admiring my top hat, aren't you?' Hannah grinned and nodded. The man's eyes twinkled and he bent forward, resting his hands on his knees. 'Well, you see, that's my sign of authority in this place. When folks see my top hat coming, they know they've to be working hard.' He winked and chuckled. 'But I'm sure I'm not going to have any trouble from you four, now am I?'

They smiled a little uncertainly as Mr Scarsfield scrutinized them. *Dear me*, he was thinking as his glance rested upon Jane, *they're sending them younger and younger. This little one looks no more than eight years old.* 'From the workhouse, are you?'

'Yes, sir,' Hannah answered, once again taking the lead.

39

'You needn't call me "sir", lass. You call Mr Critchlow "sir".' He sniffed, 'And Mr Edmund too, I suppose. But you call me "Mr Scarsfield". Now, follow me and I'll take you to Mr Critchlow's office. You have to sign a paper first and then we'll see what jobs we can set you to do.'

They followed him across the yard and in through a door at the end of the main building, up spiral stone steps to the first floor.

At another door, Ernest Scarsfield paused and turned to say, 'This first room is what we call the counting house. It's where Mr Roper sits to do all the bookwork. Beyond that is the master's office. Mr Nathaniel Critchlow is the owner of the mill, but his son, Mr Edmund, is in the business too now. He's the manager of the mill, really.' He leaned a little closer and lowered his voice, as if imparting a confidence. 'The old man still likes to keep his hand in, but it's really Mr Edmund who runs the place.' Ernest straightened up and winked. 'With me to help him, of course.'

The children smiled dutifully, yet they were all feeling apprehensive, not knowing what to expect. Even Hannah felt her knees trembling.

Ernest knocked on the door, and, hearing a murmur from within, opened it, standing aside to usher the children ahead of him. Finding herself once more in the lead, Hannah took a deep breath and stepped into the room. Jane, though still clinging to her hand, managed to hide behind Hannah. The two boys followed, with Mr Scarsfield bringing up the rear and closing the door behind him.

A man – thin, sour-faced and already balding though only in his thirties – was perched on a stool at a high desk, hunched over it, and writing in a thick, leather-bound ledger. He was dressed in sombre black from head to foot, the only relief being his stiffly starched white collar and blue silk cravat.

'Morning, Roper,' Mr Scarsfield said cheerfully, but he didn't pause in moving the children on towards a door halfway down the left-hand side of the room.

The man at the desk glanced at the children with grey, lifeless eyes over the top of his small, steel-framed spectacles. His only reply to Ernest Scarsfield's greeting was a disapproving sniff.

Mr Scarsfield opened the door to the inner office and stepped in first this time.

'Good morning, sir,' he greeted the man sitting behind the desk in the centre of the room. This time, Hannah noticed, his tone was far more deferential.

'Morning, Scarsfield.' His glance rested on the four youngsters. 'Well, well, and who have we here?'

The portly man, with a red face, thinning grey hair and long bushy side-whiskers, spread his podgy hands on the desk in front of him. He was dressed in a black frock coat, dark grey trousers and a light grey waistcoat, with a black stock knotted beneath a white, stand-up collar. Hannah had never seen anyone dressed so grandly in all her life.

'Mr Goodbody's latest arrivals, sir,' Ernest Scarsfield said. 'Now, tell Mr Critchlow your names. You first, lass.' He tapped Hannah's shoulder.

The children spoke in turn. Jane's voice was scarcely audible and Daniel mumbled, but Hannah and Luke spoke up fearlessly.

'Have they brought everything they should have?' Mr Critchlow glanced towards his overlooker.

'I'm sorry, sir. I haven't checked with Mrs Bramwell. They only arrived late last night.'

Mr Critchlow looked impatient. He turned back to Hannah. 'You've been given some clothes?'

She nodded.

'And two guineas?'

Reluctantly, Hannah nodded.

'Have you got it with you?'

The four youngsters glanced at each other and then nodded. All of them had had the sense to carry it, fearing that if they left it in the apprentice house, it might disappear. They'd no way of knowing at this moment just how honest their fellow apprentices were. If their life in the workhouse was anything to go by, then they should trust no one.

'It's to be handed to my clerk, Mr Roper, as you go out.'

'But it's ours,' Hannah burst out.

Mr Critchlow frowned. 'It's to pay for any fines you might incur.'

'Fines? What – what fines?'

'We call them stoppages. We fine you for bad behaviour, lateness or poor work.' He frowned at them over his bushy eyebrows. 'And of course, the more serious the crime, the more you will have to pay. Mr Roper keeps a ledger. Now,' Mr Critchlow went on briskly. 'We've a paper for you to sign. Has it been explained to you what this paper is?'

Four heads shook in unison.

Nathaniel Critchlow reached into a drawer in his desk, and brought out eight sheets of paper covered in small, neat writing. He cleared his throat. 'This is what we call an indenture. It's a legal piece of paper. We each have a copy and we each have to sign both copies.' He pointed a finger towards them and then at himself. 'You and me. You' – his finger pointed again

42

at the children – 'are promising to bind yourself to me and my heirs for a fixed term of years – usually that's until you reach the age of eighteen. You're promising me that you will be a good and faithful apprentice, that you will not leave or absent yourself from your place of work without my consent. You will not steal, damage or destroy anything that is my property. You will obey all the rules and behave at all times in a manner befitting your station as an apprentice. And providing that you keep your side of the agreement, in return, I' – his finger now turned towards himself – 'and my heirs promise to employ you for that number of years in a suitable occupation and teach you all you need to know. Now,' he smiled down at them. 'Is that all clear?'

'Please, sir,' Hannah asked. 'What wages do we receive?'

'Wages?' Mr Critchlow frowned. 'We don't pay wages to apprentices.'

'Then – then how are we to live?'

His face cleared. 'Oh, I see. Didn't I say? We provide you with accommodation and all your food – and clothes.' The last item was added as if this were a great benevolence.

Ernest Scarsfield leaned forward. 'You can earn a bit doing overtime. You'll be paid for that.'

'A-hem, oh yes, of course. But it'll be a while before they're useful enough to do that, Scarsfield. Don't mislead them.'

'No, sir, of course not,' Ernest said dutifully, but out of sight of his employer, Hannah felt him squeeze her elbow and understood that, as soon as he could, he would likely put some work their way so that they could earn a few coppers.

But Mr Critchlow's next words dampened even that hope. 'And don't forget the stoppages ledger, Scarsfield. Make sure they understand that anything they break or do wrong will have to be paid for.'

'Sounds as if we'll end up paying to work here,' Hannah muttered. She felt a sharp dig in the ribs from Luke and another squeeze on her elbow from Mr Scarsfield. This time it was a warning.

'What? What did you say, girl?' Mr Critchlow demanded.

'Nothing, sir,' she replied, but she was thinking quickly, debating whether to sign the paper that would bind her here for six long years. She thought of her mother, who had begged her to behave, to work hard and learn a skill. 'It's a great chance for you, Hannah,' Rebecca had said in her gentle voice. 'Take it.' And it was a chance too, the young girl reminded herself, to find employment for her mother. Then they could be reunited.

Hannah smiled brightly and stepped forward. 'Where do you want me to sign, sir?'

A few moments later, when they'd each laboriously scratched their names (or, in the case of Jane, made her mark – an untidy, squiggly cross), they watched whilst Mr Critchlow filled in their names in the appropriate blank spaces in the document. At the bottom of the paper he added the date, his signature and a big, red seal of wax.

'There, that's all done, and now Mr Scarsfield will show you around the mill and then what work he would like you to do.' He looked up at his overlooker. 'Come back here later, Scarsfield. We've matters to discuss.'

'Yes, sir,' Ernest Scarsfield nodded as he led the

children out of the room, Hannah once more bobbing a polite curtsy and bestowing her most beaming smile on the man whom she was now bound to serve for the next six years.

Six

'Now,' Mr Scarsfield said, smiling down at them as they clattered back down the stone steps and into the yard once more. 'We'd better find you all a job to do.' He looked them over, assessing them. 'We usually start the apprentices off just sweeping up and keeping the place tidy. After a while, we'll try you on other jobs so's you work your way up, see?'

Four heads nodded.

'You three' – he pointed to the twins and Jane – 'are small enough to crawl under the machines to sweep the fluff up, but you . . .' Now he pointed at Hannah. 'You're a bit tall for that. I don't want any accidents.' He frowned. 'The mill is a dangerous place, 'specially for you youngsters and 'specially' – he laid emphasis on the word – 'when you're crawling about under the machines. Watch your heads and your backs and you, Pickering, mind your hair is plaited and covered by your bonnet.'

'What about me?' Hannah asked. 'What am I to do?'

'I think I'll try you scutching.'

Hannah blinked. 'Whatever's that?'

Ernest laughed and his brown eyes twinkled. 'It's part of the preparation of the raw cotton. Come on, let's set these three to work and then I'll take you and show you.'

He led the children into the mill. Now the noise of machinery was much louder, and the newcomers were tempted to put their hands over their ears to block out the din.

'You'll get used to it,' Ernest mouthed at them. 'And you'll soon learn to lip read an' all. It's the only way you can hold any sort of conversation in here. Mind you, don't let me catch you chatting, though.'

'Fat chance,' Luke muttered, though above the noise, the overlooker didn't hear him.

Ernest led them into a long room where dozens of machines were working. The noise was now deafening, but the workers standing before the machines didn't seem to mind. Ernest was pointing at a small girl darting between the machines and then crawling beneath them to sweep the dust and fluff collecting under each one. The newcomers stood watching for a moment and then the two boys picked up a brush and emulated the girl.

Jane clung to Hannah, whimpering. 'I can't do that. I'm frightened.'

The overlooker put his hand on the young girl's shoulder, but she cringed away from him, burying her face against Hannah.

'Don't be frightened of me, young 'un. I'll not 'urt yer.' He bent closer so that she could hear what he said. 'Look, just today, you can sweep the floors all round the machines, but mind you don't get in the way of the operators. They'll likely box yer ears if yer do.'

Jane trembled and tears ran down her face.

'Come on,' Hannah coaxed. 'You know we've got to work. We signed that paper and Mr Scarsfield's trying to find you something easy to do to start off.'

47

Jane sniffled and nodded. She took hold of the broom that Ernest held out to her.

'I'll just have a word with one of the women. Ask her to keep an eye on the little one.'

He glanced beneath the machinery before adding, 'The lads look to be doing fine.'

After a few brief words with the woman at the nearest machine, Ernest nodded to Jane, who began to sweep the floor with tentative strokes. The overlooker cast his eyes to the ceiling as if in despair, but then smiled as he and Hannah left the room.

Away from the noise, Hannah said, 'She's only ten and small for her age. She'll be all right once she gets used to it.'

'Aye well, we'll see,' Ernest said, sounding none too hopeful.

He led the way out of the main building again and across the yard into the one set at right angles. As they walked he said, 'The bales of raw cotton are stored in a room on the ground floor beneath the counting house. It's Mr Roper's job to check them all in. Then the lads carry them across the yard to this building. This is where the preparation is done.'

They entered a room where other children were working; some of them Hannah had seen in the apprentice house. They were unpacking bales of raw cotton, pulling it and then sorting it into different piles.

'That's called "blending",' Ernest explained. 'They're sorting into different qualities so that each pile consists of the same quality of cotton.'

Hannah nodded.

'Now, what I want you to do is to remove all the

seeds and the dirt from the cotton. It's a boring job, but you've got to start at the bottom, luv. But I reckon you're bright and quick and I'll keep me eye on you. You'll soon be moving on, I've no doubt.'

'That's "scutching" then, is it?'

'Aye, then the cotton's spread into a flat sheet before it goes into the next room where there's a carding engine. I'll show you that another time. Bentley!' Ernest raised his voice and beckoned one of the girls over. 'This is Francis. She's to start with the scutching. Show her what to do, will yer?'

'Yes, Mr Scarsfield,' the girl said meekly.

Just as he turned to go, Ernest reminded Hannah, 'Oh, and tomorrow morning, make sure Pickering plaits her hair and puts it up under her bonnet.'

Now it was Hannah who nodded, and said, 'Yes, Mr Scarsfield.'

'D'you know, I can't hear a thing,' Luke began as the four of them walked home after their first day's work in the mill.

''Cept them machines,' finished Daniel. 'I can still hear 'em banging in my head even now we're out in the open.'

'It hurts my ears,' Jane murmured, slipping her hand into Hannah's. 'And everybody shouts so.'

'They have to, don't they, to make themselves heard above the noise.' Luke grinned and added, 'There's one good thing.' He poked Hannah in the ribs. 'We can't hear your singing no more.'

Playfully, Hannah punched him on the shoulder.

At that moment there was a clatter of clogs behind

them and they heard Nell's voice. 'Come on, you lot. You've got school for two hours now and jobs to do before any of us get any supper.'

'School?' Luke said. 'Now? After working all day?'

'Jobs?' Daniel added.

'I'm tired,' Jane whimpered. 'I want to go to bed.'

Hannah squeezed her hand. 'Come on, Jane. Let's go and meet the teacher.'

'I don't want to. I don't want him rapping me with his cane.'

'You 'ave to go until you're thirteen. I don't any more. I'm fifteen. But you'll be in trouble if you don't go. It's the law and even the Critchlows have to abide by it,' Nell said. She sniffed. 'Mind you, I reckon they'd get out of it if they could. A schoolmaster needs paying, and the Critchlows don't like parting with their money.'

'Does the master teach the girls an' all?' Hannah asked as they neared the schoolroom.

Nell nodded. 'There used to be a schoolmarm for the girls, but she left, all sudden like.' She cast a swift glance at Hannah as if trying to convey some sort of message, but Hannah was mystified. No doubt the teacher had found better employment, she thought. 'And they didn't appoint anyone else,' Nell went on. 'So now Mr Jessop teaches everybody.'

For the next two hours the weary children were obliged to sit on the long benches behind the tables and draw letters in the sand trays. The more able were given slates. Several of the children's heads drooped until they were resting on the desk. Until, that is, Mr Jessop brought his cane down with a sharp crack.

Hannah kept nudging Jane, trying to keep her awake, but the child was so tired that at last Hannah let her sleep. The schoolmaster came to stand over her. He raised his cane and Hannah held her breath. Mr Jessop bent down, looking closely at the pale, drawn face of the little girl. He lowered his cane and turned away, leaving her to sleep. Hannah smiled to herself. Perhaps this place wasn't so bad after all. There seemed to be one or two people prepared to be kindly now and then – Mrs Bramwell, Mr Scarsfield and now the schoolmaster. But she doubted there was much compassion in Mr Roper, and she feared that Mr Critchlow would be a greedy taskmaster. Perhaps his son, Mr Edmund, would be nice. She daydreamed until her wandering thoughts were brought sharply back to her work by the crack of Mr Jessop's cane on her desk.

After the requisite two hours, the children were released to return to the apprentice house.

'Come along, come along. There's work to be done.' Ethel Bramwell was standing at the back door, clapping her hands to hurry them along.

'Do we really have to do jobs now?' Hannah asked Nell. 'Before we get any supper?'

''Fraid so. The boys have to sweep the yard and fetch logs and coal in, and we have to sweep and tidy the dormitories and Mrs Bramwell's private rooms. Then there might be darning and mending to do. On Monday and Tuesday nights, we have to do the ironing.'

'What about Mary? Doesn't she do all that?'

'She does the washing on a Monday, but she has to do all the cooking for about eighty of us. There's fifty girls and twenty-nine boys as well as the Bramwells and Mary herself. I tell you, I wouldn't swap jobs with her, even if it is hard in the mill.'

'What do you do, Nell?'

'I'm a piecer.'

'Oh!' Hannah was about to ask more, but Jane was tugging at her arm.

'I'm tired, Hannah.' Hearing the list of chores recounted by Nell had made her feel even more exhausted. 'I just want to go to bed.'

'Maybe Mrs Bramwell won't make you younger ones do jobs,' Hannah began, but Nell laughed.

'Don't you believe it. If she thinks Jane's trying to get out of any work, she'll give her the hardest job that'll take her twice as long.' Nell smiled down at Jane and took hold of the child's other hand. 'Come on, little 'un. We'll help you if we can, but it won't do you any good, or us, if we're spotted.'

'Let us with a gladsome mind . . .' Hannah sang as she knelt and scrubbed the floor, summoning up all the energy she could muster.

'And just what do you think you're doing, girl?'

Hannah looked up to see Mrs Bramwell standing over her.

'Washing your floor, ma'am.'

'I can see that,' the woman said testily. 'But this task was given to Pickering. Why are you doing it?'

Hannah stood up. 'She's dead on her feet, ma'am. I've told her to go to bed and that I'd do it for her. I've finished the job you gave me.'

'You've no right to say who may go to bed and who may not.' Ethel Bramwell pursed her thin lips. 'I can find another job for you if you've finished the one I set you.'

'Why? Why can't I help Jane?' Hannah was almost shouting now. 'She's only ten.'

Ethel's lip curled. 'That's nothing. In the past children have worked in this mill from the age of eight.' She sniffed and beneath her breath muttered, 'And younger, if the truth be known.'

Open-mouthed, Hannah stared at her and Ethel continued. 'Pickering must learn to do her share.' For a moment, she seemed to soften, even using the girl's Christian name for once. 'I know you mean well, Hannah, but you're not doing the girl any favours.'

'But she's tired, exhausted and, and . . .' Hannah faltered. She'd been going to say that the child was homesick. How anyone could be homesick for the workhouse was beyond Hannah, yet she knew that Jane was missing her friends from the only home the little girl had ever known. But maybe, given time, this house might be more of a real home than a workhouse could ever be. She would try to make Jane see that. But, just now, all she could do was to help the child physically.

Suddenly, Hannah put her head on one side and smiled. 'Please, Mrs Bramwell, won't you let me help her just tonight? Just this once? And then I'll tell her she'll have to manage. And I'll do the other job too. Whatever it is.'

Ethel Bramwell stared at her. She'd never met a girl like this before. Usually, it was a battle of wills to get any of the children to do the household chores after long hours in the mill and two hours' schooling too. And now here was a new arrival begging to do even more work than she'd been asked to do. The girl was slim and dainty, yet she must have an inner strength

53

that was not immediately apparent. There were dark shadows of weariness beneath her own eyes, yet Hannah had the will power to drive herself on – just to help another. The sound of this girl singing in the punishment room had stayed with the superintendent, and she was sure she'd heard her again just now.

'Is Pickering a relative of yours?'

Hannah shook her head. 'No, but we're best friends. I've known her ever since we went into the workhouse.' At the reminder of the workhouse, the sudden longing to see her mother threatened to overwhelm her. But she lifted her chin and met the superintendent's gaze. 'We went in three years ago, but Jane'd been there all her life.'

'I see,' Ethel said, relenting. 'Well, all right then, but mind you make sure she understands that it is just this once.'

Hannah beamed. 'Thank you, ma'am.' She knelt down once more to finish her work, but then looked up to ask, 'What's the other job you want me to do?'

Now Ethel smiled, and some of the severity left her face. She waved her hand. 'Oh, never mind about that.'

As Hannah left the room a few moments later, Ethel gazed after her and bit her lower lip. That girl would be a beauty one day, she thought with a sudden shudder of apprehension. And that day wasn't far away. God help her then when Mr Edmund laid eyes on her.

'Well, I never,' Nell remarked, staring down at the sleeping Jane when the other girls trooped wearily upstairs to their beds. 'She'll be in trouble in the morning when Mrs Bramwell finds out she's not finished her work.'

'No, she won't,' Hannah said, 'because I've done it.'

Nell stared at her. '*You've* done it?'

Hannah nodded.

'Then you'll be in trouble an' all.'

'No, I won't. Mrs Bramwell knows all about it. She let me do it. Just this once, she said.'

Nell gaped. 'She – she *let* you?'

Hannah nodded.

'Well – well . . .' For a moment the girl was lost for words, then with a shrug she said, 'She must be going soft in her old age.' She laughed. 'Well, now we know who to come to if we want to get round her.'

Hannah grinned. 'I don't think it will work very often.'

'Oh, I don't know. Mrs Bramwell has her favourites. You tek Joe Hughes – you know, the lad your friends said was in the next bed to them?'

'The one who snores?'

Nell giggled. 'That's him. The whole dormitory complain about him. Well, he's one of her favourites. The things he gets away with, you wouldn't believe. If the rest of us did half what he does, we'd end up in the punishment room.'

Hannah laughed. 'Don't forget I've been in there already. I quite expect to spend half me life in there.'

Nell shuddered. 'That time was just a warning. You wait till they decide to really punish you.'

Seven

Hannah met Joe Hughes the next morning as they all hurried down to the mill.

'Is this the girl you were telling us about?' he asked Luke.

'Yeah. This is Hannah. Hannah – Joe Hughes.'

Hannah smiled at him, but none of them slowed their pace. Already they could see Mr Scarsfield waiting by the door.

'Pleased to meet yer, Joe Hughes.'

'And you, Hannah. Come for a walk up the hills on Sunday afternoon, will yer?'

Hannah glanced at the hills, shrouded in early morning mist. But she'd already seen how beautiful they were when the sun shed its golden light upon them.

'Yeah. All right. We'll come.'

'Oh, I didn't mean—' the boy began, but they'd reached the door and Ernest Scarsfield said, 'No talking now. Get to your work and look sharp about it.'

The children parted, the twins and Jane going into the main mill. Hannah skipped across the yard to the preparation room in the nearby building with Joe Hughes trotting beside her. He worked the carding machine in the room next door.

However boring the job, Hannah was meticulous in her work, but it wasn't long before she noticed that

56

the other girl was not as careful to get every seed and bit of dirt out of the cotton.

'You've missed some bits there, Millie,' she pointed out.

The girl looked up at her, her dark eyes flashing anger. Her lips twisted as she said, 'Oh, got a boot-kisser here, 'ave we?'

Hannah gasped. 'How dare you? I was only trying to help.'

'I'm supposed to be the one helping you – not for you to come in here trying to lord it over me. Reckon you know better than me how to do it, d'yer?'

Hannah nodded towards the pieces of raw cotton the girl had put on the heap that was supposed to have been cleaned. 'If that's the way you do your job, then yes, I do.'

The girl leaned towards Hannah. 'Well, I can make your life a misery in here – and in the house. No one likes a bootkisser.' She smiled maliciously. 'That's what I'll call you. "Boot". And if anyone wants to know why, then I'll tell 'em.'

For a moment Hannah stared at her. The years rolled back and once again she was a bewildered little five year old standing in the street near her home, being taunted with cruel names. Only at that time she hadn't known the meaning of the names they called her. But she recalled how she had learnt to deal with the insults.

She threw back her head and laughed aloud, amused at the look of confusion on Millie's face. Then Hannah began to sing, but this only incensed the other girl further. She shook her fist in Hannah's face. 'Aye, go on sing. Sing your heart out, girl, 'cos when you've been here a bit, you won't feel like singing. I promise you that.' She flung a handful of cotton in Hannah's face. 'And since you're so clever, you can do all the scutching on yer own. I'll do the blending and spreading.'

Hannah's only reply was to sing louder than ever.

About mid morning, the door to the preparation room opened and three men came in. Hannah knew two of them: Mr Critchlow and the overlooker, Ernest Scarsfield. Her gaze rested briefly on the third. He was a tall, handsome man with dark curly hair, his age about forty or so, she guessed. He walked with a graceful ease and held his head in a proud manner. Expensively dressed in a maroon frock coat, fawn trousers and matching waistcoat, he had high cheekbones above a firm, square chin and thick, black eyebrows that shadowed his dark brown eyes. He had neatly cut sidewhiskers but, though his mouth was well shaped, there was a discontented downturn to his lips.

For a brief moment their eyes met, and Hannah saw his eyebrows draw together in a frown. He strode towards her, his face thunderous.

'What's all the noise? Concentrate on your work, girl.'

Ernest was beside her at once. 'She's new, Mr Edmund. Only arrived yesterday.'

'That's no excuse. She should know her place, and her place is attending to her work, not singing.'

'I'll see to it, Mr Edmund.'

'Mind you do, Scarsfield.' He was about to turn away when his glance rested on some of the raw cotton that Millie had been working on. He picked up a handful. 'And what's this? Supposed to be finished is it?' He flung it at Hannah. 'You'd better learn to do your work a lot better than this, else you'll be back to the workhouse. And Goodbody will *not* be pleased to see you. Scarsfield, you're to stop her a shilling from her pay —'

Hannah's blue eyes flashed. 'How can he stop money out of my pay? I don't get paid.' She pointed her finger at the older man. 'Mr Critchlow said so.'

There was a breathless silence whilst everyone in the room stared at her.

The tall man stepped close to her, glaring down at her from his superior height. He grasped her chin with strong fingers, forcing her head backwards. He held her like that for several moments, gazing into her eyes, his glance roaming over the whole of her face.

'Answer me back would you, girl? We'll see what a night on the floor of the punishment room will do for you.'

He released her suddenly so that she staggered backwards. He turned away. 'See to it, Scarsfield. No supper and you can take a shilling from the money she brought with her.'

Hannah opened her mouth to protest, but she caught Ernest's warning shake of his head. The angry stranger brushed imaginary fluff from his jacket and strode into the room next door, followed by Mr Critchlow.

'I'll see you later, Francis,' Ernest said before he hurried after them.

Spreading out the cleaned cotton fibres into a flat sheet, Millie smiled triumphantly. 'Serves you right. You should know better than to cheek Mr Edmund.'

So, Hannah thought as she picked up the cotton he had flung at her, that was Mr Edmund Critchlow. The man she had been warned about.

A little later, Ernest Scarsfield came back alone. He stood with his arms akimbo, glancing between the two girls. 'Now, which of you two was supposed to have scutched that piece of cotton the young master found? Come on, I want the truth.'

Hannah met his gaze fearlessly, but she said nothing.

'It weren't me, mester,' Millie whined. 'I've put 'er on the scutching. I'm doing the blending and the spreading now.' She cocked her head on one side and smiled winningly at the overlooker. 'If that's all right with you, Mr Scarsfield. See, you 'ave to know what you're doing with the blending, don't you, Mr Scarsfield? We don't want all different qualities mixed up together do we, sir?'

Shocked, Hannah gaped at the girl. Millie was lying quite blatantly. She pressed her lips together and shot the girl a vitriolic glance, but still she said not a word.

'Hmm,' Ernest said thoughtfully, stroking his moustache. 'Very well then, but you'd better both mind what you're doing. I don't want any slacking else I'll have to fine the pair of you.'

With a stern glance at each of them in turn, Ernest Scarsfield left the room, banging the door behind him.

Once she was sure he was out of earshot, Hannah turned on the girl. She grasped her arm and swung her round to face her. 'Don't you dare tell lies about me again. I don't tell tales on others and I always tell the truth about meself. If it'd been me that'd sorted that cotton, I'd've owned up.'

Fear flickered in Millie's eyes. 'Le' go, you're hurting my arm. I'll tell—'

'No, you won't. You hear me. You won't tell any more tales about me – or anyone else – and if I hear you have . . .' Her grip tightened until the girl cried out in pain. Then Hannah released her grasp, flinging Millie away from her. 'If it's anyone slacking around here, then it's you.'

Hannah returned to her work. Not another word passed between them for the rest of the day. And Hannah was too angry to sing.

Sunday was the only day of the week when the mill workers were allowed any time off. The adults who worked there mostly lived locally and had the day to be with their families. They were expected to attend the Methodist service held in the schoolroom at the mill, but afterwards there was time for the younger men and women to go courting.

The apprentices, though, were still under Mr and Mrs Bramwell's authority. They too had to attend the morning service, but afterwards there was more schooling and household tasks for them. Pauper apprentices, it seemed, had no free time at all. Even in the workhouse, Hannah thought truculently, there had been exercise time. Though they were not allowed outside the confines of the workhouse walls without permission from the master or the matron, at least all the inmates went out each day into the fresh air to walk, to chat or just to sit in the sun on warm days.

'You know you asked me to go walking with you on Sunday afternoon?' Hannah said to Joe as they fell into step on their way to work the following morning.

61

Joe grinned at her. 'Yeah.'

'Well – how? Or when? We don't seem to be given any time off.'

Joe shrugged. 'We just go.'

'And end up in the punishment room when we get back, I suppose?' Hannah had spent an uncomfortable night there. Given no supper, she had lain on the bare floor with only one blanket to wrap herself in. She had hardly slept and this morning she was both tired and ravenously hungry.

'We can either sneak off after the service – there's an hour or so before dinner – or we can go after.'

Hannah pulled a face. 'Mrs Bramwell says she teaches the girls sewing on a Sunday afternoon.'

He grinned. 'And that's going to stop you?'

Hannah laughed. 'Not really, no. I'll risk it.'

'Tell you what, we'll just have a short walk between chapel and dinner.' He winked at her. 'Don't want you moving into the punishment room permanently.'

Hannah pulled a face. 'Me neither.'

Eight

'I don't want to come, Hannah,' Jane said, when told of the proposed outing with Joe Hughes as they came out of the schoolroom after the service on the first Sunday morning. 'I'm so tired I could cry.' Indeed, tears of exhaustion filled the young girl's eyes. 'I just want to go home and sleep.'

'I know.' Hannah hugged her. 'You go on then. I'll wake you up for dinner when I get back.'

'Where are you going?' Jane asked worriedly. 'You'll be in trouble again.'

'Only for a little walk. Joe's promised to show me the waterfall behind the mill.'

Jane returned her hug fiercely. 'You don't mind me not coming,' she said, her voice muffled against Hannah's shoulder.

' 'Course not.'

They pulled apart and smiled at each other. 'Besides,' Jane said, coyly, 'I think that Joe Hughes wants you to himself.'

'Eh?' Hannah was startled, then she laughed. 'Don't be silly.'

'I'm not.' Jane yawned, already thinking of their bed in the dormitory with longing. 'I reckon he likes you.'

'Don't be daft, he . . .' Hannah started to say, but Jane was already walking away from her, too tired to stand talking any longer.

'There you are!' Joe came towards her, walking with a swagger, his hands in his pockets. 'Just walk slow, so we end up at the back. Then, when we get to the bottom of the hill, there's a little path that runs at the back of the mill just below the cliff. If no one's watching, we nip through there.'

Hannah nodded, her eyes shining at the thought of an hour or so of freedom.

'Hey, Hannah, wait for us.'

'Oh no,' Joe muttered. 'Not that pair.'

Hannah turned and saw Luke with Daniel trotting close behind him.

'Off for a walk, a'yer?'

'How did you know?' Joe said belligerently.

'Heard you ask her the other day.' Luke grinned.

'Yeah. I asked her,' Joe glowered. 'Not the whole blooming lot of yer.'

Hannah laughed and slipped her arm through theirs. 'Oh, come on, let's all go. It's too nice a day to argue. Let's just enjoy ourselves while we can.'

'I'm tired, Luke,' Daniel muttered. 'I want to go home.'

Luke glanced at his twin. 'All right. See you later.'

Daniel blinked. 'What – what do y'mean?'

'You go and have a sleep. I'm going with these.'

Daniel glanced from his brother to Hannah. He and his brother were never apart. They went everywhere together. But now, Luke was choosing the company of others rather than him. Daniel didn't like it, and he was blaming Hannah. She could see it in his eyes.

'All right,' he muttered sulkily. 'I'll come an' all.'

'No, you go back if you want to—'

'I don't,' he snapped back. 'Not on me own.'

Joe was disgruntled too now. He'd wanted to walk out with Hannah on his own, not have the twins tagging along. Joe was older than the other three. At fourteen, he fancied himself old enough to start courting. He liked the look of this new girl whose blue eyes sparkled when she laughed. She'd left her long blonde hair flying loose this morning, cascading down her back in golden waves and curls that glinted in the sunlight. She was lively with boundless energy and she laughed often. And sing! He'd heard singing in the room next door to where he worked in the carding room. In the service that morning, her voice had risen, clear and pure, above all the others. She was a bit young yet, but she'd grow, he told himself, and he reckoned she'd grow into a beauty an' all.

'Come on then. Here's the path . . .' He caught hold of Hannah's hand and was elated at the look of fury on Luke's face.

They skirted the base of the cliff on which the row of houses containing the school and the apprentice house stood, and came to a place where a stream ran under the path to the waterwheel, whose power turned all the machinery in the mill.

'They call this the "head race",' Joe told them importantly. 'They constructed this to run from the mill pool down to the wheel.'

Hannah's gaze followed the line of the man-made stream that surfaced beyond the path and ran towards the paddles of the great wheel, which stuck out like sharp, hungry teeth. The wheel was silent today.

'So how do they stop the water,' Luke asked with boyish curiosity, 'when the mill's not working?'

'There's an iron hatch at the top of the race where it leaves the pool. When they want the wheel to work they just open the hatch. The water flows down the race to work the wheel and then it comes out the other side and flows down the tail race back into the river.'

'But where does the water go when the hatch is closed?' Now Daniel took up the question.

'There's a weir out of the pool straight back into the river. I'll show you.'

A few paces further on they came to where the River Wye widened out into the huge lake that Joe called the mill pool. Then, walking to the left, they stood a moment on the narrow footbridge watching the white foaming water cascading over the edge of the weir and rushing on down the rocky riverbed. Ahead of them was a steep climb up rocks to the hillside above.

Joe, still holding Hannah's hand, began to climb, pulling her after him. 'From up here you can see all the mill and some of the village.'

They climbed, puffing and panting, until they gained a narrow path running along the hillside overlooking the mill. Far below them now, it seemed small. They walked on along the sheep tracks, climbing higher.

They stood a moment to catch their breath.

'That way,' Joe waved to their right, 'is up to the Wyedale Arms.'

'We saw that the day we came,' Luke said.

Joe ignored him as if he hadn't spoken. 'And the other way,' he pointed in the opposite direction, 'leads to another mill about a couple of miles away.'

'Another mill!'

'Yeah. You can walk to it by a path on the other side of the mill pool.' He squeezed Hannah's hand and lowered his voice. 'I'll show you that another time. It's a lovely walk by the river. Very quiet and peaceful.' He glanced about him and then added, 'But we ought to go back now. If we're late for dinner, we'll all be in trouble.'

'Don't expect *you* will be, though,' Luke sparred. 'Not with Mrs Bramwell, anyway.'

Colour suffused the other boy's face. 'Have it your own way then,' he muttered moodily and looked directly at Hannah. 'I was only thinking of you. You've been in trouble already, haven't you?'

Hannah lifted her face to the sunshine, closing her eyes and luxuriating in the feel of the breeze on her face, rippling through her hair. 'You're right, Joe. But it's so lovely out here. It's almost worth risking a spell in the punishment room just for an hour or two of freedom.'

'Well, I'm going back now.' Joe let go of Hannah's hand. 'I don't fancy a beating from Mr Bramwell. You lot can please yourselves.' He thrust his hands in his pockets, turned and began to walk back the way they had come.

Worriedly, Daniel said, 'Come on. We ought to do what he says.'

'I'm not going back just 'cos *he* says so,' Luke scoffed. 'Come on, Hannah, let's walk a bit further. It's a great view from up here. Much better than walking on the road. You can see everything.'

'I don't think we ought to,' Daniel murmured, frowning.

Now it was Luke who grasped her hand. 'Well, you go, Dan. We'll see you later,' he called back cheerfully to his twin. Now – just as he'd wanted all along – he had Hannah to himself.

Joe Hughes had spent most of his life in the work-house and then in the mill. Places where segregation was the rule. And although he was younger than Joe, from his early years spent on a farm Luke, even at eleven years old, probably knew more about the natural instincts of animals – and human beings – than the older boy did. And Luke's natural instinct was to contrive to be alone with a pretty girl, to hold her hand, to put his arm around her. Even, if he was greatly daring, to kiss her.

And the prettiest girl he'd ever seen in his life was walking beside him right now.

'D'you like Joe?' he asked her suddenly.

'He's all right,' she said carefully. 'Why? Don't you like him?'

Luke pulled a face. 'He's a bit of a know-all.'

'Well, he's been here a few years now. I think he's only trying to be friendly.'

'The other lads say he's Mrs Bramwell's favourite.'

Hannah laughed. 'That's what Nell said an' all.'

Suddenly, Luke grinned. 'Mind you, it might do us a bit of good – to be on his right side.'

'Oh, Luke! How could you possibly think such a thing?' Then she giggled deliciously. 'But you could be right.'

'Look,' Luke said suddenly. 'Isn't that the Grundys' farm down there?'

'I think so. Yes, it's near the crossroads, but doesn't it look small from up here.' She laughed. 'And look at the cows in the field. They look like ants.'

'And look up there. Joe's right, that is the Wyedale Arms where the carter dropped us off.'

'Mm.' Hannah's voice was suddenly wistful. 'I wonder,' she began, and then stopped.

'If you could get a lift back again one day?'

Her eyes widened. 'How – how did you know?'

Luke's expression softened, and he was no longer teasing as he said, 'Because if I had a mam back there, then I'd be wanting to go back to see her sometime.'

'You would?' Hannah breathed.

Luke nodded. 'And if you ever want to – *really* want to – then I'd help you do it.'

'Even if . . . even if you got into trouble?'

'It'd be worth it – for you to see your mam,' he told her earnestly.

Hannah felt a blush creep up her neck and into her face. Tears prickled her eyelids. 'Oh, Luke,' was all she could say.

He squeezed her hand. 'We'd best be getting back an' all now. Look, there's a path here going right down to the farm. I 'spect it's one the sheep have worn on their way back home. Let's follow it. We'll go back this way. It'll be quicker. We can run on the road.'

Feeling a thrill of daring, they followed the path down the hillside towards the river. Hand in hand they ran across the footbridge over the water and up the lane bordered by the Grundys' farm. A man stood in the yard, watching their approach. He took his cap off, scratched his head and replaced it. He moved towards the gate and leaned on his arms on the top of it.

'Now where're you two off to in such a hurry? What've you been up to, 'cos you've got "guilt" written all over your faces.'

'A' you Mr Grundy?' Luke said as they stopped by the gate.

'Tha's right. And who're you then to know my name?'

'Your wife was very kind to us when we arrived the other day,' Hannah said. 'She gave us some lovely stew.'

'Ah,' said the burly man as understanding dawned. 'From mill, a' yer?'

The two youngsters nodded.

His expression softened. 'Out for a bit of an airing, a' yer. 'Spect there's not much fresh air in that place.'

'It's very dusty, isn't it?' Hannah said. 'With all the cotton bits floating in the air.'

The man nodded. 'I'll give you a tip. Whenever you wash, bathe your eyes with clean water. A lot of the youngsters get trouble with their eyes. And if they get very sore, you come and see my missis. She'll give you some eye lotion to use, 'cos that old skinflint won't spend an 'apenny on having a doctor visit if he can avoid it.'

'Thank you, Mr Grundy. That's very kind of you.'

The man smiled. 'Coming in to see the missis, 'a you? Nice joint of lamb we've just had for dinner.'

The children's mouths watered, but regretfully Hannah said, 'That's ever so kind of you, but we ought to get back. If we're missed, we'll be in trouble. And it's the best meal of the week today. Boiled pork and potatoes.'

'On yer go then. I'll tell the missis I've seen you.'

Bidding him goodbye, Hannah and Luke began to run. They didn't stop until they were in sight of the mill.

'I reckon Joe and Daniel'll both be in a huff with us.' Luke grinned, looking not particularly bothered.

'They'll get over it.' Hannah laughed. 'At least, Daniel will. He'll not stay mad at you for long. As for Joe – he can please himself.'

Luke felt a warm glow. When they arrived at the back door of the apprentice house breathless from running, Hannah turned to Luke.

'That was wonderful.' Her cheeks were pink, her bright eyes glowing and her hair flying free. Luke caught hold of her and gave her a swift, fumbling peck on the cheek.

Then, as they opened the door and burst into the kitchen, eighty or so pairs of eyes turned in their direction.

Near the range, with her hands folded and her mouth pursed, stood Ethel Bramwell. Slowly, she walked towards them. There was not a sound in the room. The children, seated on benches on either side of the four long tables, stopped eating to watch what was about to happen.

Ethel Bramwell reached them. 'And where might you two have been when there's work to be done? You're not allowed out of this house without permission. You should have come straight back here after the service. Why didn't you? I know you are both comparatively new here, but you know the rules, don't you?'

Hannah and Luke glanced at each other. 'Yes, ma'am,' they murmured in unison.

'If it hadn't been for Joe telling me that he'd seen you going up the hill,' Mrs Bramwell went on, 'I might've thought some accident had befallen you and sent people out to look for you. You'd've been in serious trouble then.'

Hannah felt a flash of anger. So, Joe was a telltale an' all, was he? It seemed there was no one here she could trust, except the three children who'd come with her from the workhouse. And maybe Nell. She liked

Nell. Daniel would never in a million years tell tales about his twin. He'd rather take punishment himself. But Joe, it seemed, had no such scruples. Hannah guessed that he was miffed at Luke having taken Hannah away from him on the walk *he* had planned. And now, he'd taken revenge.

Her glance raked the tables until she saw him. He was the only one with his gaze averted. He dared not look her in the eyes. Well, Hannah promised herself, she'd sort him out later, but her attention was dragged back to what Mrs Bramwell was saying.

'I can't let this go unpunished even so. There'll be no dinner for either of you. You' – she pointed at Hannah – 'will spend the rest of the day in the punishment room on bread and water.' Her glance turned to Luke. 'And we'll see what a beating will do for you.'

She stepped between them and laid a hand heavily on their shoulders. 'Come along.'

As they were led away, Hannah caught sight of the tears coursing down Jane's face, of Nell's anxious look and Joe's scarlet cheeks.

Not until the next morning as they hurried to work were Hannah and Luke able to speak to each other.

'Was it very bad, Luke? Did she hurt you?'

'It was him – Mr Bramwell – not her. He beats the boys and she punishes the girls.'

'Did it hurt?'

'It wasn't too bad. I've 'ad worse from old Goodbody.' The lad grimaced and Hannah knew he was being brave. 'I'm sorry I led you into trouble, Hannah, but it was great out there on the hills, wasn't it?'

'Yeah, it was. And it's not the first time I've been in trouble and I doubt it'll be the last.' She grinned at him. 'I'm just sorry we didn't stop and have Mrs Grundy's roast lamb, aren't you?'

As they parted in the yard to go to their separate places of work, Ernest Scarsfield saw them laughing together. He'd heard about the previous day's escapade and now he shook his head in wonder. Was there nothing that would tame this girl? Because the way she was going on, she was going to spend half her days in trouble. And the more trouble she got into, the harsher the chastisement would become. He didn't want to see a pretty, bright little lass like her forever being punished, yet he couldn't help but secretly hope that her spirit would never be broken. He'd seen it all over the years. Undernourished, overworked children cowed and old before their time, many of them never even reaching adulthood. The work was arduous and only the strongest endured. He devoutly hoped Hannah was a survivor.

Nine

The following Sunday as they walked back from the morning service in the schoolroom, Luke whispered, 'Are we going out again?'

Hannah shook her head. 'It's not that I don't want to, or that I've suddenly turned into a bootkisser like Millie calls me.'

Luke grinned. 'Fat chance!'

Hannah smiled too. 'But I do want to keep in Mrs Bramwell's good books for a bit, if I can. You know what she's like.' Suddenly, Hannah clapped her hands and mimicked the superintendent. ' "Come along, come along. There's work to be done." Well, I'm going to do whatever she asks me. You see, I want to go and see me mam. And they won't let me if I keep getting meself into trouble, will they?'

Luke pulled a face. 'I don't think they will anyway. 'Specially not yet. We've only been here a couple of weeks.'

'Well, I'm going to try in another two weeks' time,' Hannah said determinedly. 'But in the meantime, I'm going to behave myself.'

Luke laughed aloud. 'I'll believe that when I see it. By the way,' he added, 'have you seen Joe?'

'Not to speak to. I've seen him in the yard but he scuttles out of my way whenever he catches sight of me.' Her eyes sparkled with mischief. 'Reckon he's scared to face me.'

'Me an' Daniel thought about giving him a thumping—'

'Oh, don't do that, Luke. You'll end up in more trouble.'

He nodded. 'That's what Daniel said. So instead we've got all the other lads to ignore him for a bit. None of 'em can stand him, so maybe that'll teach him a lesson.'

Hannah laughed. 'Poor Joe,' she said, but there was not much sympathy in her tone.

The four children had been living and working at the mill for a month. Apart from still trying to help Jane with the evening's household chores when the younger girl was almost dropping on her feet with tiredness, Hannah had been a model of good behaviour. Every day, except Sunday, was the same. All the children, regardless of their age, were woken at five thirty in the morning and had to be at work by six. Their breakfast of porridge and oatcake was brought to them in the mill by the overworked Mary from the apprentice house, but the children were allowed an hour at midday to go back to the house for their dinner. They then returned to the mill and worked until six o'clock in the evening, followed by two hours' schooling, household chores, supper and bed. The food was reasonable – better than the fare in the workhouse. There was a regular supply of fresh vegetables from the field in front of the mill, in which the boy apprentices worked on Sundays under Arthur Bramwell's instruction whilst the girls sewed and darned under his wife's direction. They were given meat two or three times a week and there was plenty of milk from the Grundys' cows.

Hannah remained fit and healthy. She'd taken Mr Grundy's advice and bathed her eyes night and morning, which seemed to prevent her suffering from the eye infections that plagued many of the mill's workers. And sometimes, when the atmosphere became dense with the floating dust from the cotton, she would tie a piece of clean rag around her mouth and nose.

'Look at Lady Muck here,' Millie would jeer, but it wasn't Hannah who went home at night with rasping breath and her mouth caked with fuzz.

At the end of Hannah's fourth week at the mill, Mr Scarsfield came into the preparation room. 'I'm going to try you as a piecer, Francis. You've made good progress in here and—'

Overhearing, Millie piped up. 'What about me, Mr Scarsfield? I've been here longer than Boot. I should be—'

Ernest Scarsfield frowned. 'Boot? Why on earth do you call her Boot?'

Millie blushed. She'd called Hannah the derogatory name ever since that first day. Usually she remembered to call her by her proper name in front of their superiors, but in her indignation at being passed over, as she thought, the nickname had slipped out.

'I – I . . .' the girl faltered, but Hannah laughed.

'It's nothing, Mr Scarsfield. It's only a bit of fun. I've got a name for her, an' all.' Her eyes twinkled with merriment. 'But I'm not going to tell you what it is.'

The overlooker glanced between the two girls. He was well aware that there was animosity between them; he'd seen it from that first day. That was partly why he was looking to move Hannah to another job.

He'd taken to this girl. She was a willing worker and a quick learner, even if she was a bit rebellious at times.

'Hmm,' he glanced at Millie. 'I'll think about it. Maybe I'll try you as a tenter working on the carding machine with Hughes. In the meantime, I'm putting a new girl with you. You can teach her to do your job and then we'll see.' Millie's eyes flashed resentment but she had the sense to keep silent. The overlooker's voice took on a note of warning. 'She's come from the village, not from a workhouse. Her *parents* work here in the mill and they've apprenticed her.' Without saying so, he was indicating that it would be unwise to try bullying the new girl; she was not alone in the world. 'She starts on Monday, so you,' he turned back to Hannah, 'come to me first thing on Monday and I'll take you to Hudson. She'll show you what to do.'

Hannah smiled broadly. 'Thank you, Mr Scarsfield.' She liked Nell Hudson. The bed she shared with Jane was still next to Nell and her sleeping companion, and there were often muffled giggles in the night between the four of them.

'It's all right for some,' Millie muttered begrudgingly. 'I've been here a lot longer than you. I should be getting a better job, not you.'

'Who says it's a better job? It's not bad in here. At least it's away from all that noise.'

'You'll've more chance of being offered overtime, that's what,' Millie spat. 'You'll be able to earn money instead of just your keep and a new set of clothes once a year.'

'Well, if you weren't such a slacker, you might get the chance. The bosses aren't stupid, y'know. Keep yer nose clean and you might get the chance to work with Joe next door.'

'I don't want to work with *him*. Mrs Bramwell's pet. I'm no bootkisser,' Millie sneered. 'You 'n' Joe Hughes make a good pair.'

Now Hannah didn't respond. Since the day he'd carried tales to Mrs Bramwell, Hannah had heard it from some of the other children that he was not only the woman's favourite but that he deliberately sucked up to her. Joe still attempted to be friendly with her, but Hannah gave him the cold shoulder. Luke, she'd decided, was the one she wanted as her friend.

'Come to think of it, that Hudson girl's one an' all.'

Hannah's eyes widened. 'Nell? Never!'

'You'll find out. Only it's not boots she's kissing,' Millie said smugly and refused to say more.

The rest of the day passed in silence between the two girls, but at six o'clock, Hannah ran out of the yard and up the hill, excited to tell her good news to Jane and Nell.

'I'm coming to work with you,' she cried, grabbing hold of Nell about the waist and whirling her around. 'Mr Scarsfield says I can be a piecer and you're to teach me what to do.'

Nell's dark eyes lit up. 'That's wonderful. Marvellous!' She flung her arms around Hannah and they danced the length of the dormitory, laughing and singing together.

'What's got into you two?' one of the other girls asked as, one by one, they trudged wearily into the room. 'Come into a fortune, 'ave yer?'

'They're leaving. I bet that's what it is,' said another.

'Nah.' Millie, coming into the room, overheard the remarks. 'They're a couple of bootlickers, the pair of 'em. 'Er,' she pointed at Hannah, 'has got Mr Scarsfield wrapped round her little finger. And as for 'er – well, we all know who'd she'd lift her skirts for, don't we?'

The two girls stopped dancing and looked at each other, their merriment dying. Hannah made to pull away from Nell and lunge herself at the smirking Millie, but Nell caught hold of her. 'No. Leave it. She's not worth it. Not worth losing this chance over. You come and work with me. We'll be all right together.'

'Yeah, 'course you will,' Millie sneered. 'His pimp now, a' yer?'

Hannah started forward again, but Nell's grip tightened. 'I said, leave it.'

The rest of the girls averted their eyes or hurried out of the room. Hannah said no more, but the vindictive Millie had spoiled her exciting news.

'Mrs Bramwell, please may I go to see my mother one Sunday?'

The superintendent stared at Hannah in amazement. 'Go – to – see – your – mother?' she repeated.

'Yes. I haven't heard from her since I came here.'

Mrs Bramwell sat down suddenly, her shocked gaze still fastened on Hannah's face. 'Well, I never heard the like.'

Hannah put her head on one side and stared at her, puzzled by the woman's reaction to what, to the girl, seemed a simple, straightforward question. 'May I go? Please?'

'Oh no, no.' Mrs Bramwell shook her head. 'It's out of the question. Dear me. The very idea.'

Now Hannah frowned. 'Why? Why can't I go? It's not so far. I could do the journey in two days. There one day and come back the next. I just want to see her.'

Mrs Bramwell laughed wryly. 'Oh, my dear child, don't you know what signing that indenture means?'

'What's an in – indenture?'

'The piece of paper you were asked to sign when you arrived here.'

'Oh, that. I'd forgotten what it was called.'

'Yes, that.' Mrs Bramwell's tone was flat. 'Signing that paper means that you're bound to Mr Critchlow until you're eighteen. And he doesn't allow anyone to leave here. Not even for a day.'

Shocked, Hannah stared at Mrs Bramwell. 'You mean – you mean I can't go to see my mother for – for *six years*?'

Mrs Bramwell nodded.

The twelve-year-old child felt a lump in her throat and her eyes smart with tears. 'Why? Why not?'

Mrs Bramwell bit her lip as she considered her answer. This young girl was spirited, some might say wilful. If she put ideas into the girl's head, then . . . 'It's – it's the rules here,' she said lamely, ducking giving a full answer.

Now Hannah was angry with the uncontrolled rage of a young girl. Her blue eyes sparkled defiantly. 'Then they're cruel rules that keep a child from its mother. *For six years!*' She whirled around and ran from the room, and though Mrs Bramwell called after her, the girl didn't stop, ignoring the possibility of a night in the punishment room for her disobedience.

Left alone, Ethel Bramwell sighed. For once, she'd take no action against the girl. For once, she sympathized with her.

Hannah ran on, out of the house and down the hill to the mill. She would see him. She would seek out Mr Critchlow – the man who made these harsh rules. She'd tell him exactly what she thought of him.

Moments later she was banging on the door of the outer office. When a voice bade her enter, she thrust open the door and marched into the room. The clerk, Mr Roper, looked up from his desk. He blinked at her over the top of his spectacles.

'What do you want, girl?' he asked gruffly. 'You've no right to be in here. Have you been sent for? In trouble, are you?'

'No, but I want to see Mr Critchlow.'

'See – Mr Critchlow?' Mr Roper was startled, just as Mrs Bramwell had been, at the girl's audacity. Hannah thought for a moment that he was going to say, just like Mrs Bramwell, 'Well, I never heard the like.' But instead, he pursed his mouth. 'You've got cheek, I'll give you that. But in this place, that'll only earn you a punishment – not admiration.'

Hannah bit back a hasty retort. She swallowed her anger, realizing suddenly that belligerence would gain her nothing.

'Please, sir,' she said, modifying her tone, her whole attitude. 'Please, could I see Mr Critchlow?'

'He's not here. He's gone for the day.' Mr Roper paused and then added, slyly, 'but Mr Edmund's here. You could perhaps see him, if you like.'

In her innocence, Hannah nodded. 'Yes, please.'

Josiah Roper was a strange, complicated character. He had been born into relatively privileged circumstances.

He'd attended private schools and had been set to enter Oxford or Cambridge University until the day he'd learned that the family fortunes had been drunk and gambled away by his ne'er-do-well father. Josiah had been obliged to seek gainful employment. He was intelligent and able, but the doors that once might have been opened to him by way of his family's standing were now slammed in his face. Seventeen years earlier, as a desperate young man of eighteen, Josiah had sought out Edmund Critchlow, who'd been one of Josiah's father's more fortunate gambling cronies. Mistakenly, Josiah believed the man might feel some pangs of guilt, perhaps some sort of responsibility that he'd been involved in the downfall of the Roper family. Whilst Edmund did persuade his own father to employ Josiah as their clerk, his reasons were far from charitable. Edmund was ambitious. He couldn't wait to take over the running of Wyedale Mill from his father. Roper, he assumed, would be eternally grateful and utterly loyal to him. The impoverished young man, Edmund believed, would be his eyes and ears throughout the mill. People would tend to ignore the quiet man, to look upon him as a mere clerk. But they would be mistaken, Edmund schemed, for there would be nothing happen in the mill that he wouldn't hear about from Roper.

Josiah was indeed grateful to take the position, but his appreciation was short-lived. Though he did his job conscientiously, he was resentful of his benefactors, seeing his lowly position as an insult to his intelligence and none of his own making. In his twisted, embittered attitude, he took a perverse delight in hearing the quarrels and troubles that took place within his hearing in the inner office. As he went about the mill, ostensibly on office business, he picked up titbits of gossip, overheard private conversations, witnessed quarrels between workers and saw problems arise. And all of this he carried back to his office to calculate how he could best use such information. If he could manipulate a situation to cause trouble for someone – anyone, it didn't matter who it was – then his day was all the brighter. It relieved the monotonous drudgery of his enforced servile position. Yet, with his tale-bearing he was unwittingly fulfilling the very act that Edmund wanted of him.

And now here was this girl, who'd been in the mill but a few weeks, standing in his office demanding to see the master. Josiah's lip curled. It lightened his day. Well, she could see the young master. That'd stop her gallop and no mistake. She was a bit young at the moment, but Edmund would mark her out, and in three or four years' time . . .

Josiah rose slowly from behind his desk and straightened up. 'I'll ask if Mr Edmund will see you.' He moved deliberately slowly towards the door to the inner office, knocked and entered without waiting for a reply. He closed the door behind him and Hannah was left alone. She looked about her.

The offices were on the top floor of an annexe attached to the main mill. As she looked out of the windows, Hannah could see the building at right angles to this one and then, directly in front of her, the third one. The room itself was dark and dreary, furnished only with Mr Roper's high desk and an odd chair or two. A candle stood on the corner of his desk to give him a little extra light by which to write in his fine, spidery hand. The walls were lined with shelves, overflowing with ledgers and files and papers. No doubt Mr Roper knew where everything was, but to her, the place looked a muddle.

After what seemed an age, the door opened again, and Josiah beckoned her inside. Nervous now – the waiting had robbed her of her daring – Hannah stepped forward until she was standing before the man she'd seen only a few times walking through the mill. Mr Roper retreated from the room and softly closed the door.

Mr Edmund kept her waiting several minutes whilst his pen scratched across a sheet of paper before him. At last, he looked up, his thick, black eyebrows meeting in a frown. Then, as he realized who it was, he leaned back in his chair and linked his fingers.

'Well, well, well, the little blonde girl whom Scarsfield thinks fit to promote to piecer, even though she couldn't do her first job properly.'

Hannah's chin lifted defiantly. 'I hadn't done the piece of cotton you picked up.' She paused deliberately before adding, 'Sir.'

Edmund's eyes glittered. 'Hadn't you, indeed? Are you telling me that the other girl had done it?'

Hannah shook her head. 'No, sir. I'm just saying that you picked up a piece that I hadn't worked on.' She met his gaze, outwardly fearless yet inside she was quaking, her knees trembling uncontrollably.

He was a frightening figure, tall, commanding, and he held her life in his hands. His power was absolute and yet here was this slip of a girl daring to stand up to him. Strangely, it amused Edmund. He leaned forward, resting his arms on his desk, 'So – to what do I owe this pleasure?'

Hannah ran her tongue around her dry lips. 'Please, sir, I would like permission to visit me mother.'

Edmund frowned. There was a long pause, before he said slowly, 'Your – mother? You have a mother?'

'Yes, sir.'

'Goodbody told me you were orphans. The four of you.'

'The other three that came with me are, sir. But I've still got me mother.'

'And where is she?'

'At the Macclesfield workhouse, sir.'

'And how do you propose to go all that way to visit her?'

'I . . . I thought if I went on a Saturday afternoon and came back on Sunday night—'

He smiled sarcastically. 'You think you could walk all that way in that time?'

Hannah shook her head. 'I thought I could get a lift with the carter who brought us.'

'That costs money, girl.'

'But I have money, sir. The two guineas—'

'Ah yes. The two guineas.' His cruel smile broadened. 'That money is to pay for any stoppages you incur. It is not to be frittered away.'

'And that's frittering? Wanting to see me mother?' Hannah cried rashly, growing red in the face.

Edmund regarded her. *This girl is a little wild-cat*, he was thinking. *And wouldn't I just like the taming of her.* He smiled, but his smile was at his own thoughts. He was imagining Hannah a few years older . . .

He shook his head, pretending regret. 'I'm sorry, my dear, but it will not be possible to allow you to travel all that way to visit your mother.'

'But, sir—'

He held up his hand to still her protest. 'Perhaps, by now, she may have moved on. Found employment—'

'She'd've let me know. She'd've written to me.'

'Would she, indeed? She can write, then?'

'Well, no, but she'd've got someone else to do it for her. She'd've let me know somehow.' Hannah was insistent and incensed enough to demand boldly, 'Why can't I go to see her?'

'Because you signed a paper promising to be a loyal employee.'

'But I am a loyal employee. I'm not trying to leave. Just to go and see me mother. Just for a day. Other children see their parents. Several go home on a Sunday even though they live in the apprentice house in the week.'

'Not the workhouse paupers.'

She flinched to hear herself described that way.

'You see,' he went on, 'those other children live locally. They've been apprenticed by their parents, who've signed the paper on their behalf. So it is the *parents* who are legally bound to ensure their children keep to the agreement. Now, in the case of children from the workhouse, we have only the signatures – or the crosses – of the apprentices themselves. If we were to allow them to go wandering all over the country, well, we'd have no way of knowing if they'd come back.'

Hannah gaped at him. 'But of course I'd come back. I've promised you, and I don't break my promises.'

'Very laudable, I'm sure.' Edmund leaned back again. He regarded her thoughtfully for a moment. 'And do you know,' he said, sounding as if the admission actually surprised him. 'I think I believe you. But it's not possible. If we were to allow one to go, then all the others would want to go too.'

'But most of them don't have family. Most of the children, who've come here from the workhouse, don't have anyone. They're orphans. I'm not.'

'But you should be,' Edmund said. 'Goodbody is supposed to send only orphans.' His face darkened. 'Otherwise we encounter this very problem.' His lip curled. 'Children wanting to see their parents.'

Hannah bit her lip. 'Then – will you let me write to her? Will you see that my letter is sent?'

Edmund looked at her thoughtfully. He felt the familiar stirrings. One day, he promised himself, he would have this girl. Deciding to appear benevolent, he smiled, 'Of course, my dear. You write your little letter and bring it to Mr Roper. He'll make sure that it's sent to your mother.'

There was no more to be said. Hannah could see that no amount of pleading was going to change his mind. If only, she thought, she could have seen the older man, Mr Critchlow senior, then . . .

As if reading her mind and without looking up, Edmund added, 'And don't go asking my father if you can visit her. The answer would be the same.'

As she turned and marched towards the door, his final words followed her. 'And don't think about running away, will you? Our punishments are very severe for runaways.'

Hannah looked back over her shoulder, staring at him for a moment.

She hadn't thought of doing any such thing. At least, not until he had put the idea into her head.

Ten

'So.' Nell smiled. 'Are you ready to become a piecer?'

Hannah nodded. The previous evening she'd written her first letter to her mother. It was nestling in her skirt pocket. She planned to take it to Mr Roper at dinnertime. But for now, she must concentrate on what Nell was telling her.

'We work for the women who operate the spinning machines – mules, they're called. You'll be with me and Dorothy Riley to start with. Then, when you're good enough, you'll work with someone else.'

Hannah smiled. 'What do we have to do?'

'When a thread breaks we have to twist the ends back together again. But you have to be quick, 'cos they don't stop the machine.'

'Isn't it dangerous?'

Nell shrugged and pulled a face. 'Not if we're quick. And the women are good. They shout a warning.' Nell leaned forward and lowered her voice. 'The women get paid for every piece they produce, and if we can mend the broken threads without the machines having to be stopped, they can earn more. Sometimes, at the end of the week, they'll give us a few pence out of their own wages 'cos we've helped 'em earn more, see? We'll be working with Mrs Riley. She's ever so generous. She'll see us right. And you need nimble fingers.'

She flexed her own long, slim fingers and laughed. 'Mr Edmund says I've got nimble fingers.'

'Mr Edmund? I thought it was Mr Scarsfield who told us what work we're to do.'

Nell stared at her for a long moment, then seeing the genuine look of puzzlement on the younger girl's face, she gave a small sigh and said flatly, 'Yes, yes, of course it is. That's what I meant to say. Mr Scarsfield.' She smiled and linked her arm through Hannah's as they moved into one of the spinning rooms, where the clatter of machinery was deafening. Hannah grimaced but she saw Nell was laughing. 'You'll soon get used to it,' the girl mouthed at her.

For the morning, Hannah just observed Nell watching the rows and rows of yarn being drawn and twisted. The girl never took her eyes off the machine, and the moment a thread snapped, she swiftly twisted the broken ends together. By dinnertime, Hannah had a slight headache from staring at all the fine strands of cotton and the noise all around her, but she kept the fact to herself. Not one word of complaint would pass her lips. The job was a good one for a child of her age and – like Nell said – she was sure she would get used to it. Nevertheless, she was pleased to escape into the fresh air in the hour's break for dinner. She ran lightly across the yard and up the stone steps to the counting house. At his 'come in' in answer to her knock, Hannah opened the door and stepped inside to stand meekly before Mr Roper's desk, waiting until he should condescend to look up and acknowledge her presence. He kept her waiting – deliberately, she thought – for what seemed an age, until Hannah was afraid she'd be late back to her work.

'Don't fidget, girl. What is it you want?' he snapped, looking up at last.

'Please, sir, Mr Edmund said you'd see that a letter's posted for me.'

Hannah gave him what she hoped was her most winning smile, but it was lost on the embittered man. He merely glanced at her briefly over his spectacles and grunted sourly, 'Leave it there. I'll see to it.'

'Thank you, sir. Thank you very much.'

As Hannah left the office, Josiah Roper picked up the letter and, for a moment, weighed it in the palm of his hand. He glanced at the door, listening to make sure she had gone. He could hear her footsteps clattering down the steps and her sweet voice echoing back up the stairs. Josiah's mouth curled with disdain. Singing, indeed! How anyone could feel like singing in this place he couldn't imagine. He unfolded the letter to read her neat, childish handwriting.

'*Dearest Mam, I hope you are well. I am fine and now working as a piecer with Nell, who is my friend.*' The letter went on to describe the apprentice house and Mr and Mrs Bramwell and some of the other children. She made no mention, Josiah noticed, of the Critchlows or the fact that she'd already been confined to the punishment room on several occasions and that stoppages had been made out of her precious two guineas now in Josiah Roper's keeping. He smiled wryly. The child made this place sound idyllic, but, he realized, the girl wanted her mother to believe her well and happy.

Perhaps she was, Josiah thought, surprised. If her wretched singing was anything to go by.

The letter finished with a plea. '*I do wish you would write to me. I long to hear from you and know*

*that you are all right. Perhaps matron would write a
letter for you.'*

Josiah frowned thoughtfully. The matron. Matilda
Goodbody. Ah, now there was an idea – if it should
become necessary. He glanced at the door once more
before slowly tearing the letter into small pieces. He
was not taking this action on his own initiative;
Edmund had given the instruction.

'Destroy them, Roper,' he'd said. 'And make sure
no incoming letter reaches her.'

Josiah smiled cruelly, deliciously anticipating what
the girl might do when no answer to her letters
arrived.

As Hannah and Nell left the mill that evening and
crossed the yard, they passed a boy talking to Ernest
Scarsfield. The newcomer was tall and very good-
looking in Hannah's eyes. He had dark brown hair
and eyes to match. He looked a little solemn, but
then, she thought, he might well if he had any idea
what he was coming to. She bent towards Nell to
whisper, 'Do you think he's come for a job?'

'Eh?' Nell gaped at her in surprise. Then she
laughed. 'Don't you know who that is?'

Hannah shook her head.

'That's the next Critchlow. Adam. He's Mr
Edmund's son. We don't see much of him though.
He's away at school most of the time. Just now and
again he comes to the mill when he's home for the
holidays.' She grinned. 'To check his inheritance, I
expect.'

Hannah glanced back over her shoulder and stared
at the young man. He looked a little older than she

was. Fourteen or maybe fifteen, she thought. She could see now that he had the look of his father, the same dark colouring. Yet there was a marked difference: the boy had no cruel, sardonic twist to his mouth. As if feeling her scrutiny, Adam Critchlow turned and their eyes met. Embarrassed, a faint blush crept up Hannah's face and she looked away swiftly.

'Well, I'm off to the schoolroom,' she said, deliberately changing the subject.

'Not for much longer you won't be. You're not allowed to go after you're twelve.'

'Oh.' Hannah bit her lip. She was twelve already, almost thirteen, but she loved the two hours in the schoolroom after work each day. It was the only place she never got into trouble. Though the master was strict, Hannah so enjoyed soaking up the knowledge that her attention never wavered. She could write neatly, spell reasonably well and was above average at arithmetic. Some of the children, even at her age, still couldn't write their name in the sand tray, let alone be allowed to move on to use a slate. But Hannah was surprisingly alert even after long hours in the mill.

For the teacher, who laboured with children too exhausted to take in anything he was telling them, Hannah was a joy to teach. The elderly schoolmaster found his stern ways softening towards this able pupil. He had never before encountered such an enthusiastic child amongst the pauper apprentices at the mill. So, when later that same evening Hannah approached him as the other children escaped the classroom, he smiled at her. The girl didn't return his smile.

'What is it?' he asked. 'Something amiss?'

'Please, sir, I understand I'm not supposed to come to school any more. I'm thirteen next month.'

'Ah.'

'But I don't want to stop coming for lessons, Mr Jessop. That book you're reading to us – *Swiss Family Robinson* – I love it. I want to know what happens. I want to hear the end.'

The man was thoughtful for a moment. 'Has anyone said anything to you? Mr Critchlow, Mr Edmund or the Bramwells – about you not being able to attend classes any more?'

Hannah shook her head.

A twinkle came into Mr Jessop's eyes. A twinkle that very few of his pupils ever saw. He leaned towards her. 'Then we'll carry on until someone tells us to stop, eh?' He pointed his forefinger at her. 'You don't know the rule about stopping at twelve, and I,' now he pointed towards himself, 'don't know how old you are.'

Hannah's eyes shone. 'Oh, thank you, Mr Jessop.'

'Just one thing, mind,' he added. 'You won't be able to tell anyone that it's your birthday.'

'I don't mind. I'd rather keep coming to school.'

Mr Jessop nodded. 'Very well, then. Our little secret, eh?'

It would be six months before anyone realized that Hannah should no longer be attending the school, but in that time Mr Jessop had finished reading the story and started another. When she was forced to stop attending, he lent her books from the schoolroom. And whenever Hannah found herself destined for a spell in the punishment room, she hid the current precious book beneath her skirt and was lost in another world away from the stark confines of the bare room.

Little did anyone know that, apart from constant hunger, Hannah now quite enjoyed her spells of solitary confinement.

As Nell had said, Dorothy Riley was more than just 'nice', she was generous with her pay at the end of the week.

'There you are, my pets,' she said, slipping a few coppers into the girls' hands outside the mill gates. 'Can't promise it every week, but you've done really well considering it's your first week. Mind you,' she laughed, eyeing them, 'I don't think you'll be at the job long. You'll soon be a mite too big to nip in and out. Besides, old Scarsfield's got his eye on you two to go up in the world.'

Nell and Hannah exchanged glances. 'You think so, Mrs Riley?'

'I know so, luv. So, you keep on the way you are and you'll soon be earning proper money of your own.'

Hannah pulled a face. 'Well, Nell might. She's older than me, but I've a long way to go before I'm out of my indenture.'

Dorothy laughed. 'Don't you worry about that, luv. Our Ernest has ways and means of getting round that if he finds a really good worker amongst the apprentices.' She tapped the side of her nose knowingly. 'You mark my words.'

The two girls were to find that Dorothy Riley was even more generous in sharing her knowledge and experience with her two young piecers. When the machine was running smoothly, she made them watch her every move and explained everything she did and everything that happened. Before long, Hannah was working with another woman, Mrs Martin, who was as generous as Dorothy Riley.

'And when we get a machine of our own,' Hannah asked Dorothy, 'might we get paid then?'

'You should do, but now *he's* running the mill, he's put a stop to all that. Ernest told me himself. He's mad about it an' all, but there's nowt he can do. Sorry, luv.' Hannah pulled a face, knowing Dorothy was referring to Mr Edmund. 'Ah well, what you never have, you never miss, eh?'

Dorothy laughed. 'So they say, but I've never quite believed it myself.'

Hannah had settled in quickly to her new work and, whilst she still sang, no one else could hear her now above the noise of the machinery. Hannah sang on, hopeful every day that word would come from her mother. But the days and weeks turned into months, and still no answer came to her letters. At last, worried out of her mind and longing to see Rebecca, Hannah made up her mind to go back to Macclesfield to the workhouse and find out for herself.

'Oh no, Hannah, don't do that. You'll get into such trouble.' Jane's eyes filled with tears and she clutched Hannah's hand. 'They put children who run away into that awful room for a week. And they might beat you.'

Hannah wished she had not confided in the younger girl.

'I know you must want to see your mam,' Jane

went on. 'But she wouldn't want you to get into such trouble. You know she wouldn't.'

Hannah bit her lip. That much was true, but she was so worried about her mother now. Why had she not heard from her? Something must be wrong. After the conversation with Mr Edmund three months ago now, she'd written four letters, dutifully taking each one to the office and handing it to Mr Roper. She was not to know that, as with the first, moments after she'd left the room her loving letter lay in shreds in the bottom of Mr Roper's waste paper basket.

'I have to go,' was Hannah's simple answer to Jane. 'But forget I ever told you. And don't tell anyone else. If they ask, you mustn't tell them anything.'

Miserably the younger girl nodded. 'I wish you hadn't told me,' she whispered.

So do I, Hannah thought, and vowed not to tell anyone else.

Eleven

'Coming for a walk this afternoon?' Luke asked her as the apprentices trooped back from the schoolroom one Sunday morning. The service was not just for the apprentices, but for the whole village. Sometimes a man who lived in the village led the worship, and sometimes they had a visiting preacher. Hannah's favourite was the local doctor who lived in the next village. Dr Barnes was a portly figure with a round, red, beaming face and bushy side-whiskers. He was a benevolent preacher, gently exhorting his congregation to try to lead a blameless life. He didn't make Hannah feel sinful by just being alive like some of the other preachers did, thumping poor Mr Jessop's desk and shouting at the cowering youngsters in a thunderous voice that echoed to the rafters.

'I'd like to, Luke,' Hannah said, 'but I've got something else I have to do this afternoon.'

'What?'

She grinned at him. 'Never you mind.'

'I do mind. I thought you was my girl. You meeting some other feller, then? It's that Joe, I bet.' His jealousy was real. If an adult had overheard them, they might have roared with laughter at such a conversation taking place between two children. But the twelve-year-old boy (the twins had had a birthday since their arrival at the mill, though, like Hannah's, it had passed unnoticed) and the thirteen-year-old girl, working as hard as they did in the mill, considered themselves more grown up than others thought them.

'I talk to everybody, haven't you noticed?' Hannah said saucily.

He grinned ruefully. 'Yeah. All right, you do.' He paused and then asked, 'What's so important then that you won't come out, though? Got my socks to darn, 'ave yer?'

Darning socks was one of the many tasks Hannah had to tackle in Mrs Bramwell's sewing class. Strangely, the woman turned a blind eye if some of the girls did not present themselves in the kitchen every Sunday afternoon. It was the only occasion on which she showed leniency. Earlier that morning she'd called Hannah into her sitting room. The girl had stood in front of her, sighing inwardly and raking through her mind to think what she was in trouble for this time. But Ethel Bramwell was smiling. 'I don't mind you going out on a Sunday afternoon, Francis. In fact, if I'd my way, you children ought to be encouraged to walk out on a Sunday afternoon.' She sighed. 'But I have my orders as I'm sure you know.'

It was the closest the superintendent would come to criticizing their employers to one of her charges. But for some reason, Ethel Bramwell trusted this girl. She couldn't explain why. Maybe it was the girl's spirit that refused to be cowed or her open honesty. Whatever Hannah did, she would always own up to it and take her punishment cheerfully. She had even been known to take the blame for something someone else had done – if that someone was one of her close friends.

'But,' Mrs Bramwell was saying, 'you're one of the

neatest workers I've got. Your darning is as good as mine. The simple truth is, Hannah, I need your help.'

Hannah, noticing the woman's use of her Christian name, knew her words were sincere and her praise genuine.

'So,' Mrs Bramwell went on. 'How about you and I strike up a bargain? You come to my sewing classes on alternate Sundays and you're free to go out into the hills on the other days.'

Hannah beamed, delighted that, for once, she was not going to have to break the rules.

'Thank you, ma'am,' she said simply, and vowed to work twice as hard as anyone else on the days she tackled the piles of mending that Mrs Bramwell laid in her lap.

Now, Hannah punched Luke playfully on the shoulder for his impudence. Impulsively, and breaking her promise to herself, she turned to face him. 'Luke, don't tell a soul, but I'm so worried about me mam. I've written four times and not a word's come back. I have to go and see her.' Her words came tumbling out. 'I went to see Mr Critchlow – to ask permission – but there was only Mr Edmund there and he wouldn't let me go.'

Luke shook his head. 'The old man wouldn't've done either. Don't do it, Hannah. Please. It's not that bad here if you behave yourself, but they're devils if you don't.' He was still remembering the beating he'd had.

Anguished, Hannah cried, 'But what else can I do? I've got to know if me mam's all right.'

Luke bit his lip, thinking. 'Why don't you ask Mrs Bramwell to see if she can find out for you?'

Hannah shook her head. 'She'd only say the same

as Mr Edmund. "If we do it for one, they'll all want it." That's what he said about letting me go to see her.'

'Oh.' Luke had run out of ideas. He bit his lip worriedly. 'So – what're you thinking of doing then?'

'Going anyway,' she said firmly.

'What? This afternoon?'

'No – I was going to see Mrs Grundy. See if she'll help me. She might know if I can get a ride to Buxton . . .'

Luke shook his head. 'It might make things awkward for her.'

'How . . . how do you mean?'

'She'll know we're not supposed to run away. She wouldn't help you do something wrong like that.'

'She's nothing to do with the mill, is she?'

Luke shrugged. 'They supply the milk and other food. The Critchlows might cause trouble for her.'

'Oh,' Hannah said. 'I hadn't thought of that.'

They walked on in silence.

'Look,' Luke said. 'We could still go and see her this afternoon. I'll come with you. We could sort of bring the talk round. Tell her you're that worried about yer mam. She might think of something.'

Now Hannah stopped and turned to face him. 'You really mean you'll help me? You'll not try to stop me going?'

Luke regarded her solemnly. 'I don't think you should go. You'll get caught and brought back here and punished. You might not even get as far as the workhouse to see yer mam and then it'll have all been for nothing.'

'But I'll have tried, won't I?'

Luke nodded. 'Yeah, and I can't blame you for trying. If I was in your shoes, I'd do exactly what you're doing.'

Hannah squeezed his arm in gratitude.

'Hello, my dears. This is a nice surprise. Come away into the warm. Blustery old day even for October, isn't it? Winter's coming early this year, I reckon. There's a nice piece of beef and roast potatoes left from our dinner.' Lily Grundy reached out and pinched Luke's cheek playfully. 'You must have known there were leftovers.'

She chuckled as she ushered them into her warm kitchen and sat them at the table. Though the fare at the apprentice house was adequate, it was never enough to assuage growing appetites, and the two youngsters fell to eating the food she placed in front of them with gusto.

'Where's the mester?' Luke asked, his mouth full and gravy oozing out of the corner of his lips.

'In the front room fast asleep. Just like he always is on a Sunday afternoon. You'll see him later,' she laughed. 'If you can stay long enough.'

'He works very hard. I 'spect he deserves a sleep on a Sunday,' Luke remarked, popping another loaded forkful into his mouth.

'This is wonderful, Mrs Grundy,' Hannah said. 'I haven't tasted meals like this since – since . . .' Her voice faltered and for a moment tears filled her eyes. She blinked them back hastily, but not before both Luke and Mrs Grundy had noticed.

'It's because of Hannah we've come to see you,'

Luke rushed in. 'See, her mother's still in the work-house we came from, but Hannah's never heard word of her since we left. She's worried about her.'

Mrs Grundy's face sobered and she looked first at one and then the other anxiously.

'Hannah asked for permission to go and see her mother,' Luke went on. 'But—'

Mrs Grundy's generous mouth pursed as she finished his sentence. 'They won't let her go.'

'I asked Mr Edmund,' Hannah said, trying to keep her voice steady. 'But . . . but he said no.'

'Huh! Him! He would!' Mrs Grundy's tone was scathing and there was a bitter note to her words. She sighed heavily and sat down at the table, resting her arms on its surface. 'I don't often talk about this, but you both seem nice enough young 'uns.' Her glance roamed over Hannah's face as if assessing her.

Hannah dropped her gaze in embarrassment. Not so bashful, Luke grinned. 'We are.'

Mrs Grundy gave a faint smile, but it faded as she went on. 'We've never been blessed with children, me and the mester, but we've nephews and nieces. My brother's got a boy and a girl, but they live away. Right down south, so we don't see much of them. But Ollie's sister lives up the hill.' She nodded her head in the direction of Millersbrook, the village perched on the hillside above the mill. 'She'd a lad and – and a little lass.' She paused a moment and wiped a tear away with the corner of her apron. 'The lad – Ted – works here on the farm with Ollie. He's a good boy and – because we've no family of our own – this farm'll be his one day.' For a moment she pressed her lips together to stop them trembling. 'But their Lucy, she went into the mill.' She paused again as if the telling of this tale was painful. 'She was apprenticed and, just like you are I expect, she was given all the rotten jobs to start with. She had to crawl under the machinery. One day, there was an accident and her lovely hair got caught.' The woman closed her eyes, screwing up her face as she relived the agony. 'Tore it off her head, it did. Scalped her.'

The two youngsters stared at her with absolute horror. 'Did she – I mean – was she . . . ?'

Mrs Grundy nodded and her voice was a whisper. 'Yes, she died. Poor little mite. Only twelve, she was.'

There was silence between them, the only sounds the singing of the kettle on the hob, the settling of coal in the grate and a sudden flurry of sparks up the chimney.

At last Mrs Grundy cleared her throat and, her voice stronger now, said, 'So, if you want any help, Hannah, any time, you come to me and Ollie. We'll help you. We've no time for them at the mill. No time at all.'

'But . . . but I thought you supplied the milk an' that?' Luke asked.

Mrs Grundy's mouth was grim. 'We do. It goes against the grain, in a way, but we argued it out. One,' she ticked the reasons off on her fingers, 'it's business. We've a living to make. Two, we've nowt against the Bramwells. In fact, I'm quite friendly with Ethel Bramwell, and Ollie has a drink in the Wyedale Arms with Arthur. They were as upset as anyone over the accident. And three, we reckon if we supply the house, then we know you youngsters are getting good food. We . . . we reckon it's what our little Lucy would've wanted.'

There was logic in their reasoning, Hannah supposed,

though she thought she'd have been hard put to have anything further to do with the place if that had happened to one of her relatives or someone she cared for.

She said nothing as Mrs Grundy repeated, 'So, we'll help you whenever you need it – if we can.'

Luke spoke up for Hannah. 'She wants to go and see her mother. She knows that she'll probably be caught and punished, but she'll risk that, if she can just find out if her mother's all right.'

Mrs Grundy eyed Hannah. 'So, what do you want to do exactly?'

For a moment, Hannah gazed at her. Could she really trust this woman? Would she and her husband really help her or would they take her straight back to the apprentice house where she'd be locked in the punishment room? Luke, sensing her misgivings, reached across the table and touched her hand. 'It's all right, Hannah. Go on, tell Mrs Grundy.'

The woman's eyes softened. 'It's all right, dear. We won't let you down, I promise.'

'I . . . I thought if I left late one Saturday after work and walked through the night to Buxton, I could maybe get a lift on the carrier's cart from there. But I don't know the way. I know we came from Buxton to here, but I don't know which road to take to get back there.'

'All them corners and hills, I 'spect you lost your sense of direction,' Mrs Grundy said.

Hannah wasn't quite sure what she meant, but she nodded.

''Course,' the woman went on, musing aloud. 'If you was walking, the best way is up through the village and go by the country roads. But a little lass, on your own and in the dark, you could easy get lost.'

'I could go with her,' Luke began, but Hannah interrupted swiftly.

'No, I won't have you getting in trouble because of me. Thanks, Luke, but I've got to do this on me own.'

'Well,' Mrs Grundy said slowly. 'There's another way. Ollie could take you as far as Buxton in the cart and then you could make your way from there. Mebbe you could catch the coach from there. Or beg a lift with a carrier going to Macclesfield.'

The two youngsters stared at her. 'Would Ollie – I mean, Mr Grundy – do that for me?'

Mrs Grundy shrugged. 'I dunno, but we could ask him.' She began to rise as if to go and ask her husband there and then, but Hannah touched her arm, 'No, please, don't wake him.'

Lily Grundy sat down again, smiling comically. 'P'raps you're right. He'd not be in the best of moods to be woken from his Sunday afternoon nap.' She thought for a moment before saying, 'I tell you what you could do. You might beg a lift with the chap who fetches our milk every morning. Mind you, he's here early. One or two folks from the dale beg a lift with him now and again. He won't charge you anything and he'll take you nearly to Buxton. You could walk the rest of the way. Mind you –' she was thinking aloud now – 'you'd need some money to get a ride from there to Macclesfield.'

Hannah pulled a wry face. 'I haven't got any.'

'You've still got your two guineas from the work-house, ain't yer?' Luke reminded her.

'Well – yes, but . . . but Mr Critchlow,' she smiled

ruefully, 'or rather Mr Roper has charge of that. They'd likely demand to know what I wanted it for. Besides,' she grimaced ruefully, 'Mr Edmund said it's to pay for stoppages and I reckon Roper's taken some out of it already.'

'I'll lend you some, luv,' Mrs Grundy offered. 'And then you pay me back when you can. Few pence a week. I wouldn't mind.'

Hannah's eyes filled with tears at the woman's kindness. Mrs Grundy scarcely knew her, yet she was offering her far more than anyone at the mill would. She hesitated, but Luke urged her to accept. 'Go on, Hannah. You've got the chance of earning a bit now you're a piecer, and Mrs Grundy wouldn't offer if she didn't mean it.'

'It's very kind of you and I will pay you back. Every penny.'

Mrs Grundy patted her hand. ''Course you will, luv. I know that. So, when are you going to go?'

'Next Saturday,' Hannah said firmly, before she could lose her nerve.

'Right. Well, you'll need to be up at the top near the Arms by five o'clock in the morning. Ollie always takes our churns up there for him. And I'll get you the money now. Enough for coming back, an' all.'

'I don't know how to thank you.' Now Hannah allowed the tears of gratitude to spill over.

Twelve

'What are you two whispering about?'

Hannah and Jane looked up guiltily at Nell's question. The older girl's smile faded when she saw their expressions. 'Hey, I was only joking, but you really are up to something, aren't you?' She pursed her lips. 'I just hope it's nothing that's going to get us all into trouble, that's all.'

Hannah forced a laugh. ''Course it isn't.'

Nell moved closer. 'What then? What's going on? Is one of you in trouble already? Is that it?'

'No, but she will be if she does what she says she's going to,' Jane burst out, her face red.

'Jane!' Hannah cried, but the damage was done. Now Nell wouldn't let the matter drop.

Suddenly, she was very anxious. 'You're not going to run away?' This was the unthinkable. It was what carried the severest of punishments. Even a girl could be beaten for that.

'No,' Hannah said reluctantly. 'I'll come back.'

'So – what are you going to do?'

'She's going back to Macclesfield to see her mam,' Jane blurted out. 'She's never heard from her all the time we've been here.'

Nell looked at Hannah with a mixture of pity and fear. 'I can understand you wanting to go, but you won't half be in for trouble when you get back. And you probably won't even make it to Macclesfield. They'll catch up with you long before you get there and they'll never believe that you meant to come back.' She pulled a face. 'Not many of us would, if we once got out.' She paused, hoping she'd made the girl change her mind, but seeing the determination on Hannah's face, Nell sighed and asked flatly, 'So, when are you going?'

Hannah put her hand warningly on Jane's arm to stop her saying any more and faced Nell. 'It's best you don't know.'

Now Nell was indignant. 'Don't you trust me?'

Hannah was quick to say, ''Course I do, but – like you say – there's no need for anyone else to be in trouble. Only me.'

Nell nodded towards Jane. 'Well, she will be. She sleeps with you, and the rest of us can hardly say we haven't noticed you're missing.'

'I'll go early, while you're all still asleep. All you've got to do is to know nothing when they ask you.' She laughed. 'You can say you thought I was in the punishment room. I spend enough time there.'

Nell snorted. 'You'll be spending a lot more in there an' all when they catch you.' Then she sighed and relented. 'But we could cover for you for a bit. Give you time to get right away.'

Hannah shook her head. 'It's good of you, Nell, but I'd rather none of you knew. There's just one thing. I've decided to go early on a Saturday. It'll give me two days. I know how I can get a lift part of the way and I'll get back – somehow – on Sunday night. Thing is, Mr Scarsfield'll miss me at work.'

'He might not. He doesn't come round so much on a Saturday. Spends the morning with the bosses in the office. Planning next week's work. I know, 'cos—' Nell stopped suddenly and bit her lip. A faint blush tinged her face. 'Anyway,' she went on swiftly, 'me and Jane'll play dim, and the rest of them really won't know anything. And I'll cover your machine for Mrs Martin. I'll tell 'er you're not well or summat.' Now Nell glanced severely at Jane. 'So don't go telling anyone else, see.'

Jane shook her head, red-faced and tearful that she had given away Hannah's secret. 'I'm sorry, Hannah.'

Hannah put her arms around her and hugged her. 'It's all right. No harm done.'

She hoped fervently that she was right.

On the Saturday morning, very early, Hannah slipped out of the bed she shared with Jane, managing not to disturb the sleeping child. Carrying her clothes, she tiptoed out of the room and dressed on the landing outside the dormitory. It was still dark as she crept down the stairs and into the kitchen. The noise, as she opened the back door, seemed to echo through the house. She held her breath a moment, listening, but there was no movement from above that might mean someone had heard her. As quietly as she could, she pulled the door shut behind her and set off down the hill, then along the wall side and past the pillared gate leading into the mill. Once clear, she began to run up the lane. Passing the Grundys' farm, she could hear sounds from the cow shed but she didn't dare to linger. She wasn't sure of the time and she didn't want to miss the man who collected the milk.

At the top of the hill she bent over to catch her

breath but was relieved to see that Mr Grundy's churns were still standing against the low stone wall. She sat down beside them, leaning her back against the rough stones. As she waited she watched the dawn streaking the sky with a rosy peach colour and the world around her grew lighter. She listened, straining her ears for the sound of the rattling wheels of a cart that might herald the carrier's arrival.

She had no means of telling the time and she began to worry that she'd missed him. Perhaps the churns were empty, returned for the farmer to refill the next day. She tapped the side of the one nearest to her and heard the dull sound that meant it was full of milk. She breathed a sigh of relief. But then she heard another sound – a sound she dreaded hearing. Footsteps were coming up the last stretch of the hill, nearer and nearer. Someone else was coming from the valley to beg a lift too. She watched as a figure, climbing the last few feet, appeared. Hannah drew in a startled gasp. The man was walking with his head bowed. She couldn't see his features, but there was no mistaking his hunched stance. Shocked, she couldn't move. And then it was too late to run as he lifted his head and saw her.

'You!' Josiah Roper came towards her slowly, his beady eyes never leaving her face. As he drew closer she could see that he was smiling with sadistic pleasure. 'Running away, are you?'

Now her boldness returned. She stood up, facing him and saying stoutly, 'No, I'm not. I'm coming back tomorrow tonight. I'm going to see my mother in Macclesfield.'

For a brief moment even Josiah Roper seemed fazed by her bold, yet polite retort. But he recovered quickly to say, 'I thought I heard Mr Edmund tell you distinctly that you couldn't go?'

There was a brief silence before Hannah muttered, 'He did. But,' she added, more strongly, 'I mean to come back. I'm not a runaway, Mr Roper, truly I'm not.' She stepped closer, trying to appeal to the man's better nature – if he had one. 'I have to see my mother. I have to know if she's all right. I haven't heard a word from her ever since I came here. And you know I've written four times.'

'That's as may be, but you cannot go without the master's permission . . .'

At that moment, they both heard the sound of the carrier's rattling wheels.

'Oh, please, Mr Roper, let me go. I beg you. I swear on my mother's life that I'm coming back tomorrow night. I *promise* you.'

But he was smiling nastily. 'I don't believe you. I'll have to take you back.'

'But – but you'll miss your ride too. Please, Mr Roper . . .'

But delivering an errant child back to the punishment that awaited her would bring Josiah Roper far more satisfaction than his monthly weekend trip to Buxton to see his widowed mother.

'Mr Roper.' Mrs Bramwell's face was puzzled as she opened the back door of the apprentice house to the man's loud knocking. Then her glance travelled down a little to see the girl standing beside him and saw that he was gripping Hannah's arm tightly. For a clerk who sat hunched over a desk all day, Josiah was surprisingly strong.

111

'Francis?' Now there was an anxious question in her tone as if she already knew – and feared – the answer.

'I found this girl at the top of the hill, waiting – would you believe? – for a ride with the milk cart. And where, I'd like to know,' Josiah put his head on one side and smiled accusingly, 'did she get the money to take a trip all the way to Macclesfield?'

Mrs Bramwell's mouth dropped open and she glanced from one to the other. 'Well, you needn't look at me like that, Mr Roper. I know nothing about this, believe me.'

Josiah grunted. 'Really. Then in that case you've shown a serious dereliction of your duties, Mrs Bramwell. Because you should've known and put a stop to it.' He gave a mock sigh, pretending that what he was about to say pained him. 'I shall be obliged to report the matter to Mr Edmund.'

Ethel Bramwell stared at him before saying bitterly, 'Oh, I'm sure you will, Mr Roper. Nothing'll give you greater pleasure, will it?'

'It's not Mrs Bramwell's fault,' Hannah cried. 'She knew nothing about it. No one did.' She looked up at Ethel. 'And I wasn't running away, Mrs Bramwell. I was coming back tomorrow night. I was only trying to see my mother.'

'A fine tale,' Josiah snorted. 'Since when did any child voluntarily come back if they once got away from here?'

'Me.' Hannah glared up at him. 'If I say I'll do something, then I'll do it.'

The adults looked down at her. She could see that Mrs Bramwell wanted to believe her, but there was no softening in Josiah Roper's attitude. 'Where did you get the money? Did you steal it?'

'No,' Hannah gasped, horrified that anyone could think such a thing of her.

His grip tightened painfully on her shoulder and he bent menacingly towards her. 'Then where did you get it?' His face close to hers, Hannah stared into his beady eyes and shivered fearfully.

But now Hannah couldn't answer truthfully. She wouldn't involve Mrs Grundy. 'I . . . I saved it. It was mine.'

'Saved it? How? You came from the workhouse and all they give you is the two guineas you handed to Mr Critchlow.' He smiled maliciously. 'And I still have that in my safekeeping.'

'That he took off us, you mean,' Hannah said rashly and earned herself a clout across the side of the head from Josiah.

'I asked you where you got the money,' he shouted, but now Mrs Bramwell intervened.

'That's enough, Mr Roper. You've no right to touch this girl. No right at all. She's my responsibility.'

Josiah turned on the woman. 'Then you'd better start doing your job, Mrs Bramwell, or else—'

'Oh yes, Mr Roper, or else – what? You lay another finger on this girl – or any of the children in my charge – and I'll be the one doing a bit of reporting to the master. To Mr Nathaniel Critchlow.'

They glared at each other, whilst Hannah stood watching, biting her lip and chastising herself for her wayward tongue. It'd got her into trouble before and it looked as if she'd made matters worse now.

Josiah turned away, but as he did so, he wagged his

finger in Mrs Bramwell's face. 'You watch out, Ethel Bramwell. You just watch your step, that's all I'm saying.'

As he turned to go, Mrs Bramwell reached out and dragged Hannah into the kitchen and slammed the door. 'And now, young lady, I'll deal with you.'

Thirteen

'It's out of our hands. There's nothing we can do about it, Arthur.'

Mr and Mrs Bramwell were standing either side of the kitchen table, arguing over the girl who sat between them calmly eating her porridge. They glanced at Hannah with expressions of anger tinged with pity. They were cross with her for – as they believed – attempting to run away. They, as well as she, would be in trouble. But more than the concern for themselves, they pitied the golden-haired girl for the punishment they knew awaited her – a punishment of which she was, at this moment, blithely unaware.

'Roper knows. He brought her back. He'll waste no time in telling the master or Mr Edmund.'

Arthur Bramwell regarded the girl sorrowfully. 'The old man's away. It'll be Mr Edmund he tells.'

'Ah!' Ethel let out a deep sigh and murmured, 'Poor child.'

Arthur leaned on his hands on the table, large, capable hands that had never been afraid of manual work, hands that were just as ready to caress as to chastise the apprentices in his care. He was a big man, broad and strong and quiet, and when he could he protected the youngsters. Sometimes he had to beat them, but he made sure he did not damage them physically. It was humiliation he wished to inflict rather than actual hurt. Just to make them toe the line. But when it came to the matter of a child running away, he was powerless to prevent the inevitable punishment.

'Why did you do it, Francis? Why did you try to run away?'

Hannah swallowed the last mouthful and laid her spoon in the empty bowl. She looked up at them both, first at Mrs Bramwell's anxious face and then at the big man's. During the time she'd been here, she'd come to like and respect this couple. They were strict, but fair, and she knew they really cared about all the children. She was sorry to have caused them trouble and said so, adding, 'But I wasn't running away. I just had to go and try and find out how me mother is. I asked for permission, but Mr Edmund refused me.'

'So,' Arthur said in his deep rumbling voice. 'You went anyway?'

Hannah bit her lip and nodded. 'I'm sorry,' she said huskily. 'But you've got to believe me, Mr Bramwell, I was coming back.'

'Do you really mean that?' It seemed as if Arthur Bramwell couldn't quite believe what he was hearing.

Hannah nodded. 'I like it here. The work's hard, but I don't mind that. And I like the people.' She pulled a face. 'Well, most of them. All except Mr Roper.'

She didn't like Mr Edmund either, but she thought it wise not to say so at this moment.

Husband and wife glanced at each other and, though they said no more, Hannah could see that neither of them really believed her. And if they didn't, then there was not the remotest chance that either of the Critchlows would, especially Mr Edmund.

116

'Well, we'd best get it over with,' Ethel Bramwell said. 'Come on, girl.'

'Want me to go with her, Ethel?' Arthur straightened up and looked across at his wife, but she shook her head. 'No, no, Arthur. The girls are my responsibility. It'll not be the first time I've had to stand there and take his abuse – nor will it be the last.'

Again they both looked down at Hannah. 'Mebbe he won't be so hard on her,' Arthur murmured, intending that Hannah should not hear him, but her sharp hearing caught every word. 'She's a pretty little thing.'

But Ethel answered swiftly, 'I'd sooner see her spend a week in the punishment room than anything else he might have in mind.'

'Well, keep your eye on her. She's just the sort he goes for. Give her another year or two and – well . . .'

His voice petered out as Mrs Bramwell took hold of Hannah's shoulder and propelled the girl in front of her. 'He'll have to get past me first. He can get up to his tricks with the mill girls from the village if he likes. They'll have to look out for themselves, but he's not having his way with any of my girls. Not if I can help it. Mind you,' she lowered her voice. 'I don't seem to be managing it with young Nell.' She raised her voice. 'Come on, you. Let's get it over with.'

Hannah wasn't sure who was trembling the most as they stepped into the inner office.

Even though it was Saturday morning, Edmund Critchlow was sitting behind his desk, leaning back, rocking slightly as he regarded them through his dark, hooded eyes.

'So, girl, you thought you could defy me and get away with it, did you?'

'Mr Edmund—' Mrs Bramwell began, but the man

held up his hand to silence her, his glance never leaving Hannah's face.

'Well, what have you to say for yourself?'

Hannah lifted her chin and met his eyes boldly. Inside she was quaking, but she was determined not to let this man see her fear. 'I'm truly sorry, Mr Edmund, that I disobeyed you. I just wanted to see my mother.'

'Don't you think all the children here would like to see their mothers? Why should you be different?'

With an outward calmness, Hannah answered, 'Most of the children in the house have no mothers – or fathers. They're orphans. I'm not. I have a mother. I wanted to see her. I've written to her four times – like you suggested – and brought the letters to Mr Roper to send, but I've not had a word back. I just want to know she's all right. That's all.'

It was quite simple to the girl's mind. She couldn't understand why no one else could see it. And worse still, she couldn't understand why anyone would deliberately want to keep a child from its mother.

Edmund leaned forward, tapping the desk with his forefinger. 'I thought I'd made it clear last time. When you came here, you signed a paper. You remember?'

'Yes, sir.'

'And do you know what that paper was?'

'An indenture, sir.'

'Quite right. And what did it mean?'

'That I'm apprenticed to you for six years.'

'Exactly. Six years. And that means you do not run away during that time.'

'I wasn't running away, sir. I keep trying to tell you – and everyone – I was coming back tomorrow night. As soon as I'd seen my mother.'

118

For a moment, Edmund stared at her and then his lip curled, 'You really expect me to believe that?'

Hannah met his gaze steadily. 'Yes,' she said simply, 'because it's the truth.'

'She's a good girl usually, sir,' Mrs Bramwell began but Edmund snapped.

'Hold your tongue, Bramwell. I'll have more to say to you later. I hold you responsible for all this.'

'Mrs Bramwell had nothing to do with it, sir,' Hannah spoke up. 'She knew nothing about it. I let myself out of the back door this morning, really early. Before anyone was up.'

'That's no excuse. You shouldn't have been able to get out. The door should have been locked and the key hidden.'

Mrs Bramwell opened her mouth to protest, but at the sight of the young master's glowering face, she closed it again.

His mouth was tight, his thick black eyebrows drawn together almost hiding his cruel eyes. 'Well, we have a way of dealing with runaways here.'

Hannah opened her mouth to say, 'I'm not a runaway,' but further protest was useless. No one would believe her.

Hannah roused to hear a soft tapping on the door.

She was lying on the cold hard floor of the punishment room with not even the rough blanket for covering. There was nothing in the room now except a jug of water to drink and a bucket for her to relieve herself in. She pulled herself up slowly. Every bone in her body ached, every muscle screamed for relief and her buttocks stung from the wheals inflicted by the thin cane. Mr Edmund had delivered the beating himself, despite Mrs Bramwell's valiant protests.

'You've no right, sir,' Ethel had cried. 'Not a girl.'

'No right? No right, you say. I've every right, Bramwell. I own her – body and soul. I own all of them, every last one, and I will do with them as I please.'

With that, Edmund had grabbed hold of Hannah and hauled her towards his desk. Swinging her round, he had grasped the back of her dress, and in one swift movement torn it open to reveal her naked back and bottom.

'No, sir, no,' Ethel had tried in vain, terrified by the madness in the man's eyes. He had raised the cane, and though she lunged forward, trying to wrest it from his hand, he had pushed her roughly out of the way so that she overbalanced and fell to the floor. Then with a vicious delight he had brought the cane down on the girl's pink young flesh again and again until her skin was raw and bleeding.

Ethel had sat on the floor where she had fallen, closed her eyes and moaned aloud. But there was no sound from Hannah. Not a whimper, not a word of protest or entreaty. She had stood with her face buried against her arm as she was held over the desk, and made not a murmur. It had incensed Edmund further. 'I'll teach – you – to run – away,' he had shouted between each cutting stroke. 'We'll see how you – sing after this – eh?'

On and on he had gone, stroke after stroke, until Hannah's legs had given way and she had crumpled to the floor. At last, he had stopped, standing over her, breathing hard whilst Ethel Bramwell scrambled across the floor to gather the girl into her arms.

At last Hannah had made a sound. Quite plainly they had both heard her trembling words.

'Rock of ages, cleft for me . . .'

Ethel Bramwell had looked up at the man towering above them both, and almost laughed hysterically to see the incredulous look on his face.

'Hannah? Hannah – you there?' The voice came again, rousing her.

Despite her terrible state, Hannah wanted to laugh and reply, 'Where else do you think I'd be?' But she quelled the retort and struggled to the door. She pressed her face to it and whispered, 'Luke?'

'Yeah, it's me. I've brought you some food, but there's no key. I can't open the door.'

Again a sharp retort sprang to her lips but remained unspoken. Instead, she said, 'That's nice of you, but I can't open it either.'

There was a long silence and Hannah thought he had gone, but then she heard Luke say, 'Can you open the window?'

'I . . . I'm not sure. It's so cold in here, I haven't tried.'

'Well, have a go because . . .' His next words were lost to her as, stiffly, she moved across the small room and pushed at the window. She pushed and shoved, and slowly, protestingly, it opened. She went back to the door.

'Yes, I've opened it, but why?'

'Listen, when it's dark tonight I'll get a rope and throw it up to you. Then I'll tie a cloth with some food wrapped in it and you can pull it up.'

'Oh, Luke, you'll be in trouble if you're caught.'

'Ne'er mind about that. You're hungry, aren't you?'

At the mere thought of food, Hannah's stomach rumbled, but Luke was whispering urgently, 'I'll have to go. But watch out tonight.'

She heard a brief movement on the other side of the door and knew he was gone. Now she felt lonelier than ever.

It worked better than Hannah had imagined it possibly could. The punishment room was at the top of the house in the attic, but she'd reckoned without Luke's determination. It took four attempts before she caught hold of the rope and hauled it into the room.

'Wait a bit,' Luke called up in a loud whisper. 'I've got to tie it on this end.' A moment's silence and then she heard him say, 'Right, pull away.' Slowly and steadily she hauled on the rope until the bundle came level with the window.

'And what, may I ask, is going on here?'

Hannah gasped, startled by the voice that came up through the darkness from below the window. Oh no! she thought. Not him again. Swiftly she dragged the bundle in through the window and squatted down out of sight. She held her breath, listening intently through the open window.

'Evening, Mr Roper,' she heard Luke say brightly, but Josiah Roper was not to be fooled so easily.

'I asked you what you were doing, boy?'

'Tekin' a stroll like you, Mr Roper. Nice evenin', ain't it?'

There was a moment's silence when Hannah visualized Josiah glancing up towards the window of the punishment room. His next words confirmed her fears. 'I hope you're not communicating with that girl?'

'What girl, Mr Roper?'

Despite her pain, Hannah had to stuff her fist into her mouth to silence the laughter bubbling up inside her. Luke sounded so innocent.

'You know very well "what girl",' Josiah snapped. 'I think I'd better report this to Mrs Bramwell . . .'

Hannah heard no more. Swiftly she opened the bundle to reveal a piece of cold meat pie and some bread and cheese. This wasn't the sort of fare the apprentices were given. She hoped Luke hadn't stolen it. He'd be next in the punishment room if he had. She heard them move away, and now, ravenous, she stuffed it into her mouth.

By the time footsteps sounded outside the room, the door flung open and light from the lamp that Mrs Bramwell carried flooded the room, making Hannah wince against the sudden brightness, all trace of the food was gone and the cloth it'd been wrapped in hidden beneath her clothing. The rope was the only thing that might have given them away, but she'd thrown that out of the window, hoping that Luke would have the sense to retrieve it as soon as he could.

Ethel glanced round the room and then, seeming satisfied, she nodded, 'You'll be coming out in the morning. Mind you're ready for work.'

The light disappeared and the door slammed shut again. Hannah sighed and lay back on the floor trying, in vain, to find a comfortable position. Tomorrow night, she thought, she'd be back in her own bed snuggling close to Jane.

*

When she appeared in the dormitory the following morning, Jane ran to her and hugged her hard. 'Oh, I've missed you so.'

Hannah hugged her in return and then said, 'Come on, we'd best hurry. I don't want to be late on me first morning back.'

Hand in hand they left the house and ran down the hill, joining the other apprentices already making their way through the early morning mist, scarcely awake and rubbing their eyes with weariness.

Ernest Scarsfield counted them in. 'Oh, you're back with us, Francis, are yer? Not do that again in a hurry, I'll be bound.'

Hannah glanced up at him. 'Why will no one believe me, Mr Scarsfield?'

'Eh?'

As she explained, his blank look turned to one of incredulity. He laughed. 'You trying to tell me you really meant to come back?'

Hannah nodded. 'Yes, I am.'

Ernest pushed back his hat and scratched his head. 'Well, if that don't beat all. I've never heard the like.'

'It seems as if no one expects someone to come back if they once get away,' Hannah said solemnly.

Ernest nodded. 'That's about the size of it, lass.' He paused and then stared at her again. 'You really did mean to come back once you'd seen yer mother?'

'Yes, I did.'

For the first time someone really seemed to believe her. The overlooker smiled and bent towards her. 'Look, I'll try to see what I can do to help yer. I've got a mate in the village who goes through to Macclesfield about once a month. Would yer like him to ask around for yer? See if he can find out about yer mother?'

Ernest Scarsfield was rewarded with Hannah's wide smile. Her blue eyes sparkled with grateful tears. 'Oh, thank you, Mr Scarsfield. You're so kind. I don't know how to thank you.'

He straightened up, feeling an unaccustomed lump in his throat. 'There, there,' he said awkwardly. 'Don't fret. I'll see what I can do.' He patted her shoulder. 'Run along into work now.'

As he watched her go, Ernest stroked his moustache, still marvelling over the child. Not only had the young girl done something remarkable – she'd made him involve himself in the life of one of the workers, a thing he'd vowed he'd never do – but for some reason he couldn't explain, he believed her story. He actually believed the child had meant to return to the mill.

And that, to him, was the most incredible part of it all.

That morning, despite the soreness of her back that would take some time to heal, Hannah sang at her work.

At last, someone really believed her.

Fourteen

Hannah had to be patient – something she wasn't very good at. Ernest Scarsfield had said he'd try to make enquiries for her and she believed him, but the wait was agonizing. She busied herself with work, trying to keep her mind off thoughts of her mother, even asking Mrs Bramwell for extra chores in the evening. 'Jane's so tired. Please let me do her jobs.'

Ethel Bramwell was amazed at the resilience of this girl. After a beating like she'd taken, many another would have moaned and begged to be excused from work for weeks. But Hannah made no complaint even though her back was smarting and she would always bear a faint scar or two where the cane had cut the deepest. Ethel believed Hannah's story now and was secretly trying to think of a way to help the girl find out about her mother. They were all supposed to be orphans that came from the workhouse. It was Goodbody's fault for sending Hannah, no one else's and certainly not the girl's.

'Can we do something, Arthur?' Ethel asked her husband. 'I can't help liking her. I know she's a bit of a rebel.' She smiled with something approaching fondness. 'But I have to admire her spirit. We don't get many like her in this place. You should have seen that beating he gave her.' The woman shuddered. 'He was like a man possessed.'

Arthur's kindly face was grim. 'I expect there was a bit more to it than that.' He nodded knowingly at his wife. 'You know what I mean, love. Beating a young girl. Gave him a thrill, I expect. By, he's a nasty piece of work and no mistake.'

'I know she's a handful, but she didn't deserve that. She's a funny little lass. She's – she's . . .' Ethel sought the appropriate way to describe Hannah. 'She's rebellious for the right reasons.'

Arthur nodded. 'I know exactly what you mean.'

'So?' Ethel prompted. 'Is there anything we can do to help her?'

'I'll have a word with Ernest. He's a decent bloke. Mebbe he can think of something.'

Ethel smiled. 'D'you know, she's still doing all her little friend's chores at night? The little pasty-faced one. Pickering.'

'And you let her? Spoiling the other lass though, isn't it?'

Ethel grimaced and shrugged. 'Like Francis says, the other child's dropping on her feet when she gets back from the mill. It's plain to see and I can't argue with it. I have to let the little 'un rest else she'll not be fit for the mill and then you know what'll happen. It'll be us to blame. As usual.' They exchanged a glance, then Ethel asked, 'D'you know what job Pickering's doing?'

Arthur shrugged. 'No, but I'll mention it to Ernest. See if he can put her on something a little less tiring.'

They met in the Wyedale Arms at the top of the hill – Ernest Scarsfield, Arthur Bramwell and Ollie Grundy. Several of the male mill workers also climbed the steep

127

slope two or three times a week. The ale was worth the tough climb and the walk back home was easy, unless of course one too many had been imbibed and then there was the danger of falling and rolling home quite literally.

The three of them tucked themselves away in a corner and almost before they'd got settled with their pints in their hands, Arthur said, 'Now, Ernest, my missis has made me promise to ask you about that little lass who's desperate for news of 'er mother. You know, the one that ran away and spent a week in the punishment room for her trouble.'

Ollie Grundy pricked up his ears, knowing at once that it was Hannah they were talking about.

Ernest was nodding soberly. 'He beat her himself, didn't he?'

'Beat her? Who?' Ollie had spoken aloud before he could stop himself.

'One of the lasses tried to run away,' Arthur explained. 'She *said* it was to see her mother in the workhouse, that she meant to come back—'

'Oh, she did,' Ollie said, without thinking. 'She did mean to come back.'

'Eh?' Ernest stared at him.

Ollie sighed, realizing he'd said too much. Now he'd have to explain. 'My missis helped her. Lent her some money. Lily trusted her – believed her.' He faced the other two fiercely. 'And so do I.'

Ernest and Arthur exchanged a glance.

'But who beat her?' Ollie persisted.

'Mr Edmund,' Arthur said. 'Thrashed her till she bled, my missis says. I've never seen the wife so upset over any of the young 'uns.'

Ollie's face was grim and Ernest shook his head sadly.

'But d'you know what?' Arthur said, leaning forward. 'Ethel said that he only stopped when the little lass fell to the floor almost in a faint, but she was still trying to defy him. She was still trying to sing.'

The three of them sat in silence, until at last Arthur said, 'Well, then, is there anything we can do to find out about her mother for her? She's a good worker – at least she is at the house. Even does some of the jobs for her little friend. And that's another thing – that little girl Pickering is fair done in when she gets home at night. A' you working 'er too hard, Ernest?'

'I wouldn't be at all surprised,' Ernest remarked, drily. 'But you know I don't make the rules, Arthur.'

There was silence between the three of them whilst Ernest took a long swig of his ale. Ollie was saying nothing now, but he was listening intently. His Lil would certainly want to hear about all this. Ernest wiped his mouth with the back of his hand and then twirled the ends of his long moustache. 'As a matter of fact, I've already asked a pal of mine to inquire at the Macclesfield workhouse about her mother.'

Arthur beamed. 'That's good o' yer. The missis'll be pleased.' He shrugged and gave a wry laugh. 'Don't know why 'cos Francis is a troublesome little baggage, but the missis has taken a liking to her. I 'ave an' all, if truth be known.'

Ernest laughed. 'I know what you mean.' He leaned towards Ollie. 'D'yer know, she sings hymns. All day long while she's working.'

'Aye. She does at the house, an' all,' Arthur put in.

Ollie, who had promised himself to say no more,

could contain his curiosity no longer. 'Sings, you say? In that place? What on earth has the poor little lass got to sing about?'

'Francis is a good little worker,' Ernest said. 'I've already set her on as a piecer alongside Nell Hudson. You know Hudson, don't you, Arthur?'

'Oh aye. I know her,' Arthur said wryly.

'And the two lads that came at the same time – the twins,' Ernest went on. 'They're doffers now. But that other little lass you're on about – Pickering. She's not making much progress. She's still sweeping up.'

Ollie's face was grim. 'What, under them machines?'

The two mill employees glanced at each other uncomfortably. They remembered only too well what had happened to Lucy Longmate, Ollie's niece.

'I'll watch out for the little lass,' Ernest said gently.

Two days after this conversation had taken place, Hannah woke with a start as Arthur came into the girls' dormitory, banging the ends of their beds with his stick as he always did. She sprang up, wide awake at once. She never seemed to suffer the weariness that the others did. Some had to be fairly dragged out of their beds every morning. And Jane was one of them.

'Let me be,' she whimpered as Hannah shook her awake. 'I can't get up. Not today. I really can't. I'm so tired.'

It was the same complaint every day and Hannah took no notice. 'Come on. Up you get. If you want me to plait your hair, you'll have to get up now.'

There was no answer – Jane was asleep again.

With a sigh, Hannah ran to the bowl and ewer at

the end of the dormitory and splashed her face with the cold water. She liked to be first to use it; by the time fifty girls had washed their sleepy faces in it, the water was cloudy with scum. Hannah dressed quickly and tied up her own long hair. Then she bent once more over the sleeping girl. 'Do come on, Jane. We'll be late.'

'I'd leave 'er,' Nell commented. 'Let Mrs Bramwell find her. She can deal with her. She's a pain, that one.'

'She's just tired out.'

'So's a lot more that work in the mill. She's nobody special.'

'She is to me,' Hannah snapped back.

'Oh, sorry I spoke, I'm sure.'

'No, I'm sorry, Nell,' Hannah said quickly, not wanting to fall out with the girl who had become such a friend to her. To them both, if it came to that. 'It's just that I don't want to see her in trouble. The work's more than she can manage without being put in the punishment room.'

Nell moved to the other side of the bed. 'Come on, then. I'll give you a hand.'

Together, they pulled back the thin grey blanket, grasped Jane on either side and hauled her upright. The girl's head lolled to one side.

'Come on, you,' Nell said sharply. 'Up with you, else I'll throw that bowl of mucky water all over you.'

They got her standing, and Nell held her whilst Hannah pulled on her skirt and blouse. Jane just stood there, swaying limply, her head down, her eyes closed. If they hadn't held on to her, she'd have fallen over. She was quite literally asleep on her feet.

Hannah grasped hold of her hair and began to separate it into three hanks ready to plait it.

'You haven't time to do that now,' Nell said. 'We'll all be late. Everyone else's gone already.'

Hannah bit her lip, but she couldn't argue.

'Put her bonnet on and tie it tightly. That'll have to do her today.'

Together they dragged the girl out of the room, stumbling awkwardly down the stairs with Jane between them.

The blast of cold morning air seemed to wake her, and she pulled herself free of Hannah and Nell to walk on her own. She pulled her shawl closely around her and hurried into the mill.

'Thanks for your help,' Nell muttered sarcastically, her eyes following Jane, but it was said with a grin. She linked her arm through Hannah's. 'Come on, there's a lot of broken threads waiting for our fingers.'

'They're late with the breakfast, aren't they?' Nell said, when they had been worked for over two hours.

'I dunno, I left me gold watch at home this morning,' Hannah mouthed.

'Oh, very funny, but I wish they'd hurry up. Me stomach thinks me throat's been cut.'

'You carry on here,' Hannah suggested. 'I'll just pop me head outside and see what's happened.'

To her amazement, groups of workers were standing about the yard, whispering together, their faces solemn. But there was no sign of Mr Scarsfield. She saw Luke and ran to him. 'What's going on? Why's everyone out here? And where's breakfast?'

As Luke turned to face her, Hannah was shocked to see tears in his eyes. Fear gripped her insides. 'What is it? What's happened? Is . . . is it Daniel?'

Luke shook his head. He took hold of her hand. 'It's Jane. She . . . she got her hair caught in one of the machines . . .'

Hannah felt as if the breath had been knocked from her body. The colour drained from her face, and her legs gave way beneath her. If Luke hadn't caught hold of her, she would have crumpled to the ground.

There was no hope that the child could survive. Though she was mercifully unconscious now, her injuries were so terrible, the loss of blood so much that by the time the doctor arrived, Jane was slipping away. Her unplaited hair had escaped from beneath her bonnet, and as the exhausted child had crawled beneath the clattering machines, she'd failed to keep her head low enough. The cruel machine had caught at her hair and whipped it up. Jane's petrified screams had been heard even above the machine noise. The operator had stopped the machine immediately, but the damage was done. They had pulled her out to find hair and skin torn from her scalp and blood flowing everywhere. Luke had been there when it had happened. He'd been the one to crawl underneath to release her. His eyes were dark with the horror of what he'd seen as he told Hannah about it.

Then, for the first time since he'd known her, Luke saw Hannah cry. She burst into noisy sobs and clung to him. 'It's my fault. It's all my fault. I didn't plait her hair. We were l-late and I . . . I didn't do it. And . . . and I always do it. Oh, Luke – Luke – it's all my fault.'

He put his arms around her and held her close, not caring who saw them. But everyone was dealing with their own shock at the horrifying accident.

'Of course it's not your fault. It's not up to you to look after her.'

'Yes, it is. It is. I always look after her. She's so little and pale and gets so tired.'

'That's not your fault. It's them. They shouldn't work her so hard. A little thing like her. And if anyone should see she's got her hair plaited, it should be Mrs Bramwell.'

Luke's words were meant to comfort her, but they didn't. Hannah blamed herself and there was nothing anyone could say to her that would ever take away her guilt.

Fifteen

'I want to see her. Let me be with her.' Outside the room where Jane lay, Hannah tussled physically with Mrs Bramwell, who was trying to restrain her.

'You can't do her any good, Hannah.'

'She's going to die, isn't she?'

The woman nodded.

'Then let me be with her,' she begged. 'Let me hold her hand. Please!'

Mrs Bramwell was firm. 'Promise me you'll stay here if I go and ask the doctor.'

Hannah swallowed and nodded reluctantly. 'All right,' she said hoarsely. 'Tell him . . . tell him that I'll do whatever he says, but if she's going to die, I want to be with her. I'm her best friend. She'd like me there. I know she would. Even though . . . even though . . .' Fresh tears welled.

'Even though – what?' Mrs Bramwell asked gently.

Hannah pulled in a deep shuddering breath. 'Even though it's all my fault.' The words came out haltingly and Ethel Bramwell could see the agony haunting the girl's eyes. 'I didn't plait her hair this morning like I always do. She was so tired – she wouldn't get up. Me and Nell had to drag her out of bed. It made us late and – and . . .'

'And you didn't plait her hair because you were so

135

afraid of being a few minutes late,' Mrs Bramwell finished softly.

Miserably, Hannah nodded.

For the first time ever, Ethel Bramwell was moved to enfold one of the pauper children into her arms. Hannah leaned against her and closed her eyes. For a moment she could imagine it was her mother holding her, Rebecca who was comforting her. She laid her head against the older woman's shoulder and wept silently. She was no longer hysterical, just dreadfully sad and burdened with a heavy weight of guilt.

At last, Mrs Bramwell patted her back, trying to give a little comfort, even though she realized the gesture was futile. She released Hannah and turned away, wiping a tear from the corner of her eye. She'd never met a girl like Hannah before. Most of the children who came here were just out for themselves. They'd rob each other of their last piece of bread, their last ha'penny, given half a chance. But here was Hannah Francis caring for a weaker child more than she cared about herself. Look how she'd done the younger child's household chores just because little Jane had been dead on her feet after her first day in the mill. And she'd gone on doing Jane's work whenever the child couldn't cope with the tasks. Ethel Bramwell felt a shudder of shame. It should've been her looking out for the younger, weaker ones. And now here Hannah was again, bravely wanting to sit beside the dying child, even though she was blaming herself for the accident. She was ready to put herself through the torment of seeing her friend die before her eyes, just to bring whatever comfort she could to the little girl.

As Ethel entered the room, Dr Barnes turned to her

and shook his head gravely. 'I'm sorry. She's so badly injured—'

'I know,' Ethel whispered and then swiftly explained Hannah's request.

'I don't want an hysterical child in here.'

'She won't be. I promise you. She – she . . .' Ethel paused, searching for the right words to describe Hannah to the doctor. 'She's a remarkable girl. I've never met anyone quite like her – not one so young, anyway. She's been punished recently.' Ethel dropped her gaze in shame. 'Most severely, I'm afraid – for running away to try to see her mother, who's still in the workhouse. But Hannah's adamant she wasn't running away, that she intended to come back. But, of course, no one believed her.'

The doctor said bluntly, 'Well, if this place is run so badly that you all can't believe anyone would voluntarily return if they once got away, then it's high time things were changed. That's all I can say.' He nodded grimly towards the bed. 'And if this sort of thing can happen to a child, if we can kill a little mite by tearing her to shreds all in the cause of making money . . .' The usually genial doctor spat out the words with a bitterness that made Ethel Bramwell flinch. 'Then what is the world coming to?'

She was obliged to agree. 'You're quite right, of course.' Mrs Bramwell sighed. 'It's high time there were some changes. But it'll never happen. Old man Critchlow – Mr Nathaniel – just carried on running the mill the way his father did.' She shrugged. 'Oh, he abides by the law – or nearly so.'

Dr Barnes eyed her keenly. 'Are you quite sure about that? This wretched pauper apprentice system has been abandoned in most of the mills. New laws made it too expensive, as I understand it. Mind you, the new laws are better for the children, aren't they? They raised the minimum age and cut the number of daily working hours. So why not here, I'd like to know? How come the Critchlows are still running the scheme?'

Ethel Bramwell ran her tongue around dry lips. She was sailing in deep waters now, risking her own livelihood and that of her husband's by speaking her mind. But she rarely got the chance to unburden her deep anxieties to someone who understood, to someone who wouldn't betray her confidence. Though she didn't know the doctor well – the Critchlows were too mean to call upon his services except in the direst emergency, even for their staff – Ethel felt she could trust him. 'Some mills are running twenty-four hours a day, with a shift system. That's never happened here, though. Mind you, when me 'n' Arthur first came here more than twenty years ago, children as young as nine used to work eight hours a day in the mill – longer if they wanted to do overtime to earn a few pence. And that left very little time for any education. By the time they were thirteen they worked twelve hours a day and no more schooling.'

The doctor grunted. 'Hmph, still not good enough in my opinion. What's the law now? No child under eight can work at all, is it?'

The superintendent nodded. 'And youngsters can only work between six in the morning and six at night and for no more than ten hours a day.'

'Oh, that's spoiling them rotten,' Dr Barnes said sarcastically. He glanced at the still form of Jane in the bed. His tone softened. 'And this poor creature? She only looks seven or eight. How old is she?'

'Ten. At least, that's what Mr Goodbody said.'

'Goodbody? Who's he?'

'The master of the workhouse where . . . where the children come from.'

The doctor's expression hardened. 'So – it really is still going on here then?'

'The pauper apprentice system? Oh yes,' Ethel Bramwell said bitterly. Then she sighed. 'I've very mixed feelings about it all, Doctor, I don't mind admitting. We haven't quite so many as we used to have. At one time we had over a hundred children; now there's only about eighty.' She smiled thinly. 'Of course if they close the house, Arthur and me will be out of a job, but even so . . .' She bit her lip. Ethel was warming to something that had bothered her and the kindly Arthur for years, yet it was the first time she'd ever dared to voice her misgivings to anyone apart from her husband. 'I don't like being part of something that could be described as – well – as cruel. Of course, I have to be strict with the children. Eighty youngsters all living together – they can get out of hand. It's part of my job to keep them in line, but in here . . .' She laid her hand over her heart. 'I do feel for them. I . . . I try to be fair. That's why when the girl you're about to meet always did little Jane's household chores for her after work at night – well – I let her. The – little one,' she gestured with a trembling hand towards the child in the bed, 'was always so exhausted.'

The doctor grunted. 'Well, if they'd let me see the children now and again, I could maybe have helped. They do it in some mills, y'know. There's one in

Cheshire that's got a marvellous reputation for caring for its workers.'

Ethel sighed. 'Yes, I've heard of it too, but there's not an earthly chance that Mr Edmund would ever agree to anything like that here.'

'Well, sadly, I don't believe there's a law – yet – that says they have to provide regular medical checks for their workers, but,' he eyed her keenly, 'are you telling me, Mrs Bramwell, that the Critchlows do bend the law when it suits their own purpose?'

The woman, torn between telling the truth and yet risking her own position by doing so, nodded. Casting caution aside now, she went on heatedly. 'They work the children far longer than the hours they're supposed to. They get less schooling than is laid down by the law. They're supposed to get at least three hours a day until they're twelve, but it's only ever two at the most. And whilst they're apprentices, bound to the Critchlows by that wretched bit of paper they're made to sign when they arrive, they only get their bed and board. The only way they can earn money for themselves is by doing overtime on top of the already long hours. And believe me, Doctor, most of them don't even understand what that paper really is that they're signing.'

'And how are the children treated?'

'If they do anything wrong, the boys are beaten, the girls locked in the punishment room and half starved for days. And on rare occasions – very rare, thank the Lord – a girl will be beaten.'

'On whose orders?' Dr Barnes barked. 'I didn't think Mr Critchlow was a bad master.'

'Oh, he's not so bad. But his son – Mr Edmund – is another matter.' Her voice dropped to a whisper. 'He's

140

... he's evil, Doctor. The day he takes over the running of this mill, may God help us all.'

There was a long silence whilst they both pondered the appalling prospect. Then, as the child in the bed stirred and whimpered in pain, the doctor cleared his throat. 'Fetch this remarkable young lady in then, but I suggest you stay with her, Mrs Bramwell. It's a hard thing to do. To sit and watch your friend die.'

When Mrs Bramwell opened the door and beckoned Hannah inside, the doctor looked up, intrigued to see this unusual girl of whom the superintendent had spoken. At once he was struck by the young girl's demeanour. She walked into the room, her head held high, her face calm. It was only on closer inspection that the doctor could see the anguish in her blue eyes and the blotchy marks on her cheeks of recently shed tears. Hannah wished herself anywhere – back in the mill, even back in the punishment room – anywhere but here. Nevertheless, she sat down beside the bed and gently took hold of Jane's hand, steeling herself to face the terrible sight – the blood-soaked bandages, the scarcely recognizable face.

'I'm here, Jane,' she whispered, swallowing the bile that rose in her throat. 'I'm here now. It'll be all right. Don't be frightened. I'll stay with you. I won't leave you.' She whispered the comforting, reassuring words with such mature composure that the two listening adults glanced at each other.

'See what I mean, Doctor?' Ethel murmured, and the man nodded, 'Indeed I do, Mrs Bramwell. Indeed I do. A most remarkable child.'

He took out his pocket watch and murmured. 'I think I'll stay a while. I've more calls to make, but they'll wait.'

'I'll get another chair. We can sit over here in the corner, but we'll be close by if . . .'

She stopped and faced the awful truth. It wasn't a matter of 'if' but 'when'.

Mrs Bramwell slipped quietly out of the room and returned with a chair. Then she and the doctor sat in the far corner of the room, silently watching.

Jane stirred and opened her eyes and Hannah leaned closer. 'I'm here, Jane. I'm here.'

Weakly, the girl whispered, 'It wasn't your fault, Hannah.'

'It was. I should have plaited your hair. I—'

Jane tried to shake her head and then winced at the terrible pain. She cried out and screwed up her face. 'No, no, I . . . I don't want you to blame yourself. You . . . you've always been so kind to me. Looked after me. Please, Hannah, sing to me. I want to hear you sing my favourite . . .' It seemed as if she might have said more but the effort was too much, the pain unbearable. Her eyelids closed and she drifted away.

Her voice shaking and with tears streaming down her face, Hannah began to sing, 'The Lord's my shepherd, I'll not want . . .'

Mrs Bramwell wept openly, and even the doctor wiped a tear from the corner of his eye as the little girl's life ebbed away.

As Hannah's voice faded away at the end of the hymn, the doctor rose quietly from his chair and went to the other side of the bed. He felt the child's pulse and then looked down into Hannah's upturned face.

His voice deep with emotion, Dr Barnes said, 'I'm sorry, my dear. She's gone, but she's out of pain now. That's how you must think of it. She's at peace.'

Hannah laid her cheek against Jane's hand and

sobbed. She could not in all honesty have prayed for her friend to survive. Jane was hurt beyond all hope, so dreadfully injured that any life would have been a living hell. Better that her little friend was, like the kindly doctor said, at peace.

They gave her a few moments, and then it was Dr Barnes who put his hand on her shoulder. 'Come, my dear. Mrs Bramwell will look after her. There are things she must do. But she'll be gentle with her.'

Hannah knew what that meant. She had to lay out Jane ready for the rough pauper's coffin. She pulled herself up and bent over to kiss Jane's cheek one last time. Already, it felt cold beneath Hannah's lips, but perhaps that was her imagination.

The doctor's arm supporting her, she stumbled from the room. Outside the door, Luke was waiting and she fell into his arms. Above her head, Luke and the doctor exchanged a glance.

'Look after her, son. She's a very special girl.'

Luke, unable to speak for the huge lump in his throat, nodded.

'Come on,' he whispered at last. 'Let's get out of here. Let's go up on the hill.'

'What . . . what about Daniel?' Even in her distress, Hannah spared a thought for the shy boy. He depended on his twin just like Jane had depended on her. But she'd let her little friend down. She didn't want to be the cause of trouble between the brothers.

'He's still working. He'll be all right. Just this once. Come on.'

They left the house and began to run down the hill and along the path leading to the weir. Then, turning away from the mill, they scrambled up the rocky track, slipping and sliding, to the narrow steep path on the hillside high above the mill pool and the river. Luke took hold of her hand and held it tightly as they walked on in silence. Before they rounded the curve of the hill that would take them out of sight of Wyedale Mill, they paused and looked back.

'It don't look such a bad place,' Luke murmured.

Hannah sighed. 'It's not the place. The mill's – what's the word? – majestic. Yes, that's it, the mill's a majestic building.' Her glance roamed away, down the dale, following the winding river. 'And the valley's lovely. So peaceful, so . . .' Tears blurred her eyes. The terrible sight of her friend was still so fresh in her mind. It would haunt her for ever. She swallowed hard and said huskily, 'It's the people who run it. The Critchlows. It's all their fault. But it's such a shame. It could be such a happy place. The workers are good people.'

'It'll never be a happy place with Mr Edmund around. And I 'spect his son'll be just like him when he grows up.'

Hannah thought about the young, solemn-faced, dark-haired boy she had seen just the once. She'd've liked to have thought that he might grow up to be different. But it wasn't very likely.

She sighed sadly. 'Yes, I expect you're right.'

They turned their backs on Wyedale Mill and walked on, following the winding path worn into the steep hillside by the sheep that grazed there.

'See that big house across there.' Luke pointed to the cliff on the opposite side of the dale. 'That's the Critchlows' place. Millersbrook Manor.'

The house was perched halfway down the steep hillside a little way from the village itself.

'Do they all live there, then?'

'Yeah. The old man, Mr Edmund and Master Adam – when he's home.'

'From school, you mean?'

'That's right. He's away at some fancy boarding school. That's why we never see him much. He only comes home in the holidays.'

'How do you know all this?'

Luke forced a grin. He was trying hard to draw Hannah's thoughts away from the sadness they were both feeling, take her mind off what was happening back at the apprentice house. ''Cos I'm a nosy beggar.'

'Who else lives there, then? Is there a Mrs Critchlow?'

Luke shook his head. 'No. The old man's wife died years ago and Mr Edmund's wife died having another baby.'

'Oh yes. I'd heard that.'

'It's a houseful of men.'

'They've got servants though? They'll have a house-keeper, surely?'

'Oh aye,' Luke said airily. 'But servants don't count, do they?'

'No,' Hannah said soberly and her thoughts came back to Jane. The little girl's life hadn't counted with the Critchlows.

Sixteen

By a strange coincidence, it was Adam Critchlow whom they saw first when they dragged their feet reluctantly back to the mill.

'What's he doing here?' Luke muttered.

'He must be home from school,' Hannah said.

The young man was standing in the middle of the yard looking up at the mill. At the sound of their footsteps, he turned. He didn't say anything until they drew level with him. They were about to pass by, but he spoke, bringing them to a halt.

'I heard about the little girl.' His voice was soft, gentle almost, though Hannah could hardly believe such a word could describe any of the Critchlows. She pressed her lips together to stop the tears flowing again, yet her action had the look of disapproval.

Adam's eyes clouded. 'Tell me,' he said suddenly, his gaze on Hannah's face. Luke was ignored. 'What happened? Tell me it all. I want to know.'

Hannah did so, sparing him nothing. She was gratified to see him wince, yet at the same time his response surprised her. Perhaps this Critchlow did have some feelings. If so, he was the only one who did, she thought bitterly.

But it seemed that Adam believed differently about his family. 'My grandfather's distraught.'

Hannah's eyes widened in disbelief and, beside her, she heard Luke give a derisory snort. Adam glanced at him briefly, but dismissed his presence. His attention returned to Hannah. 'He is,' he persisted. Even though Hannah had not spoken, he could read her thoughts plainly written on her face. He stepped closer to her, cutting Luke out. 'I know perhaps he seems harsh to you, but there are other mills a lot worse than this one, you know. They don't have good food or the medical attention we provide.'

'Medical attention? What medical attention? We never see a doctor from one month to the next. They only called him in this time because they had to. Because . . .' Her tears spilled over again. 'Because they knew she was going to die. He couldn't save her. No one could have done except not to've let it happen in the first place.'

Adam dropped his gaze and shuffled his feet. 'I know and I'm sorry.' He lifted his head again and stared into her face, holding her gaze. 'But one day it'll all be different. One day – when the mill's mine – it'll be very different.'

'Aye,' Luke spoke for the first time. 'But how long have we to wait before that day comes? And in the meantime, once the old man's gone, it'll be your father in charge.' He paused and added pointedly, 'Won't it?'

To this, it seemed, Adam had no reply.

News of the child's accident and subsequent death spread through the mill, and a sadness descended over the workforce. Though everyone carried on with the work expected of them, there was an undercurrent of resentment flowing beneath the surface. The workers were suddenly not as biddable. There was a feeling of unrest, and Nathaniel Critchlow was alarmed by it.

'It's just like that other time when a little girl got killed. What can we do?'

'Do?' Edmund snapped at his father. 'Why, nothing, of course. As long as they're doing their work. And Scarsfield will see to that, else he'll have me to answer to.'

Nathaniel spread his hands. 'But I like my workers to be happy. They work better. Maybe we should have a doctor visiting the apprentices regularly. I've heard there's a mill in Cheshire where—'

'Nonsense, Father. You're too soft. They respect a firm hand, not a weak one.'

Nathaniel regarded his son soberly and not without a little disappointment. 'There's a vast difference between a firm hand and a callous one, my boy. It'd be no bad thing to look after their health. And,' he added pointedly, 'to be seen to be doing so.'

Edmund's mouth twisted. 'I'm not one for philanthropy.'

His father shook his head. 'Outsiders – and even the workers themselves – might see it as philanthropic. But think about it for a moment, Edmund. A healthy, happy millhand will work better. We need to keep them on our side.' He frowned worriedly. 'It's what your grandfather believed and so do I.'

'Our side,' Edmund scoffed. 'Workers will never be on "our side", as you put it. It's us and them, Father. Always has been, always will be. And for most of them, the more they produce, the more they earn. Isn't that incentive enough?'

'Not for the apprentices. They're not paid at all unless they do overtime.'

'Huh! We feed and clothe the little brats. And we have to educate them – thanks to all the blasted new laws they keep bringing in.' Edmund wagged his finger at his father. 'Their lives are better here than if they were still in the workhouse, but as for pandering to them with regular health checks, well, that's an unnecessary expense to my mind.'

'It's not pandering to them. They have a right to—'

Edmund stepped closer to his father's desk and leaned across it. Prodding his forefinger on the surface of the desk, he said, slowly and deliberately, 'They have no "rights". When they work in this mill, when they sign their indenture, they belong to us. We *own* them. Body and soul.'

Edmund swung round and marched out of the room, slamming the door behind him.

Nathaniel stared after him with a growing sense of foreboding. How, in God's name, he asked himself, had he reared such a heartless and, yes, he had to admit it, cruel son? A shudder of apprehension ran through him. He had a sudden, awful, premonition of how the mill would be run after his own demise. It was a picture that filled him with fear. He sighed deeply. We should be looking to improve conditions, not going back into the past, Nathaniel thought. It's bad enough I've let him persuade me to carry on the scheme with Goodbody long after every other mill owner has abandoned it. They were breaking the law, he knew. The children in Wyedale Mill worked longer hours, had less schooling than anywhere else. If a government inspector should call . . .

'There's only one thing for it,' he murmured aloud. 'I'll just have to live long enough to see Adam grown up and come into the business.' But then his musings came to a halt. The boy was certainly tender-hearted, but would Adam be strong enough to stand up to his ruthless father?

Nathaniel groaned aloud and, resting his elbows on the desk, dropped his head into his hands. He felt suddenly dizzy and sick at the thought of what might happen to the mill his own father had begun.

From boyhood, the mill had been Nathaniel's life. He could still remember so vividly the day they had found Wyedale. They'd been touring the Derbyshire countryside on horseback, just he and his father, Moses, looking for a place to build a cotton mill.

And they had found it. At the end of the long, curving valley where the River Wye tumbled in a natural waterfall, Moses had found the perfect place to build a mill for his son to inherit. And it would pass down the generations, Moses had dreamed. From father to son with always a Critchlow at the helm.

Nathaniel could still remember that day so clearly – his father sitting astride his horse, his tall and imposing figure hiding a stern yet kindly disposition. At the top of the hill, he had taken off his hat and waved it in the air, his dark brown hair blowing in the wind. They had ridden down the steep mud track, past the smattering of houses – the farm and a few cottages – right to the end of the dale, where there was room to build a mill beside the river that would provide the power for the great wheel.

'This is it, my boy,' Moses had cried jubilantly. 'This is where the Critchlows' mill will stand for generations. For you, Nathaniel. For your sons and even for their sons.'

'But, Father,' Nathaniel had said, looking around

him at what appeared to him to be a bleak and desolate place. 'There are no houses. Where will you get the people to work in the mill?'

Moses had laughed, the wind whipping away the sound and carrying it through the dale. 'We shall build houses. Up there.' He had pointed to the cliff face rising steeply at the end of the valley. 'We'll bring workers from the city slums. From the workhouses. We'll give them a good life – a better life than they've ever known or ever expected. And in return,' Moses had smiled down at the young Nathaniel, 'they'll work hard for us and make us rich men.'

And everything that Moses had promised had come to pass. He'd built his fine mill and the houses on the cliff for the workers, and Millersbrook village above Wyedale Mill was born. He had built an apprentice house and a schoolroom and brought pauper orphans from the workhouses in the nearest towns and cities. And many had stayed on to work in the mill as adults and to live in the cottages in the village, to marry and bring up their families there.

Moses was a strict but fair employer. The list of rules and the fines posted up about the factory were those he had drawn up, and they were still in force to this day.

Remembering all this, Nathaniel groaned aloud.

The sound carried through the door to the outer office, and Josiah Roper smiled.

Three days later, though he was quaking inside, Mr Critchlow stood up to his son. 'You're to let anyone who wants to go attend that child's funeral.'

Edmund glowered and opened his mouth to speak, but Nathaniel Critchlow held up his hand. 'We'll have a rebellion on our hands if you don't.'

Edmund appeared to think for a moment. 'I'll allow her closest friends to go and the Bramwells. Maybe Scarsfield as well, but no others. We'll have the whole mill grind to a halt if they think they can all wangle time off.'

'Very well, then,' Mr Critchlow agreed to the compromise. 'Are you going?'

Edmund laughed without humour. 'Me? Attend a pauper's funeral? Hardly!'

Nathaniel's hand shook visibly. 'I should go,' he murmured. 'But . . . but I can't face it. I don't feel well.' He passed a hand over his forehead as he felt the dizziness and the headache he had been experiencing for the past few days – ever since the child's accident – sweep over him.

But to everyone's surprise, there was a Critchlow at the funeral.

As Arthur Bramwell and Ernest Scarsfield pushed the coffin on the handcart up the steep hill to the burial ground beyond the village, the few – the pathetically few – mourners fell into step behind them. Mrs Bramwell, Hannah and Nell in the front, followed by Luke and Daniel, as ever walking side by side.

As they began to move off from the apprentice house, Adam Critchlow stepped out from behind the mill's pillared gateway and fell into step at the back. Hannah didn't notice him. Walking between Ethel Bramwell and Nell, she kept her eyes firmly fixed on the small coffin and quietly prayed that her little friend had truly found peace.

'Did you see him?' Luke asked her later when it was

all over and they were sitting in the kitchen at the house, drinking tea as a special treat on such a dreadful day.

'At the back,' Daniel put in. The four youngsters were sitting together whilst the three grown ups had gone into the Bramwells' sitting room to partake of something a little stronger than tea.

'Who?' Hannah asked listlessly, cupping the mug in her hands to warm them. She was still shivering, though it was more from her inner misery and the terrible burden of guilt rather than from the cold day.

'Master Adam,' Luke said. 'He followed us all the way to the cemetery.'

'At the back,' Daniel repeated. 'He walked behind us and then stood at the back when we was all round the grave.'

'Did he?' Hannah was surprised and, even against her will, a little moved. She wanted to think badly of the Critchlows, yet was there one amongst them who was actually showing some compassion?

'Did you speak to him?'

'No,' Luke said and Daniel shook his head.

'I wonder,' she mused, 'just why he came?'

No one could answer her.

'I'm sorry, Francis,' Ernest Scarsfield stopped Hannah as she was leaving the mill three days after Jane's funeral, 'but my mate can't find out anything about yer mother. He went to the workhouse, but they wouldn't tell him anything. He saw someone called – now, what was it? – Good, was it?'

'Mr Goodbody,' Hannah said, the disappointment

spreading through her already. She'd had such hopes that word would come any day from Mr Scarsfield's friend. Since Jane's death, Hannah had not felt like singing – not once – and news from her mother had been the only thing she'd looked forward to.

'Aye, that was it. Well, he more or less ordered him out of the place. "Can't divulge information about inmates," he said. Miserable old bugger. It wouldn't've hurt him to send word to a little lass about her mother, now would it?' He looked to Luke for agreement. Luke was always at Hannah's side these days with Daniel never far behind.

Luke nodded. 'He's a right bastard.' And Daniel nodded grim agreement.

For a brief moment, Ernest Scarsfield looked taken aback, then he frowned. 'Now then, lad, none of that sort of language here. You know the rules. By rights, I should fine you thruppence for that.' Then, realizing that he had just been swearing himself, Ernest smiled. His admonishment was gentle. These three had been through enough already in their young lives. He ruffled Luke's hair as he added, 'But I know what you mean.' He turned again to Hannah. 'I'm sorry, lass.'

Hannah tried to smile, but her voice wobbled as she said, 'Thank you for trying, Mr Scarsfield.'

She turned away, but Ernest called after her. 'You could see Mr Critchlow. The old man, that is. He *might* help. He's not a bad old stick – most of the time.'

'Thanks. I will.' But she didn't hold out much hope.

*

'We'll have to go and see Mrs Grundy. I haven't dared go yet, but I should,' Hannah told Luke and Daniel the following Sunday.

Luke nodded. 'You'll have to tell her that they've taken the money she lent you. And kept it.' He paused a moment. 'It'll take you years to pay it back.'

'I know,' Hannah said miserably. 'I'll be old and grey by the time I do.' She sighed. 'Still, let's get it over with. Let's go and see her.'

'Can I come an' all?' Daniel asked.

Luke's face sobered and he shook his head, but not, as Hannah thought at first in answer to his brother's question, but to her suggestion. 'We can't go. None of us.'

Hannah stared at him. 'You ... you mean you won't come with me? Oh, Luke!'

'No, no, it's not that. Of course I'll come with you.' He paused, then added, 'When you can go.'

'But I want to go today. Now.'

He shook his head. 'You can't.'

'What do you mean? It's Sunday. We'll go this afternoon. Mrs Bramwell will understand.'

'You can't. You're not allowed out. Not even to go to the service with the rest of us.'

'Not – allowed – out? Nobody's said anything to me.'

'I heard Mrs Bramwell telling Mary that you'd be staying with her this morning and that she'd tell you to help get the dinner ready.'

Hannah, angry now, whirled around. 'I don't believe this. I'll go and ask her myself.'

'Hannah, don't . . .' Luke called after her, but Hannah paid no heed.

She knocked sharply on the door of Mrs Bramwell's sitting room, indignation lending her boldness.

'Come in.'

Hannah flung open the door and marched into the room. 'Is it true?' she burst out. 'Is it true I'm not allowed out? Not even to go to the service?'

Ethel Bramwell sighed, rose and came to stand in front of the girl. 'I'm sorry, Hannah. Truly I am. But that's Mr Edmund's orders. We're under his strict instructions, see. Me, Mr Bramwell and even Mr Scarsfield. We've not to let you out of our sights, so to speak. I'm to keep you here and Mr Bramwell's to see that you go to the mill every morning. Then Mr Scarsfield's to keep his eye on you all day until you come back here at night.'

Hannah's gasped and her eyes widened. 'But . . . but that's like being in prison.'

'Aren't we all?' the older woman murmured.

'Well, I won't be a prisoner. Not here. Not anywhere.'

'You've no choice, child.' Ethel Bramwell said, but there was sadness in her tone. 'None of us have. The Critchlows own us – all of us.'

Hannah frowned. She knew she was fastened to the Critchlows for the term of her indenture, but surely the Bramwells weren't.

'Why do you say "all of us"? You and Mr Bramwell can leave any time you like, can't you? You're not under any kind of indenture, are you?'

Mrs Bramwell shook her head. 'No, but think about it, Hannah.' Without realizing it, Ethel Bramwell called the girl by her Christian name. 'How would we find other employment? If we just upped and left, where would we go? How would we ever get another position without a reference?' She leaned closer. 'And how would we get a reference? Mr Critchlow would

156

never give us one in a month of Sundays if we said we wanted to leave even though we've served him for over twenty years.'

Shocked, Hannah stared at her. She hadn't realized that everyone here – including the Bramwells, even Ernest Scarsfield and Mr Roper – were all virtual prisoners of the Critchlows.

'Now, you be a good girl and do what they say for a week or two and then we'll see. Likely, they'll've forgotten all about you by then.'

Hannah pursed her lips and shook her head. 'I'm not staying locked up in here even for a week or two. First thing tomorrow morning, I'm going to see Mr Critchlow.' Then she swung round and marched from the room again, leaving Ethel Bramwell staring after her and sighing deeply. 'Oh, my dear child. You don't understand what you're doing. You really don't.'

Seventeen

Hannah ignored their warnings. She paid no heed to Mrs Bramwell or to Luke. Not even to Ernest Scarsfield. They tried to stop her – tried to warn her.

'And if you run into Mr Edmund, well . . .' They all said exactly the same thing, and all left the sentence hanging in the air unfinished. Hannah was determined, but she was trembling as she knocked on the door of the outer office and stepped in to face Mr Roper.

Josiah Roper did not, of course, try to dissuade her. He had good reason not to. He wanted a few fireworks to brighten his dull routine. He didn't care if this wilful child, who'd spoilt his weekend away from this place, was locked in the punishment room again. He was smiling as he ushered her into his master's office and closed the door behind her. He didn't return to his desk, but leaned close to the door to listen.

Inside the inner office, Hannah faced Mr Nathaniel Critchlow. She breathed a little easier to find him there and not his son.

'Please, sir, I'd like your permission to go to morning service with the others on Sunday.'

The old man frowned at her. 'So you can run away again, eh?'

Hannah shook her head. 'I wasn't running away, sir. I keep telling everyone, but no one will believe me. I just wanted to find out how my mother is, that's all.

158

I haven't heard from her since I came here even though I've written several letters to her. I was coming back, sir. Truly I was.'

The man gazed at the young girl's fresh face, at her clear blue eyes, at the golden hair cascading down her back. He sighed. She was going to be a real beauty in a few years' time. She was now, but she was not quite old enough ... He shuddered. Maybe he shouldn't keep her here. Maybe he should let her go back to the workhouse. He could tell Goodbody that she wasn't suitable, even though she was actually one of the best child workers they had. She was shaping up very nicely. Soon, she would be shaping up in an entirely different way and then his son would really start to take notice of her ...

With unaccustomed impetuosity, he said, 'Would you like to go back to the workhouse, my dear – for good?'

'Oh no, sir. I signed that piece of paper for you and I intend to keep my promise. I mean to stay here. But all I want is to know how my mother is.'

Now Nathaniel Critchlow stared at her in amazement. 'You want to stay here?'

Hannah nodded. 'I didn't – when Jane—'

'Yes, yes,' Nathaniel said and his own voice was husky. He hated any kind of accident in his factory. And this had been a bad one – the very worst. Though he'd shied away from seeing the child for himself, he still trembled at the mere thought of Jane's injuries.

'I wanted to run away then,' Hannah was saying, 'because I blamed myself for not tying her hair up properly for her like we'd been told.' The man and the girl stared at each other, their faces filled with sadness at the tragedy. They each felt a sense of guilt that the accident could have been avoided.

'I just can't understand why my mother hasn't answered my letters. She can't write herself, but she'd have got someone to read them to her and then sent me word.'

Nathaniel leaned forward and rested his elbows on his desk, linking his fingers to stop their shaking. 'I'll tell you what I'll do,' he said slowly, 'but first, you have to give me your word that you won't try to run away—' As Hannah opened her mouth to protest once more, he held up his hand. 'Not even just for a day.'

Hannah took a deep breath. 'It depends what you're going to do.'

Nathaniel smiled wryly. The boldness of this girl was truly amazing and yet it was not insolence. Even from his lofty position as her master – the man who owned her body and soul now – he had to admit that she was only standing up for what she considered her rights. Her rights, indeed! Edmund would say that she had none and Nathaniel was tempted to tell her as much. But as he gazed again on her pretty, open face, the retort died on his lips.

'Well, providing I have your promise, I'll write to Cedric Goodbody myself and ask for news of your mother. We might even arrange for her to visit you here.'

The ecstatic delight on the young girl's face was like the appearance of the sun after storm clouds. 'Oh, sir, would you really do that for me?' She clasped her hands in front of her. 'Oh, thank you, *thank* you.'

Nathaniel cleared his throat and said gruffly. 'So, will you give me your promise? No more trying to sneak off to see her for yourself.'

'I promise, sir. Oh, I promise.'

'Now, just to show me that you mean what you say, you're to stay in for another two weeks. Then you can go to the Sunday services again.'

Hannah nodded and thanked him again. At that moment she would have done anything he asked her. Anything at all.

'I'm so sorry, Mrs Grundy, about the money. But I will pay you back every penny.'

Three Sundays later, the three youngsters – Hannah, Luke and Daniel – were sitting in the warm kitchen at the farm.

Mrs Grundy shrugged. 'Don't worry about it, love. I shan't lose any sleep over it. I'm just sorry you didn't get to see your mother.' Her usual merry face clouded. 'That Josiah Roper – he's a nasty piece of work. He could've turned a blind eye. Could've let you go when he found you at the top of the hill. I remember our Lucy hated him. He was always creeping about the mill, watching an' listening and then telling tales to Mr Edmund.'

She looked into the sad faces opposite her. 'I heard about your little friend,' she said gently. 'Just like our Lucy, weren't it?'

Hannah nodded, looking stricken.

Lily Grundy sighed heavily and heaved herself up to get them a drink and fetch a fruit loaf from her cake tin. Changing the subject away from matters that grieved them all, she said, 'So, what are you going to do now about yer mam?'

'Mr Nathaniel's been quite good,' Luke said taking up Hannah's tale. 'He's promised—'

'To write to Mr Goodbody himself,' Daniel finished.

For a moment, Mrs Grundy glanced between the three of them, with a puzzled expression. Then her face cleared. 'Oh, him at the workhouse, you mean? Where you came from? But I thought you'd already written to him.'

'Not exactly. I wrote to me mam.'

'And she's never replied?'

'Well, no. She can't write. But I know she'd've got one of the others to write for her.'

Mrs Grundy handed round mugs of thick creamy warm milk and slices of cake before she spoke again. She sat down and pulled her cup of tea towards her, stirring it thoughtfully. 'I don't suppose that someone along the way has been stopping your letters. Either going out or coming in.'

The three youngsters stared at her. 'Would . . . would they do that?' Hannah asked indignantly.

Mrs Grundy snorted and took a sip of her tea. 'I wouldn't put anything past that lot up at the mill – if it suited their purpose. Anyway, love, it'll soon be Christmas. Maybe your mother will send you a letter then, eh?'

'Do you think anyone would really do that?' Hannah asked the two boys again as they walked back to the apprentice house as dusk descended into the dale. 'Stop someone's letters?'

'Mr Edmund would,' Luke said.

'And Mr Roper,' Daniel volunteered.

'But I don't think old Mr Critchlow would, do you?' Hannah said. 'I'm sure he wouldn't.'

The two boys glanced at one another but did not

answer, and the three of them walked the rest of the way in silence.

Christmas came and went, marked only by a little more food at dinnertime and a couple of hours' free time in the afternoon. The pauper children in the apprentice house scarcely noticed the difference, though the feasting at the Manor lasted three days and left Nathaniel Critchlow suffering from severe indigestion and an even worse headache from the drink he had consumed.

Struggling to his office at the mill on the fourth day, he sat at his desk, his head in his hands. 'I don't know what to do,' he murmured.

Josiah, hovering on the other side of the desk, asked, 'Can I help, sir? You don't look too well. Perhaps you should go home.'

'I should speak to Edmund,' the old man murmured.

'Mr Edmund won't be back from Manchester until late tonight.'

It was from the merchants in Manchester that the Critchlows bought the bales of raw cotton, that started life on the *Gossypium* plant in the southern states of America, its fluffy bolls picked by slave labour and transported all the way to Liverpool and by canal to Manchester. Edmund was a shrewd and clever negotiator – no one could deny that – and Nathaniel had been happy and relieved to hand over that side of the business to his son.

'Are you sure I can't help, sir?' Josiah asked again. His seeming concern was persuasive. Nathaniel sighed and confided, 'It's the girl.'

'Which girl might that be, sir?' Josiah feigned ignorance, yet he'd already guessed.

'Francis.'

'Ah!' Josiah said, a wealth of understanding in that simple utterance. 'She is somewhat – er – wilful. What has she done now?'

'It's not so much what she's done as what's happened.'

Nathaniel Critchlow raised his head slowly and sighed deeply. 'When she ran away that time, it seems that all she was trying to do was to see her mother. She's not had word from her mother – or even *of* her – since she came here. And the child's worried. It's only natural, I suppose. She's written several times, she says, but no word has come.'

Josiah smiled but said nothing. All Hannah's letters had been unanswered because they had only left his office in shreds.

'Until now,' Nathaniel finished heavily. He picked up a sheet of paper and held it out for Josiah to read. 'This arrived this morning. It's from Goodbody. The child's mother died only a few weeks after the girl's arrival here. All this time and no one thought to tell us so that we could tell the poor child.'

Nathaniel's face crumpled and he dropped his head into his hands once more. Brokenly, he said. 'It's all getting too much for me. I can't bring myself to tell her.'

Josiah looked down at his master and felt a thrill of jubilation. The old man was past it. High time he retired and handed over the running of the mill to his son. And with Edmund in charge – Edmund, who was Josiah's mentor and friend, then . . .

164

'Why don't you leave this to me, sir? I'll attend to what needs to be done.'

Nathaniel looked up gratefully. 'You will? Thank you, Roper. You're a good man.'

He pulled himself up and stood swaying unsteadily. Josiah put out his hand and took hold of his arm. 'I think you should go home, sir. I'll get one of the hands to bring the pony and trap to the door. Here, let me help you with your coat.'

Solicitously, Josiah helped the old man shuffle to the door, down the stairs and into the trap.

'See him right home, Baldwin,' he ordered one of the mill workers. 'Mr Critchlow isn't well.'

'Your father doesn't seem well, Mr Edmund,' Josiah greeted him on his return late that night. Knowing Mr Edmund's habit of returning straight to his office after a successful buying trip to the city, the clerk had stayed late in the office deliberately. Sitting there in the semi-darkness, Josiah had hatched a plan. But it would need careful handling.

'You still here, Roper?' Edmund said, shrugging himself out of his coat and striding into the inner office and towards the waiting whisky bottle in his cabinet. He poured himself a double measure and sat down in his father's chair. Leaning back, he rested his feet on the corner of the desk, crossing his ankles. 'What's the matter with him?' His eyes gleamed, matching the excitement glittering in Josiah's eyes. 'Serious, d'you think?'

'I hope not, sir,' Josiah said dutifully, but they both knew it to be a lie. They both wanted the same thing – Edmund to be in full control of the factory.

By God! they were each thinking. *Then we'll see things happen.*

'This letter,' Josiah went on, holding out the piece of paper, 'seemed to upset him. It's from Goodbody. About the Francis girl. It seems your father wrote to him to make enquiries. At the girl's behest.'

Edmund dropped his feet to the floor with a thud and sat up. 'Did he, b'God?'

'It seems,' Josiah went on smoothly, 'that the mother died only a few weeks after Francis came here. And – um – nobody seems to have thought to let us know.'

'I see.' Edmund's eyes narrowed as he regarded his clerk thoughtfully. Josiah licked his lips before saying carefully, 'I think your father was reluctant to tell the child. Didn't want to distress her further. She . . . she's a trifle wilful, I believe.'

Edmund snorted and took another mouthful of the burning liquid. 'She's trouble. I've a good mind to send her back to the workhouse and let her stay there.' He was silent for a moment, thoughtful. Despite the trouble Hannah had constantly caused, Edmund was no fool. The girl was a good worker. Scarsfield had said so. Soon, she would be capable of carrying out an adult female's work at no extra cost. Besides, he was confident that the Bramwells or Scarsfield fined or punished her appropriately for her misdemeanours. And now, she was truly an orphan.

Josiah's humble tones cut into his thoughts. 'If you'll permit me, I'd like to make a suggestion, Mr Edmund.'

'Eh?' Edmund roused himself from his thoughts. 'Of course, Roper.'

Josiah licked his lips again. 'I've been thinking over

the problem, sir. You see, if the girl finds out her mother's dead, she could do anything. Cause a riot amongst the apprentices, run away. She might,' he emphasized, 'even take the matter to the authorities. Anything . . .'

Edmund's eyes narrowed. 'So – what is your suggestion?'

'That we don't tell her.'

Edmund pulled a face. 'But won't she go on asking? Won't she try to run away again to find out for herself? Just like she says she did the last time?'

With smooth deliberation, Josiah said, 'Not if she starts to receive regular letters from her mother.'

'Eh?'

'If I may be so bold, I believe your – er – relationship with Mr Goodbody is such that the man would be prepared to participate in a little harmless deception. I say harmless, sir,' he hurried on, 'because, after all, we have the child's best interests at heart, don't we? We want her to be happy and settled in her work. And I'm sure she would be, Mr Edmund, if she were to receive a letter every now and again from her mother telling her to be a good girl and not to even think of running away.' Warming to his theme, Josiah hurried on. 'She'd be reassured that her mother was in good health and . . . and I think she'd be obedient to her mother's wishes as expressed in the – er – letters.' He cleared his throat. 'It seems, sir, that the girl's mother cannot read or write and would have to ask someone to write for her. So, there is no chance, you see, that she'll question why someone else has written in her mother's stead.'

Edmund stared at the man in front of him. 'Well, well, well, Roper. What a devious mind you have.' His eyes gleamed and he smiled. 'But a clever one, even I have to admit. And yes, you're quite right. Goodbody will do whatever I ask him. I'll write to him. But not a word to my father, mind.'

'Of course not, sir,' Josiah said with a little bow. He laid the letter on the desk in front of Edmund. 'If there's nothing else, then I'll bid you goodnight, sir.'

'Goodnight, Roper,' Edmund murmured absently, as he picked up the letter from the master of the workhouse and began to read it for himself.

The following week, Josiah Roper sent for Hannah.

'Come in, girl, come in.' He beckoned her forward and motioned her to stand in front of his tall desk.

'Mr Critchlow has asked me to tell you—'

'Has he heard from Mr Goodbody? Is my mother all right?'

Josiah frowned. 'If you'll give me time, girl, I'm getting to that.'

'Sorry, Mr Roper,' Hannah smiled at him winningly, but her prettiness was lost on the cold-hearted man.

'Mr Critchlow – Mr Edmund Critchlow, that is – has asked me to see you. His father is unwell at the present time and all correspondence is now being dealt with either by Mr Edmund or – myself,' he added loftily. He was deliberately dragging out getting to the point. He was enjoying the girl's agitation. She was hopping impatiently from one foot to the other and pressing her lips together as if to prevent further questions bursting forth.

Slowly, he held up a piece of paper. 'This letter purports to be from your mother, child. Mrs Good-

body, I understand, has been kindness itself in under-
taking to write to you on behalf of your mother.'

Joseph believed that in matters of deceit, the nearer
the truth one could keep to, the better the chance there
was of the lies being believed. Mrs Goodbody had
indeed penned the letter, but under the instruction of
her own husband, who'd explained tersely the necess-
ity of keeping on the right side of Edmund Critchlow.

Hannah sprang forward and snatched the sheet of
paper from Josiah's bony fingers. She scanned it
eagerly and, as Josiah watched closely, a smile spread
across her mouth. There were tears in her eyes as she
looked up at him.

'Oh, thank you, Mr Roper. You don't know how
much this means to me. Please – will you thank Mr
Critchlow for me? I don't know how I can ever repay
him.'

'You can repay him, girl, by working hard and
keeping yourself out of trouble. And no more thoughts
of running away, eh?'

'Oh no, Mr Roper.' Her bright blue eyes were
glowing with a happiness that had been missing for
weeks, ever since Jane's death. She'd never forget her
little friend and she would always carry the feeling of
guilt. But with news she believed to be from her
mother, Hannah could allow herself to look forward
again.

'Fall for it, did she?' Edmund demanded, opening
his door as soon as he heard Hannah leave the clerk's
office.

Josiah smiled maliciously. 'Oh yes, sir. She fell for
it.' *And so*, he thought as the young master's door
closed again, *have you. Another Critchlow secret in
my keeping.*

At that moment, Hannah was skipping down the stairs back to her work, the precious letter clutched against her breast and, for the first time since Jane's tragic death, she was singing at the top of her voice.

But the next day, a rumour flew through the mill that struck dread into the heart of each and every worker. Mr Nathaniel Critchlow had suffered a serious seizure. For days, his life hung in the balance, but when the news came that he would live, there was little rejoicing. The man was paralysed and would never again sit behind the desk in the mill office. From that moment, Mr Edmund was in full control of Wyedale Mill, and there was only one person who revelled in the news.

Josiah Roper.

Eighteen

As the months and years passed, Hannah moved from job to job in the mill, working as a bobbin winder and then as a drawer.

'I could leave you on the mule with Mrs Martin,' Ernest told her, 'but you're a quick learner and I want you to learn as many jobs as you can. Then, if I'm short anywhere, you can always fill in for me, lass.'

Hannah beamed at him and nodded. She always found a new interest in her work, always found something to sing about. On alternate Sundays, she, Luke and Daniel climbed the hills above the mill, to breathe in the fresh air and taste freedom, even for only an hour or so. When it snowed and the hillsides were clothed in white, they still climbed, slipping and sliding and clinging on to each other, laughing and shrieking in delicious enjoyment. Most weeks they called to see Mrs Grundy, Hannah taking a few of her hard-earned coppers whenever she could. Slowly, the debt was being repaid.

And still the letters that she believed were dictated by her mother to Mrs Goodbody arrived regularly. Hannah could imagine her mother speaking the words aloud – she could almost hear Rebecca's gentle, loving voice exhorting the girl to be good and to stay at the mill.

'*Don't be trying to come to see me,*' the letters

always said. '*I'm well and happy to know that you are too. You are so fortunate in your position. It was so kind of Mr Goodbody to arrange it all for you and we don't want to upset either him or Mr Critchlow, who has been so good to you too, do we?* She signed all her letters, *Your loving mother*, and this was followed by an untidy cross.

Hannah would hold the place where she imagined her mother's fingers had touched the paper against her face, close her eyes and pretend that her mother was tenderly caressing her cheek.

'Mrs Goodbody must write them all for her,' Hannah told Luke and Daniel as the three of them stood on the top of the hill overlooking the dale. She showed them the growing bundle of precious letters from her beloved mother that she carried in her pocket.

'They're all in the same handwriting.' She paused and then added wistfully, 'It's lovely to hear from her and know she's all right, but it's not the same as being able to see her and talk to her and . . . and hug her.'

With one accord as if pulled by the same string, the two boys turned and Daniel began to run down the hill, slipping and sliding in his haste to get away. Luke paused for a moment to look back at her.

'At least you've still got a mam,' he said harshly and then he ran after his brother.

Hannah stared after them, tears welling in her eyes. 'Oh, how stupid I've been. How unkind. I never thought . . .'

At suppertime, she sought them out. Never one to shirk doing the right thing, she stood in front of them. 'I'm so sorry. It was thoughtless and hurtful of me to keep going on about my mother. You helped me so much at first when I was so worried about not hearing from her that I hadn't realized every time I talk about her it must remind you of . . . of . . . Well, I'm sorry.'

The two boys glanced at each other and then looked at her with identical grins on their cheeky faces. ''S all right,' Luke said. 'We were being daft an' all. It's not your fault we've no mam and dad.'

'And we are glad for you that your mam's all right,' Daniel added.

'Friends then?'

''Course,' the twins chorused.

Summer came round once more, Hannah's fourth in Wyedale. Letters from her mother came spasmodically, but Hannah wrote faithfully every month. On alternate Sundays, whatever the weather, she roamed the hills or walked beside the river with Luke and Daniel, and her friendship with Nell, too, deepened. Ernest Scarsfield had noticed how well the two girls worked together, so when it was time for them to learn yet another job, he put them together once more.

'We're to learn to be throstle spinners,' Nell told her excitedly. 'Oh, I've always wanted to do that. We're to work on one of the machines that produces the warp thread.' Nell hugged her. 'We're going up in the world, Hannah. Just like Mrs Riley said we would. You'll see. I must remember to be specially nice to . . .' She broke off. 'Come on, let's go and find your Luke and tell him.'

'*My* Luke,' Hannah laughed.

'Oh yes.' Nell's face was serious. 'He's in love with you. Hadn't you noticed?'

'Well, I love him. And Daniel and you, of course.'
She skipped ahead of Nell, singing a song of her own
making this time. 'We're going up in the world.'

Nell smiled and shook her head in wonder. Was
Hannah still so innocent and naive as she made out?
She frowned. Maybe she should have a little talk with
the younger girl, explain just how boys, and men in
particular, could be – once you started to grow up.

'Quick, she's coming,' Luke hissed. 'Get ready. The
minute she opens the door we all shout "Happy
Birthday".'

The giggling children lined up around the long
bench tables in the kitchen. It was suppertime on a
Saturday evening in August, the evening of Hannah's
sixteenth birthday. In the middle of the table stood a
birthday cake, which Mrs Bramwell had made herself.
It was something she and Arthur did on an apprentice's sixteenth birthday. Although it meant no legal
coming of age, to the Bramwells that particular age
seemed to mark a turning point in the lives of the
youngsters in their charge. If a child had already
worked four or five years – or even longer – in the
mill, by the time they reached sixteen they were doing
the work of an adult and the Bramwells believed they
should be treated as such. And if anyone had earned
that right, it was Hannah Francis. She was a hard
worker and always cheerful – well, almost always.
Mrs Bramwell was well aware that the girl still carried
a sadness in her heart over the death of her little
friend, and daily she still longed to see her own
mother. During the three years and three months that
Hannah had been at the mill, it had never been poss-

ible for Rebecca to travel to see her, and the girl – of course – had never been granted permission to return to the workhouse.

Ethel Bramwell understood that part of it. What she didn't understand was why the mother had never been allowed to visit. Parents who'd agreed to their children being apprenticed to the Critchlows were allowed to visit often.

'I expect the guardians won't pay for her fare to get here, if she's still in the workhouse,' Arthur had remarked reasonably when Ethel broached the subject with him earlier that day.

Ethel had sighed. 'It's not right. Keeping a girl from her mother for all that time with only letters to keep them both going.' Her voice had faltered a little over speaking of what was a great sadness to both her and her husband. 'If we'd been blessed with children, I know I couldn't have borne to've been separated from them in such a way.'

'No, love,' Arthur had agreed quietly. 'No more would I.' He had sighed. 'But that's the way it is. At least she's been well treated at this mill. It'd be a different story at some of the others.'

Ethel had shaken her head. 'If Mr Nathaniel had still been at the helm, then I might've agreed with you, but not now. Not with *him* in charge. I hear the children talking. The tales they're bringing back, Arthur. Things are getting worse and they'll go on getting worse now he's got no one to curb him.'

'It's been happening for years, Ethel. Let's face it, Mr Nathaniel was weak. He rarely stood up to his son even when he was still coming to the mill, now did he?'

Ethel Bramwell had shrugged. 'But when he was

still here, Edmund was away a lot in Manchester on business. Things didn't seem quite so bad then, but now he's here more of the time . . .' Her voice had trailed away.

Arthur Bramwell's face had been solemn. There was something he'd heard that had filled him with deep foreboding. He'd put off telling his wife until he knew if the rumour was true. Yet then, he had felt he must tell her. 'I'm sorry to say,' he had said slowly, 'that things are about to get worse.'

Ethel had stared at him. She held her breath, knowing she was not going to like what he was about to say.

'It seems that Mr Edmund wants to resume handling the business side of things. He'll be spending more time away just like he did before.'

Ethel had begun to smile hopefully. 'Well, that'll be better—' Seeing her husband's expression, she stopped.

Bluntly and in a flat, hopeless tone, Arthur had said, 'Ernest reckons he'll make Roper manager of the whole mill when he's away.'

Ethel's eyes had widened. 'Josiah Roper! Why him? He doesn't know the first thing about the workings of the mill. He's just a clerk. Why not Ernest or one of the other overlookers?'

With a puzzled frown, Arthur had said slowly, 'I don't know.'

'Well, if it does happen, if Roper's put in charge, then may God help us all. That's all I can say. But let's not say anything to the children,' Ethel had begged. 'Not yet. Let's not spoil Hannah's day. You can tell them when we know it's really going to happen.'

Now, as they stood waiting for Hannah, they

pushed aside all thoughts of the mill. Tonight, they would have a party for all the children in their care. For a few precious hours they'd try to help them forget the drudgery of their working days.

'She's coming,' Luke said again. 'I can hear her singing.'

A ripple of soft laughter ran amongst the children. 'We can always hear where Hannah is,' Daniel said, and everyone laughed.

'Shh,' Luke hissed, and everyone tried to stifle their laughter.

The door opened and Hannah stopped in surprise, the words of her song dying on her lips, her mouth wide open in astonishment as everyone chorused, 'Happy Birthday.'

She put her hands over the lower part of her face to hide her blushes, but her eyes sparkled with tears of surprised delight. As their voices died away, Luke and Daniel moved forward and stood on either side of her.

'Mrs Bramwell's made you a cake.'

'And now you must cut it and make a wish.'

For the next hour laughter and singing filled the kitchen of the apprentice house. At last Arthur rapped on the table for silence. 'Now, we've all had a good time, but it's time the younger ones were in bed . . .' This was greeted with a chorus of protests, but they rose obediently, helped to clear away the remains of the feast, and climbed up the narrow twisting staircase, still laughing and talking.

Hannah put her arms around Ethel Bramwell's waist. 'Thank you. Thank you so much for a lovely party. It was just like my mother used to do for me. I only wish . . .' The girl's voice broke and she buried her face against the superintendent's breast.

Ethel put her arms about Hannah. Though kindly towards all the children in her charge, she was rarely demonstrative. But her lack of any show of affection was deliberate. It didn't do to become too attached to any of the children. Her position demanded aloofness, and besides, that way lay hurt. How could she have borne to watch poor little Jane die in agony if she'd allowed herself to love the child? How could she – each and every day – watch the little ones toil to and from the mill, dragging their weary feet, coughing and spluttering as the fluff took hold of their lungs, watching as their eyes became sore, their ears hard of hearing? No, Ethel Bramwell couldn't allow herself to become a proper mother to the children. She dared not. But tonight, just for a moment, the barriers were down and she hugged Hannah to her. 'I know, my dear, I know how you must feel.'

Hannah lifted her face and smiled through her tears. 'But I wouldn't want you to think I'm ungrateful. My mother would love to've been here to join in the fun, but when I write to her, I'll tell her everything. It'll make her so happy.'

Ethel, who knew nothing of the deception being carried on by Josiah Roper and Edmund Critchlow, smiled. 'I'm sure it will. And she should be very proud of her grown-up daughter. You're a credit to her, Hannah. Now,' she said briskly, gently easing herself out of the girl's arms, 'help me clear up and then you can get to your bed.'

As the room began to empty and Ethel bustled about clearing away the last few crumbs of the demolished cake, Luke grabbed Hannah's hand. 'Come for a walk,' he whispered. 'Now you're an old lady of sixteen, you don't have to go to bed for another hour.'

Hannah giggled. 'Oh, the freedom. It'll quite turn my head.' Then impishly she added, 'But you're not sixteen yet. You'd better go to bed, little boy, or you'll be in trouble.'

'I'll risk it,' Luke grinned, but as he pulled her towards the door, Hannah glanced back. 'What about Daniel?'

'He'll be all right. I want you to meself for once.'

Hannah's eyes widened and she laughed, a faint pink tingeing her cheeks as they slipped out of the back door and into the velvet blackness of the night. 'Come on. Let's go into the wash house.'

'I thought you wanted to go for a walk.'

Through the darkness, she heard his soft chuckle. 'Not really. I just wanted to get you to meself.'

They crept into the building across the yard and shut the door behind them. Hannah shivered and Luke put his arm about her, drawing her close.

'Enjoyed your birthday, have you?'

Hannah rested her head against his shoulder and sighed. Although a year younger, he was as tall as she was now. 'Of course I have. It was lovely of the Bramwells to arrange it all.'

'With a bit of help from me an' Daniel.'

Hannah put her arms round his waist and hugged him. 'I thought as much. Thanks, Luke. You and Daniel are my very best friends besides Nell.'

His arms tightened around her. Against her hair he whispered huskily, 'I . . . I'd like to be more than friends. Hannah – I want you to be my girl.'

She drew back a little. 'Oh, Luke, I'd love that, but you know it isn't allowed. We'd be in such trouble—'

He laughed so loud now that she put her finger against his lips to quieten him. 'Since when,' he mocked her fondly, 'has that ever stopped you?'

Hannah laughed softly and leaned forward, until their foreheads were touching. Thinking back over the time she'd been here, she seemed to have been in trouble more times than not. Most of the time her misdemeanours had been nothing very serious. The worst had been the time she'd tried to visit her mother. But since letters had come frequently, she'd been, if not happy, then content to do as her mother asked her in every letter. '*Be a good girl, work hard and be a credit to me.*'

'We'll have to keep it secret, then, won't we?' Luke was saying. 'Folks are used to seeing us together. They know we're good friends. We'll just have to mind they don't guess it's a lot more now.' He paused and there was an unaccustomed hesitancy in his tone as he added, 'It *is* a lot more now, isn't it, Hannah?'

'Yes, oh yes, Luke.' She wound her arms around his neck as he leaned forward and tried to kiss her. But they bumped noses and ended up convulsed in laughter. 'Reckon we need a bit of practice,' Luke whispered. Then he bent his head to one side and his lips touched hers in their first tentative kiss.

They stood whispering and giggling and kissing until at last, Luke said reluctantly, 'We'd best go back in. I don't want Mr Bramwell coming after me with a big stick. Come on,' he grabbed her hand and together they sneaked out of the wash house once more. 'Now,' he said, letting go of her hand near the back door. 'Remember, no one must know.'

'Not even Daniel?' Hannah said.

'Daniel?' Luke was surprised that she should even ask. 'Oh, he knew how I felt about you even before I realized it meself.'

Hannah collapsed in gales of laughter and clung to him for a moment, and that is how Mrs Bramwell saw them as she opened the back door.

'There's something going on between those two,' Ethel told her husband as they undressed for bed that night.

'Which two?'

'Luke Hammond and Hannah.'

'Going on? Naw. They're just friends, that's all.' He laughed, a deep, low rumbling sound. 'Can't be much going on when the three of them go everywhere together. Can't do a lot when his twin's tagging along, can he?' He sobered suddenly. 'Unless you're implying—'

'No, no, of course I'm not suggesting anything like that,' Ethel said hurriedly.

'Thank God for that,' her husband muttered.

'But you know the Critchlows make their own rules. If word gets out they'll be sacked. One, if not both of them. Ne'er mind their so-called indenture.'

Arthur made a dismissive sound as he said, 'Ach, I know the rules, woman. But it goes on. You know it does. We see the lads and lasses walking back up the hill to the village at night after work hand in hand, now don't we?'

'There's not much he can do about those who live out, but what he doesn't like is it going on here in the apprentice house. Old man Critchlow might've turned a blind eye, but his son certainly won't. And I'll tell you something else, an' all. It'll make Mr Edmund notice *her*. She's growing up fast. And if he starts to notice her, you know what might happen then.'

For a moment, Arthur stared at his wife across the width of their double bed, then he shrugged. 'I don't think it's Hannah you've to worry about. If anyone, it's Nell.'

As Arthur Bramwell climbed into bed, lay down and closed his eyes, his wife sighed heavily. 'I've been worried about Nell Hudson for years.'

In the dormitories, most of the children were asleep, but two were wide awake, thinking of each other. Hannah snuggled down in the bed she no longer had to share, feeling the happiest she'd been since she'd come to the mill.

'Nell?' she whispered. 'Nell, are you awake?'

When there was no answer, she reared up and squinted through the darkness to the bed next to hers. To her surprise, it was empty. But far from being concerned, Hannah only chuckled. Maybe Nell's got a sweetheart too, she thought happily.

Nineteen

The day that Edmund became bored with spending most of his days at the mill, Josiah Roper believed it might be the happiest day in his life.

'I'm not getting the best prices for cotton,' Edmund ranted, pacing up and down his office.

'There's no better negotiator than you, sir.' Josiah gave a small obsequious bow as he hovered in the doorway. 'The figures certainly aren't as good as when you were doing the buying in person.'

Edmund grunted and continued to pace. 'There's nothing else for it, Roper, I'll have to start going to Manchester and Liverpool again myself. I can't trust anyone else to do it. Not properly.'

I could do it, Josiah was thinking. *I could barter just as well as you.* But the clerk held his tongue. He was an expert book-keeper – no one could ever deny that. He knew how to make the figures add up to a healthy profit on the bottom line in his numerous, neatly written ledgers. Yet no one realized that during the years he had, on the surface, faithfully served the Critchlows, Josiah Roper had been garnering a wealth of knowledge about the cotton industry. He'd learned all he could about the financial side of the trade – and so much more. He could recognize the best quality of the cotton and where it came from. On the pretext of checking deliveries, he'd seen for himself the bales of raw cotton that Edmund had bartered for and bought. He'd listened at doors, subtly questioned the workers as they passed in and out of his office. And when the machines fell silent late at night, Josiah would pass like a shadow through all the floors, seeing for himself all the processes needed to turn the raw cotton into a finished, saleable product.

But he could reveal none of this to Edmund Critchlow. He had to wait. He had to bide his time . . .

Edmund stopped his pacing and faced his clerk. 'What I need, Roper, is someone to be manager of the mill whilst I'm away.' His lip curled. 'Scarsfield would be the obvious choice, but he's far too soft. He'd have the hands running circles round him. No, I need someone with a firm hand. Someone who'll stand no nonsense.'

Josiah cleared his throat. 'Does it have to be someone who actually works in the mill itself, sir? I mean, surely, it should be someone who understands the business side too. The – er – financial side. They would know what needed to be done and merely be capable of passing on those requirements to the various overlookers.'

He fell silent, waiting for his words to permeate Edmund's mind. He watched the fleeting expressions on his employer's face. Saw the light beginning to dawn. Hardly daring to breathe as excitement flooded through him, he wondered briefly if this feeling was akin to the thrill his own father and Edmund had felt at the gaming tables. If so, then for the first time in his life, he could understand his father's addiction. The fast-beating heart, the clammy hands, the beads of sweat on his forehead.

Edmund was staring at him. 'You mean – you?' There was sarcasm in his tone.

Again the deferential bow. 'You know you can trust me implicitly, Mr Edmund. You surely cannot doubt my loyalty to you and your family.'

'But you know nothing about the workings of the mill.'

'Perhaps not,' Josiah said meekly, preferring not to divulge the extent of his acquired knowledge. 'But – like I said – is that strictly necessary?' Daringly now, he put it into words. 'I'm sure I could see that the overlookers carry out all their duties. If, of course,' he added slyly, 'you were to give me the authority.'

'Hmm.' Edmund pondered for a moment and then his face brightened. 'I've a better idea. I'll bring Adam home from school. Make him manager of the mill.'

Josiah's hopes faded. Yet he was not quite ready to give up. 'But Master Adam's only sixteen—'

'Seventeen. High time he was here learning the family business instead of idling away his time at school.'

'But won't he be going to university?'

Edmund let out a loud guffaw. 'Adam? Go to university? He's not clever enough, Roper. He'd never get in. Besides, he'd be far better here. After all, the mill will be his one day. The sooner he starts learning his trade, the better. He's too soft, of course. He's like his grandfather. But with me to guide him, he'll toughen up. I'll write to his headmaster at once.' Edmund rubbed his hands, gleeful that his problem had been solved. 'Of course,' he said offhandedly as he sat down behind his desk and picked up a pen, 'you can hold the fort until Adam gets home.'

Josiah Roper almost spat in the other man's face. He glared at Edmund's head bowed over the letter he'd begun to write. If he'd had a weapon to hand at that moment, Edmund Critchlow might not have lived to see another day. As it was, Josiah turned on his heel and left the room, his only outward show of displeasure being to bang the door behind him.

One day, he promised himself. Oh, one day, Mr Edmund Critchlow . . .

'Nell – where were you last night? Oh, you weren't in the punishment room, were you? Surely Mrs Bramwell couldn't have been so mean. Not after my party. She couldn't have been—'

'Hannah, just shut up, will you? And stop asking so many questions.'

Hannah gasped. 'But . . .'

'But nothing. Just mind your own business. All right?'

Hannah stared at her friend. Nell avoided meeting her eyes and pushed past her to get to her bed. Hannah's mouth tightened. She picked up her shawl and her clogs. 'Well, if that's the way you want it,' she said stiffly, and began to follow the others rushing to get to work. The bell had gone already. At the door, she paused. 'You'd better get a move on. You'll be late and then you'll be fined . . .'

'Just go, Hannah. Leave me alone.'

To Hannah's surprise, Nell made no attempt to follow, but climbed onto her bed and lay down, curling herself into a ball, hugging herself.

Hannah bit her lip, hesitating. 'Nell, are you ill? Do you want me to fetch Mrs Bramwell . . .'

Nell sat up suddenly, and leaned over the side of her bed to pick up her clogs. Hannah felt a wave of relief.

'Come on, then,' she began, but her relief turned to horror as Nell flung one of her clogs straight at her, narrowly missing her head. The clog banged against the wall and fell to the floor with a clatter.

'Get out!' Nell screamed. 'Just get out and leave me alone.'

Hannah went, almost falling down the stairs, gulping back the sobs. Whatever was the matter with Nell? She rushed to find Mrs Bramwell, not caring if she was late and incurred a fine.

'There's something the matter with Nell,' she burst out. 'She wasn't in bed last night before I fell asleep and she's just come in like a bear with a sore head. She's lying in her bed and won't come to work.'

Mrs Bramwell's face was grim. 'Is she indeed?'

It was a strange thing to say, Hannah thought. The woman didn't seem concerned that Nell might be ill. Just that she was not going to work.

'I think she's ill, she's holding her tummy and—'

'Leave her to me and you get to work, Francis.'

Hannah ran out of the house and down the hill, only just managing to clock in half a minute before the bell in the tower stopped ringing.

The whole day passed with Hannah having to run between the two machines, doing her own work and Nell's, trying to keep her friend out of trouble.

The day passed quickly. As she was leaving by the gate, hurrying back up the hill to the house to see how Nell was, she heard a shout behind her and saw the twins running towards her.

'Have you heard the news?' Luke began.

'Master Adam's back,' Daniel continued.

'He's to be manager—'

'Of the mill—'

'When Mr Edmund's away—'

'On business.'

As always when they were together, the two boys imparted the information in turn.

Hannah glanced from one to the other in amazement. 'Master Adam? But . . . but he's only a boy. How can he be manager?'

'Because he's a Critchlow—'

'That's why.'

'And he's about seventeen now, isn't he?'

'Oh.' Hannah wrinkled her forehead. 'Oh well, I don't suppose it will make much difference to us. Will it?'

Luke grinned. 'Things might be better. Word has it that Mr Adam is much nicer—'

'Than his father.'

'More like—'

'His grandfather.'

Hannah smiled at them in turn and then stepped between them, linking her arms in theirs. 'Come on, let's go and tell the others. And I want to find out how Nell is.'

There was excited chatter amongst all the apprentices at the news. Only Mr and Mrs Bramwell seemed preoccupied and anxious.

'Don't you think it's good news about Master Adam being made manager, Mrs Bramwell?' Hannah asked.

'What? Oh yes, I suppose so. Don't bother me now, Hannah. I've enough on my mind.'

'How's Nell? Where is she? Can I see her?'

188

'No,' Mrs Bramwell snapped. 'You can't. Nor will you. She's gone.'

Hannah's mouth dropped open. 'Gone? What do you mean, gone? Gone where?'

'How should I know?'

'But . . . but . . . you should know. You're the superintendent, you're—'

Mrs Bramwell rounded on her. Now she was nothing like the kindly woman who'd hugged Hannah on her birthday only yesterday. Now she was like a screaming banshee. 'Is it my fault if the stupid girl gets herself into trouble and gets sent away? Is it? Is it?' Mary, the kitchen maid, stopped and turned to stare at her mistress. Even she, who worked for her all day and half the night too sometimes, had never seen Mrs Bramwell in such a temper.

Hannah blinked and opened her mouth to speak, but at that moment Mr Bramwell came into the kitchen and hurried towards his wife. 'There, there, Ethel,' he soothed, putting his arm around her shoulders. 'You mustn't blame yourself. Or the poor girl, if it comes to that. We know who's to blame, now don't we, but there's not a thing we can do about it.'

To Hannah's horror, Ethel turned her face away and wept against her husband's shoulder. 'But what'll become of her? What'll happen to her?'

Hannah began to feel frightened. 'Mr Bramwell, what's happened? Please – won't you tell me?'

Arthur Bramwell looked down upon the innocent face upturned towards him. He sighed inwardly. He would dearly like to tell this honest, hardworking child the truth, but he had been sworn to secrecy and so had his wife. He'd like to warn Hannah too, but he dared not do so.

Instead, he said sternly, 'It's not your place to ask questions. Hudson's gone and she won't be coming back. That's all you need to know. Now, get about your chores else you'll find yourself in the punishment room for insolence.'

For once Hannah did as she was told, and the following morning she sought out Dorothy Riley, but the woman only shrugged. 'Best not to ask, love. Know your place, that's my advice to you.' She glanced at Hannah and then touched her face with callused, work-worn fingers. 'You're a pretty lass, more's the pity, so keep your head down. Do your work and try not to get noticed. Now come on, we've all got work to do, else we'll have Mr Scarsfield after us. And he's in a bad mood this morning, now he's a throstle spinner down.'

Again Hannah worked the two machines all day, though it wasn't easy. Tired, hot and dirty by the end of the day, she was still determined to try to find out what had happened to her friend.

The overlooker was standing next to the time clock when the bell sounded for the end of the day.

'Mr Scarsfield,' Hannah asked after she had stamped her card and returned it to its holder. 'What's happened to Nell?'

The man stared at her in surprise for a moment and then frowned. 'Ah,' he said. 'I see you don't know.' He glanced away, avoiding her clear, straight gaze.

'All I've been told is that she's gone away and won't be coming back. What I don't know is why. No one will tell me.'

'She's been sacked,' Ernest said bluntly. 'She's displeased the master and he's sacked her.'

'But . . . but how? Why?'

Ernest looked at her strangely for a moment and then muttered bitterly, 'You'd better ask him.'

'Oh, I will.' Hannah began and turned away as if to go that very minute, but Ernest caught hold of her arm and held her fast. He shook his head, his eyes full of concern for her now. 'No, lass, don't. I shouldn't have said that. That's the last thing you should do. Promise me you won't go asking any more questions.'

Hannah stared at him for a moment before saying solemnly, 'I'm sorry, Mr Scarsfield, I can't give you that promise.'

He released her with a click of exasperation. 'On your own head be it then, girl. But don't say I didn't warn you.'

Twenty

Now, on Sundays, Luke and Hannah walked alone.

'I feel awful leaving Daniel,' she said more than once. 'He hasn't any other friends.'

But Luke only grinned 'He doesn't mind. I've told him – time he got himself a girl an' all.'

'Is there anyone he likes?'

'Don't think so.'

He glanced behind him. They were out of sight of the mill now, walking round the edge of the mill pool beneath the cliff and alongside the river. Green-headed mallards, uptailed as they searched the depths for food, swam close by. Coots and moorhens darted about the surface and every so often they heard the plop of a jumping fish. Overhead, leafy trees sheltered them from the hot sun. Luke put his arm about her waist and they walked on, matching their steps to each other.

'So – what do you think to our new young master then?' Luke asked her.

'He's all right. I haven't seen much of him.'

'Haven't you? Well, I've seen him watching you at work'

'I hadn't noticed.'

'No, he minds to keep himself well back in the shadows. But he stands watching you and listening to you singing.'

192

Hannah laughed. 'I shouldn't think he can hear much above the noise all that machinery makes.'

'No – but he can look at you.'

Hannah teased him. 'A' you jealous?'

He grinned at her. ''Course I am. I don't like anyone eyeing my girl up, even if he is the boss's son.'

Hannah tweaked his nose playfully. 'Just so long as it isn't Mr Edmund. He sends shivers down my spine every time he looks at me.'

Now Luke wasn't laughing any more. He'd heard the tales about Mr Edmund and he didn't like them one little bit. And he didn't want Hannah asking him about them, especially if the latest rumour about Nell was true. Deliberately, he changed the subject. 'Have you heard from your mother lately?'

Hannah didn't answer immediately. Ever since that day on the hillside when the twins, younger then, of course, and feeling more vulnerable, had been so upset, she'd avoided talking to them about her mother. In fact, she scarcely spoke to anyone at the mill about her now. She was conscious that many of the children she lived and worked with were orphans. But now, as Luke asked her directly, she frowned and said, 'No, not since before my birthday. In fact, I didn't get a letter then and I know she wouldn't have forgotten it. She ... she always used to make a big thing of anyone's birthday.'

Gently, Luke said, 'Hannah, you didn't get a letter last year for your birthday. You were upset about it then.'

Hannah stared at him. 'You're right. But I got such a lovely one a week later that I forgot all about it. I ... I just thought that ... well ... being in there, she'd lost track of the date.' Her voice trailed away,

193

her heart aching at the thought of her mother still imprisoned in the workhouse.

'Have you written to her?' Luke prompted.

'Yes. Twice – but she's not written back.'

They walked on in silence. Luke couldn't think of any useful suggestion, and though Hannah was busy with her own plans, she had no intention of telling Luke what they were. It had been two months since Nell had disappeared so suddenly and Hannah still didn't know what had happened to her, and now she wanted to find out why the letters from her mother had stopped. And so, despite her declaration that she tried to avoid Mr Edmund, there were now two very good reasons why she needed to seek him out deliberately.

'May I see Mr Edmund, please?' Hannah asked Josiah Roper politely.

'What about?'

'I – it's a personal matter.'

The man's mouth twisted slyly. ''Bout you and young what's-'is-name, is it? Want to get married, do you?'

Hannah gasped and couldn't stop the flush rising in her face. 'I don't know what you're talking about.'

'Oh, I think you do. You'd better be careful. If Mr Edmund gets wind of it, that lad'll be out on his ear, indenture or no indenture. He'll be gone.' His impudent glance raked her from head to toe. 'Mind you, he'll not sack you. Oh no, he'll likely keep you for himself.'

'It's nothing like that. There's nothing between me and Luke—'

Josiah raised his eyebrows. 'So you do know who I was talking about then?'

Hannah's blush deepened. 'Stop trying to put words in my mouth,' she cried angrily. 'Is Mr Edmund here – or not?'

'No, he isn't.'

'Thank you,' she said, her tone heavy with sarcasm. She turned to go. As she pulled open the door to leave, Josiah said airily, 'Not had a letter lately, have you?'

Hannah stopped in her tracks and looked back at him. 'What . . . what do you mean?'

'Oh, nothing.' He paused and then added, calculatingly, 'I expect Mrs Goodbody has got sick of writing. It can't be easy making up lovey-dovey letters, pretending to be your mother.'

'Whatever do you mean? *Pretending* to be my mother?'

Josiah's lip curled. Still harbouring bitterness at Mr Edmund's decision to pass him over and bring home a mere youth to be manager of the mill, he said, 'Those letters aren't from your mother, girl. Mrs Goodbody wrote them all. Every last one of them.'

Hannah was still puzzled. 'My mother can't write herself, but—'

'Of course your mother can't write now – even if she ever could. She's dead.' Hannah clutched at the door to steady herself as Josiah continued vindictively, 'She's been dead for three years. Ever since a few months after you came here.'

Hannah felt the colour drain from her face, and felt her legs tremble weakly as if they would no longer support her. 'But . . . but Mr Edmund . . . ?'

'He deceived you. Him and Mr Goodbody wanted to keep you here. Keep you happy. They cooked up the little scheme of Matilda Goodbody writing to you – just so you'd think that your dear mama was still well and happy.'

Hannah gasped. 'I don't believe you. You're a wicked liar, Mr Roper.'

Josiah shrugged. 'Think what you like. It doesn't bother me. But what would I have to gain by telling you lies?'

She stared at him for a long moment, her thoughts in turmoil. 'I . . . I . . .' she began, but she could think of nothing to say, so she turned and ran. Ran to find Luke, all thoughts of the second reason for her visit to the office – to ask about Nell – driven from her mind.

It was not Luke she found, but Adam Critchlow.

Running wildly across the yard towards the gate, she ran smack into him and would have lost her balance and fallen had he not caught hold of her.

For a moment he held her close and then, when she was steady on her feet, though gasping for breath through her sobbing, he held her a little from him and looked down at her. His eyes darkened as he saw her distress.

'Hannah, what is it? Whatever's the matter?'

'You – you and your family. He's . . . he's lied to me. All this time, I believed him. I've been loyal. I've worked hard – and all I get in return is lies and deceit.'

'Whatever do you mean? I don't understand what you're talking about.'

'My mother's dead. And he never told me. He's lied to me. Kept me believing she was alive and well and . . . and happy and all the time . . .'

She broke into fresh, hiccuping sobs.

'No! I don't believe it. My grandfather wouldn't do something like that.'

'It wasn't your grandfather – it was your father.'

'My *father*?' His look was incredulous.

Hannah nodded grimly. 'It was all a plot hatched up between him and the master of the workhouse to keep me quiet.' Her voice broke and she sobbed afresh.

'You're saying my father did that?' Adam asked slowly.

'You don't believe me, do you? Why will no one ever believe me?' she cried passionately. She realized he was still holding her and she tore herself free. 'Let me go! Let me go! You're – you're all the same. *You'll* be just the same.'

Adam's face blanched. 'No, I won't. I promise I'd never do anything like that.' She could still hear the doubt in his voice. He couldn't believe such a thing of his own father.

Her eyes blazing now, rage drying her tears. 'Oh yes, you will. You'll be just like him. You won't be able to help yourself. When you have us all in your – in your power, you'll be as bad as him. He'll *make* you just like him. There's a lot you don't know about your father. You've not been here to see it. But things are very different for us workers since your grandfather was taken ill. Very different.'

Then she ran. Out of the gate and up the steep slope, not stopping until she'd rushed into the apprentice house and slammed the kitchen door behind her. She leaned against it, sobbing and breathless.

'What on earth . . . !' Ethel Bramwell began angrily, but when she saw the state of the young girl, she laid down her rolling pin at once and, wiping her floury hands on her copious white apron, she hurried forward. 'Oh, my dear, what's happened? Don't tell me there's been another accident.'

She led Hannah forward and pushed her into a chair near the kitchen range and then poured a cup of tea from the huge teapot sitting in the hearth. 'There, there. Tell me all about it.'

The story flooded out and even Ethel Bramwell, who'd worked for the Critchlows for years, was astonished.

'Mr Critchlow? Old man Critchlow?' Her tone was disbelieving. 'He was party to this?'

Hannah shook her head. 'I don't know. Maybe. It was Mr Edmund mainly and Mr Roper was in on it too. It . . . it was always him who gave me the letters an' . . . and posted mine. If he ever did post them,' she ended flatly. It didn't matter now whether he had or not. Her loving letters would never have reached the person for whom they were intended anyway.

Mrs Bramwell sighed. 'I don't like to think the old man knew about it. I'd've thought better of him.'

Hannah's face hardened. Her blue eyes turned cold. 'They're all the same. Every one of them. Master Adam'll be just the same, when he's older.'

Once, Ethel would have leaped to the young boy's defence. But now she could think of nothing to say.

Twenty-One

'So, you're causing trouble again are you?'

Early the following evening, Hannah was making her way round the back of the mill along the path towards the waterfall where Luke would be waiting for her. The mill was still working, the millhands trying to catch the last of the daylight. The huge wheel thundered round and round, the water rushing along the race to feed its hungry teeth. Suddenly, a figure loomed up out of the shadows, and before she could step around him, Edmund Critchlow had grasped her arm in a vice-like grip. 'You need teaching a lesson, girl.'

'You're hurting.' She tried to twist herself free, but he held her fast.

'Oh, I'll hurt you girl. I'll give you a lesson you won't forget in a hurry. Now Nell's no use to me, you can take her place. I fancy me a young tender piece . . .'

Hannah struggled, trying to free herself, trying to get away. She twisted and lashed out at him with her free hand, but he caught hold of that too. Then she kicked out, catching him on the shin. He let out a yelp of pain, but instead of releasing his hold, he gripped her even more tightly. She screamed, but no one could hear her cries above the roar of the churning water. Edmund raised his hand and dealt her a stinging blow to the side of her face. She reeled and would have fallen if he had not still been holding her. 'You little bitch,' he snarled.

The last vestige of her resistance was almost gone; he was too strong for her. And then suddenly, miraculously, a figure hurtled towards them, waving his arms and yelling, 'Let her go. Leave her alone.'

'Oh, Luke, Luke,' Hannah sobbed thankfully.

He'd been standing on the path leading to the waterfall, watching for Hannah and had seen it all. Now he stood a yard away from them, his hands clenched at his side, every sinew in his body poised, tensed to spring, but he did not touch either Hannah or Edmund. Instead, his steely eyes bored into the older man's. 'Let – her – go,' he yelled.

Edmund threw back his head and laughed. 'And who's going to stop me?' He pointed at Luke with a derisory gesture. 'You?'

Luke took a step towards them. 'Yes. Me.'

He was not as tall as Edmund or as strong. He was still only a youth, but at this moment he was defending the girl he loved. And his anger lent him strength.

For a brief moment, a flicker of uncertainty crossed Edmund's face, but then it was gone and he was once more the master, the powerful owner of the mill who ruled all their lives. But in that brief moment, Hannah had felt the tiniest relaxation of his hold on her and she twisted herself out of his grasp.

'Run, Hannah,' Luke ordered. 'Go home – to the house and stay there.'

'No – I—'

'Go!' Luke's tone was a whip crack, demanding obedience.

Hannah went, running along the path and up to the

house. 'Oh, please, please come and help Luke,' she cried as she fell into the kitchen, panting and breathless.

'What's to do?' Arthur Bramwell strode towards her and grasped her arms to steady her.

'It's Luke and . . . and Mr Edmund. Fighting,' she gasped.

'Fighting?' Arthur Bramwell was incredulous. It was unheard of – an apprentice fighting with the master. Even strong Arthur Bramwell quailed at the thought. He released her and rushed from the house. Several of the boys and a few of the girls followed, chattering excitedly. 'A fight. There's a fight between Luke and the master.'

Hannah followed, pushing her way through them to get there first.

There were other figures, looming out of the shadows coming from the mill to stand watching – and waiting. But no one moved forward.

'He'll be for it, fighting with the master.'

'Where's Mr Scarsfield? He might be able to—'

'Mr Bramwell's there. Look.'

'He'll not step in. This is mill business.'

'But the lad's from the house.'

'Help him,' Hannah begged. 'Please – help Luke.'

But no one moved.

'We'd like to, lass,' one of the men murmured. 'But it's our jobs – our homes. We daren't.'

'He's right,' another muttered. 'I'd like to give that Mr Edmund a taste of his own medicine. Been wanting to punch him in the face for years, but I've me wife and young 'uns to think of.'

'I'm sorry, lass. The lad's on his own.'

Hannah cast about wildly, but no one moved. No

one went to Luke's aid. But there was one who she knew would come running.

'Where's Daniel?' she cried.

'Working. He's on the late shift. Best leave him, Hannah. If you fetch him here, he'll be in trouble too. Luke wouldn't want that. He'll deal with this on his own.'

She tugged at Mr Bramwell's arm. 'Stop them. Oh, please, stop them.'

The big man shook his head sadly. 'I can't. It's out of my hands.'

Hannah bit her lip and a sob escaped her. She stood with her hands over her mouth, watching the scene with terrified eyes.

'Oh, please, Luke, don't,' she cried.

The muttering fell silent as the onlookers watched the two figures stalking each other like a pair of fighting cocks.

'Taking wagers, are we?' someone murmured, but no one took him up on the suggestion. No one spoke. All eyes were riveted on the two men. This was a serious business.

Edmund, six inches taller than Luke, looked down at him disdainfully. Above the roar of the water, he shouted, 'Go on, then. Hit me. If you dare.'

Luke's eyes were glittering with hatred and loathing. He would've liked nothing better than to smash this man's face to a pulp. Yet he held back. He had rescued Hannah. That was what mattered. They'd have to think what to do next – after this – but for the moment, she was safe.

'I've no wish to hit you, sir, but you've no right to touch the girls. Specially not my Hannah.'

Edmund laughed humourlessly. 'Oho, your Han-

nah, is she? Well, well. We'll have to see about that.
Fornication in the apprentice house? Dear me. The
Bramwells have been neglectful in their duties. They'll
be out on their ear—'

'There's been no . . . no fornication. I love Hannah.
I wouldn't hurt her.'

Edmund thrust his face close to Luke's. 'You won't
get the chance. You're sacked. You'll be on your way
back to the workhouse before this night's out. Back
where you belong. You and your mealy-mouthed
brother.'

It was the insult to his twin that finally tipped Luke
over the edge. He swung an ungainly right hand at
Edmund's chin and caught him a glancing blow as
Edmund ducked. Though a big man, Edmund was
quick and light on his feet. Rumour had it that as a
young man at university he'd indulged in all the raffish
pursuits: drinking, gambling and a little bare-knuckle
fighting. And anyone who'd had a wager on Edmund
Critchlow to win had always gone home a happy man
at night.

Now, Edmund's fist landed in the centre of Luke's
face with a sickening crack. Bone splintered and blood
spurted from the younger man's nose. Luke tottered
backwards, but then the vision of Edmund grasping
Hannah so roughly, dragging her along, swam before
his eyes. He straightened up and lunged at Edmund,
but he was no match for the older, stronger man. Luke
had little knowledge of fighting. In the odd boyish
scrap in the workhouse yard, there had always been
the two of them. Him and Daniel against the world.

Where was Daniel? Why wasn't he here, standing
shoulder to shoulder with his twin?

Edmund's blows rained thick and fast. Two more

to the head, one just below Luke's ribs, knocking the wind out of him and causing him to bend double. And each blow drove him backwards. There was no let up. A blow to the side of his head sent him reeling, closer and closer to the edge of the bank above the wheel. The watchers moved forward, shouting, but above the roar of the churning water neither Edmund nor Luke could hear them. Luke was almost senseless, still on his feet but only with tremendous willpower. And on Edmund's face was murderous intent.

The watchers knew it was going to happen. They could see it. Hannah, Arthur Bramwell and one or two others ran forward, shouting a warning, but it was too late. With one last vicious blow, Edmund sent Luke flailing backwards over the edge and down, down into the cavernous centre of the giant wheel. His body was tossed and tumbled until his features were scarcely recognizable.

The wheel ploughed on relentlessly, but Edmund stood on the edge looking down, watching with fists clenched, jaw hard and unrepentant, and making no move to stop it.

Hannah rushed towards the edge and would have fallen in too, but Arthur Bramwell caught hold of her. She struggled against him, screaming, 'Stop the wheel. Stop it.'

Others arrived at the edge, staring helplessly down at Luke being thrown around the inside of the wheel.

Arthur's grasp tightened on her arms briefly. 'Stay here,' he ordered and then he ran into the mill.

The wheel was slowing, the water settling. A gasp rippled amongst the onlookers as they saw Luke's battered body fall to the bottom and lie there, a mass of blood and shattered bone.

And then Hannah began to scream as if she would never stop.

'It's all your fault. If it hadn't been for you, I'd've been with him.'

Hannah gasped. Her eyes were blotchy from two days of constant weeping. She was inconsolable, but Daniel was angry, vitriolic.

'And now he's dead – all because of *you*!'

She had no answer.

'I'd've been with him,' he ranted on. 'We were always together. Always. Until you came along. Then he'd rather be with you than with me.' He glared at her, hatred in his eyes. 'I 'spect you were making a play for the master, were you?'

Now, Hannah was startled out of her lethargy. 'No.' She was horrified. 'How can you even think such a thing of me? I loved Luke. You know I did.' Tears welled again in her eyes and she covered her face and sobbed. 'How can you even think that, Daniel?'

He was silent, unapologetic. He was hurting, just like Hannah, and his only weapon was to lash out at her to try to assuage his own guilt at not being at his twin's side when Luke had needed him the most. But it wasn't working. He could not pass the guilt onto her shoulders. Daniel would carry the burden for the rest of his life. And so would Hannah, for she blamed herself just as much as Daniel did.

Her sobs quietened and for the first time since the tragedy, calmness came over her. 'It wasn't your fault,' she said in a flat, emotionless voice. 'And it wasn't really mine, even though I shall feel it was for the rest of me life. There's only one person to blame and that's

Edmund Critchlow, and as God is my witness, I'll pay him back for this.' Her tone took on a steely edge and even Daniel was forced to believe her. 'I'll never forgive and I'll never forget. And one day, I'll make him pay.'

Twenty-Two

Luke was buried in a pauper's grave alongside Jane.

The mill worked on as usual and no one was granted official leave to attend the funeral. Only those who dared to defy the rules and take time off from their work were there. Daniel, Hannah and Ernest Scarsfield together with Ethel and Arthur Bramwell, even though they all knew they'd be fined for doing so.

They'd thought that no one from the Critchlow family would have the audacity to show their faces, yet as they followed the coffin on its final, sorrowful journey, another figure fell into step at the very back just as he had at Jane's funeral.

Adam Critchlow.

He was an unwelcome presence, but later, as Arthur Bramwell remarked, 'The lad was brave to come. Think about it. His father caused Luke's death. We all know that. And there were enough of us there to bear witness, yet there's been no inquiry. It's all been hushed up. There's a few bribes changed hands, if you ask me.' It was the first time that Hannah had ever heard the taciturn Arthur Bramwell speak out against his employers. 'The poor lad's been pushed into a pauper's grave and forgotten about. The Critchlows haven't even had the decency to pay for a proper burial for him.'

Listening to the conversation, Ethel put in, 'I 'spect they thought it'd be like admitting guilt if they did.'

Arthur glanced at his wife and nodded. 'You've a point there. Aye, I see what you mean.'

There was silence for a moment before Hannah said softly, but in a tone that was like a vow, 'Well, he won't be forgotten about. Not by me.'

'No,' Arthur agreed. 'Nor by us. And he'll never be gone whilst Daniel's around, will he? Like two peas in a pod they are. I could never tell the difference between them. I'd never have believed two people could be so alike.'

Hannah said nothing. To her the two boys had been very different. Daniel was nothing like the merry, outspoken Luke, but a mere shadow of his brother. But she felt for him. What was poor Daniel going to do now without his twin?

Mrs Grundy wept openly. 'Another death. When are the authorities going to do something about that place?'

'There's not much they can do, love.' Ollie Grundy patted his wife's shoulder and glanced sympathetically at Hannah.

'Well, there ought to be. Isn't there someone we can report it to?'

Ollie shrugged his huge shoulders. 'I wish there was. D'you know, I'd even risk that part of our livelihood – losing that trade – if it meant saving them poor children up there any more hurt.'

Hannah, believing him, smiled weakly. 'It wasn't so bad when old man Critchlow still ran things. It's only since *he's* taken over.' She paused and then added,

'You've heard the news, I suppose, about Mr Nathaniel?'

The Grundys glanced at each other. 'No.'

'When he heard the news about Luke, he had another seizure. A really bad one. He's not expected to live.'

'Aye,' Lily Grundy said bitterly. 'Well, there you are then, that puts Mr Edmund in full control an' no arguing with it now. And he's likely to be there for years to come.' She paused and looked directly at Hannah. 'You ought to get away from that place – from *him* – whilst you've the chance. We'll help you, won't we, Ollie?'

Hannah stared at them, glancing from one to the other in amazement. 'But . . . but I haven't even paid you all the money back you lent me last time. With all the stoppages I get, I haven't been able to manage even a few pennies recently. I still don't get proper wages.'

Lily flapped her hand. 'Don't think any more about that. We've got it all planned, me and Ollie.' Husband and wife glanced at each other like conspirators. 'He'll take you to Buxton on the cart on Friday morning and you can get a ride from there on the carrier's cart – or the coach, whichever you like – back to Macclesfield. There must be folks there you know who'd help you.'

Hannah was doubtful. 'We were in the workhouse. I daren't go back there. Mr Goodbody'd have me sent straight back here.'

'What about where you lived before you went into the workhouse? Can you remember?'

Hannah sought back through her mind to being eight years old and even before that. 'I can remember me gran – just. She looked after me when me mother went out to work. I . . . I can remember her dying and

209

the coffin outside our house in the street, on a cart – a handcart – and the men pushing it. And . . . and the neighbours. They all came out and I watched me mother walking behind it down the street. I wanted to go with her but I wasn't allowed and . . . and someone was holding onto me to stop me running after her . . .'

'Can you remember who that was?' Lily tried to prompt her memories.

'I . . . I think she lived next door. I called her Auntie – Auntie – oh, I can't remember.' Hannah rubbed her forehead in frustration as if the action would massage her brain to work better.

'Can you remember where you lived – the name of the street? She might still be there.'

Hannah shook her head. 'It was a narrow street with tall terraced houses.'

'Well, there'll be dozens of streets just like that one in a place like Macclesfield,' Lily said. 'That don't help much.'

'Is there anything else you can remember?' Ollie pressed, trying to help. 'Did you live near anything like a church or the place your mother worked or . . . ?'

Hannah frowned. 'I . . . I think we lived a couple of streets away from the mill where Mam worked.'

'The mill? Your mother worked in a mill?'

'Oh, not like the one here. It was a silk mill. I do remember that.'

'A *silk* mill! Well, I never.' Ollie was thoughtful for a moment before he said, 'That might help. You could ask at the silk mills. There might be people there who'd remember her.'

Hannah smiled wryly. 'There might well be, but I don't know if they'd kill the fatted calf, exactly.'

Ollie and Lily glanced at each other. 'What do you mean, lass?'

Hannah pulled a face. 'I think the reason we ended up in the workhouse was because we lost the house after me gran died.'

'Why?'

'Me gran was the tenant – not me mam.'

'Couldn't your mother have taken it on?'

Hannah shook her head. 'No – she was sacked from her job.'

Gently, Lily asked, 'Do you know why?'

'No. Not really. But . . . but . . . I always thought it had something to do with me.'

'With you?'

Hannah nodded, the shame flooding through her as she whispered, 'I haven't got a dad, you see.'

Lily laughed, and it was a genuine laugh – the first Hannah had heard since Luke's terrible death. 'Well, there's plenty of your sort about, love. I shouldn't let that worry you. Most o' them orphans up at the mill'll be just like you, I'll be bound.'

Hannah smiled weakly. 'Well, yes, they are. And there were plenty of us in the workhouse. It . . . it was only then I realized I wasn't the only . . . only bastard in the world.'

'Aw, lovey.' Lily gathered Hannah to her bosom. She rocked her and the girl felt comforted. 'There's one thing though, lass, that perhaps you hadn't thought of. *Somewhere* you've got a dad. How about trying to find him, eh?'

Hannah drew back from the woman's embrace and stared up at her in surprise. 'I – I'd never thought of that.'

'Now, hang on a minute,' Ollie said, suddenly concerned. 'D'you think that'd be wise? I mean – there might be all sorts of complications.'

Lily's face was set. 'Such as?'

'Well,' Ollie floundered, glancing helplessly from one to the other. 'I dunno. I just think—'

'I'm not suggesting she should go marching up to his door demanding to be taken in as his daughter. But if she could find him, he just might be willing to help her. She can only ask.' They were talking now as if Hannah was not in the room. But she was and hanging on every word.

'Aye, and how will she feel if he sends her off with a flea in her ear? She'll be hurt all over again.'

'Not if she prepares herself that that might happen. She'd be no worse off than she is now.'

'Huh! Just rejected again, eh?'

'Oh, Ollie, you're a lovely man.' Lily reached up and patted his cheek. 'But sometimes, just some-times—'

'Yes, you are, Mr Grundy.' Hannah smiled. 'But Mrs Grundy's right. I've nothing to lose. That's what I'll do. I'll find my father.'

Over the next few days, Hannah made her plans carefully. She was determined not to be caught this time. There was only one person she confided in. Daniel. Though he was still offhand with her, she still counted him as her closest friend in the house now. How she wished Nell was still here. She would have helped her, advised her. But Nell was gone and no one would tell her where or why.

'You'll only be caught and brought back like last

time,' Daniel muttered morosely. 'And don't expect me to be passing up food to you in the punishment room like Luke did.'

'I'm not going to get caught. Not this time. I've got help.' She bit her lip, not knowing if she could trust him enough to confide in him that much. He was still very bitter. But he guessed anyway. He stared at her for a moment and then gave a little nod. 'Oh aye, the Grundys, I suppose.'

Hannah caught hold of his arm. 'Don't tell a soul. Please, Daniel.'

'All right,' he agreed grudgingly, and she had the awful feeling that if he'd dared, he would dearly like to give her away.

'Why don't you come with me?' she said rashly. 'Get away from this place? Surely, you don't want to stay here now? Not after what's happened?'

He glared at her. ''Course I'm staying here. I can't leave Luke here all on his own, can I? I can never leave here. Not now. But you go. Oh yes, you go and forget all about us.' He jerked himself out of her grasp, turned and hurried away.

'Oh, Daniel,' Hannah whispered, tears in her eyes.

Hannah couldn't follow the same escape pattern as on the previous occasion. Security at the house was much tighter since that time, but she planned to leave late one Thursday evening and go to the Grundys' farm. Then early on the Friday morning, before she was missed, Ollie would take her to Buxton. So, when everyone else was in bed, Hannah took a blanket from the bed that had been Nell's and bundled it beneath her own to look as if she was sleeping there, nestled down beneath the covers for warmth. Then picking up the bundle of her few belongings, she slipped down the stairs and into the kitchen.

Ethel Bramwell was busy in front of the range, her face red from the heat. For a brief moment, Hannah hesitated, wishing she could say goodbye. Ethel and her husband had been as kind to her – and the others – as their position allowed. She was surprised to realize just how fond she'd become of them both.

Ethel straightened up from bending over the fire and was about to turn around as Hannah slipped unnoticed out of the back door. She hurried along the path and down the steep slope, past the gate into the mill. Even from here she could hear the rhythmic clatter of the machinery as it worked through the night. From the rumours she'd heard, it seemed Edmund had plans to have the mill running non-stop – twenty-four hours a day, seven days a week, even on a Sunday.

'He's got young master Adam drawing up plans to have us working in relays,' Hannah had overheard Ernest Scarsfield telling Arthur Bramwell one night over a tankard of ale at the kitchen table. 'And he's lengthening the hours we've to work. Breaking the law, he is, but what can any of us do about it?'

Nothing, Hannah thought bitterly. *Mr Edmund considers himself above the law, even that of murder.*

'Sit down, sit down,' Lily Grundy greeted her, bustling about the warm kitchen.

'I ought to hide,' Hannah said anxiously, standing just inside the doorway, still holding her bundle. 'If they come after me—'

'Look, love, sit down. I've something to tell you.' Mrs Grundy was avoiding looking directly at her, and

Hannah felt a moment's panic. Then she calmed herself. If the worst came to the worst, she could always go back now, before she was missed. No one would be any the wiser.

'My Ollie had a bit of an accident. Hurt his leg, silly man – stabbed himself in the foot with a pitchfork.'

'Oh, I'm so sorry. Is it bad?'

'He'll be all right, but he'll be laid up for a day or two.'

'Tell him not to worry. I'll go back now – this minute. We'll wait till he's better.'

'No, no, our Ted's going to take you. He'll be here early in the morning. And in the meantime, we'll hide you here. In the hayloft, if necessary. They can't come searching our place. Oh, they can come and ask, but that's as far as they'll get.' She sniffed. 'They'll get short shrift from me if they try searching my place without so much as a by-your-leave.'

She was so adamant, so sure, that Hannah believed her.

'Now,' Lily said briskly, as if it was all settled. 'Sit down and eat your supper. I'll just take a plate up to his lordship and then you and me can sit down and have ours together. That'll be nice, won't it?'

'Yes,' Hannah said meekly, and sat down.

As they finished their meal, they heard the dog begin to bark. Hannah leaped to her feet. 'It's them. I know it is. They've come after me.'

'Quick. I'll let you out the front door. They'll likely come to the back. I'll ask 'em in and you nip round to the barn and up the ladder into the loft. I'll hide this,'

215

Lily said, snatching up Hannah's bundle of belongings from the floor and moving with surprising agility. 'Look sharp, now.'

Hannah ran. Out of the door on the opposite side of the house and around the corner. Here she paused, listening to the voices as Mrs Grundy opened her back door and ushered the visitors into her kitchen. Then Hannah ran softly across the yard to the barn. Inside it was gloomy, but she could just see the ladder up to the hayloft. Gathering up her long skirt, she climbed up. Her knees were shaking, not from the climb up the rickety ladder, but the fear of being caught by the ankles and dragged down again. She reached the top and scrambled across the hay-strewn floor to the furthest, darkest corner, where she huddled into a ball, her heart beating so loudly, she was sure that if they came into the barn below they would hear it.

Minutes passed and she heard voices. Voices that came nearer and nearer.

'She's not here, I tell you. What would she come here for, I might ask?'

'You helped her before. And you've helped others an' all.' Hannah recognized Arthur Bramwell's voice. 'Don't think we don't know, Lily. It's only 'cos we've kept it from the master that he hasn't stopped you supplying us.'

'Huh!' was Lily's scathing reply.

'Look, love,' Ernest Scarsfield's tone was placating. 'We're mates, me 'n' Arthur here and your Ollie.'

'Aye, drinking mates,' Lily put in, but there was amusement rather than resentment in her tone.

Hannah heard the two men chuckle. 'Aye well, mebbe so, mebbe so, but we wouldn't want to do anything to harm your living. You know that, so if you know anything about the girl, tell us.'

'I don't.'

'If you see her, you'll let us know?'

'I'm sorry, Ernest. I know you mean well, and I 'preciate it, but, no, I won't come telling tales to the mill about her or anyone else from that place. You know full well what happened to me niece and I've no time for the Critchlows, not one of 'em. So there you have it.'

'Well, you're straight, Lily Grundy, I'll give you that. But it'd be the best for the girl herself. Where's she going to go? Back to the workhouse, eh? She'll not get a welcome there, I can tell you. The Critchlows and Goodbody have got a nice little scheme still going that they're not about to let go of. She'll be sent right back here to spend a week in the punishment room. And God knows what else Mr Edmund might think up to punish her.'

'He's evil, that one,' Lily spoke up. 'The old man was bad enough, letting accidents happen and young lasses get killed, but he was a saint compared to that son of his.'

To this, the two men made no reply.

Hannah held her breath as she heard a scuffling in the barn below and then, when they spoke again, their voices were further away and she began to breathe more easily. Several minutes passed before she heard Lily below calling up. 'Come on down, Hannah. Coast's clear. They've gone.'

Hannah peered down from the hayloft. 'They might come back.'

'No, I don't think so.' Lily chuckled. 'I reckon they

know very well you're here. Maybe, deep down, they sympathize with you, love. Come on down, they're not coming back. I'm sure of it.'

Reluctantly, Hannah climbed down and, as she reached the bottom of the ladder, Lily put her arm around the girl's shoulders. 'Now come on, you snuggle down in the bed in the spare room and I'll bring you up a nice mug of cocoa.'

Impulsively, Hannah hugged her. 'Oh, Mrs Grundy, you spoil me.'

Embarrassed, Lily patted her shoulder. 'Aye well, mebbe so. But it's nice to have someone to spoil and I reckon you deserve it, love.'

Hannah couldn't remember when she'd last slept in such a comfortable bed nor been cosseted and pampered by anyone. Her memories of life with her mother and grandmother when they'd lived in their own home were dim and fleeting. It was as if all the traumas of the past three and a half years had blotted out some of her happy memories – more, if she counted her time in the workhouse too. But she fell asleep in the soft feather bed dreaming of soft hands and gentle voices and the shadowy unknown figure of a man – her father.

Twenty-Three

The Grundys' nephew, Ted, arrived the following morning as the first fingers of light crept over the top of the hills. He was fair-haired, small and wiry, with a grin that seemed to stretch across the whole of his face. He reminded Hannah poignantly of Luke.

'Hello there,' he greeted her, and held out his hand to help her onto the seat on the front of the cart. 'Aren't I the lucky one? It's not every day I get to drive a pretty girl into the countryside.'

Lily Grundy bustled up. 'Now then, Ted, none of your flirting with this one. She's special, she is.'

Ted's grin widened even further if that were possible. 'I can see that.'

'And just mind you get her well away from here before anyone from the mill is likely to be about. I don't want her running into Roper – not this time.'

The young man's face sobered and his tone became serious. 'I know, Auntie. I've put a pile of sacks in the back. If the worst happens, she can hide under them.'

Lily smiled and patted his shoulder. 'Good lad. I've packed some food up for you both and mind you let her take some with her when you drop her off in Buxton, Ted. We don't know if she's going to get anywhere to sleep tonight. And I want you to have this, Hannah.' Lily unfolded a thick, warm shawl and tucked it around Hannah's shoulders.

'Oh, Mrs Grundy—'

'Now, now, none of that. It's a gift. I don't want it back.'

Ted's face was a picture of concern as he glanced up at Hannah sitting, a little impatiently, on the front of the cart. 'Haven't you got anywhere to go?'

'Only the workhouse – and I don't fancy going back there. Mr Goodbody will send me straight back to the mill.'

'She's going to try to find the street she used to live in years ago,' Lily put in. 'There might be a neighbour there who'll remember her and give her a bed for the night.'

Ted glanced worriedly from one to the other. 'Wouldn't it be better if I took her all the way to Macclesfield? Stayed with her till I see she's got somewhere?'

Lily frowned and glanced up apologetically at Hannah. 'I'd like to be able to say yes, lass, you know I would. But I need him back here. With Ollie laid up, I can't manage everything on me own.'

Hannah smiled down at her. 'Of course you can't. It's very good of you to let him take me at all. Come on, Ted, the quicker we get off, the quicker you can get back.'

He gave a mock sigh and climbed up beside her. 'Oh well, I'm no match for two determined women.' He pulled a comical face. 'I never was for me auntie anyway.' He picked up the reins and slapped them against the hind quarters of the huge carthorse between the shafts. 'We'll be off then. See you later, Auntie Lily.'

The horse climbed the steep hill steadily, its great shoulders pulling strongly on the harness. Their progress was laboured and slow, and Hannah bit her lip, expecting any moment to hear a cry from behind them and running footsteps. Once or twice she glanced back anxiously, but the road sloping away behind them was empty.

As they reached the top of the hill, Hannah took one last glance back at the hills and the river winding through the dale – the place where she and Luke had escaped from the daily grind of the mill to snatch a few hours of freedom and real happiness. The early morning sun cast pale light on the hillsides and touched the trees with delicate fingers, but it was not the glorious colour she'd seen on the day she'd arrived here. Pauper's gold the man who'd brought them had called it. Well, she'd known some golden days with Luke and Daniel and little Jane. If she closed her eyes now, she could still see the four of them running alongside the river, or racing each other up the steep slopes, to stand at the top looking down on the mill below them. It had been like standing on the top of the world and they'd thrilled at the feeling of freedom, even if only for a few precious hours.

But already two of her friends were dead and Daniel had turned his back on her. She couldn't stay, didn't want to stay, for she feared Mr Edmund's vindictiveness. Even those who might try to protect her were helpless against his authority. If Master Adam were older, it might be different. But he wasn't. He was little more than a boy himself and as much in his father's power as the lowliest pauper apprentice.

It would be so easy to turn her back on it all, to set her face forward and never think about Wyedale and its mill again. At that moment as she looked back and said her silent goodbyes, she was very tempted to do just that. But instead, Hannah made a vow to herself. *I'll come back one day, Luke, I promise. Mr Edmund might have wriggled out of the law with the help of all his cronies, but he's not going to get away with what he did to you.*

One day, I'll pay him back. I don't know how and I don't know when. It might take a lifetime, but one day, I'll bring him down. I'll see him rot in Hell!

The road levelled out and the horse picked up a little speed.

'Why are you leaving now, 'cos you've been there for a few years, haven't you?' Ted asked conversationally. 'I'd've thought you'd have gone a long time ago.'

'I did try. Once. But not to run away, just to go back to . . . to see me mother.'

'Oh aye, me auntie told me about that. You ran into Roper, didn't you? Bit of bad luck, that.'

There was silence for a moment before Ted prompted, 'So did you ever get to see your mother?'

Hannah bit her lip and didn't answer immediately. 'No,' she said huskily. 'I . . . I never saw her again.'

'Is that why you're going now then? To try to find her?'

Hannah pressed her lips together to stop them trembling. She shook her head. 'She – I think she's dead now. That's what I've been told. Unless, of course it's another lie.' She'd like to hope it was, but she didn't dare.

Ted was apologetic. 'I'm sorry, I shouldn't have asked.'

Hannah sighed. 'It's all right.'

There was a pause, but the young man could not hold back his curiosity. 'So why are you going now?'

Hannah was silent again for a moment and then, haltingly, she began to explain. And then it all came in a torrent, like the waterfall behind the mill, the words just came flooding out. She told him everything, finding it strangely easy to talk to a comparative stranger. She told him about her early life, how she had vague memories of a much happier time and then how she and her mother had gone into the workhouse.

'I don't really understand what happened then. I know me gran died – I remember that.' She wrinkled her brow. 'I ought to remember more. I was eight when that happened. I *ought* to remember, but all I can think of is the time in the workhouse.'

'Why did you end up in the workhouse?'

'Mam lost her job at the mill.'

'The mill? What mill?'

'One of the silk mills in Macclesfield.' She went on then, describing her life in the workhouse. 'It was hard, but it was the same for everyone and there was a sort of . . . a sort of friendliness amongst the inmates.'

'Inmates? Is that what they called you?'

Hannah smiled. 'Mm, but it wasn't so bad in a lot of ways. If you were young and strong and could work, you were all right.' Her face clouded. 'But if you were ill or old, it must've been terrible to think that you were going to spend the rest of your days in there.'

'Bit like the mill, then?' Ted was referring to the Critchlows' mill – the only one he knew. 'That's what they all say about the mill. Once you get in there,

there's no way out.' He was silent for a moment, before he said seriously, 'I do know how lucky I am that me uncle's given me a job. And he's promised me the farm. He's got no kids of his own, you see, and auntie's no family to speak of. I think she had a brother but he lives down south and they've lost touch. Sad, that, isn't it? So, there's only our family. Uncle Ollie is me mother's brother.'

Hannah nodded. 'I know. It was your sister that . . . that—'

'That got killed in the mill? Aye, it was.' Ted's voice hardened in just the same way that Lily Grundy's tone always did when she spoke of the mill. 'Poor little Lucy. She was a lovely little kid. Bright and merry – you know – real fun to have around. We still miss her.'

'I know how you feel. I expect you heard about my little friend, Jane?'

Ted glanced at her. 'Yeah. Same thing that happened to our Lucy, weren't it?'

Hannah nodded and they travelled for a while without speaking, each lost in their own thoughts.

'I suppose you had a rough time when they caught you that time you tried to go to see yer mother,' Ted broke the silence at last.

'He beat me.'

'Never!' Ted was scandalized.

'And then I was put in the punishment room for a week. Mind you, it wasn't so bad. Luke sent food up to me on a rope.'

'Luke. Who's Luke?'

Tears sprang to her eyes and the sudden lump in her throat stopped Hannah answering for a few minutes.

'He . . . he was my friend. My . . . my very *best* friend.'

'Was?' Ted prompted, but his tone was gentle.

'Mmm,' Hannah nodded. Tentatively, at first, but then with a growing need, she confided some more in this friendly young fellow, ending, 'I thought your auntie would've told you.'

Ted shook his head. 'We don't talk about the mill in our family. Not unless we really have to because of the business side.'

'I'm sorry, Ted. Here I've been rattling on. I never thought. I'm so sorry. I didn't stop to think how painful it must still be for you.'

'And you, too. You've had a rotten time there. Losing your friends, an' all.' He glanced at her. 'And I don't mind you talking about it, Hannah. Not if it helps you.'

Gratefully, she touched his arm. 'Thanks. You're kind. Just like your auntie and uncle.'

The young man felt a warm flush rise in his neck. 'Go on with you,' he said, suddenly embarrassed. 'I'm just nosy. Me auntie's always telling me to keep me nose out of other people's business else I'll get it chopped off one of these days.'

Hannah laughed and their mood lightened. With every stride of the horse's long strong legs, she began to feel safer. As the sun rose higher in the sky, Ted glanced up. 'I don't know about you, but I'm hungry. Shall we stop for a bit? It's time the horse had a rest and a nosebag or a graze on the side of the road.' He glanced at her, reading the anxious look that flitted across her face. 'We're far enough away now, I reckon.'

Hannah nodded and climbed down. 'Yes, I'm hungry

too and I could do to nip into that field behind a bush.'

Ted laughed and covered his eyes. 'I promise not to look.'

'You'd better not,' Hannah said spiritedly.

It was a warm, bright day for October and later, having eaten, they lay back in the grass and dozed a while. When they aroused, they had no idea of the time, but Ted squinted up at the sun. 'Must be nigh on midday, I reckon. Come on, we'd best be on our way, if I'm to get back home tonight.'

'How much further is it?'

Hannah had only travelled this road once before and she'd no memory of the distance. She hadn't even known on that occasion exactly where they were going. It saddened her to realize that of the four of them that had travelled together that day, two were already dead and the remaining two were left with the bitter taste for revenge.

'Not far.' Ted interrupted her thoughts.

Just over an hour later, they reached the outskirts of the town.

'Where is it you want to be? The railway station?'

'No. Your auntie said I'd best find a carrier or a coach. She's given me some money to pay someone.'

'There's often market traders travelling between the two places, I've heard tell. There's a chap who travels here from Macclesfield every Monday morning, his cart loaded with goods. He stays the week and then goes back at the end of the week and loads up ready to come back on the Monday morning. He might be leaving today. If we could find him . . .'

Hannah's expression was doubtful, but Ted was full of bright ideas. 'If we ask at some of the shops in the town, mebbe someone will know him – know where we might find him.'

Hannah didn't hold out much hope, but she supposed it was possible. 'All right then. Where do we start?'

'Town centre, that's where,' Ted said, slapping the reins. 'Come on, we've a man to hunt down before it gets dark.'

Twenty-Four

Hannah had not believed it possible, but they found the man, a Mr Dawkins, who lived in Macclesfield, but who travelled between the two towns just as Ted had said. It took an hour of trekking round several shops but at last they met someone who knew him.

'Aye, tha's right,' the burley shopkeeper said. 'Bin here less than half an hour ago. He's tekin' a load back to Macclesfield for me. Me son's got a shop there and we often use old Dawkins to take stuff back'ards and for'ards for us. Only just missed him, you 'ave.' At the sight of the two youngsters' crestfallen faces, the man laughed. 'But I can tell you where he is. In the pub, that's where. Likes to wet his whistle before he travels home on a Friday night. Reckon that horse of his knows the way home better 'n he does.'

'Come on,' Ted said, grabbing her hand. 'Thanks, mister.'

'Don't mention it, lad. Want him to tek summat for yer, d'yer?'

Ted grinned. 'This lass needs a lift to Macclesfield and I remembered hearing about this feller. D'you think he'd take her?'

'Should think he'd be glad of the company of a pretty young wench.' He winked at Hannah. 'But don't worry, luv. He's a good family man, is Dawkins, with lasses of his own. He'll look after you all right.'

They found him sitting in the corner of the smoky tavern, a kind-faced man in his forties.

'Aye, that'll be all right, duck,' he said at once. 'You just wait outside whilst I finish me pint and me bit of baccy and I'll be with you. We'll be travelling through the night, but you can bed down in the back of the cart under the horse blanket.' He laughed. 'That's if you don't mind the smell.'

As they waited outside, Ted said, 'Now, are you sure you've got enough money? 'Cos me auntie'd box me ears if I let you go without enough. I can lend you a couple of shillings, if that'd help.'

'You're very kind, but your auntie's already given me some. I'll be all right.' She touched his arm. 'But thanks all the same.' Her face clouded. 'It'll be finding somewhere to stay that'll be the problem. I daren't go to the workhouse, and apart from that I don't really know where to start.'

'I'll tell you where. The police station.'

Hannah's eyes widened in sudden fear. 'The . . . the police station. But . . . but wouldn't that be dangerous? I mean – if the Critchlows have reported me running away.'

Ted threw back his head and guffawed. 'The Critchlows report you? Not likely. They'll not want the police sniffing around. Making inquiries.' As Hannah looked mystified, Ted went on. 'Look, we've always reckoned that the Critchlows and that fellow at the workhouse . . .'

'Mr Goodbody.'

'Yes, that's him. Well, we reckon they had a good thing going between them, but maybe it wasn't exactly legal, if you know what I mean.'

Hannah shook her head. 'No, I don't.'

229

'All them little pauper apprentices coming to the mill. Well, years ago it was a common practice with all the mills, but not lately. With all the changes in the laws, it became too expensive. Yet the Critchlows kept the system going. Now, why do you suppose that is, eh?'

Hannah shook her head. 'I don't know.'

'Somehow, they were making themselves a bit of money. I reckon Critchlow was paying Goodbody to provide him with cheap labour.'

'Cheap labour? How do you mean, cheap labour?'

'You were signed up for so many years, when you got to the mill, weren't you? I bet he made you sign a paper, didn't he?'

Slowly Hannah nodded. 'Yes, I was bound to him for six years.'

'Thought so. And I bet he doesn't pay you anything – still being an apprentice – even though you've been there over three years.'

Her eyes widened, as realization began to dawn.

'*And* I dare bet you're doing an adult's work now, aren't you? Same as some of the women from the village that work there?'

Hannah nodded and now her lips tightened.

Ted shrugged. 'There you are then. Cheap labour, 'cos he'll have to pay the women. But you're an apprentice and will be for the six years. And even then, you'd be lucky if you could get him to give you a proper wage. 'Specially now Mr Edmund's in charge. So, like I said, go to the police station. They might be able to tell you where to find a lodging house. And if they can't,' he grinned suddenly, 'they might let you sleep in one of their cells.'

'Oh, thanks.' Hannah laughed.

'No, I'm serious. A mate of mine got stuck in Manchester one night and couldn't get home so he went to the police and they let him sleep in one of their cells – just for the night. Honest,' he added as he saw Hannah's sceptical look. 'And besides, they wouldn't want a young lass like you roaming the streets at night.'

'Yes, well, I'll see.' Hannah was doubtful but his suggestion sounded sincere enough. And, after all, the police were supposed to be there to help you. They weren't just about catching criminals.

'Besides,' Ted went on, warming to his theme. 'They might be able to help you find that long-lost neighbour of yours.'

But that, it seemed, was beyond the burly policeman who stood behind the desk in the station. He scratched his head as he looked down at the slim young girl standing before him.

Hannah had enjoyed the ride through the spectacular countryside, passing from Derbyshire into the county of Cheshire. She'd slept for the first part of the way, but in the early hours of the morning, the cold had woken her and she'd clambered up to sit beside the carter. They'd chatted amiably but she'd not been drawn to confide much in him. All she'd told him was that she was returning home after some years, but that her mother had died and she needed to find a place to stay until she could find work.

'Ted – that's the young feller who brought me to Buxton – reckoned I should ask at the police station. Do you think that's a good idea?'

'I do, duck. They'll know of reputable lodgings for

a young 'un like you. They might even know if there's jobs going somewhere.' He sniffed. 'Surprising what the peelers on the beat know. A mite too much sometimes.' He paused and then asked, 'Where did you live before?'

'That's just the trouble, Mr Dawkins,' Hannah said. 'I don't know. I *ought* to remember, but I just can't.'

As they came down the last hill, Hannah was fascinated by the sight of the town spread out below them. A feeling that she was coming home flooded through her as her gaze took in the huge, square buildings and tall chimneys, church towers and spires and the roofs of hundreds of houses. She sighed as she swept her arm in a wide arc. 'I used to live somewhere down there – if only I knew where.'

Beside her, Mr Dawkins laughed. 'Well, I don't reckon it was anywhere near us, duck. I'm sure I'd've remembered a pretty little thing like you. But your friend had the right idea. The police'll help you. I can't take you right there – it's up the hill, near that church with the square tower – St Michael's. See?' He pointed with his whip. 'But I'll show you how to get there.'

They travelled another half a mile or so in silence until Mr Dawkins asked, 'Recognize anything yet?'

Hannah bit her lip and shook her head. She was disappointed. She'd so hoped that once she saw the town again, her memories would come back. But nothing looked familiar.

'Do you remember the railway?' Mr Dawkins asked. 'Or the Bollin? The river?' he explained when she looked puzzled.

'No.'

'We're just passing over the Bollin now, but you can't see it. It was covered up along here when they built the railway. There's still places where you can see it though. Now, this 'ere's the Waters. It's where I live.'

She looked at the wide open space surrounded by houses and larger buildings with tall, smoking chimneys. In the centre stood a square public house with a sign outside – the Cross Keys. A coach, drawn by two horses with prancing hooves, rolled by. Men on horseback clip-clopped past and two men driving four cows tipped their caps to Mr Dawkins, who waved in return to their greeting

'Why's it called the Waters?'

Mr Dawkins pulled a face. 'Place floods from time to time. It's by the river. If we get heavy rain, this whole area's like a lake.' He laughed and pointed at the Cross Keys. 'I remember a few years back, before the railway came, the pub getting flooded. Lost all their barrels of beer in the cellars, they did. A right to-do there was.'

Hannah frowned. She couldn't remember anything like that happening in her childhood.

'But we're used to it,' he went on, grinning like a man completely happy with his lot.

Pulling his cart to a halt at the bottom of a long flight of stone steps, he said, 'If you go up these, duck, you'll come out near the church, and the police station is on the other side of the church in the basement of the Town Hall. You can't miss it.'

He glanced at her apologetically. 'I wish I could take you home with me, duck, but our little house is fair bursting at the seams already. I've four young 'uns and another on the way and what the missis'd say if I turn up on the doorstep with a pretty young wench like you in tow, I daren't think.'

'It's all right, Mr Dawkins, honestly. And I can't thank you enough for bringing me this far. Are you really sure you won't let me pay you?'

'I wouldn't dream of it. It's been my pleasure. I've enjoyed your company.'

Hannah climbed down, and picked up her bundle from the back.

'I hope you've got plenty of puff, lass. There's an 'undred and eight of them steps. I know, 'cos I counted 'em as a lad.'

He was still laughing as the cart rattled away and Hannah turned to begin the long climb. Just as he had said, she was breathless by the time she arrived at the top of the steps. Before her was the dark stone of the church and, walking round it, she found the pillared entrance to the Town Hall and her way into the basement beneath it.

So here she was standing in front of the desk and looking up into the fatherly face of the constable.

'Well, love, if you don't know the street you lived on, nor your neighbour's name, then you've set me a real problem. Can't you remember anything about where you lived?'

Hannah frowned. She felt rather foolish. After all, she'd been nine years old when they had finally been forced into the workhouse. She ought to be able to remember where she'd lived before that. But for some reason, it was all very hazy. Just flashes came back to her, but nothing that seemed helpful. Now she knew what the phrase 'racking her brains' meant. Her head almost hurt with trying to think, trying to remember. Then suddenly, her face brightened. 'There was a pub just round the corner down the next street.'

'Ah, now we're getting somewhere. What was it called?'

'I – um – I don't know.'

The big man smiled at her. 'Oh dear, I thought we had it then. You see, love, there's lots of streets with pubs just round the corner. If we was to tramp round them all, we could be a week or more. Now, best thing you can do today is to have a wander round the town. See if anywhere seems familiar. But if you don't find somewhere to stay, then come back here. Now promise me you'll do that before it gets dark. I don't want to think of you wandering about the streets at night.'

'Do you know of a lodging house?'

The big policeman scratched his head. 'I know of a few, but some you wouldn't be able to afford. No offence, luv.'

'None taken.' She grinned ruefully at him as she hitched her bundle onto her shoulder. 'I'll go and have a look round then.'

'You do that,' he nodded, 'and yer can leave yer bundle here if you like. Pick it up later. No need to be carrying that around all day.' He stowed it safely in the back room as he added, 'Good luck.'

'Thanks. I think I'm going to need it.'

His gaze followed her as she left the station. He was curious about her. He'd already guessed she was a runaway, probably from a bad home or a harsh employer, but his instinct and his experience told him that she was no criminal on the run.

It was no surprise to Constable Robinson to see Hannah standing before his desk once more just as it began to turn dark. In a way, he was pleased to see her. For one, it meant she'd nothing to hide from the law, and secondly, she'd had the sense to come back where she would be safe.

'Now, love, no luck then?'

Hannah shook her head. She'd tramped the streets all day and now she was tired and hungry and frightened. Frightened that she would not be able to find a place to stay or work and that she would be sent back to the mill. Tentatively, she asked, 'Er – I don't suppose I could sleep in a cell tonight, could I?'

He blinked at her, obviously surprised by her request, yet, as he thought about it, he nodded slowly. 'I don't see why not. I'll have to check with my superior, because things can get a bit busy here on a Saturday night. But you sit down over there, love, and I'll go and ask.'

Hannah sank wearily onto the bench and leaned her head against the wall. It had been a long day and she hadn't slept well for the last two nights, but now that there was a good distance between her and the Critchlows, she could relax – a little, at least. And, ironically, if they let her stay, she'd be safe in the police station.

The officer was back in only a few minutes. 'Yes, that's all right. One night only, though, he says. But he don't like to think of a young girl like you wandering the streets. We've both got daughters of our own. Come on then.' He lifted the hatch in the counter and beckoned her through. 'You can share my bread and cheese with me.' He chuckled and patted his rotund belly. 'The missis always makes me too much anyway.'

The back room was a hive of activity. Two men were packing papers and books into crates whilst

Hannah sat and ate the policeman's crusty bread and creamy cheese.

He sat down too. 'Now then—' His tone was still kindly and concerned, yet there was a trace of firmness too. 'Are you going to tell me who you're running away from?'

Hannah stopped chewing for a moment and stared at him. 'How . . . how did you know I was?'

He chuckled. 'I've been in this job a few years now, love. A young girl like you doesn't just turn up in a place for no reason.' He glanced her up and down, taking in the state of her boots, the hem of her dress. 'You've not travelled far, nor have you been sleeping rough. So, where have you come from and why?'

'Are you going to make me go back?'

He shrugged his huge shoulders. 'Depends, love. I can't break the law, however much I might want to help you. And I do. Let me tell you that here and now, I do want to help you best I can.'

As Hannah munched, she eyed him speculatively. She was trying to decide whether to trust him or not. The very worst that could happen was that he would have her sent back to the mill – and the waiting punishment room. She gave an involuntary shudder.

The kindly man must have noticed for he asked gently, 'So very terrible was it?'

She sighed and decided that she had little choice. And there was just the chance that – for once – she'd found someone who might believe her.

So, she told him everything. At the end of her tale, the officer sat looking at her and stroking his chin thoughtfully.

'Well, by rights, you should go back to the mill, love. You've broken the terms of your indenture and I think I'm right in saying that this Critchlow fellow has the right to make you complete the term you signed up for.'

'I know,' Hannah said sadly, 'but surely, there's some law to say that they shouldn't lie to you about your mother. And I can't understand why more wasn't done to look into Luke's death. Jane's accident, I can understand. There's always accidents and that's exactly what it was – an accident. But Luke falling into the wheel wasn't. Edmund Critchlow struck him and he fell backwards.'

The policeman shook his head. 'Ah well now, I'd be inclined to agree with you there, but since it's outside our area and it's all been done and dusted, I don't think there's much we can do. Won't bring the lad back, will it?'

'No,' Hannah said grimly, 'but it won't make Mr Edmund pay for what he's done either.'

Constable Robinson eyed her as he said softly, 'I reckon you've got it in mind to see that he does – one day – haven't you?'

Hannah stared at him. Was he a mind reader?

He chuckled. 'It's written all over your pretty face. "I'll get him back one day," that look says.'

Hannah smiled a little sheepishly. 'I'll have to mind what my face is showing then, won't I?' And they laughed together. But more seriously, the man said gently, 'Well, love, just mind how you do it. Don't break the law, will you? Now then,' he went on more briskly as he pulled his huge frame to its feet. 'Let's get you settled in a cell before I go off duty. I'll make sure they leave the door open so's you won't feel you're being locked up for the night. And in the morning – well – we'll see, eh?'

It was strange lying alone on the hard bed in the tiny room. She was so used to sleeping in a large room with lots of other people, hearing their snuffles and snores. Yet it was far from quiet in the cell; sounds from other policemen on night duty drifted down the corridor. And from a neighbouring cell came the raucous singing of a drunk, arrested for disturbing the peace. Hannah smiled to herself in the darkness. He was still disturbing the peace in here – her peace. Yet gradually, the volume of his singing decreased and he murmured the words softly to himself.

It was strangely comforting for the girl who'd always loved to sing, even if it was the ramblings of a drunk.

Finally, wearied by the events of the long day, Hannah drifted into sleep, lulled by the crooning of her companion in the cell next door and wondering what the next day would bring.

Twenty-Five

The following morning, having shared in the station's breakfast in the back room, Constable Robinson introduced her to a young, fresh-faced officer. 'This 'ere's Jim Smith. How would you like to walk along with him on his beat and see if you recognize any of the streets?' He turned to the young man putting on his tall hat and straightening his knee-length blue frock coat. 'Now, Jim, if it gets to afternoon and you haven't found the place this young 'un is looking for, take her to Ma Boulton's. She takes in lodgers and she keeps a decent house.' He glanced archly at the young fellow. 'If you know what I mean.'

The young constable grinned at his superior and then swivelled his glance to include Hannah. 'I'll look after her, sir. Come on, then – Hannah, is it?'

She nodded.

As they came out into the street, the young man confided, 'You've done me a favour. I'm glad to get out of there. The station's moving to new premises with accommodation for our inspector so's he can live above the shop, you might say. We're all getting roped in to help pack everything up. So,' he winked at her, 'thanks for giving me a proper job to do. Right then,' he went on briskly, 'I reckon the best place to start is right here in the Market Place. Something might look familiar.'

As they began to walk along, Hannah kept silent, knowing that the young man was on duty, but he opened the conversation. 'Constable Robinson says you can't remember much about the place you used to live.'

Hannah frowned, trying again to drag up her childhood memories. 'I can't remember the names, but I've got a sort of picture in my mind. I . . . I think I might recognize the street.'

Jim pulled a wry face. 'If we can find it. Macclesfield's a big place.'

'I know,' Hannah said quietly. 'I'm sure I tramped most of it yesterday.'

'But you didn't see anything familiar?'

Hannah shook her head.

'Mr Robinson said your mother worked in one of the silk mills. Did you live near where she worked?'

'I think so. Just a couple of streets away.'

'Which mill was it?'

'I can't remember.'

'Did you ever go to the place where she worked? Would you recognize the mill?'

'I – don't think so. I used to stay home with my gran.'

'Did you go to school?'

'Oh yes. Me gran used to give me a penny and I'd go on a Sunday.'

'Ah, now that gives me a bit of a clue. Come on. I've got an idea.'

The tall young man began to lengthen his stride and Hannah had to trot to keep up with him. But she was smiling now. Suddenly, thanks to the kindly constable in the station and now this nice young man, she had real hope.

241

They'd walked quite a distance from the Market Place along a main street before Jim turned right into a narrower street. Still he said nothing until they came to a halt before a large building.

'This is the Sunday school,' Jim said.

Hannah stared up at the long rows of windows. Her mouth dropped open. 'That's it! That's it! This is where I went to school.'

Jim grinned down at her. '*Now* we're getting somewhere. So, can you remember your way home?'

Hannah's face fell as she looked wildly about her. There was a catch in her voice as she said, 'No, no, I can't.'

'Don't worry,' Jim said calmly. 'We'll do what Constable Robinson calls "acting it out".'

Hannah looked up at him, puzzled, but Jim's grin only widened. 'It's what we do when we want to try to figure out how a crime happened.' He leaned closer and, his eyes dancing as he teased her, added, ''Specially if it's a *murder*.'

If he was aiming to shock her, he was trying the wrong person. Hannah grinned at him and despite her anxiety, said impishly, 'I bet that's exciting – when you get a murder.'

He blinked and then laughed. 'By heck, you're a feisty little piece, aren't you? Most girls go all daft and squeamish when I talk about it.'

'So, what do I have to do to "act it out"?'

'Go right up to the main door there and pretend you're just leaving at the end of the day.'

Hannah looked at him blankly for a moment, then shrugged her shoulders and did as he suggested. She walked to the main door and then turned and looked back towards the young man standing at the gate.

Vague memories stirred in her mind. She closed her eyes a moment and she could almost hear the sound of other children, laughing and shrieking as they ran, pell-mell, towards the gate. She opened her eyes and began to run too. Reaching the gate, she didn't pause, but ran on, turning to the right and on up the street.

'Hey, wait for me.' Grinning, the young policeman took off his hat and pounded after her. Hannah glanced back and laughed aloud, realizing what it must look like to passers-by. She was hurtling along the street being pursued by a policeman. She slowed her pace and stopped to wait for him. When he reached her, she was bending forward, catching her breath but still laughing.

It was the first time she'd laughed with such abandon since Luke's death. Somehow, being miles away from the place where it had happened made it possible to put it out of her mind for a short while. But not for long; she couldn't imagine ever being able to forget about Luke for very long.

Puffing, Jim said, 'By heck, you can't half move for a girl.'

She chuckled. 'I thought I'd better stop. Folks might think you were trying to arrest me.'

He laughed too. 'You're right at that. But as long as it hasn't stopped you remembering where you're headed.'

Hannah straightened up. 'Oh no. I can remember very clearly now. We go right to the end of the road and then turn left.' She frowned. 'But I can't remember anything after that.'

'You will when you get there,' Jim said confidently. 'Come on. It sounds as if it's Bridge Street we're wanting.'

But when they turned the corner, Hannah was still puzzled.

'This is a silk mill on the left here,' Jim prompted helpfully. 'Is this where your mother worked?'

Hannah stared up at the building. 'I . . . I seem to remember it. I suppose it could be.'

'Maybe it's only familiar because you walked past it on your way home from the school.'

They walked a little further, and then suddenly, Hannah stopped on a corner where another street crossed Bridge Street. She stood looking down the sloping street to her left.

'This is Paradise Street,' Jim said. He waved his arm to the other side of the road. 'It carries on up there as well.'

Her voice was little more than a whisper, but there was no denying her excitement. 'This is the street where we used to live.'

'You sure?'

She nodded. 'It was very clever of you to suggest retracing my footsteps like that.'

He smiled and shrugged off her compliment, yet she could see he was gratified. Her face sobered and she frowned. 'You'd've thought I ought to've remembered the street names. After all, I lived here till I was nine. And I ought to remember the people we lived near. How dim am I?'

'Well, mebbe you sort of . . . sort of blocked it out. Didn't want to remember it. You know?'

She wasn't sure she understood what he meant, but he continued, trying to explain. 'Folks sometimes try to forget unhappy times in their lives.'

'But I wasn't unhappy. Not here.'

'But when you left here,' Jim persisted, 'you went into the workhouse, didn't you?'

'Yes,' she said slowly.

'Well, that's not a very happy experience, is it? Maybe you've tried to blot that out from your mind and the rest's gone as well.'

'There's worse things that can happen,' she murmured. There was suddenly a bleak, haunted look in her eyes. The last few weeks at the mill had been far more traumatic than life at the workhouse, grim though that had been. Luke's death had been the worst thing – the very worst thing – that had ever happened to her. Guiltily, she realized that his death had affected her far more deeply than hearing that her own mother had died. She supposed she could accept the death of her mother – although not the fact that it had been kept from her – because it was the natural progression of life. What was hard to bear was the loss of her young sweetheart, the boy she'd hoped to marry one day.

Jim glanced at her and saw the tears brimming in her eyes. 'Yes,' he said softly. 'I'm sure there is.'

Hannah took a deep breath and brushed her tears away with an impatient gesture. 'But I see what you mean. And maybe you're right.' She lifted her face and smiled bravely. 'It's all coming back now and it's thanks to you.'

Hannah stood a moment, gazing down the street at the terrace of tall, three-storey houses. The longer, small-paned windows on the top storey were the tell-tale sign that they were weavers' garret workshops. One of those very rooms had been where her own grandfather had worked, Hannah thought.

Children played in the roadway and women stood in front of their houses, keeping an eye on the youngsters and gossiping with their neighbours. Suddenly, Hannah's glance came to rest on a woman standing at the bottom of the three steep steps in front of her house and leaning against the railing, a small, round woman with her arms folded across her ample bosom. She was chatting to another woman standing on the pavement beside her.

'Auntie Bessie,' she whispered, then louder and louder until she was shouting and running down the street, her arms outstretched. 'Auntie Bessie, *Auntie Bessie!*'

She flung herself against the woman, who, taken by surprise, sat down suddenly on the bottom step.

''Ere, what d'you think you're . . . ?' the woman began indignantly as she grasped the railing and hauled herself up. But Hannah put her arms around the woman's plump waist and hugged her hard, pressing her cheek against her.

'What a' you doing?' The woman grasped Hannah by the shoulders and prised her away. She did not throw her off entirely, but held onto her, looking down into her upturned face. Behind them Jim had caught up with Hannah in time to hear the woman add, 'Who are you?'

He stood quietly, watching and waiting.

Hannah opened her mouth but before she could speak, the thin, grey-haired woman who had been gossiping with Bessie suddenly cackled with laughter and prodded Hannah with a bony finger. 'I know who you are, girl. I'd know you anywhere.' She glanced at her friend. 'Can't you see it, Bess? You know who she is, don't you?'

Bessie stared at her friend. 'No, I don't know.' She glanced between the thin woman and Hannah, seeming not to know quite which of them to ask. In the end, she asked them both. 'Who is she, Flo?' And turning again to the girl, 'Who are you?'

'It's as plain as the nose on her face,' Flo piped up, and cackled again with laughter at her own joke. 'Though it's a pretty little nose. Good job you didn't get his nose as well as his blond hair and blue eyes.'

'Flo,' Bessie was becoming impatient now, 'just cut the funning, will yer, and tell me who she is?' She turned back to Hannah and, still holding her shoulders, gave her a little shake. 'Or you tell me.'

Hannah grinned up at her. 'It's me, Auntie Bessie. It's Hannah. We used to live next door to you. I used to come into your house when me mam was at work.'

'Hannah,' Bessie said wonderingly. '*Hannah!* Aw, love—' Suddenly, Hannah was swept into the woman's arms and pressed against her softness. 'Fancy me not knowing you. Aw, I'm sorry, I'm sorry.' She held her at arm's length again. 'Let's 'ave a proper look at you.'

Hannah had no choice but to submit to her scrutiny. Beside them, Flo said softly, 'See what I mean, Bess? You remember *him*, don't you? She's his kid, all right, even if Rebecca would never say. There's no mistake now. Not now, there ain't.'

Hannah glanced at Flo, the question written on her face.

Bessie frowned. 'Shut up, Flo,' she muttered. 'You've said enough. More than enough, by the look of it.'

'Oh, sorry, I'm sure,' Flo said huffily. Then she bent towards Hannah. 'You remember me, ducky, don't yer? I'm yer Antie Flo.'

Hannah stared into the thin face, the grey eyes, the gaunt cheeks, the beak-like nose and the thin-lipped mouth. Oh, she remembered her all right. She remembered Florence Harris. How she'd called after Hannah and her mother, calling them names as they walked down the street. 'No better than you ought to be, Rebecca Francis. And that girl of yours'll be the same. It's in the breed. Her father's a good-for-nothing woman-izer and you're nothing better than a whore!'

Oh yes, Hannah remembered her now, but instead, she smiled sweetly into Flo's face and said, 'No, sorry. I don't. I only remember Auntie Bessie. She was always so kind to us.'

Flo straightened up and with a disgruntled 'Huh!' turned away. She began to walk back to her own house, next door, but with a parting shot, she pointed at the young constable and said, 'What's he doing here, then? In trouble already, is she? It'll be no more than you could expect. You want to be careful of her, Bess. Bringing trouble to your door. That's what she'll do.'

But Bessie was chuckling softly. 'That's put 'er nose out of joint. You come along in and tell me what's been happening to you. But first,' she glanced up at Jim. 'What is this bobby doing here? Are you in bother?'

'No, no, Auntie Bessie. He's been helping me find you. Well, helping me find where I used to live. I . . . I couldn't remember . . .' Her voice faltered and faded.

'Couldn't remember?' Bessie seemed shocked.

Jim stepped forward and, clearing his throat, he spoke for the first time. 'I think she's blotted a lot out of her mind. She – well, she'll no doubt tell you herself – but she's not had it easy . . .' Now, he too stopped, unsure what to say next.

'Ah,' Bessie said and nodded, catching on quickly. 'Well, let's go inside and we'll all 'ave a nice cup of tea and a bit of a chat, eh?' She grinned at the constable, her merry eyes almost lost in her round, red cheeks. 'You too, young feller. I ain't never 'ad no cause to be frightened of the bobbies and I ain't goin' to start now.'

Jim smiled back. 'Ta all the same, missis, but I'd best be getting back on me proper beat, else it'll be me in the trouble.' He nodded towards Hannah. 'But I'll keep in touch. I'd like to know how she goes on.'

Bessie chuckled inwardly. *I bet you would*, she thought, as she saw the way the young man's eyes rested on Hannah's pretty face. *Oh, I bet you would.* Aloud, she said, 'Well, lad, like I say, you're welcome in my house any time you like. In or out of your uniform.'

Hannah turned to him. 'Thank you so much for all your help. You . . . you've been wonderful. And please – thank Mr Robinson for me too, won't you?'

'I will, miss. And . . . and good luck,' he added as he put on his hat and turned away, raising his hand in farewell as he strode away up the street. 'By the way, don't forget to collect your bundle of things from the station, will yer?'

'I won't. And thank you.'

'Now, love,' Bessie said, putting her arm around Hannah's shoulders. 'Come along in. It's high time you and me did some catching up.'

Twenty-Six

Two hours later they were still sitting either side of
Bessie Morgan's table, tea grown cold before them,
exchanging their stories of the years since they'd last
seen each other. Hannah had poured it all out – every
bit of it – and she, in turn, had listened to Bessie's
tale.

'Your gran was always good to me, love, 'specially
when I lost one of me little 'uns with the scarlet fever.'

'I remember that,' Hannah said gently. 'I wasn't
allowed to play with Peggy for weeks.' She leaned
forward. 'Is . . . is Peggy all right? I mean . . .' She
faltered. It was difficult asking about Bessie's large
family. Perhaps there had been more tragedies. There
had. Bessie wiped her eyes with the corner of her
apron. 'She's all right.' Bessie's generous mouth was
suddenly tight. 'Far as I know, that is.'

'Far as you know . . .' Hannah began and then
stopped. But she had gone too far to pull back now.
'What . . . what do you mean?'

'I don't see her. I don't even know where she's
living. Not for sure.'

Hannah waited. The questions were tumbling
around in her mind, but she held them in check,
waiting for Bessie to continue in her own time. 'Peggy
was always a wild one,' Bessie was saying, and Hannah was remembering the bright, fair-haired tomboy

250

she had played with. 'She met this lad when she was fifteen. I didn't like him. He was an idle beggar. Into all sorts, he was. Him and all his family and not always on the right side of the law. But she wouldn't listen to me. It was about – about the time I lost my Bill.'

Hannah gasped. She hadn't thought to ask about Bessie's quiet, unassuming husband, Bill.

'Oh no, not Uncle Bill.'

Bessie nodded and her eyes filled with tears again. 'He got injured at work in 'fifty three and died just before Christmas.'

'That was just before they sent me to the mill,' Hannah murmured, but Bessie was lost in the telling of her own tale now.

'What I'd have given to have your gran and your mam still living next door,' she went on, 'I can't tell you. And that was when madam,' Hannah guessed she was referring to her wayward daughter, Peggy, 'decided to up sticks and leave. Packed 'er bags, she did, and off she went with 'im. Went to live with his parents in Davies Street. Well, I say parents. His dad's in gaol, by all accounts.'

Hannah touched the woman's hand. 'Oh, Auntie Bessie, I'm so sorry to hear all this. You've had it worse than me.'

'No, love, no. Things like that shouldn't happen to a young girl. When you get older – to my age – well, you expect to 'ave to take a few knocks.' She smiled through her tears. 'Worst of it is, though, they've all left home now. The lads are working away. Ben is in Manchester and Micky went to London. Doing very well, he is. Got a job in an office, so he says. He writes regular, but he can't get home much. Neither can Ben, even though he's only in Manchester, it might as well be a million miles away.

'What about the others?' Hannah asked tentatively, fearing more bad news.

'Young Billy's at sea. Joined the navy, 'ee did, and Sarah's married.' Bessie was smiling now. 'Got a babby. Bonny little girl. Called her Elizabeth after me. Beth for short. But they live in Liverpool. Her husband works on the docks, so I don't see a lot of them either.' Her face fell again. 'It's hard, you know, Hannah, when you've had a house full of family and then, all of a sudden, you turn round and there's no one left but you.' Bessie forced a smile as she added, 'But I should count my blessings. The landlord let me stay in me home, even though I don't work in the weaving trade any more. Not now poor Bill's gone. There's a nice feller rents the garret.' She jerked her thumb upwards, indicating the attic rooms of her house. 'But he's a quiet sort. Comes and goes and I never see him.' She pulled a face. 'No company there, if you know what I mean.'

Hannah could hear the loneliness in Bessie's voice. She held Bessie's hand and leaned forward. 'Well, I'm hoping to find a job in one of the silk mills and stay in Macclesfield.' She pulled a wry face. 'As long as Edmund Critchlow doesn't catch up with me and have me dragged back to serve out my term. Anyway,' she went on briskly and with more hope in her tone than she was feeling inside. 'I'll come and see you often. I promise.'

Bessie smiled. 'Where are you living?'

'Nowhere yet. That's me next job. Find lodgings.'

Bessie's face lit up. 'Then you've found 'em, love. You can stay here and I won't take no for an answer.'

Now it was Hannah's eyes that filled with tears.

'Oh, Auntie Bessie, I'd love to,' she cried and, hugging her, Hannah felt as if she had come home.

With her husband and one of her boys dead and the rest of her family gone, Bessie's only source of income was to take in washing. But those who lived nearby were as hard up as she was and the work was spasmodic.

'We're doing each other a favour,' she assured Hannah. 'If you get a job and pay me a bit of board each week, you'll be saving me from the workhouse.'

Hannah's eyes widened in disbelief, but Bessie nodded, 'You will, I tell you, you will. The lads send me money now and again, but it's not fair to expect it.' She laughed suddenly. 'You don't see the chick scratching for the old hen, do you?'

Hannah put her arms around her and murmured, 'I'll scratch for you, Auntie Bessie, just like I'd've done for me mam, if only . . . if only . . .'

Bessie hugged her close. 'Aye, love, I know. I know.'

Hannah settled in quickly with Bessie Morgan. For the first few weeks they decided she should not go in search of work.

'You keep your head down, just for a week or two. There'll be time enough for you to look for a job after Christmas. In the meantime, you can help me with the washing and ironing. I reckon everyone's decided to have their sheets and blankets washed for Christmas. I've even got three pairs of curtains, would you believe? I don't know where all the work's coming from all of a sudden. I really need your help, Hannah. You couldn't have turned up at a better time.'

'What about Mrs Harris? You . . . you don't think she'll report me to Mr Goodbody, do you?'

'Not if she knows what's good for her,' Bessie said grimly. 'Don't you fret, love. I'll have a word with her. Make sure she keeps that runaway mouth of hers tight shut, else she'll have me to reckon with.'

Hannah smiled, suddenly feeling a lot safer. She wasn't sure whether Bessie was telling the truth about needing her help, but she worked hard alongside the older woman over the copper and the tub in the wash house in the back yard. At night, when Bessie put her swollen legs up, Hannah tackled all the ironing. The next day, she tramped the streets to return the fresh laundry and collect more work.

It was on a cold January morning, when she walked to the very end of Bridge Road, turned left into Chestergate and continued out onto the Prestbury Road, that she saw the workhouse. She stood before the main entrance, looking up at the imposing stone building, at the plaque above the door bearing the date that building began – 1843 – and up again to the clock tower and the weather vane on the very top. Then her glance took in the numerous windows and the tall chimneys. Hannah shuddered. She remembered this place all too well.

She wondered if the Goodbodys were still there and asked herself if she dared to knock on the door and ask for the truth about her mother. Hannah bit her lip and turned away, her eyes filling with tears. Though she longed to find out about her mother, it was too big a risk.

*

254

'What's the matter, love?' Bessie asked. Hannah had hardly said a word since her return from taking and fetching the laundry and now she was picking at her supper with little or no appetite. 'Are you poorly?'

Tears spilled down Hannah's face.

'Aw, love, what is it?' Bessie was round the table in a trice and enfolding the girl in her loving embrace.

'I . . . I saw the workhouse today and . . . and it brought all the memories about Mam back. I know they said she was dead, but was it true? Perhaps it was another lie.' She lifted her tear-streaked face. 'Auntie Bessie, what if she's still in there?'

'Well, we'll go and ask, but don't get your hopes up, love, will you? Because, to be honest, if your mam was still alive I reckon she'd've got in touch with you somehow. I can't believe she'd let nearly four years go by without a word.'

'But they stopped my letters.'

'Aye, I know. You told me,' Bessie said grimly.

'You see,' Hannah said, 'I want to find out the truth but I daren't go to the workhouse in case Mr Goodbody's still there. He'd have me sent back to the mill. I know he would.'

Bessie beamed suddenly. 'Then leave it with me, love. I've nothing to fear of that place – only of having to go in it to stay. But not now. Not now you're here. So I'll find out about your mam for you.'

'But . . . but what will you say? Won't he suspect I'm with you? He might already have heard from Mr Edmund that I've run away.'

Bessie frowned thoughtfully. 'Aye, well, I won't mention you . . .' she began, but then a gleam came into her eyes. 'Tell you what – it might be better if I *did* mention you.'

Fear crossed Hannah's face. 'Oh, Auntie Bessie, please don't—'

'No, no, love, listen a minute. If I go to Goodbody and ask where your mam *and you* are, then he won't suspect I've seen you, will he? I'll just say I'm trying to find out about my old friends.' Her face was suddenly sad. 'It broke my heart the day you left to go into that place, Hannah, but there was nothing we could do. We'd've helped you if we could've done. We 'adn't the room to take you in here.'

'I know, Auntie Bessie, I know you'd've helped if you could've. But,' she went on, coming back to the idea of Bessie visiting the workhouse, 'what if the master asks you outright if you've seen me?'

Bessie looked her straight in the face and said, 'I'll say I haven't set eyes on you from the day you left our street to enter the workhouse.' Suddenly she beamed, 'I'll just not add, "until now".'

Hannah's mouth twitched, she smiled and then she laughed out loud. 'Oh, Auntie Bessie!' And then suddenly, out of the past came the phrase that her gran had used fondly when speaking of Bessie Morgan. 'Oh, Auntie Bessie, you're a caution, you are.'

But the following day, when Bessie put on her best hat and coat and set off for the workhouse, Hannah was on tenterhooks. She couldn't settle and paced about the house like a caged animal. At last, with nothing to occupy her, Hannah picked up a parcel of clean laundry and set off to deliver it.

As she retraced her steps to the terraced house she

now called home, Hannah paused again outside the school. She wondered if there were any of the teachers there who would still remember her. She almost stepped into the building, but then turned and hurried away, realizing that the more people who knew she was back here, the more chance there was of Goodbody finding out about her. And then . . .

Hannah bent her head and hurried home.

'There you are.' Auntie Bessie was at the door, looking anxiously up and down the street. 'You had me worried.'

'Oh, sorry, Auntie Bessie, but I was that restless after you'd gone. I just had to get out for a bit. I've delivered Mrs Brown's laundry.'

Bessie nodded. 'That's all right then. Now come on in and we'll have a nice cup of tea and I'll tell you all about it. I'm parched, I am. It's me one bit of luxury. Tea.'

Hannah laughed. 'We only got given it in the apprentice house if we were ill.'

Bessie chuckled. 'Well, I hope you didn't get it very often then.'

Hannah had to hold in her impatience for Bessie's news just a little longer, until the older woman had lowered herself into her chair and drunk half her cup of tea. 'There, that's better.'

'Did you see Mr Goodbody? Did he ask about me?'

Bessie shook her head. 'I didn't see him, but I saw his wife.'

Hannah pulled in a startled breath. 'Oh! Oh dear!'

But Bessie was smiling and leaning towards her. 'I'll tell you something, Hannah. She's far more frightened of you than you are of them.'

'Eh?' Now Hannah was mystified.

Bessie sat back and said triumphantly, 'She was real jittery when I asked about you and your mother.'

Hannah shook her head wonderingly. 'Why? Why ever should she be frightened about me?'

'Because they lied to you, didn't they? Kept you thinking your mother was still alive and well and writing to you? I expect if you were to ask your policeman friend about that, you might find that it was against the law in some way. I don't know what they'd call it, but I'd call it criminal, wouldn't you?'

'I suppose so.' Hannah was doubtful. She'd lived her whole life under the rule of others and she couldn't imagine having any power over anyone else. Others wielded the power in Hannah Francis's world – not her. But a tiny sliver of determination and hope began to grow. 'What did she say, Auntie Bessie?'

'Well, when I got there I asked the porter if I could see Mr Goodbody, and he said he was away, but would I like to see Mrs Goodbody. "She's the matron," he said. "She can admit folks when the master's away."' Bessie sniffed. 'Likely he thought I was wanting to go in to stay.' She paused a moment, reflecting how close at times she'd come to having to do just that.

'And did you see her?' Hannah prompted.

Bessie nodded. 'Oh, I saw her all right. She soon came off her high horse when she realized I wasn't another pauper at her gate. And when I said I was inquiring after my old friend, Rebecca Francis, and her daughter, Hannah, she went white.'

Hannah's mouth dropped open. Bessie nodded, 'Oh yes, believe me, Hannah, she went white. She's frightened of her part in the deception coming out, I could tell. I don't reckon you've much to fear from her.'

'Maybe not,' Hannah murmured, finding her voice through her surprise. 'But that's not him, is it?'

'True, but I don't reckon they've heard about you running away. She told me that Rebecca died only a few months after you were sent to the mill. That seemed genuine, but then she seemed to get nervous. Just said that as far as she knew you were still there. When I pressed her and asked if she'd sent word to you that your mother'd died that was when she went white and began to stutter. "My husband deals with all that sort of thing," she said.' Bessie laughed aloud. 'Oh, Hannah, I couldn't resist it, I said, "I'd've thought that you being the matron, like, that it'd've been your job to let the poor girl know."' Bessie rocked with laughter until the tears ran down her cheeks. 'Oh no, no, she said. That was her husband's job. She was quick to put the blame on his shoulders, I can tell you.' Bessie wiped her eyes. 'Anyway, love, as I was coming out, this young woman comes running after me across the yard. She said she'd heard I was asking after Hannah Francis and her mother. Goodness only knows how she knew.'

Though she now had to accept that her mother was truly gone, it was no great shock. Deep inside, she'd known it to be the truth. 'News travels fast in there,' she said with a small smile. 'I reckon the inmates know what's happening even before the master does. Go on, Auntie Bessie.'

'This girl said she'd known you at the mill and that the last time she'd seen you, you'd been fine but that you'd been anxious about your mother as you'd never heard from her. She said she'd written to you herself after she heard in the workhouse that your mother had died. But she didn't know if the letter had ever reached you as you'd never replied.'

'No, it didn't,' Hannah said grimly.

'Doesn't surprise me,' Bessie said. 'I expect with their little scam going on between Goodbody and this Critchlow fellow, they intercepted *any* letters addressed to you.'

'Mmm,' Hannah frowned. 'I wish I knew who'd really done that. I can't believe it of old man Critchlow. He seemed so nice . . .'

Bessie snorted. 'Huh! They all do, until it comes down to money. You were money to them, love. The Critchlows likely paid Goodbody a handsome sum to apprentice you for the pittance it cost them to keep you. Neither of them would want to lose it.'

Hannah was silent for a moment, then she asked curiously, 'Who was the young woman who said she knew me?'

'Nell Hudson.'

'Nell!' Hannah stared at Bessie. 'Nell is in the workhouse?'

And when Bessie nodded, Hannah breathed, 'Oh no! Not Nell. Oh, Auntie Bessie!' She clasped Bessie's hand across the table. 'I have to get her out of there. I just have to.'

Twenty-Seven

'But I don't know what you can do,' Bessie said, though her eyes were full of sympathy for the girl. 'You haven't got a job yet yourself.'

'I will do and I won't be long about it.'

Bessie smiled at the young girl's confidence, marvelling at her determination, her resilience after all the cruel blows that life had dealt her. 'No, love, I'm sure you won't. You're young and strong and willing, and anybody'd be a fool not to employ you, but – but you can't expect to support a household of four on a woman's wage. Your friend could come here and with pleasure, but—'

'Four? What do you mean – four?'

'Didn't you know? Your friend Nell has got a baby. A little boy. He's about a month old.'

Hannah stared at her for a moment and then nodded slowly. 'Yes, yes, it all fits now. No wonder Mrs Bramwell wouldn't tell me why she'd gone away.' Her eyes filled with tears as she remembered. 'And why Nell was so short with me the very last time she spoke. She must've known, must've realized what they'd do. Oh, poor, poor Nell. But I wonder who—?' Then shook herself. 'No time for that now. I have to think of a way to get her out.' She looked Bessie straight in the eyes as she asked, 'So, if we could get enough money to support ourselves, you'd have her here? As another lodger? Her and her baby?'

'Oh yes.' Bessie smiled without hesitation. 'It'd be lovely to have a little one about the place again.'

'And supposing, just supposing that both Nell and me could get work, would you . . . would you look after her child?'

Bessie's eyes sparkled. 'Oh, I would. I would.' And the lonely woman clasped her hands together in thankfulness, blessing the day the young constable had helped Hannah find her old neighbour.

The very next day, Hannah tramped the streets looking for work but she returned home at night disappointed and dispirited.

'Did you try all the silk mills?' Bessie asked.

'Well – one or two,' Hannah said vaguely. She'd wanted to avoid mill work if she could, but it seemed if that was all that was left open to her, she'd no choice. At least she could offer some kind of experience that was allied to that trade. Silk work couldn't be so very different from cotton, could it?

'Anybody home?' came a voice from the door, and Bessie cast her eyes to the ceiling.

'Yes, come in, Flo – if you must.'

'Well, that's a nice greeting, I must say.' Undeterred, Flo Harris entered and sat down at the table. She reached across for a cup and saucer, picked up the teapot and poured herself a cup of tea.

''Elp yourself, why don't you?' Bessie muttered. 'As if I've the money to buy luxuries for half the street.'

Flo cackled with laughter. 'I will, ta, Bessie.' Then

she turned her attention to Hannah. 'Well, girl, gettin' yer feet well and truly under Bessie's table, a' yer?'

Refusing to be daunted by the woman's sharp tongue, Hannah grinned. 'That's right, Mrs Harris. Just like you.'

Now it was Bessie who roared with laughter. 'Now, now, come on you two. Let's not be 'aving any bickering. And as for you, Flo Harris, Hannah's living here with me now, so you'd best get used to the idea.'

Suddenly, Flo smiled. ''S'all right by me. It'll be summat to keep the neighbours gossiping about for a week or two. Gregory's whore's daughter back home. She comin' an' all, is she? Rebecca?'

Bessie banged her fist on the table so hard that the cups rattled in their saucers and the teapot lid bounced. 'Now, look here, Flo. There's no call for you to talk like that. Whatever happened in the past, it's not young Hannah's fault anyway, now is it?' She paused, waiting for Flo's agreement. When it was not forthcoming she banged the table again, demanding loudly, 'Is it?'

Flo jumped and blinked. She could see that Bessie meant business and if she wanted to keep on the right side of her neighbour then she'd better alter her tune. 'No – no, you're right, Bessie,' Flo said, calling upon all her acting skills. ''Course you are.' She turned to Hannah. 'Tek no notice of me. It's just my way. I don't mean no harm.'

Hannah was not taken in by Flo's apology, which had been dragged out of her by Bessie – she remembered her of old – but she smiled thinly and nodded.

'And in answer to your question,' Bessie said quietly now, 'no, Rebecca won't be coming back. She died in the workhouse.' She glared at Flo. 'And I reckon we're all a bit to blame for that happening when we didn't lift a finger to help when she was forced to go in there along with her little girl.'

Flo opened her mouth to make some retort but, seeing the look on Bessie's face, thought better of it. Instead, she turned to Hannah and muttered, 'I'm sorry to hear that.'

Now Bessie cleared her throat and changed the subject. 'Well, Hannah's been job hunting today, but she's not 'ad much luck. Do you know of anywhere where they're taking folk on, Flo?'

The woman appeared to give the question thought, but then pulled a face. 'Sorry, I don't.' Then a sly look came across her face. 'Why don't you go and ask your father to give you a job?'

'Now that's enough, Flo,' Bessie said, and Hannah could see that she was angry now. 'I'm warning you.'

'Oh, sorry, I'm sure.' Flo pretended huffiness. 'I was only trying to think of something to help. Forget I said anything.'

But Hannah was not about to forget. 'My father? You *know* who my father is?' She turned from Flo to Bessie and asked, almost accusingly, 'Do you know him?'

Bessie shifted uncomfortably. 'Well – er – you see, love . . .'

'Auntie Bessie, do you know him?'

There was a brief pause whilst both Hannah and Flo stared at Bessie, who, at last, sighed and said flatly, 'Yes, love. I know him.'

'We all know him,' Flo added triumphantly. 'We've always known who he was, even though Rebecca would never say.' She touched Hannah's hair with bony fingers. 'And now there's no mistaking it. You've got his hair colouring and his bright blue eyes. Oh, there's no mistaking Jimmy Gregory's bastard.'

Hannah flinched, not at Bessie's sudden banging on the table once more but at the cruel name Flo had called her.

'Now that is enough, Flo Harris,' Bessie roared. 'If you can't keep a civil tongue in your head, you're not welcome in my house no more.'

Flo knew that she'd gone too far this time. She'd no wish to fall out with Bessie. Oh, they had their spats and Flo was renowned for her sharp tongue, but they'd never really fallen out – not seriously. Now, however, it looked as if young Hannah was a serious threat.

'I'm sorry, Bessie,' Flo whined. 'I meant no harm.'

'Well, mind you don't,' Bessie snapped. Then she was silent for a moment, thinking. 'Mind you,' she said slowly at last, 'you've got a point – even though you could've found a kinder way to say it.'

'How do you mean?' Hannah pushed aside the insult. It wasn't the first time she'd had the cruel name hurled at her and she doubted it'd be the last.

'Well, I suppose you *could* go and see your father.'

'See my father? Why?'

'He's manager at Brayford's silk mill.'

'And he married Brayford's daughter,' Flo put in. 'Oh, done very nicely for himself has Jimmy Gregory.'

Bessie cast her a warning glance but said, 'Yes, she's right. Your father is now in a position of importance.' She leaned towards Hannah. 'He's in a position to help you, love.'

'If he will,' Hannah said bitterly. 'He evidently

didn't want to help my mother when she was expecting me, did he? Or later, when we were turned out of our home.'

There was a strained silence in the room whilst Bessie and Flo exchanged a look. Then came the words that shocked Hannah and broke her heart.

Bessie touched her hand gently and said softly, 'He couldn't, love. He was already married.'

Twenty-Eight

'I'm sorry you've had to find out, love,' Bessie was still trying to console Hannah late that evening. The girl had not cried, but she had gone very quiet, withdrawn into herself, and the older woman was distraught to think that she'd been the cause of the sparkle dying in the girl's eyes. Hannah was only just coming to terms with the death of her childhood sweetheart and the news of her mother, and now here was Bessie being the cause of further grief.

But Hannah took a deep breath and summoned up a tremulous smile. 'It's all right, Auntie Bessie. Honestly. I'd've had to've known sometime and if I'm to go and see him then . . . then I'd better know what to expect.'

Bessie chewed at her bottom lip, but nodded. The girl was right. Painful though it might be, it was better that she knew the truth, especially if she was to meet him.

'Will you do something for me though, Auntie Bessie?'

'I will if I can, love. You know that.'

'Will you tell me everything you know? About me father?'

'Aw – well – now, I don't—'

'Please. I need to know. It can't harm Mam now. If she was still alive, I wouldn't be asking. But I need to know.'

Bessie let out a huge sigh. 'Aye, well, I suppose you've a right to know – now you're older. Trouble is, love, I don't know very much really. See, your mam would never tell anyone who your father was. We *think* we know, but I have to say, it's all guesswork on our part.' She paused and her glance roamed over Hannah's face. 'But looking at you now, love,' she murmured. 'It does look as if we might be right.'

'Just tell me, Auntie Bessie.'

Bessie took a deep breath. 'There was this chap at the mill where your mam worked. Jimmy Gregory.' A small smile played on her mouth. 'Handsome devil, he was, I have to admit. But a one for the ladies. You know what I mean.'

Hannah nodded. She knew only too well what 'a one for the ladies' meant. Unbidden, the image of Edmund Critchlow was in her mind.

'By all accounts,' Bessie went on, 'there was something going on between him and yer mother. Folks used to see them together. And she used to stay late at work sometimes – I know that for a fact. Of course she could have been working . . .' Bessie's voice trailed away. Hannah could tell she didn't really believe that.

'But you think she was meeting him?'

Bessie nodded. There was silence until Hannah prompted, in a flat, unemotional tone, 'And he was married? To the boss's daughter.'

'Oh no, not then. He was only the supervisor then and married with a child, I think.'

'So,' Hannah mused, 'somewhere I have a half-brother or sister.'

'His first wife and the child died. It was the cholera.

Like your Gran Grace died of. And about the same
time too. But you have got a half-brother and a half-
sister by his present wife.'

Hannah digested this. From thinking herself an
orphan and completely alone in the world, she was
now having to come to terms with the knowledge that
she had a father and siblings.

'But he didn't come looking for my mother then?
When his wife died, I mean?'

'No,' Bessie said grimly. 'But I've a feeling your
mother went looking for him.'

'How . . . how do you mean?'

'I think she expected that he would marry her, now
that he was a free man.'

'But, obviously, he didn't want to know.'

Bessie sniffed disapprovingly. 'No. I remember her
coming home, her face swollen with crying. Bless her.
She really hoped—'

'Why do you think he didn't want to marry her?'

'By then, he reckoned he had better fish to fry. No
disrespect to your mam, love, but you know what I
mean.'

Hannah nodded. 'He'd got his eye on the boss's
daughter had he?'

'Not the boss at the mill where he and your mother
worked. No. He left there and went to work for
Brayford's as manager. That's when he got to know
Miss Emmeline Brayford. And, of course, after he'd
left, your poor mam got finished at the mill. Her
protector had gone.'

'You wouldn't have thought her father – Miss
Emmeline's, I mean – would have allowed it. I mean,
he can't be considered to be in the same class as her.
Can he?'

Bessie shook her head. 'No, but by all accounts, Miss Emmeline is a very spoilt young woman. Her mother died when she was a baby and her father indulges her. Whatever she wants, she gets. And she wanted Jimmy Gregory.' Bessie laughed wryly. 'Mind you, I bet he's had his wings clipped since he married her. He'll not get away with any of his hanky-panky now.'

'I don't suppose his new wife will take very kindly to his bastard knocking on his door.'

Bessie put her arm around Hannah. 'Don't call yourself that, love.'

'But it's what I am, Auntie Bessie.' She lifted her chin and added, defiantly, 'And she'll just have to get used to the idea. And he will, 'cos that's just where I'm going. Knocking on his door. I need a job. It's the least he can do for me. The very least.'

Hannah stood in the pillared porch of the imposing house. Her courage almost failed her. Almost, but not quite. Indignation carried her up the step to lift the heavy knocker and let it fall with a resounding thud. She waited for what seemed an age, hopping nervously from one foot to the other. The door opened and a maid looked her up and down. 'You should've gone round the back. What do you want?'

'I want to see your master.'

'Who shall I say it is?'

'Never mind that.' Hannah was reluctant to give him advance warning. He might refuse to see her at all. 'Just tell him it's a personal matter.'

'Are you one of the mill girls? He'll not see you here. You'll have to see him at work.'

'No, no. I'm not.'

'You after a job then? Because if you are, he'll only see you at the mill—'

'There are reasons why I think he would prefer to see me here.'

The girl blinked. 'Oh. Oh, all right then. I'll ask him. You'd better come in, I suppose. Wipe your boots.'

While she stood in the hallway waiting for the maid to return, Hannah heard the sound of children's laughter and footsteps pounding on the staircase. She looked up to see two youngsters, a boy of about five and a girl a year or so younger, chasing each other down the stairs.

'Wait for me, Roddy. Wait for me,' the little girl cried plaintively.

'Come on, Caroline. Keep up.'

At the bottom of the stairs, the boy looked up to see the stranger standing there. The little girl cannoned into him from behind and then she too saw Hannah.

The boy smiled. 'Hello. Who are you?' He was dark-haired with hazel eyes, but it was the little girl who caught and held Hannah's attention. Startled, Hannah let out a little gasp and covered her mouth with her fingers. The child had long, blonde curling hair, and the eyes that were regarding Hannah curiously were bright blue. Even her features strongly resembled Hannah's own. There was no denying that this child was Hannah's half-sister.

But before either of them could say more, the maid returned to say, 'The master says you're to come this way.' She turned to the children. 'And you two, go and see cook in the kitchen.'

With one last glance at Hannah, the two children

clattered down the passageway leading to the rear of the house, the visitor forgotten, chattering in their high-pitched voices.

The master and mistress of the house were still at breakfast. He was seated at one end of the table, his wife at the other end. As Hannah followed the maid into the room, they both stared at her. Hannah's heart fell. She hadn't wanted to meet his wife. Indeed, she hadn't wanted to meet his children – especially one that looked so like her. She hadn't wanted any of his family to be present when she said what she had to say.

She bobbed courteously towards the woman. 'Begging your pardon, ma'am. I – I just wanted a word with the master.'

The woman was beautiful – there was no denying it. Her skin was flawless and her hair was a glorious colour – a bright red. It was not a colour Hannah had ever seen before and she was fascinated by it. The woman's mouth was perfectly shaped, though to Hannah's mind, her lips were a little thin. Her hazel eyes were cool and she raised one clearly defined dark eyebrow quizzically.

'And to what do we owe this intrusion? One of your mill girls in trouble, is it, James?' She rose gracefully from the table and moved towards the door. 'I hope this has nothing to do with you.'

As she passed close by Hannah, she glanced down, and then she faltered on her path out of the room. A small frown puckered her smooth brow as she stared into Hannah's face. Then her glance swivelled towards her husband and Hannah saw the fleeting anger cross the woman's face. Through gritted teeth, Emmeline muttered, 'Quite obviously, it has.'

Then with an angry swish of her long skirts, she left the room.

'I'm sorry,' Hannah faltered. 'I shouldn't have come.'

'Then why did you?' the man asked harshly, standing up and throwing the newspaper he had been reading at the breakfast table to the floor. He strode towards her to stand over her, angry and intimidating. But Hannah stood her ground.

She looked up into his face, into the bright blue eyes, sparkling with anger. And whilst his hair was thinning now and greying at the temples, she could see that it had once been thick and golden and curly.

There was no point in prevaricating. Even his wife had seen the striking likeness of this stranger to her own daughter. Another daughter who also took after her father.

Hannah licked her lips. 'I . . . I believe you are my father.'

James frowned. 'Do you indeed? And what makes you think that?' He was trying to avoid the obvious and they both knew it.

'Because my mother was Rebecca Francis.'

James looked startled. 'Was?' His surprise was not at Hannah's existence, but at her use of the past tense when speaking of her mother.

'She's dead,' Hannah said baldly, and was gratified when he winced. 'She's been dead for almost four years, but a fat lot you cared.'

'I . . .' he began and then stopped. He could not deny his callous treatment of Rebecca, and his defiant, stony-faced daughter, now standing before him, was living proof.

Put on the defensive, he said harshly, 'So, what do

273

you want now? To be welcomed into the bosom of my family, I suppose. Well, you can think again. My wife—'

'Ah yes, your wife. She seemed to suspect the truth very quickly, didn't she? And I've just seen your children.' Hannah put her head on one side, regarding him with calculated impudence. 'I think she saw the likeness between me and your daughter. Your *other* daughter.'

He stared at her. 'You're out to make trouble, I can see that.'

But Hannah shook her head. 'No, I'm not and – you probably won't believe me – but if I'd known that I would run into your wife and that she would see the likeness, I wouldn't have come here. Really I wouldn't.'

'So – why did you come?'

'I need a job. That's all I want from you – a job. Nothing more. Except maybe—'

'Ah – I thought there would be more.'

'Except maybe a job for a friend of mine. A girl called Nell. We've both worked at—' She had been about to state the name of Wyedale Mill, but then something held her back. Maybe he knew the Critchlows. Maybe in his anxiety to be rid of her, he would send word to Mr Edmund.

'In a cotton mill,' she went on. 'I'm sure the work can't be so very different.'

'You expect me to give you a job in my mill?' His tone was incredulous. 'And have all the workers gossiping. Have you any idea what you're asking?'

'Yes. I'm asking you to make up for getting my mother pregnant when you were already married. For not marrying her when you could've done. For letting her – and me – be sent into the workhouse without lifting a finger to help us. For letting her die there.'

James flinched and glanced away. 'Well,' he said gruffly, 'when you put it like that, I suppose I do owe you something.' For a moment, he was thoughtful. 'I'll see what I can do. It won't be at my mill. I can't have that. But I do have contacts at other mills in the town. I'll ask around.'

'Thank you. And don't forget – something for my friend too.'

He stared at her. 'By, you're a feisty little thing, aren't you?'

'I've had to be,' she told him grimly, and James Gregory had the grace to look ashamed.

'So – how did you get on?' Bessie was anxious to know. 'Tell me all about it.'

So Hannah told her it all in detail. 'And his little girl. She's the image of me. Can you believe that?'

'Aye well, it happens, love. I've known cousins – and distant cousins at that – be like two peas from the same pod.'

'I asked him to get Nell a job an' all.' Hannah bit her lip and looked at Bessie worriedly. 'Do you think I should've done that? D'you think I've pushed me luck?'

'Nah, love. It's no more than he owes you. You could have demanded a lot more. Just mind you stick to your side of the bargain, though. Once you get your job – and one for Nell – you keep right away from him and his family.'

'Oh, I will. There's nothing more I want from him,' Hannah declared stoutly. But deep in her heart, she knew that there was. She wanted him to be a father to her. A real father. But, young though she still was, life's knocks had put an old head on her shoulders. Hannah knew that her dearest wish could never be.

Smiling bravely so that this kindly woman would not guess her heartache, Hannah asked, 'So, when can we fetch Nell and her little boy?'

Bessie beamed. 'How about right now?'

Twenty-Nine

'Do we have to pay anything to get them out, Hannah, 'cos I haven't any money?'

It was the only thing worrying Bessie. As far as having them come to live with her, she couldn't wait. Especially having a little one running around again. Children had been her life and she missed them dreadfully. To Bessie, life had no meaning without a child about the house.

'I don't know,' Hannah said. 'Goodbody's a grasping devil. I think there was some sort of "arrangement" between him and the Critchlows – if you know what I mean.'

'I can guess,' Bessie said grimly, as she rammed her Sunday-best hat on her head and stuck a hat pin in it to hold it firm. She squared her shoulders as if ready to do battle – as indeed she was. 'Right then, I'll be off.'

Hannah hugged her. 'Oh, Auntie Bessie, you don't know how much this means to me. Nell was so good to me – to us – when we first arrived at the mill. I do so want to help her now. I only wish I could come with you, but I daren't. I just daren't. If Goodbody was to recognize me—'

'No, no, love. You stay here. I'll do my best.'

'I know you will.'

*

After Bessie had left, Hannah roamed around the house, once more restless with anxiety. In her mind, she travelled every step of the way with Bessie. She imagined entering the gates of the workhouse and being met by an unhelpful and belligerent master. She could see him shaking his head and ordering Bessie off the premises. Already she could see Bessie trudging home alone, defeated and dispirited. But Hannah's imagination was running riot and Bessie was faring better than the girl feared. Getting Nell and her son out of the workhouse was easier than either of them had anticipated.

Bessie's determination carried her all the way to the back gate of the building where she demanded admittance. 'You again!' the porter greeted her. 'Taken a liking to this place, 'ave yer?'

Bessie's answer was a derisive snort. 'Not likely. I ain't coming in, if that's what you're thinking. I've come to get someone out.'

The old man laughed. He still had enough spirit to joke with her. 'Aw, teken a fancy to me, 'ave yer? Come to tek me home with yer?'

Bessie smiled. 'I wish I could, love. I wish I was a millionaire and could tek the lot of you in here home with me. 'Cos if I could – I would.'

The porter's face softened, his expression wistful. 'Know what, missis. I believe yer.' He sniffed, drew the back of his hand across his face and said, 'So, how can I help you? 'Cos if you're fetching just one poor sod out of this place, I'll help you in any way I can.'

'It's two. At least, I hope so. A girl called Nell and her little boy.'

The man's face brightened even more. 'Aw, that's grand. She's a lovely lass and he's a grand little babby.

Shouldn't be in here. Shouldn't have been born in here. No one should.' He sighed. 'But there, that's how it is. Poor girl got taken in by some bastard, I suppose, who didn't want to know?'

'That's about the size of it,' Bessie murmured.

'Well, you're a good 'un to take 'em on.' He nodded at her. 'Relation of yours, is she?'

Bessie shook her head and pressed her lips together. She was on the point of telling him everything, all about Hannah and Nell and even about the master and mistress of this place, but it wouldn't do. Instead, she smiled. 'But I'm hoping we'll be like family.'

'She's a lucky lass,' he said gruffly. 'I hope she's properly grateful to you.'

Now Bessie said nothing. She didn't know Nell, didn't really know how they'd all get along together. But she was fond of Hannah, very fond, and she was doing this for her.

'Right then, I'll take you across to see the master.'

Bessie followed him as he hobbled painfully across the yard, into the back door of the building and through what seemed like a maze of dark passages until they came to a door. The porter raised his hand and knocked sharply. On being bidden to enter, he opened the door and poked his head around it.

'Someone to see you,' he said curtly. Bessie could tell at once that there was no love lost between this man and the master of the workhouse.

'Show them in then, man,' Bessie heard the thin, high-pitched voice demand from beyond the door.

Bessie stepped forward, nodding her thanks to the porter as she passed into the room. As she heard the door close behind her, she moved towards the desk. Sitting behind it, crouched over papers spread out upon its battered surface, was the man Hannah had described to her. Thin, hunch-backed with a rat-like face, beady eyes and a sharp nose. This was Cedric Goodbody.

Bessie licked her lips. 'Good morning, Mr Goodbody.'

The man grunted, pulled a blank piece of paper towards him and reached for a pen.

'Another mouth to feed,' he muttered. 'Name?'

'Mrs Elizabeth Morgan,' she said and he began to write.

'Age?'

'Why do you need to know that?'

He looked up and smirked. 'You drop your pride at the door when you come in here. Age?'

'But I'm not coming in here. I've come to get someone out.'

The man's eyes glinted. 'Have you indeed? And who might that be?'

'Nell Hudson and her son.'

A strange look crossed the man's face. 'Have you indeed?' he said again, but there was a different intonation in his voice now: surprise and a curious kind of wariness, as if he'd never expected anyone coming to ask for Nell Hudson.

He cleared his throat, dipped the pen into the ink once more and said, 'Well, I'll still need to ask you a few questions. Er-hem – for the information of the guardians, you understand.'

That's a lie for a start, Bessie thought, but she held her tongue and merely nodded.

'Where will the girl and her child be living?'

'Here in Macclesfield.'

'Can you support her?'

Now it was Bessie's turn to lie. 'Yes.'

He eyed her keenly. 'You have a husband? A man to support you?'

Now she couldn't lie. 'No, but I work.'

'Oh yes. Where?'

Again, she felt unable to lie. 'At home. I take in washing.'

The man's thin lips curled.

'And . . . and I have a lodger. She works and . . . and she's found a job for Nell an' all.'

'Ah, now that does throw a different light on the matter.'

Cedric bowed his head for a few moments. He was in a quandary. Nell Hudson had been orphaned and brought to the workhouse at the age of eighteen months. At ten she had been dispatched to the Critchlows' mill, but had recently been sent back to the workhouse when she had become pregnant. Though he had never been told officially, he suspected that Edmund Critchlow was the child's father. Nell had been the second girl to be returned to the workhouse from Wyedale Mill, heavy with child and calling Edmund Critchlow all the filthy names she could lay her tongue to. But Cedric Goodbody was beholden to the Critchlows. He'd taken the girls back into the workhouse and held his tongue, silenced by a nice little sum that passed each time from Edmund Critchlow into Cedric's bony hands.

'And you make sure they stay there,' Edmund had warned. 'It'll be the worse for you, Goodbody, if I ever set eyes on them again.'

Now Cedric raised his beady eyes and glared at Bessie. 'And where is she going to work?'

Bessie swallowed. Her throat was painfully dry. All this lying was hard work. 'At the mill.'

'What mill?' Goodbody snapped.

'One of the silk mills.'

'Here? In Macclesfield?'

When she nodded, he seemed to relax a little, though a deep frown still rutted his forehead. At last, after several moments of deep thought, which seemed an age to the waiting Bessie, he said, 'Very well, then. I will release her into your care. But you'll have to sign a paper that you take full responsibility for her.'

Now it was Bessie's turn to be anxious about what she was taking on. Then she shrugged her shoulders. Oh well, what did it matter. She'd been heading for the workhouse in her old age anyway before Hannah had appeared. If they all ended up in here, so what? It was no more, no less than she'd expected would happen one day. And in the meantime, well, she'd have a family of sorts to care for again.

That, more than anything, was worth the risk.

'Where do I sign?' She beamed at him.

'But I don't know who you are.' Nell's eyes were wide with fear. Much as she wanted to get out of the workhouse, this was like taking a blind leap off a mountain into the unknown. 'You . . . you could be anybody.'

Bessie chuckled, not in the least insulted by the girl's misgivings. She'd feel exactly the same in Nell's shoes. 'You'll just have to trust me, love, that's all. There's a home and a job waiting for you. Tek it or leave it,' she added, hoping that the girl wouldn't take her at her word and refuse to go with her. She couldn't explain it all, for Goodbody was still in the room. And even if he hadn't been, walls had ears as far as Bessie was concerned. She'd no intention of so much as mentioning Hannah's name until they were well clear of this place.

But Nell was still hesitating and Bessie began to grow a little impatient. She'd've thought the girl would have jumped at the chance to get out of the workhouse. She knew she would've done.

Then suddenly, Nell said, 'Wait a minute. I've seen you before. You came here the other day—'

Bessie gave a little shake of her head, trying to warn the girl to say no more. Swiftly, she interrupted. 'No, no, that wasn't me. Never been here before in me life, and I'd rather not have to come again, if it's all the same to you.'

'Oh,' Nell murmured, still staring at her. 'I was sure . . .' Then she shrugged. 'I must have got it wrong.' There was a pause before Nell went on, 'But why me? You don't know me. Why do you want to help *me*?'

'Well – er – see, it's like this. Me own family's all gone. Left the nest. And I'm all on me own.' It was the truth but not the whole truth.

Nell was still suspicious. 'Last time I left here, I thought I was going to be set up for life. Going to be well looked after in a good job. And look where that got me. Back here in a few years and ruined. Oh aye, ruined. I love me little baby, I won't let anyone say I don't, but I'd've sooner he'd never been born than end up in here.' She thrust her face close to Bessie's. 'Has Edmund Critchlow sent you? Is there a gang of thugs waiting for me outside to make sure I'm put out of harm's way for good? Me and little Tommy?'

Bessie was appalled. 'No, love. I promise you. Nothing like that.' She bit her lip. This girl wasn't

283

about to go willingly with her unless Bessie confided a bit more. But how could she with Cedric Goodbody's ears flapping? She touched the girl's arm. 'Look, you'll just have to trust me, that's all I can say.'

Nell glanced at Goodbody. 'Can I leave Tommy here whilst I go and see what this is all about? Can I come back for him?'

Cedric hesitated. He wanted the girl gone. In fact he couldn't understand what was holding her back. For a young 'un, she had a very suspicious mind. But he could see that for two pins she'd refuse this woman's offer. Cedric couldn't care less what was going to happen to her or her bastard. He just wanted them both out of here so that when he reported the fact to the guardians that there were two fewer mouths to feed he would receive their smiling approbation. And maybe that approbation would take the form of a monetary bonus. It had in the past.

He smiled thinly, but there was no warmth in his eyes, only swift, self-interested calculation. 'Of course, my dear. Very sensible of you. You go with this – er – lady and see what she's offering. Then, if all is well, come back and fetch your little one.' If she didn't come back, he was thinking, even if she left the boy here, at least it was one gone. And the baby would probably soon pine away without his mother.

'Right, I will.' Nell turned to Bessie. There was still wariness in her eyes as she said, 'Let's be seeing what this is all about then.'

They walked outside into the yard and then, with a cheery wave to the porter, they were outside the gate and walking down the path. Nell was nervous, glancing anxiously about her, and when Bessie took hold of her arm, the girl actually flinched with fear. 'It's all right, love. Honestly, it is. Just a few more yards away from this place and I'll explain it all.'

'Explain?' Nell came to a halt, wrenching her arm out of Bessie's grasp. 'I knew it. There is more to this than you've said. I knew this sort of luck doesn't happen to someone like me.' There were tears in her eyes. She'd dared to hope. How foolish she'd been.

Bessie leaned close, keeping her voice low. 'D'you remember someone called Hannah at the mill?'

'Hannah?'

'Shh, keep your voice down,' Bessie hissed, glancing nervously up at the high windows.

Nell lowered her voice. 'Of course I remember Hannah.'

'Well, let's just keep walking and I'll tell you.'

Still a little reluctantly, but now with increasing curiosity, Nell fell into step beside Bessie.

'Hannah and her mother used to live next door to me,' Bessie began. 'Years ago, before they came into the workhouse.' Her face fell into sad lines. 'I only wished I could've prevented that, but I had all me own brood at home. I couldn't.'

Nell said nothing, so Bessie continued. 'I didn't know what'd happened to them. Hannah and her mother. I didn't know Hannah'd been sent away to that mill in Derbyshire. I didn't know Rebecca – her mother – had died in the workhouse. I knew nothing at all until Hannah turned up on my doorstep.'

Again Nell stopped and turned to face Bessie. 'Hannah? Hannah's here? In Macclesfield?'

Now Bessie stopped too and turned to face the girl. Smiling, she nodded, 'Yes, and waiting like a cat on hot bricks at my house. It's her you've got to thank, love. Soon as I said I'd seen a girl called Nell here – and yes, it was me that came the other day.'

'I thought it was. I thought I wasn't losing me marbles already. Mind you,' she added tartly, 'that place is enough to make you.'

'I came to ask about poor Rebecca for Hannah. She wanted to know. And when I got back home, I said I'd seen you. Spoken to a girl called Nell, I told her. Well, you should've seen her face. A picture, it was. "Oh, I've got to get her out of there, Auntie Bessie," she said at once. "I've just got to."' Bessie smiled gently at the girl. 'She said you were so good to her at the mill. She's not forgotten that.'

'So is it Hannah who's fetching me out?'

'That's it.' Swiftly, Bessie went on to tell Nell all that had passed between her and Hannah, all the plans they had. 'Hopefully, she'll've got a job for you an' all, but I had to lie through me teeth in front of old Goodbody there. I didn't want him finding out about Hannah. We're not sure what he'd do if he found out she'd run away from the Critchlows.'

Tears were in Nell's eyes. 'Oh, how good, how kind of her. But,' she shook her head and the tears flooded down her cheeks, 'but I can't. I can't come. Tell her I'm grateful. Ever so grateful. I'll never forget what she tried to do for me. And her secret's safe with me. Tell her that. Be sure to tell her that. I won't give her away to Goodbody.'

Bessie stared at the girl in disbelief. 'But why? Why won't you come?'

Nell shook her head. 'Tommy. My baby. I couldn't leave him behind.'

Bessie stared at her for a moment and then she

threw back her head and laughed aloud. 'Aw, love, we wouldn't expect you to do that. We wouldn't want you to do that. Of course, Tommy's to come an' all.' She threw her arms wide and enfolded the girl whilst Nell sobbed against her shoulder. But now her tears were of happiness and relief.

And there were yet more tears when they turned into the street and saw Hannah waiting outside Bessie's front door.

'Hannah, oh, Hannah,' Nell cried, and began to run.

'Nell!' Hannah spread her arms wide and ran towards her friend. They met and hugged each other, dancing and swinging each other round in sheer joy, whilst Bessie waddled down the street towards them, beaming from ear to ear.

Thirty

Two hours later, Nell had fetched her son from the matron's care and, together with their few belongings, they were installed in Bessie's second best bedroom. Hannah was to have the tiny boxroom next to it.

'It doesn't seem fair, us taking this room and you crammed into there,' Nell said.

'It's all I need,' Hannah reassured her, hugging her swiftly. 'It's so lovely to have you both here. I don't care where I sleep. Besides, you and Tommy are having to share.'

'Do you think I mind that? I've been separated from him ever since he was born. I'm not going to let him out of my sight now.'

'Oh er – well, I know how you feel, but we'll both have to work.'

Nell laughed. 'Oh yes, but you know what I mean.'

Hannah smiled with relief. For a moment she had thought that Nell had meant it literally.

They waited impatiently for two days but no word came from James Gregory.

'I'll just have to go and see him again,' Hannah said.

'Give him time, love,' Bessie said. She refused to worry. She was happier than she'd been for years. A lot of laundry work had come her way again in the last two days and now she had two strong lasses to help her, it was done in half the time.

'It's the fetching and taking back I can't do. All the walking. Me legs are getting bad.'

'Well, me an' Tommy can do that,' Nell offered. 'The fresh air'll do him the world of good.' The smile that hardly left her face now broadened. 'He's never seen the outside world much. High time he did.' She glanced from Hannah to Bessie and back again. Her face sobered. 'I can't tell you what this means to me, you know. I'll never, ever be able to repay your kindness.'

'No need, love,' Bessie said. 'You two have made my life worth living again. It's me should be thanking you both.' Her eyes softened as she glanced down at Tommy lying kicking on the hearthrug. 'And that little man there.'

'And it's me who should be thanking both of you. Nell was like my guardian angel when we first arrived at the mill. Showed me the ropes. And now you, Auntie Bessie, taking in a waif and stray. How can *I* thank *you?*'

The three of them clutched at each other, laughing together.

'Now then,' Bessie said at last, wiping the tears of laughter from her eyes. Oh, how good it was to laugh again and to have someone to laugh with her. She'd always loved the company of young people; preferred it to the likes of Flo Harris any day. And these two lasses were as bright as buttons and sharp as a packet of needles. 'I'd best get started else Mrs Montgomery won't get her washing delivered back by tonight and she's a tartar an' no mistake.'

'Right, I'll get the copper going,' Hannah volunteered and Nell said, 'I'll clear away the breakfast things and then I'll help.'

About mid-morning the door from the passageway into Bessie's back yard opened and a grubby urchin poked his head round it. 'A' you Hannah?'

Nell, pegging washing onto the lines stretched across the yard and with her mouth full of pegs, flicked her head towards the wash house.

The lad grinned and, weaving his way through the wet clothes, stood in the doorway and repeated his question.

Hannah, elbow deep in soap suds, glanced up. 'Yes.'

'Message from the mister.'

Hannah paled and her heart thudded. 'The . . . the master?' Her first thought was that Cedric Goodbody had found out that she was back here, but as the boy spoke again her heart slowed in relief and colour flooded back into her face. 'Yeah, the master. Mr Gregory. He's sent word you're to go to see a Mr Boardman at the mill in Brown Street. There might be a job going there for you.'

Hannah smiled. 'Thanks.'

'And there was summat else.' The boy frowned, trying to recall the rest of the message. 'Oh aye. Your friend is to go to the house. His house. Not you, he said, just your friend.'

'Nell?'

The boy shrugged. ''Ee didn't say her name.'

'No,' Hannah said slowly and thoughtfully. 'No, I don't think I told him it.' Then she roused herself from her wandering thoughts enough to say, 'Thanks for coming.' She paused, taking in the boy's skinny legs and thin wrists, the grubby bare feet. She smiled. 'Would you like a bowl of soup?'

The child's eyes widened. 'Ooh ta, miss.'

Hannah dried her hands on a rough piece of cloth and led him towards the back door of the house and into the kitchen. Nell followed them in as Hannah led the boy to the table, her hand resting on his shoulder. 'This young man's earned himself a bowl of soup, Auntie Bessie. He's brought us some good news. I'm to go to the mill just round the corner and you, Nell, are to go to my – to Mr Gregory's house.'

'His house? Why to his house?'

They all looked towards the boy, but he was now so intent upon slurping the soup into his mouth that he didn't even notice them looking at him.

'I don't think he knows,' Hannah murmured. 'But Mr Gregory's made it clear that I'm not to set foot near his house again.'

There was no mistaking the edge of bitterness in Hannah's tone.

Mr Boardman, the supervisor, turned out to be a tubby, jovial man.

'Worked in a cotton mill 'afore, I hear. Where was that, then?'

Hannah bit her lip. She was sure the man was just asking out of interest, to find out what her previous experience was. So, she answered swiftly. 'A mill in Derbyshire. I don't expect you know it.' She rushed on, telling him about all the jobs she had done, not giving him time to ask for the actual name of the place. 'I was a scutcher, then a piecer and a bobbin winder for a short while. The last job I had there was as a throstle spinner.' As she rattled on, he nodded, seeming pleased with her knowledge and the skills she'd learned. At last he said, 'Well, Mr Gregory has vouched for you. Says he'd employ you himself, but he's no vacancies at the minute and you need a job now.'

Hannah nodded. 'If you please, sir.'

'Right then. I'll take you on a month's trial and see how you go, eh? You'll be winding the skeins of silk onto bobbins.' He told her the wage and all the rules and conditions. 'And you can start tomorrow morning. How about that?'

'Thank you, sir. Thank you very much.'

For the first time in months, Hannah sang out loud as she hurried home to share her good news with the two most important people in her new life – three if you counted little Tommy.

But there was still one person she would never forget. The memories of Luke were locked away deep in her heart: poignant, heart-wrenching memories of a tender, innocent love that had never been given the chance to blossom. Cruelly cut down by a tyrant. And she could never forget him either. One day, she promised, her vow burning as strongly as ever. One day, I'll have my revenge on you, Edmund Critchlow.

'So, what did he want? What did he say to you? Why did he want you up at the house instead of at his mill?'

Hannah's questions tumbled over each other as Nell stepped in the back door.

'Hey, give me a minute to catch me breath,' Nell laughed, but her eyes were sparkling.

Hannah grinned and pulled a wry face. 'Sorry, but I can hardly wait to hear all about it.'

'I gathered that,' Nell teased.

'Here's a cup of tea, love. Special treat.' Bessie was no less anxious to hear about it all than Hannah but her approach was more patient. 'Tommy's fine. He's having his afternoon nap upstairs.'

They sat around the table, waiting whilst Nell had taken a sip of her tea.

'Do you know,' she began, surprise in her voice as she glanced at Hannah, 'he's quite nice?' Hannah smiled thinly but said nothing. 'I'd expected someone like Mr Edmund, but he wasn't a bit like that.' She nodded at Hannah. 'But no wonder he doesn't want you up there – at the house. You can see in a minute that you're his daughter. You've got his hair and his eyes, haven't you?'

Now Hannah nodded and said huskily, 'And did you see his little girl?'

Nell shook her head.

'She's about three or four and she looks just like me. I'm sure his wife saw it too. Anyway, what did he say? Is he giving you a job at his mill?'

'No, he's no jobs going there at the minute. But . . .' Nell paused dramatically, 'He's offered me a job as nanny to the children.'

Hannah's mouth fell open and Bessie murmured, 'Well, I never.'

'But – but – I thought – I mean,' Hannah spluttered, 'I thought he didn't want us anywhere near his house?'

Nell touched her hand and said gently, 'It's you he doesn't want there, not me.'

'But surely, you'll remind him – and her – of me.'

'Ah, now,' Nell glanced away, suddenly embarrassed. 'Well . . .' She paused, not knowing quite how to put the next bit.

'Go on,' Hannah prompted.

'I'm sworn to secrecy. I'm not to let on that I've anything to do with you, that I even know you. And I'm sorry, Hannah, but you must never visit me there or try to contact him again in any way.'

The look on Hannah's face was bleak. If she'd secretly hoped for any kind of relationship with her father, then those dreams were dashed.

'He did say one thing though.'

'Go on,' Hannah muttered through gritted teeth. She was trying desperately not to let the tears that were welling up behind her eyes come spilling out.

'He said, "The reason I'm offering you this job is . . ." now what word did he use? Ah yes, "twofold". Yes, that was it. That's what he said. "The reason I'm offering you this job is twofold." '

'What on earth does that mean?' Hannah cried.

'Means he's got two reasons,' Bessie put in. 'Go on, Nell.'

' "My wife," he said, "can be a bit difficult to work for. And the two children aren't easy. We've had more nannies than I've got workers in the mill." ' The three of them smiled thinly at his wry witticism, then Hannah's smile faded. 'Oh, Nell, you don't want to be working for someone like that.'

'Wait a minute, wait till I've finished telling you. You see, the other reason was that he said it would be a link between you and him. "If ever she needs anything," he said, "you'll be able to let me know." '

Hannah stared at her. 'He never said that.'

For a moment, Nell looked hurt that her friend

294

could think that she would lie to her. But then, she imagined herself in Hannah's place. The girl's father had never shown the slightest interest in her, had deserted her mother and left them to fend for themselves, had never lifted a finger to help them in their direst need. And even when they'd finally met a few days ago, he'd forbidden her to try to see him again. Why, then, should she believe that he'd had a change of heart? No, she wouldn't have believed it either. So she said gently, 'That's what he said, Hannah. I wouldn't lie to you.'

Now Hannah was contrite. 'Oh no, no, I'm sorry. I shouldn't have said that. It . . . it just came out because . . . because I couldn't believe it.'

'Mebbe when he saw you, love, he had a change of heart,' Bessie suggested softly.

'Huh! It was a big one then, 'cos the other day he didn't want to see hide nor hair of me ever again.'

'Well, that's what he said, Hannah, I promise you.'

Hannah was torn now. 'But I still don't like the thought of you working for a tartar just so that I've got a link with my father. I'd sooner you got a job alongside me at the mill.'

'Wait a bit. There's more.'

'More? Go on, then.'

'I was honest with him. I didn't think there was much point in being anything else. I told him I'd got a little boy and he said that would be fine. I could take him with me sometimes if I wanted.'

'By heck,' Bessie blurted out. 'They must be desperate for a nanny if he offered that. But you know you can leave him with me, love. You don't need to take him there unless you want to.' Suddenly, her face fell. 'Oh – you mean, they want you to live in?'

'Not exactly. I'll be given a room of my own there – and a bed in it for Tommy too – and they might want me to stay so many nights of the week, two or three maybe.'

Bessie was struggling with her feelings. It was like being desperately thirsty and being handed a cup of water only to have it snatched away again before being able to take even a sip. Yet she couldn't stand in the girl's way and little Tommy would live in the lap of luxury compared to her humble home.

She felt Nell's touch. 'I'm not going to live in, Auntie Bessie. I don't want to. She'd have me at her beck and call all day and all night too. And I don't want Tommy learning those kids' bad ways, 'cos they must have got a few if they can't keep a nanny for long.'

'Are you sure, Nell? I mean it'd be much better for you both living in a nice house.'

'Maybe,' Nell agreed. 'But there'd be no laughter, no fun – and no love.'

Bessie was thoughtful for a moment. 'Have you thought, Nell, that that's probably what those kiddies need? A bit of love? Children are sometimes naughty just because they want someone to take a bit of notice of 'em.'

Hannah and Nell glanced at Bessie and then at each other.

'You know, she could be right, Nell. Folk like them don't have much to do with their children. Look how the Critchlows sent Adam away to school. He was hardly ever at home, now was he?'

Bessie gave a snort of laughter. 'Well, Jimmy Gregory wasn't born into that sort of class, but I expect he thinks he's one of them now.'

296

'Yes,' Hannah said slowly. 'I expect he does.'

'Well, I'm going to give it a go,' Nell said. 'If it doesn't work out, I can always leave. One more to add to the long list of nannies who didn't stay long. I'll tell you one thing though,' she ended as, hearing Tommy's cries from the bedroom, she levered herself up from the stool to go to him. 'I shan't stand any nonsense from the kids – or from Lady Muck, whoever she thinks she is.'

Thirty-One

The sight of a policeman knocking at one of the doors in Paradise Street was unusual on a Sunday afternoon. Though it was not one of the wealthier streets in the town, the residents were, in the main, God-fearing and law-abiding. A wayward youngster was dealt a cuff around the ear by his father or a neighbour – or even the local peeler on the beat – and no ill-feeling resulted. The community watched out for each other, helped one other, laughed, quarrelled and made up to laugh together again. But when a young constable was seen visiting Bessie's house, that was cause for Flo's curtains to twitch and the tongues to wag.

'Come away in, lad,' Bessie welcomed, and ushered Jim into the kitchen where the two girls were sewing. Little Tommy was lying on the hearthrug, looking about him and gurgling with glee.

'I was just passing.' Jim smiled, tucking his hat under his arm. 'Constable Robinson put me on this beat special-like, so's I could call in and see how you are.'

Hannah threw her sewing aside and jumped up to pull out a chair for him. 'Oh, how kind of you – and Mr Robinson. I'm fine. I've got a job at one of the mills. Been there for two months now. And this is my friend, Nell, and her little boy, Tommy. They've come to live here as well. Nell's got a job as a nanny.'

'Sit down, lad, sit down,' Bessie waved him into the

chair. 'Now, I don't 'spect your superior would mind if you had a cuppa with us, would he?'

Jim grinned. 'Not if he doesn't know, missis.' And they all laughed.

He laid his hat on the table and squatted down to Tommy to tickle his tummy. 'You're a grand little chap, aren't you?'

Tommy looked up at the tall man, startled for a moment. His baby round chin trembled and he screwed up his eyes, about to cry.

'Aw, I'm sorry. I must've frightened him. Must be the uniform. I'm usually quite good with little ones. Got nephews and nieces of me own.' He stood up and backed away, but continued to smile down at the little boy.

Nell picked Tommy up and held him against her shoulder, patting his back comfortingly.

'It's not your fault. He's not used to men, see. In the workhouse, we were segregated. He's only been around women, really.'

The smile faded from Jim's face to be replaced by a look, not of disgust or censure, but of concern. He sat down in the chair Hannah had pulled out for him. 'I'm sorry to hear you was in there. Very long, was it?'

Nell pressed her lips together. 'Since just before Tommy was born.' Tears hovered in her eyes but she smiled at Hannah. 'But thanks to my friend here – and Mrs Morgan – we're out. And,' she said firmly, 'I mean to stay out. I don't want my son growing up in that place.'

The household soon settled into a happy routine. Hannah loved her job at the mill. The other workers there were friendly and helpful and she soon fitted in. And the conditions were much pleasanter than in the cotton mill. No fluff or dust floated in the air and Hannah revelled in the sight and the touch of the silk.

'It's so shiny and all the pretty colours they dye it,' she enthused to Bessie and Nell. Bessie nodded and smiled sadly. She fondly remembered watching Bill in his garret working with the lovely yarn.

As for Nell, forthright, no nonsense Nell, she soon had the Gregory youngsters eating out of her hand.

'You were absolutely right, Auntie Bessie.' Already Bessie Morgan was 'Auntie' to Nell too, and to little Tommy she was 'Nanna'. 'Those poor kids,' Nell went on indignantly, 'are just starved of attention. That's all they need. Mind you, this job's not long term anyway. They've hired a tutor for the little boy for two years and then he's going away to boarding school when he's seven.' Her eyes darkened. 'Fancy choosing to be separated from your kids. I can't believe it. They don't know how lucky they are.'

'But there'll still be the little girl to look after,' Bessie put in, trying not to get her hopes up that Nell and Tommy would be coming back to live all the time with her.

'Not really, 'cos when the boy goes to school, they'll get a governess for the girl. Madam told me so.' She laughed. 'That's what I have to call her – "Madam". And she can be a right "madam" an' all. Mind you, I don't stand no nonsense from her. I tell her exactly what I think. She keeps asking me to go and live there full time, but I keep giving her the same answer. I'll stay there some nights but I want to keep coming home.' She glanced at Bessie. ''Cos this *is* home to me an' our Tommy. I told her I don't want

him growing up thinking he's part of that household
– that he belongs there. It wouldn't do, wouldn't do
at all. Funny thing is, she seems to take it from me
whereas her poor lady's maid gets shrieked at from
morning till night. It's a wonder she doesn't up
sticks and leave. I reckon she would if she could get
another position. Trouble is, she doesn't get any
time to get out and look for another job. Madam
keeps her working day and night. She never seems
to get any time off. And the poor kid hasn't got the
guts to stand up to Mrs Gregory. She's a mousy
little thing – from the workhouse, so I suppose she's
used to taking orders and never thinks to answer
back.' She laughed. 'Not like us, eh Hannah? Old
Goodbody and his missis couldn't wait to ship us
out of the way, could they?' Her laughter died. 'But
I turned up again on their doorstep like a bad penny
and about to give birth. He wasn't best pleased, I
can tell you.'

Nell chattered on about her life with 'the upstarts',
as she referred to the Gregorys. 'She might've been
born to that life,' she would say, 'but he certainly
wasn't. He's no better than you and me, Hannah. He
was just lucky enough to be born good-looking.'

'Yes,' Hannah said bitterly. 'A curse on all good-
looking men.' And she knew that Nell was aware she
was including Edmund Critchlow. But then Nell coun-
tered her remark by saying softly, 'He asked after you
today. Mr Gregory. Asked if you were all right – if
there was anything you needed.'

Hannah stood up suddenly and turned away. 'What
did you tell him? It'd've been nice to've had a father
when I needed one. His concern comes a bit late in the
day.'

She left the kitchen, slamming the back door and leaving Nell staring sadly after her.

'He's here again,' Bessie called from the front doorstep as she saw Jim coming down the street. 'And on his day off, an' all, by the look of his clothes. That's not his uniform or I'm a Dutchman.'

Hannah poked her head out of the door, looking over Bessie's shoulder.

'This is the third time he's come.'

'I reckon he's got his eye on you.'

'Oh no, Auntie Bessie,' Hannah lowered her voice as the young man came closer. 'It's Nell. Haven't you noticed how he looks at her?' She raised her voice, 'Hello, Jim. She's not here. She's at work.'

There was no mistaking the faint flush that coloured his face nor the fleeting look of disappointment.

'You're right, Hannah,' Bessie muttered, but then raised her voice too. 'But we're glad to see you. Come away in.'

He stayed an hour, but Nell was still not home by the time he rose reluctantly and said, 'I'll have to go. I'm on duty at six.'

'Nell will be sorry to've missed you,' Hannah said archly.

'Come an' have your Sunday dinner with us tomorrow, lad,' Bessie invited. 'She'll be here then. It's her day off.'

'Mine too.' There was no denying the sparkle in his eyes. 'Do . . . do you think she'd go for a walk with me? See . . .' He was embarrassed now, but pressed on. 'See I've got something for her. A perambulator. The lady my mother cleans for has one to sell. It's a bit battered.' He smiled. 'It's been well used, but little Tommy must be getting heavy for her to carry far now. I thought it'd be just the thing for him.'

Bessie and Hannah glanced at each other. 'That's really thoughtful of you, lad, but I don't think we could afford—'

'Oh, it's a gift,' Jim interrupted swiftly. 'I want to get it for her.' The colour on his face deepened. 'Unless you think she'd be offended.'

'Offended?' Bessie laughed uproariously. 'When it's a gift for her little Tommy? Oh no, lad. You couldn't have thought of anything better,' she assured him, and the young man went away beaming.

'It can't be me he's coming to see, Hannah, it'll be you.' Nell, when they told her that evening of Jim's visit, was adamant. 'I'm not 'alf as pretty as you and besides, I'm a fallen woman.' She gazed down fondly at her child as if the thought didn't worry her too much now that she had him. But her tone was a little wistful as she added softly, 'No one'll want me now.'

'Well, you'll see for yourself tomorrow, love,' Bessie said, winking at Hannah. They hadn't told Nell of the gift Jim intended to bring. They wanted that to be a surprise – a surprise that, in their eyes, proved his growing fondness for Nell and – best of all – for her little boy too.

When a knock sounded on the door at eleven o'clock the following morning, Bessie shouted. 'Answer the door, Nell, will yer? I'm peeling the 'taters.' She was doing no such thing; both she and Hannah were hiding in the back scullery, stifling their laughter as they listened to Nell opening the door.

'Oh – hello, Jim.'

303

'Hello, Nell.'

There was silence whilst Bessie whispered impatiently, 'Get on with it then, lad,' to be shushed by Hannah.

They heard Jim speak again, nervously. 'Mrs Morgan – er – invited me for dinner.'

'So she said,' Nell answered. 'You'd best come in.'

'Well . . . um . . . I was wondering if – after dinner, like – you'd come out with me. For . . . for a walk?'

'Oh!'

Though they couldn't see her, Hannah and Bessie could imagine Nell's face growing pink.

'That's very kind of you,' they heard her say, 'but I couldn't leave Tommy. I only get to spend time with him on me day off and—'

'Oh, I meant Tommy too.'

'Oh . . . oh.' Now they could hear that Nell was truly flustered. 'But . . . but he's getting too heavy to carry very far.'

'That's why I've brought this.'

There was a pause and Hannah and Bessie held their breath. Then they heard Nell's gasp of delight. 'Oh, Jim. A baby carriage.'

'I've brought it for Tommy. To keep, I mean. It'd be so much easier for you when you take him to work than having to carry him. Oh, Nell, do say you're not angry or offended.'

'Come on.' Bessie gripped Hannah's arm. 'Time we lent the poor lad a hand.'

Together they stepped out of the scullery and into the kitchen.

'Now isn't that kind of you, Jim? Now bring it in. We'll make a space for it here in the kitchen and he can sit in it like the little lord he is.'

The perambulator was a box-like contraption sitting on two huge rear wheels and two smaller ones at the front, with two long curved handles to push it with. Nell still hadn't spoken, and Jim was eyeing her anxiously as he manoeuvred it in through the door and set it against the wall in the space that Bessie had already cleared.

'Oh, just look, a mattress and pillow and even blankets. Put him in it, Nell, do.'

Moments later, Tommy was lying in the pram looking very much at home and beaming up at the four grown-ups watching him.

'He likes it. What a grand present,' Bessie patted Jim on the shoulder. 'And you shall carve the joint of beef I've got in special.'

As Hannah and Bessie went back to the scullery, this time no longer pretending to prepare the meal, they glanced back to see Jim taking Nell's hands in his and she looking up into his eyes.

'Now mebbe she'll believe us,' Bessie said happily.

As she stood at the sink to peel the potatoes, Bessie began to sing, and just as so many years ago, Hannah joined in.

'Let all the world in every corner sing . . .'

Thirty-Two

'Oh, my lor'! What have you done to your hair?' Bessie threw her hands in the air as Nell stepped through the back door.

They'd been sharing the house now for a year. Hannah continued to be happy working at the silk mill, though, unlike her time at Wyedale Mill, her co-workers had not taken the place of her family. Home was now with Bessie, and Nell and Tommy when they were there. Those were the best times, when the door was closed, the curtains drawn against the world and there was just the four of them. Though more often than not, it was five, for Jim was now a regular visitor to the terraced house. He and Nell had been officially 'walking out' together for most of that time.

At Bessie's exclamation, Hannah straightened up from where she had been bending over the fire in the range. At the sight of her friend, she gave a little cry, but her surprise soon turned to admiration. 'Oh, Nell, it's lovely.'

'Lovely? Lovely, you say? I'll give her lovely,' Bessie was shouting and waving her arms about. 'Spoilt her pretty hair. She looks like a whore!'

There was a sudden stillness in the room as Bessie stared at Nell in horror and clapped her hand over her runaway mouth. But the sight of Bessie's horror-struck face was so comical that Nell, far from being offended, collapsed against the doorframe, laughing helplessly.

'If I look like one, then . . . then so does she,' she spluttered. 'So does his wife. Mrs Gregory.'

'Aw, I'm sorry, love.' Bessie was mortified. 'I shouldn't have said that. It's nowt to do wi' me. But . . . but I look on you – on both of you – like you was me own daughters.'

Hannah, recovering from the surprise, moved forward to examine Nell's hair that was now a bright shade of rich auburn that shone and glowed in the lamplight. Quite seriously, she said, 'It looks even better on you than on her. D'you know, I thought when I saw her that day, it didn't look quite natural. But it is a lovely colour.'

'I've been acting as her lady's maid for a few weeks,' Nell went on. 'That poor little creature finally plucked up enough courage to give in her notice. I hope she's found someone nicer to work for,' Nell murmured, sparing a thought for the young girl, who had suffered so under Mrs Gregory's sharp tongue. 'Anyway, madam wanted me to help her dye her hair one day and she suggested I should try it. You won't believe it, but she helped me do it. I've never like my mousy coloured hair, so I wasn't going to say no, was I? She seems to've taken a liking to me. She's given me some of the clothes her children have grown out of for Tommy. And they're hardly worn. He'll look a little prince in them. She's not so bad when you get to know her. D'you know, I think she's lonely. You'd think she'd have lots of friends, wouldn't you, but she doesn't seem to have any.'

'Maybe they think she married beneath her. The so-called gentry can be a snobby lot,' Hannah remarked.

She touched Nell's hair. It felt soft and silky. 'Well, I like it, Nell.'

She turned to Bessie, who had now sunk into a chair beside the table and dropped her head into her hands. Heaving sobs shook her shoulders. The two girls glanced at each other and then hurried to her, standing one on either side and bending over her. Tommy, who had come in with Nell, pushed his way between Hannah and the table to lay his head on Bessie's lap and clutch at her knees. 'Nanna, Nanna . . .' His chubby face threatened to dissolve into tears too.

'Auntie Bessie, don't take on so,' Nell tried to reassure her. 'I'm not offended, honestly I'm not. I'd sooner you told me the truth an' if that's what you think then . . .'

But Bessie was shaking her head violently. She sat up, dabbed her eyes with the corner of her apron and pulled the little boy onto her knee to cuddle him. 'There, there,' she crooned. 'It's only your old Nanna being silly.'

Hannah poured out a cup of tea and set it on the table. 'Here, drink this. You, too, Nell. Sit down, supper'll soon be ready.'

'I should explain,' Bessie said supping her tea.

'No need,' Nell said, patting her hair with pride. 'I'm taking no notice of you anyway.'

With that, they all laughed again, but Bessie couldn't let the matter rest there. 'No, no, I shouldn't have blurted it out. Not like that, but you see it – it reminded me . . .'

She glanced uncomfortably at Hannah, took a deep breath and said, 'I wasn't entirely truthful with you, love, when you first came back. Oh, I don't mean I lied to you, but . . . but I just didn't tell you everything about my own family.' She rested her cheek against the top of Tommy's dark head and closed her eyes. 'I was too ashamed,' she whispered.

'Ashamed? You, Auntie Bessie? Whatever do you mean?'

'Do you remember, when you first came back 'ere you was asking about all my family and what had happened to them and where they were?'

Hannah nodded.

'And I told you about our Peggy running off with a young lad, going to live with his family and that I hadn't heard anything about her from that day to this?'

'Yes,' Hannah whispered.

'Well, that was the bit that wasn't quite true. She did run off with him and she did move in with him, but only for a while.' She was silent for a long moment whilst Hannah and Nell waited. 'I . . . I saw her just the once about two years later, hanging around in a rough part of the town. I wasn't sure it was her at first, because . . . because she'd dyed her hair.' She glanced apologetically at Nell once again. 'That same colour.' Bessie paused again and then continued. 'I was just about to go up to her and say, "Come home, love, and we'll say no more about it," but . . . but just before I could, I saw her go up to this toff, smiling all coyly at him, bold as yer like. They spoke for a minute and then . . . then she put her arm through his and they . . . they went off together.' Bessie closed her eyes at the agony of her memory. 'I should have chased after her. Stopped her there and then. Dragged her home by her awful hair and locked her in. But I didn't. I couldn't take it in. Not then. And then it was too late. I couldn't find her again even though I tramped the streets for several nights looking for her. But do you know the worst thing?' Her voice fell to an unhappy whisper. 'I couldn't help thinking that I was glad my Bill wasn't alive to see what his daughter had become. Now how could I have thought such a thing? How *could* I have ever been glad he wasn't here any more?' Fresh tears flowed as she looked up again at Nell, seeking her understanding, her forgiveness. 'I'm sorry, love.'

Nell smiled a little pensively now. 'It's all right, Auntie Bessie.' She sighed heavily. 'Maybe I'm not much better. I'm a fallen woman, after all.'

'No, no, don't say that,' Hannah cried, putting her arms around her friend. 'I won't let you. You must have loved Mr Edmund and thought he loved you. Just like my mother believed Jimmy Gregory loved her.'

Nell laughed wryly. 'Aye, but I should've known better. I knew I wasn't the first, but you always think it'll be different for you. That they really love you, that you can change them. But you can't,' she added bitterly. Then raising her cup, she echoed Hannah's favourite saying. 'A curse on all good-looking men.'

'And does that include Jim?' Hannah put in slyly, her blue eyes sparkling with mischief.

'Oh, my goodness,' Bessie cried. 'Whatever will he say when he sees you?'

And with that, the three of them burst out laughing, with little Tommy chortling too – even though he didn't understand a word of what they'd been saying.

To Bessie's surprise, Jim was full of compliments for Nell's new hair colour. 'I like it,' he told her truthfully. 'It suits you.'

And though they all heard Bessie's disapproving sniff, this time she kept her lips firmly pressed together.

'You don't think I look like a . . .' Nell cast a wicked glance at Bessie. 'A lady of the night?'

'Wha—?' Jim's eyes widened and for a moment he looked angry. 'Well, if you do, then so do my mother and my sister, because their hair's that colour. Only difference is, they were born with it. All you've done is to give nature a helping hand.' His tone became firm, indignant. 'Don't ever say that about yourself again, you hear me?'

'Yes, Jim.' Nell lowered her head, hiding her bubbling laughter as she saw the consternation on Bessie's face.

And there the matter might have ended, if it hadn't been for Jim's final remark on the subject. 'It does make you look different. I almost didn't know you when you opened the door.' Then he touched her cheek with a gentle gesture. 'But you're still my Nell.'

Hannah stared at her friend, seeing her suddenly through the eyes of others. Yes, it had altered her. If someone who hadn't seen her for a few years met her now, would they even recognize her? Hannah wondered. And without her being conscious of it, the germ of an idea – a daring, dangerous idea – was implanted in Hannah's mind.

Thirty-Three

Hannah, Nell and Tommy had been living with Bessie for almost two years when Jim finally proposed to Nell.

'You're a lucky girl,' Bessie assured her. 'He's a fine young man and . . .' She had been about to say more, but bit her lip and looked away.

Gently, Nell added, 'And he's a good 'un to take me *and* Tommy on. Is that what you were going to say, Auntie Bessie?'

'Well . . .' the older woman was embarrassed, flustered now.

'But you're right,' Nell said. 'To take on Edmund Critchlow's bastard as his own takes a real man, a good man. I know that. And when we're married, he's going to adopt Tommy, all legal like, so that he'll have Jim's surname.'

'Aw, Nell, love. That's wonderful. Have you . . . have you . . . ?' Again Bessie's voice faltered. Whilst she was happy for the young couple and for the child, their marriage would take them away from her. She'd come to love them as her own, especially the little boy whose endearing ways had won her heart. It'd be another loss that would be hard to bear.

'In about a month's time. We thought on Tommy's second birthday in December. Just a quiet do. After all, I've no family and Jim's only got his mother and his sister and maybe his colleagues from the station.'

Bessie tried to smile, but she couldn't hide the bleak look in her eyes. But Nell was grinning broadly. 'Oh, you're not going to get rid of us that easy, if that's what you're hoping,' she teased, knowing full well Bessie was wishing for anything but that. She moved and put her arm around Bessie's ample shoulders and hugged her close. 'There's a house down the end of this very street to rent. It's belongs to a mill owner, of course, but the old lady who lived there's just died and—'

Bessie nodded. 'Oh yes, I know who you mean. But her son works in the garret, doesn't he? What's going to happen to him?'

'He's married and they live next door to his wife's parents.' Nell's eyes sparkled. 'Luckily for us, she doesn't want to move, so he can still go on renting the garret and we can live downstairs. Jim's sorted it all out with the mill owner and he's paid a month's rent up front and it's ours from the first of December. We'll be married on that very day. Just think,' she went on, her eyes sparkling. 'We'll be in our very own home for Christmas, and you and Hannah must spend Christmas Day with us.'

As Bessie opened her mouth to protest, Nell added, 'And we won't take "no" for an answer. So there!'

Bessie's face was a picture of happiness. 'Then I'll still see Tommy if you're only down the street. You'll still let him come and see me?'

Nell laughed. 'More than that. I was going to ask you if you'd look after him whilst I carry on working for a bit.'

Bessie's eyes widened. 'Jim doesn't mind you still going to the Gregorys?'

'Not if Mrs Gregory will let me go just daily.

Besides, it's not long now until the lad goes to school and they get a governess for the little girl. I always knew the job wouldn't last for ever. Mind you, madam asks me to do a lot more for her now. Says I have a way with clothes and such.' She touched her hair a little self-consciously. 'So she might want me to continue as her lady's maid. The one she's got at the moment is less than useless – worse than the girl that was there. You should hear her shouting at her.' She laughed. 'But she never shouts at me.'

Listening to the conversation, Hannah pulled a face. 'She wouldn't dare!'

Nell had the grace to nod and say, 'That's true, 'cos I'd only shout back and walk out, and one thing she can't abide is having to look after the kids herself.'

Bessie gave a snort of disapproval. 'Some women don't know when they're well off. She doesn't know how lucky she is.'

Nell's face was sober. 'They tried to take Tommy away from me, y'know.' Hannah and Bessie stared at her. 'Told me it would be a lot better for him if I let some nice, well-to-do family adopt him. That he'd have a much better chance in life than being brought up in the workhouse.' Bessie and Hannah exchanged a glance but said nothing, allowing Nell to unburden a guilt that had lain heavily on her. 'Maybe I should've done.' She looked at the other two, tears in her eyes. 'Was I being selfish, hanging onto him?'

'No, no, you weren't,' Bessie was swift to reassure her. 'You have to do what you think best. A lot of girls in your position would've let him go and who's to say they weren't right?' Her mouth tightened. 'A lot of 'em are forced into it, either by their families or by the authorities. They don't want to give up their babies, but they're left with no choice. In fact, they're not *given* the choice.'

'I know,' Nell nodded. 'There was one poor girl in there who was desperate to keep her baby, no matter what, but they actually snatched him out of her arms and carried him off to give to some well-off pair.'

'Huh!' Hannah said bitterly. 'Another of Goodbody's schemes. I dare bet he was paid handsomely.' She glanced at Nell. 'How come he let you keep Tommy then?'

Nell smiled sheepishly. 'He knew who the father was. It was Edmund Critchlow had me sent back to the workhouse when I told him I was carrying his child. I think Goodbody was a bit unsure what to do to be right. Whatever he did could've put him on the wrong side of Edmund. So he chose to let sleeping dogs lie. He did nothing. Oh, he tried to persuade *me* to give Tommy away, but no, he didn't force me.'

'Well, you've turned out lucky, Nell. You've found a good man who'll love you *and* your son.'

'Yes, yes, I have,' Nell said, 'But I'd never've had the chance to meet him if it hadn't been for you and Hannah getting me out of that place.' Her voice was soft with love and gratitude not only for Jim, but for Bessie and Hannah too.

'Oh, go on with you.' Bessie flapped her away, pretending embarrassment, but secretly she was heartwarmed. Then, playfully, she wagged her forefinger at the girl. 'Just so long as you don't ever take little Tommy away from me.'

*

315

Nell's wedding was a quiet affair, but Bessie and Hannah had managed to scrape enough money together to give Nell a wedding breakfast at home, and to Nell's astonished delight, Mrs Gregory had given her one of her old dresses to turn into a grand wedding dress.

She and Hannah sat far into the night, cutting and fitting and stitching.

It was a merry party that returned to the house in Paradise Street, where Bessie and Hannah had put on a spread fit for a queen.

'Going to invite the neighbours in then, Bessie?' Flo Harris was hovering on the doorstep.

''Course we are,' Bessie said happily.

Flo sniffed. 'Thought the likes of us weren't welcome, seein' as how we didn't get an invite to attend the service.'

'You didn't need no invite if you'd wanted to come. Free entrance at the church,' Bessie retorted. Then she relented, adding, 'Oh, come on in, Flo and stop moaning for once in your life. And tell anyone else down the street, they're very welcome if they want to come in.'

'Ta, Bessie.' Flo smiled. 'I will.'

Half an hour later, it seemed as if half the street was crammed into Bessie's terraced house. But her neighbours came with whatever little gift they could spare: pots and pans, bed linen for the young couple's new home and all sorts of useful items. One old man, a widower, gave Nell an apron that had been his wife's. Handing it to her, he said, 'If you look after your man as well as my dear wife cared for me and our young 'uns, you'll not go far wrong, lass.'

With a lump in her throat, Nell kissed the old man's leathery cheek.

When they'd all eaten and drunk their fill and tottered back through the dusk to their own homes, there came a moment of awkwardness.

'Well, be off with you then, the pair of you,' Bessie said with brusque fondness. 'You can leave Tommy here for the night. He'll be all right with me 'n' Hannah. It won't be much of a honeymoon, but you ought to have your wedding night to yourselves.' She pulled the little lad onto her lap and cuddled him close. 'You'll be all right with your Nanna, won't you, my little man?'

The little boy, wearied by the day's excitement, put his thumb in his mouth, leaned against her and promptly fell asleep. The grown-ups chuckled softly and Jim, with a tender gesture, touched the boy's hair. 'That's good of you, Mrs Morgan. We'll fetch him in the morning.'

'No hurry,' Bessie said.

Nell laughed softly. 'For two pins I reckon she'd keep him.' Above the child's head Bessie and Nell exchanged a fond look. They both knew there was more than a mite of truth in Nell's teasing statement.

Jim put his arm around his bride's shoulders. 'Come on then, Mrs Smith. High time I carried you across that threshold.'

There were kisses and farewells all round and Nell joked, 'Anyone'd think we were emigrating to the other side of the world.' But even so, she gave Hannah an extra fond hug.

'Thanks, Hannah, for everything,' she whispered. 'But for you I'd still be locked up in that place.'

'And but for you,' Hannah murmured in return, 'I might not have survived those first few weeks at the mill, especially after Jane . . .'

'You would. You're a fighter. A survivor. Whatever you want in life, you'll get. Just be careful that you don't get hurt yourself, that's all.' She pulled back a little and looked into her friend's eyes. 'There's something still brewing in that head of yours. Something that one day you're going to do. I can see it. Sometimes you get this far away look in your eye and it frightens me, Hannah, 'cos when it happens you look so grim and determined, I know someone, somewhere, is in for it.'

Hannah tried to laugh it off, but she was startled at her friend's perception. Oh yes, she had a secret and yes, someone was going to be in for it, as Nell said. In for it good and proper, if Hannah had her way.

One day, Edmund Critchlow was going to be made to pay.

'You know, it surprises me that you haven't found yourself a boyfriend before now,' Bessie said as she and Hannah sat before the range late that night with just the glow from the fire to light the room. After an exciting and busy day, they were content to sit warming their feet against the fender. Tommy was fast asleep upstairs and they would soon be joining him. But for the moment they were enjoying the cosiness of there just being the two of them. 'If I'm honest –' Bessie chuckled – 'I'd've thought you'd have found a feller before Nell. 'Cos when young Jim first started calling, I thought it was you he was coming to see.'

'I think he did at first, but only out of kindness. I think him and that nice constable at the station wanted to know I was all right. But once he set eyes on Nell . . .' Hannah laughed.

'And you don't mind?' Bessie asked seriously.

Hannah shook her head. 'Oh no. Not a bit. I like Jim ever so much, but . . . but he wasn't for me.'

For a brief moment she closed her eyes and she could see Luke's face in her mind's eye, see them running hand in hand up the hills above the mill, could almost feel the wind in her hair.

'You still haven't forgotten that lad at the mill, 'ave you?' Bessie said softly. Her face, illuminated by the soft glow from the fire, was full of sympathy.

'No,' Hannah said huskily. 'I don't suppose I'll ever forget him.'

'Don't spend your life grieving for him, love. He wouldn't have wanted that, would he?'

Hannah sighed. 'I don't suppose so.' She was on the point of confiding in Bessie, on the point of confessing that one day she intended to go back to the mill, when a knock came at the back door.

Bessie gave an irritated tut. 'Now who can this be at this time of night?'

'Sit still,' Hannah said, jumping up. 'I'll go. And whoever it is, they'll get a piece of my mind, disturbing folks this late.'

She threw the door open, an angry remark ready on her lips. Flo Harris, her arms folded across her thin chest, stood there. 'Is Bessie still up? There's summat I have to tell 'er.'

'Can't it wait till morning? We're both dead on our feet. We've been up since five.'

'No, it won't wait. An' she won't want it to when she hears what I've got to tell her.'

Hannah sighed. 'You'd better come in, then.'

Flo marched into the house, pushing her way past Hannah. There was a strange air of suppressed excitement about her. Whatever it was, she couldn't wait to tell it, but, following her into the room, Hannah had the uncomfortable feeling that this was not going to be pleasant news for Bessie. Flo was triumphant. Yes, that was the word. Triumphant.

'Hello, Flo.' Bessie, despite her tiredness, raised a cheery smile of welcome for her neighbour. 'What brings you round at this time of night when most good folks are in their beds?'

'Ah, now you've hit the nail right on the head there, Bessie Morgan.' Flo stood on the hearthrug in front of Bessie. 'When all *good* folks should be in their beds.'

'Oh, sit down, do, Flo. I'm getting a crick in me neck looking up at yer.'

Hannah closed the door quietly and came to stand behind Bessie's chair whilst Flo took the one near the fire where Hannah had been sitting.

'So? What's this important news that won't wait till morning?'

Flo leaned forward and her eyes gleamed with jubilance. 'I've seen your Peggy.'

Thirty-Four

For a moment there was utter silence in the room, then Bessie gave a cry and fell back in the chair. Swiftly, Hannah knelt beside her. 'Auntie Bessie, are you all right?' Even in the shadowy light from the fire, the girl could see that Bessie had turned pale and she was holding the palm of her hand flat against her chest as if she had a pain.

Angrily, Hannah turned to Flo. 'Why did you blurt it out like that? You could've been a bit more tactful.'

'Huh! Sorry, I spoke,' Flo said, making as if to get up and leave, but Hannah stood up and pushed her back into her chair. Standing over her, she said in a threatening tone, 'Oh no, you stay right where you are and tell us it all.'

'When . . . when did you see her?' Bessie gasped, still holding her chest. 'And where?'

Flo settled back, enjoying her moment of glory. She was sure of their full attention now. 'It was near the pub. I'd just gone to fetch Harry his pint. He has one every night 'afore 'ee goes to bed. Just the one, mind you, I wouldn't like you to think 'ee's a drinker.'

If the situation had not been so fraught, Bessie might well have laughed out loud at this. The whole street knew that Harry Harris spent most evenings in the pub and only staggered home at closing time. The jug of beer that Flo fetched most nights from the pub in the street round the corner was for herself.

'Get on with it,' Hannah muttered through clenched teeth.

'She was hanging about outside the pub. Waiting for the fellers to come out.'

'What feller?' Hannah snapped.

Flo smirked. 'Any feller'd do, long as 'ee'd still got the price for a bit of you-know-what left in his pocket. Shouldn't be allowed. This is a decent neighbourhood, this is.'

'I know very well what my daughter is,' Bessie retorted, 'but you can't resist any chance to rub it in, can you?'

Flo laughed. 'Not my fault if I've heard tales, is it? She's been seen in some of the worst parts of Manchester and—'

'I think you've said enough, Mrs Harris,' Hannah interrupted. 'We'll bid you goodnight.' She grasped the woman's arm and hauled her to her feet.

''Ere, 'ere, what do you think you're doing?'

'I'm showing you the door, that's what I'm doing. Now you've done your dirty work, you can go.'

'Dirty work, is it? It's not me doing the dirty work. I thought Bessie would want to know.'

'Mebbe she does and mebbe she doesn't. Like I said, you could've done it in a lot kinder way. You've about given her a heart attack, by the look of her. So I'll be obliged if you'll leave. Now!'

Flo thrust her face close to Hannah's. 'You're a fine one to be handing out your orders like Lady Muck. Just remember who *you* are. Your mother weren't no better than her Peggy.'

'My mother's dead and buried. You leave her out

of this,' Hannah spat back. 'And I don't need no reminding of what I am, so there's nothing you can say that can hurt me. But you've hurt Bessie, so I hope you're proud of yourself. Go on, get out of here.'

'I'm going. And don't ask any favours of me again.'

'There's no fear of that.'

When the door banged behind her, Hannah turned to bend over Bessie. 'You all right?'

Bessie struggled to sit up. 'Aye,' she said heavily. 'Right as I'll ever be.' She clutched Hannah's hand. 'Oh, Hannah, love. Go up the street and see if you can see her, will yer?' Tears spilled down Bessie's face. 'Bring her back here, Hannah. If you find her, bring her home.'

Hannah patted her hand. ''Course I will.'

She hurried to take down her shawl from the peg behind the back door and run round the corner and along the street towards the Brewer's Arms. But there was no one standing in the shadows near the doorway. Hannah looked up and down the neighbouring streets, searching this way and that. But there was no one that could possibly be Peggy. The dark, wet streets were deserted except for the distant figure of a man, weaving his way unsteadily homewards.

Hannah bit her lip. It was almost closing time and she didn't want to be caught hanging about on the street corner. Then she made a sudden decision. She marched boldly up to the door of the tavern, pushed it open and stepped inside into the fog of pipe smoke, into the midst of the raucous laugher and the smell of ale.

Only women of a certain sort ever entered a public bar. Even Flo would go to the back door of the public house with her jug and wait there for the landlord to serve her nightly pint to her. The conversation stuttered and died, and Hannah found that every eye in the room full of men turned towards her. The big landlord stepped out from behind the bar and came towards her.

'Now, love, no offence, but I don't allow your sort in my pub. Out you go.'

He made to take hold of her arm, but Hannah said, 'I just came in to look for someone.'

'I bet you did, but like I say—'

'No, no, you don't understand. I'm looking for a girl.'

'Well, she's not here, love. I promise you that.'

Another man reeled his way towards her. ' 'Sall right, Dan. I'll look after her. And yes, yes, I'll tek her out. Now, my pretty one,' he leered at Hannah. 'Looking for company, are yer?'

The landlord turned away with a shake of his head and the buzz of conversation rose again, as the drinkers lost interest.

Hannah eyed the man now holding her arm with distaste and then suddenly, an idea came to her. She smiled. 'Isn't that what I'm supposed to ask you?' she said pertly, putting her hand on her hip and swaying provocatively. The man's smile broadened, showing a mouth of blackened and missing teeth. He put his arm around Hannah's waist and pulled her to him. Sickened by the stench of body odour and sour breath, she steeled herself not to repulse him. 'I'm looking for a friend of mine. Peggy. Someone told me she was here. Have you seen her?'

The man shook his head. 'Naw, but don't let's bother about her, my beauty. Let's go out the back.' He gave a sniff. 'Some places'd let us go upstairs. But not this landlord. Won't 'ave no goings-on on his premises, he says. He keeps an orderly house, does Dan.'

Hannah could not prevent the gleam in her eye at being given such information, but the man misunderstood it and made to pull her towards the door.

'But there's a nice little backyard 'ee's got, and whilst he's busy in 'ere . . .'

Hannah smiled into his face. 'Let me go first and see if the coast's clear.'

He grinned again. 'Tha's a good idea. Don't want to disturb anyone,' he leered. 'Or be disturbed, my lovely, do we?'

She pulled herself from his grasp and made for the door. Ribald laughter followed her, but, her heart thumping, she hurried round the corner and into the back yard of the pub. She leaned against the wall for a moment, her heart pounding, her palms sweating. The stench of the man still in her nostrils was making her want to retch. But her concern, her love, for Bessie drove her on into untold danger. If the man should choose to come after her, she was trapped with no one to lift a finger to help her.

As her eyes became accustomed to the darkness, she could see that there was no one there. There were two doors leading into low buildings across the yard and she opened each one, peering inside. They were cluttered storerooms but there was no one there.

Like a thief in the night, Hannah stole back round the corner. Not daring to linger, she picked up her skirts and ran past the barroom entrance and all the way back to Bessie's house, not feeling safe until she was inside and leaning against the closed door.

'Hannah? Is that you?' came Bessie's anxious,

quivering voice. Hannah moved forward into the room. 'Yes, it's me. I'm sorry, Auntie Bessie, but she's gone. I couldn't find her.' Swiftly, without dwelling too long on the detail of the man accosting her, Hannah explained. 'I went into the pub and even round the back, but she wasn't there.'

Bessie lay back in her chair and groaned. 'So close, so close and we've missed her.'

'Maybe she'll come another night. I . . . I could go again.' She didn't relish the idea, but she would do anything for Bessie.

Bessie let out a long, hopeless sigh. 'I don't reckon she'll come again. Maybe . . . maybe she came to . . . to look for her dad. He used to go on down to the pub sometimes. Just on a Saturday night. Maybe . . . maybe she hoped to see him.'

'Her dad?' Hannah was shocked. 'But . . . d'you mean she doesn't know about . . . about her dad?'

Bessie shook her head. 'Far as I know, she doesn't know he's dead. She'd gone before then.'

'Oh.' Hannah was thoughtful. An idea began to form in her mind, but she forbore from telling Bessie.

She had the feeling that the older woman would not be happy about it. Not happy at all.

'I need your help. I'm sorry to ask and if you feel you can't do it, Jim, because of your position an' all, I'll understand.'

'This sounds very mysterious, Hannah. Come inside and have a cup of tea with us. Nell is just home from work and I'm not on duty until ten o'clock tonight. Tommy's in bed, so you can talk freely – whatever it is. Is it Bessie? Not ill, is she?' All the time he was asking questions he was ushering her through from the front door, through their parlour, at present sparsely furnished, into the cosy kitchen at the back of the terraced house.

'Hannah!' Nell exclaimed, hugging her as if she hadn't seen her for weeks instead of only days. Whilst Nell excitedly showed her round the house and all that they had done in the short space of time, Hannah held herself in check, even though she was bursting to confide in Jim and ask his advice, ask for his help.

At last they sat down, grouped in front of the cosy fire in the range.

'Now,' Jim said, gently but firmly interrupting his wife's prattling. 'How can I help you, Hannah?'

'I'd better tell you the whole story . . .' Launching into her tale, she began by telling Jim about the night Nell had come home with her hair dyed and Bessie's outraged reaction. Nell nodded, taking up Hannah's story. 'She scared me a bit. I really thought I looked like some woman of the streets, but it turned out it was because her daughter, Peggy, had dyed her hair and . . .' Nell shot a look at Hannah. 'By all accounts, that's exactly what Peggy had become. Bessie said she'd heard bits of gossip over the years and, you could tell, she was so sad about it.' Nell paused and looked questioningly at Hannah. 'So, has something happened?'

Hannah nodded. 'The day you got married. We were just going to bed after a lovely day.' She smiled fondly at the happy couple, who exchanged a bashful glance. 'And who should come knocking at the door but Flo Harris. She couldn't wait to impart a juicy bit of gossip. She said she'd seen Peggy hanging around near the Brewer's Arms, waiting for the fellers coming

327

out, she said. Her and her vicious tongue . . .' Hannah paused a moment, imagining what she'd like to do to Flo Harris, given half a chance. Then she went on, recounting the events of that night. 'And since then,' she ended, 'Bessie's been sunk in despair. It's awful to see her. I just want to do something to help her. I want to find Peggy.'

Jim was thoughtful. 'If she's still here in the town, it mightn't be too difficult. We know most of the girls, but there's not many stay long.' He grinned. 'Not much business in this town. We move 'em on as quick as they come, that's if we can't actually arrest them. Now, if you were to say she'd been seen in one of the big cities . . .'

'She was – I mean Flo reckoned she'd been seen in Manchester.'

'Mmm, now that might be more difficult, 'cos it's a big place.'

'Bessie said she might have been looking for her dad. He used to go to that pub when . . . when he was alive.'

Now it was Nell's turn to be shocked and she repeated the very same words that Hannah had said to Bessie. 'You mean she doesn't even know her dad's dead?'

Hannah shook her head. 'Bessie thinks not.'

Nell turned to Jim. 'Oh, poor Bessie – and poor Peggy. Never mind what she's become. She was hurt by some feller and too proud to come home, I bet.' Nell touched her husband's hand. 'Not everyone's been as lucky as me,' she said huskily, 'to find someone big enough to forgive past mistakes. Jim, we have to help Hannah find her. For Bessie's sake, if nothing else.'

'But I do understand, Jim, if you can't,' Hannah put in, anxiously. 'I wouldn't expect you to risk your job.'

'No, no, I'll mind I don't do that. We're not just there to run folks in, you know. We try to help where we can.'

Hannah smiled. She, more than anyone, knew that. 'And if it's helping some poor girl off the streets, then I suppose it could be classed as part of my job.' He grinned, his kind face crinkling. 'I'll ask around. Ask my colleagues. I'll look at the charge book, an' all. See if she's ever been brought in.'

'Do you think she might be using another name though?' Hannah suggested. 'I know I would if I'd . . . if I'd . . .' She faltered. Far from condemning Peggy, Hannah was thinking, *there, but for this kind policeman and Bessie, I might have gone.* She saw, so clearly, that if she hadn't had a little help from caring people at the right moment, her life now might be very different.

Jim was wrinkling his brow thoughtfully. 'You could be right at that. D'you have a description of her? D'you know what she looks like?'

Hannah shook her head. Nell, despite the gravity of their conversation, couldn't help laughing. 'I know one thing, she's got red hair.' The other two stared at her for a moment and then joined in her laughter. It eased the tension and drove away some of the sadness. They were suddenly filled with more hope. The two girls had more faith in Jim than perhaps he had himself, but in turn, he had colleagues he could enlist in his search.

'We'll find her,' he said. 'We'll bring her home. But not a word to Bessie, Hannah. I don't want to raise her hopes until we have definite news.'

Thirty-Five

The days passed with agonizing slowness for Hannah and Nell, but each time when Jim returned home, he shook his head sadly. 'No news, love. I'm sorry, she must have left the town. The lads have kept an eye open for her, but she's skipping out of sight as soon as a policeman comes along. They do, you know, they just melt away into the shadows. I don't know how they do it.'

Nell sighed sadly. 'If you ask me, their whole lives are spent living in the shadows. I suppose the only alternative for them is the workhouse and they chose the way they did.' She paused a moment and then added bitterly, 'Can't say I blame 'em in some ways.'

Jim looked at his wife thoughtfully. Nell was loved and cared for now. She was plump and rosy cheeked, with her shining hair neatly coiled, her apron crisply starched. But it hadn't always been so. He knew a little about her past, as much as she had been able to bring herself to tell him. But he never pried, never demanded explanations. He loved her unconditionally for the girl she was now. But even though he had no conceit, he could see that her life could have been very different.

Silently, Jim vowed to redouble his efforts to find the missing Peggy. There was only one way he could think of; he would go out on his nights off in his own clothes. He would act like a man in search of female company, the kind of company to be found waiting on street corners.

But first, he knew he must confide in his older colleague. Much as he wanted to help find the girl, he was determined not to risk his career and the happiness of his little family to do so.

'Ah, well, now lad, I don't know about that,' Constable Robinson said when Jim told him of his plans. 'You could be getting yourself into a bit of bother doing that.' He chewed on his lower lip thoughtfully. 'Does it mean so much to Hannah and this – er – Mrs Morgan, is it?' He still remembered Hannah with affection. He'd been taken with the golden-haired girl with the startlingly blue eyes.

'Yes, it does,' Jim answered. 'Peggy's Mrs Morgan's daughter.'

'Ah.' The older man was suddenly full of understanding. He had daughters of his own and whilst he was obliged in his job to take a firm line with prostitutes, he was often filled with a great sadness. Some of them were hard-nut cases, loud-mouthed, vulgar and beyond sympathy, but for a few, it was the only way they knew how to survive and he could find it in his big heart to pity them. 'Tell you what, lad. I'll have to clear it with the inspector, but I don't want you going out on your own. I'll fix it so you an' me get some nights off together and I'll come with you.'

Jim stared at him. 'You'd do that?'

'Aye lad, I would. Call it my good deed for the day.' He grinned 'But not a word to the wife, mind. Far as she need be concerned, it's all in the line of duty.'

*

Jim and Constable Robinson tramped the streets on their nights off for several weeks. Not knowing anything of the efforts going on to find her daughter, Bessie grew more and more despondent, sinking further into silent misery.

Christmas had come and gone. Bessie had made a valiant attempt to rouse herself for the sake of the others, but her heart wasn't in merrymaking. And despite their own efforts, Bessie's sadness put a damper on all their spirits. Hannah, Nell and Jim discussed the matter endlessly, but they could think of nothing else to do other than what was already being done.

'I was so hoping she'd appear again at the pub round the corner on a Saturday night. But maybe, if it was her dad she was looking for, her courage failed her to do it again.'

'Or maybe someone at the pub told her he's dead,' Jim suggested.

Hannah sighed. 'I never thought of that. You could be right.'

There was silence until Jim said, 'Well, we're not giving up hope just yet. Mr Robinson is willing to carry on a bit longer and so am I.'

'Thank him for us, won't you, Jim?' Hannah said quietly.

Jim smiled and nodded.

On the next Saturday night following their talk, Hannah was restless. She couldn't explain why, but she couldn't sit still. She had to get out of the house. She felt stifled and edgy. She reached for her shawl from the peg. 'I'm just going to get a breath of air, Auntie Bessie, and I might pop into Nell's for half an hour, so don't wait up for me.'

Bessie, sitting staring into the fire, didn't seem to

hear her. Hannah sighed. Normally, such a remark might have been met with a teasing, 'Now don't you go keeping those lovebirds from their bed,' but now, there was nothing. Not even a warning to be careful out and about in the frosty darkness of the January night.

Hannah slipped out of the house and, pulling her shawl closely about her, walked around the corner. For some inexplicable reason she was being drawn towards the pub. She saw a figure walking towards her and her heartbeat quickened. But then, with a stab of disappointment, she saw that it was Flo.

''Evenin', Mrs Harris,' she forced herself to say cheerily, and she heard the woman sniff.

'Going to work, are you, love?' Flo asked sarcastically.

'Not tonight. Too cold to be hanging around street corners. Thought I'd give it a miss tonight.'

To her delight, she heard Flo gasp, 'Well, I never . . .'

In the darkness, Hannah grinned and walked on. It'd be all round the street tomorrow.

As she drew nearer the pub, her steps slowed, but taking a deep breath, she approached the door and pushed it open. Once more she was met by the stale smell of smoke and drink. One or two glanced up to see who'd come in, but this time the buzz of conversation never faltered. Hannah glanced round swiftly, anxious not to linger. She was about to turn and scan the other side of the bar room when she felt someone take hold of her arm and a rough voice speak close to her ear.

'I wondered when I'd catch up wi' you. Run out on me, would yer?'

Hannah twisted round to face the ugly face of the man from whom she had escaped the last time.

'Hello.' Hannah smiled brightly. 'Where did you get to?'

'What d'yer mean – where did I get to? It was you scarpered. I waited ages. Right till closing time.' His grip on her arm tightened. 'You want teaching a lesson, that's what you want.'

Hannah tried to twist herself free, but his grip was as tight as a man-trap as he began to drag her towards the door. Now Hannah was really frightened. 'Let go of me. I'm not what you think. I won't—'

'Oh yes, you will. Lead me on, would yer?'

'Let me go,' Hannah shouted now, her voice rising above the babble of conversation, which at the sound of her terrified tones lessened, and Hannah felt everyone's eyes turn in their direction. 'Let me go!'

'Old Sid 'aving to drag 'em in off the streets now, is he? He's too ugly even for the regular girls,' someone guffawed.

'Get 'er out of here, Sid,' the landlord called, but before he could weave his way amongst the tables to reach them, another voice spoke from behind, a soft, much younger voice.

'Let her go, Sid. She's not one of us.'

Sid gave a growl and turned to face the red-haired girl standing behind him. Hannah glanced at her too and her heart skipped a beat. The girl's face was unnaturally white and her cheeks were reddened. She wore a low-cut silk dress that had once been rather grand, but was now grubby and stained. But it was her eyes that tore at Hannah's heart. They were lifeless, defeated and hopeless. Here was a girl who had sunk to the very depths of degradation and could see no way out, except death. The girl smiled at Hannah, but the smile did not reach her eyes. 'I saw you come in here and knew you'd be in trouble. The landlord doesn't allow women in here. Go on, love. Go home. This is no place for you.'

Her voice faltered and now she stared hard at Hannah, almost as if she half recognized her. But Hannah had already guessed who she was. 'Peggy? It is Peggy, isn't it?'

The girls gasped in surprise. Beside them, the man was forgotten as the two girls stared at each other. 'Hannah? Is it – Hannah?'

'Yes, yes, it is.' Scarcely aware that the man still had a firm grasp on her, Hannah touched Peggy's arm. 'I'm so glad I've found you. We've been looking for you.'

'Looking for *me*?' She was shocked to think anyone could care enough.

'Yes,' Hannah said gently. 'We – we heard you'd been here. Some weeks back. We've been looking for you ever since.'

Tentatively, afraid of the answer, Peggy said, 'Who's "we"?'

'Your mam and me. And two other friends, an' all.' She forbore to say that one was a policeman. She was afraid that Peggy would disappear into the night without a trace.

Peggy was shaking her head. 'No, you can't mean that. They can't want to know me. Not now,' she added sadly.

'Look, are you two going to stand gossiping all night? This girl—' Sid began, but Peggy rounded on him.

'Leave go of her, Sid. Like I said, she's not one of us. I'll see you later.'

'Oh no, you won't,' Hannah said firmly. 'You're coming home with me.'

'Oho, party time, is it?' Sid leered. 'I could fancy a threesome.'

Now the two girls faced him together. 'Go away, Sid.'

Those sitting close by, listening with avid interest to what was going on, laughed. 'Come on, Sid, leave 'em alone. You're not going to get anywhere.'

Grumbling to himself, the man at last released his grip on Hannah's arm. Absentmindedly, she rubbed her arm where his fingers had bitten into her flesh. She'd have a right old bruise there tomorrow, but she didn't care.

She'd found Peggy.

'Come on,' she said, taking hold of Peggy's arm, gently but firmly. 'You're coming home.'

As they walked along the street, Peggy said hesitantly, 'Are you sure this is a good idea? They won't want me. None of 'em. And my brothers will kill me.'

'Then why did you come to the pub so close to home? You must have been hoping for – for something.'

'I just wanted to see me dad. Not to speak to him, just to see him. I heard he'd been hurt at work not long after – after I left. I just wanted to know if he was all right.' Hannah stopped and touched the girl's arm. 'Peggy – there's something you should know. There've been a lot of changes since you left.'

Peggy stared at her through the darkness. 'Oh no!' she breathed, guessing at once that it was bad news. 'Me dad, don't say me dad . . .'

'I'm afraid so. I'm so sorry. And all the rest of the family've left home. Your mam's living on her own. At least, she was until I came back.'

It took Peggy, reeling from the shocking news, a few moments to realize what Hannah had said. 'Oh yes, I remember now. You and your poor mother got turned out of your house. Mam was distraught about it.'

Hannah sighed. 'There's a lot happened in the last few years. An awful lot to tell you, but come on.' She linked her arm through Peggy's and drew her towards her old home. 'Your mam is going to be so happy to see you.'

'Are you sure, Hannah?' Peggy said doubtfully. 'Are you really sure?'

Hannah was sure and her certainty was rewarded the moment she opened the door and pushed a hesitant Peggy into the room. 'Look who I've found,' she called out. Bessie looked round and her eyes lit up. She levered herself up and lumbered, arms outstretched and tears pouring down her cheeks, towards her daughter. 'Oh, Peggy! Peggy, love.'

The girl gave a sob, 'Oh, Mam,' and fell into her arms.

Quietly, Hannah turned and slipped out into the night again, but this time she turned down the street towards Nell's home. She must tell them the good news.

Thirty-Six

Bessie was happier than she had been in years. She still mourned her beloved husband, but now she had her daughter returned to her as if from the dead. And she cared not one jot for the gossiping neighbours.

It soon became apparent that Peggy's way of life had affected her health: her skin was sallow and blotchy and she was painfully thin.

'She's nowt but skin and bone,' Bessie whispered to Hannah. 'We'll have to feed her up. Look after her.' Bessie glanced at Hannah, a question in her eyes. 'You don't mind, Hannah, do you?'

Hannah gaped at her. 'Mind? Why on earth should I mind?'

'Well, she . . . she's not going to be able to work for a while, and besides, when folks know what she's been doing, she . . . she might find it hard to get proper work. When you've led that sort of life, it . . . it's difficult to get out of it.'

Hannah touched Bessie's hand and said softly, 'About as hard as getting out of the workhouse once you're in there. Auntie Bessie, of *course* I want to help Peggy. We'll manage. When she's feeling better, she'll be able to help you with the washing.'

'As long as none of my customers know. You know what folks are like. They'll treat her like a leper for a while.'

'I can still collect and deliver for you in the evening and Nell'll still help out, I'm sure. Don't you worry, Auntie Bessie, we'll manage.'

Hannah was not feeling as confident as she made out. There was now an extra mouth to feed on her one wage. Whilst Bessie still did a lot of washing, Hannah was sure that once word got out that her wayward daughter was home, folks might well take their washing elsewhere. Bessie would suffer the stigma of the life her daughter had led. And now she was married, Nell's contribution to the household budget had gone too.

And worse than all this, Hannah, though eternally grateful to Bessie, felt the trap closing in on her. Her own plans would have to wait for a while.

The weeks and months passed, and Hannah had been working at the silk factory for almost three years. Peggy's recovery had been painfully slow, but at last her skin was clearer, she had put on a little weight, and though the haunted look would never quite leave her eyes, at least she was able to smile now. She rarely ventured out of the house – the gossips had long memories. But after she had been home almost a year, Hannah determined it was high time the girl put the past behind her and held her head up high.

As she breezed into the house one evening after work, she called out, 'Peggy, Auntie Bessie where are you? I've got some good news.'

'In here,' came Bessie's voice from the kitchen where she was laying the table for their evening meal. As she stepped into the room, Hannah lifted her face and sniffed the air. 'Mmm, something smells good.'

'Sit down. It's all ready. Come on, you too, Peg. Leave that ironing, you can do it later.'

'But, Mam, me irons are hot . . .' Peggy began, but nevertheless she set her irons back on the hob and came to the table.

'So, love, what's your news?' Bessie said.

'I've got Peggy an interview for a job at the mill.'

Peggy's mouth dropped open in surprise, but then doubt and fear crossed her face. 'Oh, Hannah, it's good of you, very good, but I don't know if I'm ready to face folk. What if—'

'Take it a step at a time, Peg. See how it goes, eh? You can pull out any time you like. Just go for the interview with Mr Boardman. If you get the job, give it a try. If it doesn't work out, you've lost nothing, have you?'

'No, but what if folk know about me? They'll likely hound me out of the place.'

'No, they won't. Not while I'm around anyway.'

Both Bessie and Peggy smiled at the little firebrand. Slim, blonde and blue-eyed, Hannah had the looks of a china doll, but her spirit was like steel. 'Look,' she went on, 'there's a girl just started in our workroom and there's been a lot of gossip about her. They say she's been on the game, got two kiddies and she doesn't even know who their fathers are. Oh, there was a lot of gossiping and nudging when she first started, but I made a point of being friendly with her and one or two more followed suit. One or two who have no reason to be calling others names, I might tell you. But it's fine now. You'll just have to brave it out for a while until it all dies down. You'll be a nine-day wonder and then they'll find summat else to gossip about.' She smiled. 'Or someone.'

'Well . . .' Peggy said doubtfully, but Bessie urged, 'Oh, go on, love, give it a try. Like Hannah says, you've nothin' to lose. And the washing's not coming in like it used to. And to tell the truth, it's getting too hard for me now. With two proper wages coming in and the little bit that Nell gives me for looking after Tommy, we could live like kings.'

Hannah bit her lip. She couldn't let Bessie go on thinking she would have her wage coming in for ever. 'Maybe there's something I should tell you. I've got plans. I – I might be leaving.'

Bessie's face fell and Peggy looked worried. 'Is it because of me, Hannah, now I've come back? Because, if it is—'

'No, no,' Hannah reassured her swiftly. 'It's something I've wanted to do for a long time. But the time's not been right. I've had to wait a while anyway, and then I wanted to be sure Bessie was all right before I left. I thought I could leave when Nell and Tommy were here.' Her smile widened. 'But then she had to go an' get married, didn't she?'

'You're going back, aren't you? Back to that mill. Why, Hannah? It'll only cause you more heartache. Put the past behind you, love. It's what you're telling Peggy to do.'

'I know – and maybe you're right. Maybe I should. But I just know that I have to go back first, before I can get on with my life.' Her mouth tightened. 'I've unfinished business there.' Her face brightened. 'But so long as I know that I can always come back here if—'

'Of course you can,' Bessie and Peggy chorused.

*

To Hannah's delight, Peggy was offered the job, and despite having to run the gauntlet of the gossiping for a couple of weeks, the girl soon settled into the routine of mill life. She was a quick and willing learner. She was quiet and unassuming, and with Hannah as her champion, she was soon accepted by the others.

Now, at last, as winter turned to spring once more, Hannah felt free to make definite plans to return to Wyedale Mill.

'Nell, can you get me some of that hair dye you use?'

Nell's eyes widened. 'Whatever for? You've got beautiful hair.'

'I'm going back.'

'Back where?'

'To the mill.'

For a moment Nell looked puzzled and then she gasped. 'To Wyedale? Whatever for?'

'I'm not going to let Edmund Critchlow get off with causing Luke's death, even if his cronies fixed it for him so he did.'

Nell's eyes were troubled. 'Oh, Hannah, do be careful. He's so powerful. What're you going to do?'

'I don't know. Not exactly. Not yet. But I don't want anyone to recognize me. I've altered a lot while I've been away. I've grown taller and filled out.'

Nell chuckled as she let her glance run up and down Hannah's shapely figure. 'And in all the right places, too.'

'And if I dye my hair, I think I'll look very different.'

'Well, yes,' Nell said doubtfully. 'But you can't hide those lovely blue eyes can you? And don't forget, blue eyes don't very often go with red hair.'

'That's a risk I'll just have to take.' Hannah was

determined, and once she set her mind to something, there was no one who could dissuade her. No one.

That night, fully grown and aged nineteen with bright red hair and blue eyes, Anna Morgan was born.

Thirty-Seven

Hannah paused at the top of the hill, looking down into the dale below. The spring sunshine slanted on the hills, tipping the trees with its golden glow.

Hannah smiled. It was just like the day she had first arrived here as a child of twelve almost seven years earlier. Pauper's gold the driver who'd brought them had called the sunlight. The scene was unchanged, but the girl who now stood at the top of the steep slope was very different from the skinny pauper child.

Today Hannah was dressed in good clothes, with sturdy new boots on her feet. She carried a heavy bag of belongings and she had money in her pocket, money she'd earned. Money that no one was going to take from her. Not this time.

Excitement fluttering just below her ribs, she set off down the hill. There was just one person in whom she was going to confide. Or rather three people. Lily and Ollie Grundy and their nephew, Ted. She couldn't bring herself even to try to deceive them. If it hadn't been for their help, she'd still be slaving in the mill, only just having completed her indenture. She wouldn't have known the happiness of the last three and a half years with Bessie. Nell and Tommy would still be in the workhouse, and Peggy ... Well, she dared not think what might have happened to Peggy by now. She marvelled at the way people's lives were intertwined with others. If it hadn't been for the Grundys' help, none of the good things of the past few years would have happened to others as well as to her.

Oh yes, she owed it to the Grundys to be honest with them if with no one else. But first, she smiled, she would have a bit of fun. She would test out her disguise on them.

At the gateway into the farmyard, she paused and looked about her again. The mill was still not in sight. It was set right at the end of the dale, around the next bend. Her heart was beating faster at the mere thought of stepping through its pillared gate once more. She wasn't quite ready to face that yet, so instead she stepped across the cobbled crewyard and knocked on the back door of the farmhouse, just like she had all those years earlier. Time seemed to tilt; for a moment it was as if the years between had never happened and she was once again that little girl, the leader of the four waifs from the workhouse, knocking on a stranger's door. She glanced over her shoulder, half-expecting to see the others, Luke, Daniel and Jane, standing behind her, scruffy, dirty urchins . . .

The door opened, pulling her back to the present. Lily Grundy had changed little; the intervening years had been kind to her. Perhaps there were a few more grey hairs, one or two more lines in her face, but the smile was still there. The welcome in her eyes, even for a stranger knocking at her door, was the same as ever it had been.

'Yes?'

'Can you tell me the way to the mill?' Hannah asked, and now she knew her voice sounded different too. When she had last said those very same words it had been with the piping tones of a child. Now her voice had deepened. It was low and husky and, though she was quite unaware of it herself, appealing.

'It's further on, love. Just keep on the way you were going. It's at the end of the dale.'

'Thank you.'

She made as if to turn away, but, as Hannah had known she would, Lily said, 'Perhaps you'd like a cup of tea and a bite to eat? You must have come a fair way.'

Hannah smiled. 'I have,' she said, but saying no more for the moment, she stepped over the threshold and into the kitchen she remembered so well. Nothing, not one thing, had changed. The smell of freshly baked bread still hung in the air. The kettle still sang on the hob near the blazing fire in the range, and Lily bustled about setting cups and saucers and a plate of home-made biscuits on the table.

'Sit down, do. Make yourself at home. It's a while since I had anybody calling on their way to the mill. Since they stopped the paupers from the workhouse coming here as apprentices, I don't get many waifs and strays passing my door.' She paused before adding simply, 'And d'you know, I miss them. Poor little mites.'

Hannah tried to hide the surprise from showing on her face. 'The . . . the pauper apprentices? What . . . was that?'

'Ah well now,' Lily settled herself down opposite and began to pour the tea. 'It began years and years ago, but it stopped . . . ooh let's see, in the late forties, I reckon, in most places, but the Critchlows kept it going at their mill –' she nodded, gesturing towards the mill further along the dale – 'for several years after that.' She leaned closer, confiding. 'We all reckon he had this scheme going with the master of a workhouse who used to send the children. They made them sign a paper binding them here for years. Poor mites didn't know what they were letting themselves in for. And then, of course, they was trapped here. They had no one to fight for them, no parents, and because they'd signed an indenture, the law was against them an' all. There was no escape, only to run away, and if they was caught, well, I hardly dare tell you some of the punishments them Critchlows meted out.' She pursed her mouth and shook her head and Hannah wanted to jump up and hug her.

'And did many run away?'

Lily smiled grimly. 'One or two. We – that's my husband, Ollie and me – and our nephew that works for us – Ted – we helped a little lass once. Nice little thing she was. Been through a lot, if you know what I mean. She deserved a bit of help.' She chuckled. 'We was risking a fair bit ourselves, mind, 'cos we supply the mill with produce – milk, butter, cheese, eggs – and it gives us a regular bit of income. But it was worth the risk – just to get one back on them Critchlows.'

'And the girl you helped?'

Lily's face lit up. 'Oh, she's all right. Wrote to us, she did. Don't know where she is, mind you,' she tapped the side of her nose, 'I've a good idea, mind, but it wouldn't do to say. Went back to where she came from and found an old neighbour who remembered her. Far as I know, she's fine.'

Hannah's smile broadened. 'She is.'

'Eh?' Lily gaped at her. 'You . . . you know her? You know Hannah?'

Hannah could not stop the laughter bubbling out now. 'It's me, Mrs Grundy, don't you recognize me?'

Lily's mouth dropped open. 'Hannah? You're . . . Hannah? But she . . . she had lovely blonde hair . . .' Her voice petered away as she stared. Then slowly she nodded. 'Yes, I see it now. You can't hide those pretty blue eyes, can you? Aw, but lass, what have you done to your hair?'

Now Hannah's face sobered. 'It's not because I wanted to. Not out of vanity. I wanted to come back, but I didn't want anyone to recognize me.' Her mouth tightened into a grim line. 'I mean to get my revenge on Edmund Critchlow. I don't know how, but I have to try. I . . . I can't lay the past to rest until I do.'

'Well I never,' Lily was still staring at her, shaking her head in disbelief. But as she took in Hannah's words, she added, 'Well, I can't blame you for that, lass. I've a few scores I'd like to settle with the Critchlows myself, but I don't expect I'll get the chance.' Her eyes gleamed. 'But if there's any way I can help you, you just let me know. All right?' She paused and reached across the table to touch Hannah's hand. 'It's grand to see you. Wait till Ollie and Ted know. I reckon Ted took a shine to you. He was always asking after you for quite a while after you went. Oh – I can tell them, can't I?'

Hannah nodded. 'Just so long as they don't tell anyone else. I'm calling myself Anna Morgan now.'

'Oh, they'll not say a word. I'll make sure of that. But you just be careful, Hannah, that's all.' Then she smiled. 'Need a bed for a few nights, do you? You're very welcome to stay here.'

Hannah's heart was thumping madly as she neared the mill. What if someone recognized her? She wasn't sure of the law regarding the indenture she'd signed. She hadn't completed it. And even though she was now nineteen and legally out of it, could they still force her to complete a further number of years because she'd run away with still three years to serve? But what did it matter if they did? she answered herself. She intended to seek work here anyway, intended to stay to exact some kind of revenge on Edmund, and that wasn't going to happen overnight. She had to move slowly and make careful plans.

As she entered the gate, she saw a young man crossing the yard, and her heart skipped a beat. For a moment she thought it was Edmund, but as he heard the sound of her footsteps and turned to face her, she could see that he was much younger, yet he had the look of Edmund Critchlow. His black hair was smoothed back from his forehead. Straight, dark eyebrows overshadowed his deep set brown eyes. His jaw was square and resolute, but his firm mouth had nothing of the cruel twist of the man who was so obviously his father. This young man's mouth curved up in a smile as he paused and then came towards Hannah.

'Adam,' Hannah murmured to herself. 'Adam Critchlow.' The boy she remembered had grown in to a man. A very good-looking young man. And what was it she'd always said? A curse on all good-looking men. The thought made her smile.

'Can I help you, miss?' he asked in a deep, friendly tone, returning what he took to be her smile of greeting.

Huskily, Hannah replied, 'I . . . I'm looking for work. I've worked in a mill before. Over . . .' Now the lies must begin in earnest. 'Over Manchester way.'

349

'What work have you done – exactly?'

Hannah reeled off all the jobs she'd done in this very mill. She was about to add that she'd worked in a silk mill too, but then thought better of it. If she told as little about herself as possible, there was less chance of slipping up.

'You need to see Mr Scarsfield. He's the overlooker, but you'd have a final interview with my father.' His smile widened. 'Or with me.'

Hannah had to press her lips together to prevent herself asking the questions that tumbled around her mind. Was he – Adam – working at the mill now? Of course! She remembered now. He'd been brought home from school and made manager of the mill just before she'd left. So he was still here and in a position of importance, it seemed. What had happened to the old man, Mr Nathaniel Critchlow? she wondered. And Mr Edmund? Was he the sole owner of Wyedale Mill now?

But there was one good thing she'd learned already. Mr Scarsfield was still here. And yet, was it so good? Ernest Scarsfield might recognize her.

Adam broke into her thoughts. 'Come along, I'll take you to see him. This way.'

As Hannah followed him into the building, she realized this wasn't going to be quite as easy as she'd imagined. For one thing, she must remember to act like a complete stranger. She couldn't be seen to know her way around the building, along passages and through workrooms that were so familiar to her. And the people that would still be here whom she knew – she must remember not to greet them, not even to smile at them.

Adam led her towards the main mill and, as he held

open the door for her to precede him into one of the workrooms, the very person she most dreaded meeting was working at the nearest machine.

Daniel Hammond.

Thirty-Eight

Daniel looked much older than the eighteen years he was now. The clatter of the machine hid the sound of their approach and Hannah was able to study him as they passed by. To her relief, he didn't even look up. The same mop of curly brown hair was still there, of course, but cut shorter now. He was still thin, and his shoulders and back stooped from long hours bending over a weaving machine. She couldn't see into his eyes from where she was standing, but his mouth was sullen and down-turned. There was no sign of the cheeky grin that had so epitomized Luke and the twin who'd copied his every move.

But the young man still reminded her so much of her lost love. Hannah felt a lump in her throat and she almost stumbled. Adam caught her arm and steadied her.

'Be careful,' he mouthed. 'The floor's uneven and it's a bit of a mess.' He pulled a face. 'It's the one thing we can't seem to do – keep the place clean and tidy.'

Hannah forced herself to smile up at him, anxious that he should not suspect the reason for the tumult of emotions coursing through her. Being back here in the dusty atmosphere, amongst the noise and, most of all, seeing Daniel was causing her a heartache she hadn't envisaged. For a moment, she wanted to turn and run. But she gritted her teeth and allowed Adam to lead her through the mill, showing her the workrooms on each floor. She tried to concentrate on what he was telling her as he put his mouth close to her ear, shouting above the din. At last he led her back out into the yard and towards the door at the end of the building that led up to the offices.

They climbed the stone steps and came to the outer office where Mr Roper had his domain. Hannah found she was holding her breath as Adam opened the door and ushered her inside. Josiah Roper was little changed, perhaps a little more bent as he hunched over his ledgers, his features even sharper and his eyes filled with the bitterness and resentment that the passing of the years had only increased. He glanced up, inquisitive as ever he had been. But Hannah deliberately kept her eyes downcast.

'This young lady is looking for a job,' Adam explained cheerily. 'Is my father in?'

Josiah sniffed with disapproval; Hannah remembered the sound so well, she almost laughed out loud. 'Do you know her?'

'No, she's just turned up at the gate.'

'We don't usually employ folks without a reference of some kind,' Josiah said loftily. 'She could be anybody.'

Indeed I could! Hannah thought wryly.

'Oh, we'll go into all that,' Adam said.

'Well, he's not here.'

Adam turned and winked at Hannah. 'Fine. Then I'll interview her.'

Josiah made a movement, but Adam glanced at him. 'Any objections, Roper?'

The man faltered, muttered something under his breath and turned back to his books.

353

'Good. Come along in, then, Miss – er . . . ?'

'Morgan,' Hannah said firmly. 'Anna Morgan.'

He drew her into the inner office and closed the door. 'I'm Adam Critchlow. Sorry about old Roper. He's been here a long time. He and my father have known each other for years and he seems to think he half-owns the place. Sit down, please,' he added, indicating a chair in front of the desk, the very same desk on which Hannah had painstakingly signed the indenture that had bound her to the Critchlows for six years. As she sat down, she felt a sudden stab of indecision. Was she being foolish, trying to retrace the past? Would it have been better to let it all go and move forward with her life? Was she stacking up a whole load of trouble for herself by coming back?

'I'm sorry my father, Mr Edmund, isn't here. He'd like to have seen you himself, I'm sure.'

At the mention of his name, all Hannah's doubts disappeared and her resolve strengthened. *I bet he would*, she thought. *But not if he knew who I really am and why I've come back.*

'You've worked in a mill before, you say?' Adam was beginning the interview in a businesslike manner, though if she could have read his mind, Hannah would've known that already he intended to employ her. There was something about this pretty girl with startling blue eyes and red hair that he found appealing; he wanted to know more about her, wanted to get to know her. And what better way than to have her working here, where he could find an excuse – a legitimate excuse – to see her every day?

Hannah licked her lips. Lying had never come easily to her, but it was a means to an end. It had to be done. 'Yes. It . . . it was a small mill in Lancashire. They . . .

they had to close.' It was the only thing she could think of to say that would stop the Critchlows trying to make contact with a former employer.

Adam pulled a sympathetic face. 'Yes, business has been difficult of late and some of the smaller mills have found it difficult to keep going. We've been lucky. My father has good contacts and work has been plentiful here. But with this war brewing in America . . . Ah well.' He smiled. 'Let's not get too pessimistic before we have to, eh? Have you brought any kind of reference?'

Hannah smiled. 'I'm sorry, I haven't got it with me. I really only came to the mill today to make an appointment to see someone. I didn't think I'd get an interview so quickly.'

'No matter,' Adam said, waving it aside as of no particular importance. 'I think I can trust my own judgement.' He smiled at her, drinking in her appearance. She smiled back, just a tentative, shy smile. Nothing too bold, she warned herself.

'Right, then. We'll go and find Scarsfield. He'll have a word with you and probably set you on for a trial period. Just to make sure you can do the job, you understand.' Suddenly, it was Adam who was nervous, at pains to make sure she understood that this was no reflection upon her as a person.

'Thank you, sir,' she said, rising and following him to the door. He opened it for her and, head held high, she swept through it, just like any lady of quality. Once more, she kept her glance averted from Josiah Roper as they passed through the outer office, and when they were in the workrooms again, Adam led her in search of Ernest Scarsfield. The overlooker hadn't changed at all. He smiled kindly at Hannah and stroked his moustache with the very same gesture she remembered so well. But thankfully, he didn't recognize her.

'Aye, Mr Adam, we'll be glad of her if she can do all she says. I've a girl gone off sick and I doubt she'll be coming back.' A meaningful glance passed between the two men and Hannah wondered what it meant. Not so naive now, Hannah could think of one or two reasons why the poor girl might not be resuming her work. She could have been badly injured in yet another accident or – as seemed more likely – she was yet another whose life had been ruined by the attentions of Edmund Critchlow, and sent away in disgrace.

Ernest Scarsfield turned to Hannah. 'Can you start in the morning, lass?'

Hannah nodded. 'I think so, if I can find some lodgings close by.'

'Try in the village. Go out of here and up the hill. Several houses take in lodgers – all mill workers.'

'Oh, what about—' Hannah bit her tongue. She'd almost asked about the apprentice house, but had remembered just in time. She stumbled for a moment and then altered her words to ask, 'My . . . my hours of working and . . . and my wage?' It seemed reasonable to ask and when Mr Scarsfield answered, she nodded and said, 'I'll be here in the morning, sir.'

'Oh, you don't call me "sir".' Ernest laughed and, just as he'd told her before, he added, 'You call me "Mr Scarsfield".'

She smiled at him. 'Thank you, Mr Scarsfield.' Then she turned to Adam and held out her hand. 'And thank you too, Mr Adam. I'll not let you down.'

He took her slim hand in his in a warm, firm handshake. 'I know you won't,' he said softly.

As she turned and walked away from them, Hannah was well aware that both men stood gazing after her, the one with admiration, the other with a puzzled look on his face.

'Mr Grundy – how lovely to see you again. And you too, Ted.'

The big man held out his arms and, without thinking, Hannah ran into his rough embrace.

'Eh, what about me? I wouldn't mind a bit of that, if there's hugs being given out.'

Hannah leaned back to look up into Ollie's face, her eyes twinkling with mischief. 'Seems your nephew wants a hug off you, an' all . . .'

'Not off him, silly. You!' Ted was quick to say, but then he saw she was teasing him and they all laughed together. Releasing herself from Ollie Grundy's strong arms, she hugged Ted too. He held her close and buried his face against her hair.

'It's great to see you again. But what's with the hair colour change? You had lovely fair hair.'

Hannah pulled away, almost having to prise herself out of his embrace. Ted was reluctant to let her go. The feel of her young, firm body in his arms had set the young man's pulses racing and his senses reeling.

'I didn't want anyone to recognize me.'

'Not recognize you? Some hope!' he laughed. 'I'd've known you anywhere, blonde or redhead. You can't hide them lovely eyes or that smile.'

Hannah's face fell. 'Really? Do you really think people will know me?'

''Course they won't,' Lily said, placing a meat and

357

potato pie on the table. 'Now come and eat – all of you. There's my special treacle tart for afters.'

'I don't suppose,' Hannah said as she sat down, suddenly feeling very hungry, 'that you know anyone in the village who'd take a lodger, do you?'

'You're staying then?' Lily's face lit up.

Hannah nodded. 'I got meself a job at the mill this afternoon. I start tomorrow morning.'

'And did anyone recognize you?' Ted asked, passing his plate to his aunt to be loaded up with a generous helping of pie and vegetables.

Hannah shook her head, but a fleeting anxious look was in her eyes. 'No. But then I only saw Mr Adam and Mr Scarsfield. Oh, and Mr Roper, but I kept my head turned away from him. I . . . I saw Daniel – you know, Luke's brother – but he never looked up from his work.'

'He'll know you.' Ted nodded with certainty.

'Mmm, maybe, but I think Daniel will keep my secret. He'll understand – if anyone will – why I've come back.'

Ted gaped at her, his fork suspended midway between his plate and his mouth. 'Why have you come back?' He grinned suddenly. 'I thought it was to see me.'

'Well, of course it was.' She smiled, playing up to him. Then her smile faded. 'But there's a much more serious reason.'

'Yes, and I'm not too happy about it,' Lily put in. 'I reckon the lass could be stacking up a load of trouble for 'erself.'

'Why?' Ollie and Ted chorused the question.

'She wants revenge on Mr Edmund, because of the accident and the death of her . . . well . . . of Luke.'

'More than just that,' Hannah said quietly and found that, suddenly, her appetite had left her. 'There's Nell too.'

'Who's Nell?' Ollie asked, still eating heartily but listening nonetheless.

'She came from the same workhouse as me, but a few years earlier. I never knew her there, but we got friendly at the mill. Then suddenly, she disappeared. None of us in the apprentice house knew what had happened to her, though I have a feeling Mrs Bramwell did. I mean, she hadn't even served out her indenture. One or two thought she'd run away.'

'And had she?'

'No.' Hannah's mouth was tight. 'She'd been sent back to the workhouse in Macclesfield because she was expecting a child.' She paused and added significantly, '*Mr Edmund's child.*'

To her surprise, Lily only shrugged and the two men looked down at their plates. 'Aye, well, she wasn't the first and I don't suppose she'll be the last.'

'Well, it's high time she was. It's high time something was done about that man. That's how Luke was killed, because he was trying to protect me. Mr Edmund was after *me.*'

Now all three looked at her.

'Trouble is, love,' Ollie said in his growly voice. 'He will be again, if you don't watch out.'

'That's just what I think, Ollie,' Lily remarked, triumphant to hear her husband agree with her.

'Then he'll have me to deal with,' Ted said stoutly and flexed his muscles.

The other three stared at him and then burst out laughing. Pint-sized Ted, though strong and sturdy, would be no match for the tall, well-built Edmund

Critchlow, but Hannah was touched by his chivalrous gesture. Wiping the tears from her eyes, she touched his arm. 'Thank you, Ted. I'll not forget that.'

The tension in the room broken, Hannah picked up her knife and fork. All at once her hunger had returned. 'By the way,' she asked as she ate, 'what happened to the Bramwells?'

'He sacked them,' Lily replied tartly. 'They'd run that apprentice house for over twenty years for the Critchlows, and just because Mr Edmund gave up the system about two years ago, they was out on their ear. He didn't even try to find them work in the mill. And I'm sure Arthur could've turned his hand to something, don't you, Ollie?'

''Course he could.'

'Where are they now?'

'Went away. To Manchester, I reckon. I 'ad one letter off Ethel, but things didn't sound too good and I've never heard again.'

'What happened to all the apprentices? Come to think of it,' she stopped eating, 'd'you know, I never thought about it before, but there weren't as many apprentices in the house by the time I left as there had been when we came. And there were no more paupers from the workhouse came after us. We were the last. I'd never realized it before, but now you mention it . . .'

Lily shook her head. 'No. As they finished their term, he didn't replace them and the last few that were there still with time to serve, he found lodgings for them in the village when he closed the house.'

'Poor Mr and Mrs Bramwell,' Hannah murmured. 'I quite liked them, you know.'

'So did we,' Lily agreed. 'I just hope they're all right.'

There was only one more thing that had to be done that night and Lily settled it as she rose to clear the table. 'You don't need to go looking for lodgings in the village. Not unless you want to, of course. You can stay here. Ollie and me's agreed. We had a little chat while you was up at the mill, when I told him you was back an' that you might be stayin'.'

'Oh, thank you, Mrs Grundy. That'd be perfect.'

Behind her, Ted beamed.

Hannah slipped into the work she was given with ease; it was as if she'd never been away. Several of the youngsters – now young men and women like herself – who'd been apprentices at the house when Hannah had lived there still worked in the mill, but no one seemed to recognize her.

There were now only two people she dreaded coming face to face with: Daniel and Mr Edmund Critchlow. And she wasn't sure which incited the most fear in her.

There were one or two other people she'd recognized, but no one to whom she'd been close. She hadn't seen Joe or Millie, and of course she couldn't ask about them. Maybe they'd left when they'd served their term.

Despite the reason for her return, Hannah was happy. She'd always liked the work at the mill, and now she was older, it was much easier. She was treated by the Grundys as a daughter and she had Ted as a friend, though he, she thought with a frown, might be trying to become a little too friendly. And her ruse seemed to be working: no one had recognized her.

But then, she met Daniel.

She was running up the stone stairs to the work-room early one morning, holding her skirts high so that she did not trip. And she was singing just as she used to, her pure voice echoing clearly up the staircase. Daniel, coming down, stopped and stared at her climbing towards him, her eyes downcast. He stepped in front of her, barring her way, and she would have cannoned into him and might have fallen backwards down the stairs if he hadn't grasped her strongly by the shoulder. She gave a little cry of alarm. As she looked up and saw who was holding her, her heart sank.

How could she have been so foolish as to be singing? Daniel, more than anyone else, would remember her singing. It'd been a joke between the three of them – four counting poor little Jane.

Daniel wouldn't have forgotten the girl who sang.

Now he was looking down into her face, into her clear, blue eyes.

'You! It *is* you. I thought I was hearing things.' He flung her away from him so that she stumbled and fell heavily against the wall and only just prevented herself from tumbling down the stairs. 'Why've you come back?' he asked bitterly. There was no pleasure in his tone at seeing her, no welcome in his eyes.

Hannah's eyes glinted and her mouth tightened. 'I've unfinished business. I told you I'd come back one day. That he wouldn't get away with . . . with what he did.'

Daniel's face was a sneer. 'Oh aye? And what d'you reckon you can do to a powerful man like Edmund

Critchlow? Don't you think that if there'd been a way, I'd've found it?'

Now that she was close to him, she could see that the years had treated Daniel harshly. His grief at the loss of his twin and the bitterness in his heart had twisted his handsome, boyish features, had eaten into his soul and made him older than his years. He was only eighteen, yet he could have been mistaken for thirty.

'Oh, Daniel,' Hannah said sadly.

He saw the sympathy in her eyes and spat, 'Don't pity me. I don't need your pity or anyone else's. You shouldn't have come back.'

'You told me before that I shouldn't be going away.'

'No, you shouldn't. Not then. You left me to cope alone.'

'But . . . but you blamed me. Said it was my fault. I . . . I thought it was better if I went.'

Daniel ran his hand through his hair. He was unsure now what he really felt. Seeing Hannah again had confused him and awakened feelings in him which he'd worked so hard to bury. But seeing her again – the girl his brother had loved, the girl that Luke had given his life to protect – had brought back all the pain and suffering. He hated her. She'd ruined his life. He'd never been able to love another human being the same as he'd loved his brother. He would never love anyone else the way he'd loved Luke.

The way he had loved Hannah.

Unbidden, the realization came to him with a jolt.

He'd watched them together and been consumed with jealousy. Older now, he recognized the feeling, and those old emotions were flooding through him again at the sight of her. He'd never known – and with a shock he realized that he still didn't know – whether the jealousy was directed at her because Luke had loved her and she'd come between the twins, or whether it was because she'd loved Luke and not him. Had be been jealous of his own brother?

Even after all these years, Daniel still did not know.

'Get out of my way,' he growled, and pushed past her to continue on his way down the stairs. 'And if you know what's good for you, you'll stay out of my way.'

Stricken, Hannah stared after him for a moment. Then lightly she ran down the stairs after him and caught hold of his arm. 'Daniel, wait a minute. Please.'

He stopped. 'What?'

'Please, Daniel, don't give me away.'

He stared at her for a long moment, gave a brief nod, pulled himself from her grasp and continued down the stairs without another word.

Hannah leaned against the wall, closed her eyes and breathed a sigh of relief.

Now – there was only Mr Edmund to face.

Thirty-Nine

'So – how's it going?'

Adam was smiling down at her as she stood in front of her machine. As she glanced up at him, she was struck once more by his likeness to his father and yet there was a difference. A very important difference. His brown eyes were warm and friendly, not cold and disdainful. His mouth curved in a smile, not in a cruel sneer.

'Fine,' she said. 'I think Mr Scarsfield is pleased with my work.'

'He is,' Adam nodded. 'That's what I've come to tell you. Your appointment is confirmed. You're no longer on trial.'

'Thank you, sir. Thank you very much.'

He leaned closer, speaking above the noise of the machinery, yet only for her to hear. 'I'd like it if you called me Adam. And would you . . . would you come out with me some evening?'

She stared at him, wide-eyed for a moment. And then quite suddenly, like a revelation, she saw her way to get revenge on Edmund Critchlow.

'I'd love to,' she said huskily.

'Saturday? You'll finish earlier on a Saturday afternoon.' He knew her hours better than she did. Hannah nodded.

'I'll meet you near the waterfall behind the mill. Do you know it?'

She nodded. She'd been here a month now. There'd been time enough for her to do a little exploring in the area. He wouldn't question it.

'I must go. See you Saturday.'

'Saturday,' she murmured.

'You gonner let me take you for a ride in Auntie's pony and trap on Sunday?'

Hannah nodded. 'That'd be nice, Ted. Where are we going?'

Ted shrugged. 'Where you like. Take you into Bakewell, if you like – if the old pony can manage the hills.'

'There won't be any shops open on a Sunday,' she said impishly.

'Oho, don't tell me you like the shops? Uh-huh! There I was, thinking I'd found me a nice girl and I find she's a spendthrift.'

Hannah laughed. 'I would be if I had the money, but I haven't.'

'Mebbe Sunday's the safest day to take you into town then.'

She chuckled. 'Mebbe you're right.'

'I'll come for you about three?'

Hannah nodded. 'Sunday it is.'

Who'd've thought it? Two young men in the space of two days. And what, she wondered, would each one say about the other when they found out?

And find out they surely would.

Saturday evening was dull with heavy April showers threatening. As she took the narrow path behind the mill and came to the footbridge across the river near the waterfall, she saw Adam waiting for her.

'I brought my father's big black umbrella,' he greeted her. 'It looks like rain.'

He took her arm and guided her along the narrow path at the side of the River Wye. On their right was the sheer face of the cliff. 'The village is on the top of this cliff. Millersbrook – it gets its name from the brook that runs in front of the mill. But I'm forgetting, you must know the village by now.'

She hesitated only a moment. 'Not – not ever so well. But I'm learning.'

'I presume you found some lodgings all right?'

'Oh yes, thank you.' Hannah bit her lip. She'd better be truthful about where she was living. 'I'm staying with the Grundys at Rushwater Farm.'

'Really?' Was she imagining a slight change in the tone of his voice at the mention of the Grundys' name? 'I didn't know they took in lodgers.' Then he murmured, so low that she could scarcely hear, 'Especially anyone working at the mill.'

'Don't they?' Hannah feigned surprise. 'Oh! Well, I don't know then. I only know that I first met them when I arrived here. I walked down the hill . . .' She was describing her arrival of years earlier, but Adam wasn't to know that. 'And I called to ask the way.' She glanced up at him. 'The carter just told us – I mean, me – that the mill was at the end of the dale, but when I came to the fork in the road, I didn't know which way to go, so . . .' She shrugged to indicate the simplicity of what had happened. 'I knocked on the back door of the farmhouse to ask the way, and this kind woman invited me in and fed me stew and dumplings.' She faltered at the memory of the four of them sitting around Lily Grundy's table, little knowing what lay in store for them. How innocent they'd all been then!

'And I suppose she liked the look of you.' He took hold of her arm on the pretext of steering her round a muddy puddle, but when they'd skirted it, he did not let go. Instead, he took her hand and tucked it through his arm. 'Can't say I blame her.'

They walked in silence, watching the ducks swimming and diving for food and the fish lying just below the surface, their heads facing upstream.

They had walked some distance when they came out of the trees overhanging the path. Before them was a building at the side of the river.

'Oh! Another mill!' Hannah exclaimed in genuine surprise. During her previous time at Wyedale Mill, she had heard tell of this one.

'Yes. This is Raven's Mill.' They stood looking up at the tall building, silent now on a Saturday evening. It was set in a narrow valley with nearby houses set beneath the cliff. 'It's strange,' Adam said, 'we have workers coming from this village to work at our mill, and I know there are one or two from Millersbrook who work here. They all use this path every day and must pass one another. I always wonder why they don't just swap jobs.'

'Mm,' Hannah was non-committal. In the past, she had heard rumours that there wasn't much to choose between the two mills as regards working conditions, but no doubt some workers believed one or the other to be better for some reason. Maybe, in the case of women workers, the owner of Raven's Mill was not a lecherous devil like Edmund Critchlow.

'Your father? Does he own Wyedale Mill?'

'Yes, but one day it will come to me.'

Hannah waited, willing him to explain. She wanted to ask about his grandfather, Nathaniel Critchlow, but she wasn't supposed to know of his existence. And yet, why not? Adam wasn't to know that she'd not heard about him from the other workers.

'Someone was saying,' she said carefully, 'that your grandfather started the mill?'

'Actually it was his father. My grandfather was a young boy when they found Wyedale together. He loved to tell the tale of how it all started.'

Adam was smiling fondly, but there was sadness in his eyes.

Gently, Hannah said, 'Is he . . . I mean . . .'

'He died almost three years ago.' It couldn't have been long after she left, Hannah thought. 'He took over the mill from his father, of course, and ran it – very successfully, I might add.'

Really? Hannah wanted to say sarcastically, but she bit her tongue.

'He had his first seizure about five years ago. There was a nasty accident. A little girl got her hair caught in a machine and she died. It really upset Grandfather. Then about three years ago there was the most terrible accident. A boy – well, a young man almost – fell into the water-wheel and was killed. There was an inquest, of course, but no one was to blame. Accidental death, they said. No one was supposed to tell my grandfather – they knew it would upset him – but,' his tone hardened, 'Josiah Roper used to come up to the Manor to see him and I think he let it slip during a conversation. I'm sure he didn't mean to, but it brought on another seizure – a bad one – and Grandfather died a few months later.' Adam's face was suddenly bleak.

'I'm sorry.' Hannah hoped her words sounded sincere. They were – for Adam. She was sure he'd been fond of his grandfather, and she couldn't really blame him for not knowing the truth about Luke's so-called accident. He hadn't been there.

'I don't think I've seen your father around the mill, have I?' It was difficult to pretend she didn't even know him, especially when his dark features were so vivid in her memory.

'No, he's away now. He left three weeks ago – just after you started. He's gone abroad for a few weeks. On business. Looking for new outlets, he said.' Now there was definitely an evasive, off-hand tone in his voice, as if the reason he was giving for Edmund's absence was not entirely the truth.

Hannah wondered if it had to do with the girl whose place she'd taken.

At that moment they felt huge spots of rain begin to fall and Adam put up the large black umbrella. 'We'd better go back.'

They were in sight of Wyedale Mill when the rain began to fall in earnest, drenching Hannah's skirt in seconds.

'Let's shelter beneath the cliff. You still have some way to go to get back to the farm.' Taking hold of her hand he pulled her beneath the overhanging shelf of the rock face. The rain was beating in the opposite direction and they were sheltered.

Adam shook the umbrella and closed it. 'I don't think it will last long,' he said, looking up at the lowering sky. 'The clouds are breaking up.'

She shivered suddenly and Adam put his arm around her. 'This wasn't a good idea. I should have taken you to some grand hotel and wined and dined you in luxury, but I was afraid you wouldn't come.'

Hannah looked up into his face, so close to hers. His brown eyes were so earnest, so open and honest that she couldn't resist teasing him a little. 'Not good enough to take to a fancy hotel, aren't I?'

Alarm crossed his handsome face. 'Oh, I didn't mean that. Please . . . please don't think—'

She laughed. 'I don't. I'm teasing you.'

There was no mistaking the look of relief on his face. 'So,' he whispered, bending closer, his lips only inches from her mouth. 'Will you let me take you out one evening?' But before she could reply, his lips touched hers and his arms were about her.

His kiss was gentle, undemanding, yet searching, questioning. 'You're so lovely, Anna,' he whispered. 'You will come out with me again, won't you?'

Hannah's mind was in turmoil. His use of her assumed name brought her sharply back to her reason for being here. She had almost been lulled into enjoying his company, into allowing herself . . . But now she remembered.

'I'd like that,' she murmured and held up her face, inviting him to kiss her again.

After the Sunday morning service that was still held in the now unused schoolroom, Hannah walked down the hill from the village, but instead of going along the lane back to the farm, she turned to the right and took the path behind the mill leading to the waterfall. She crossed the bridge and climbed the steep, rough-hewn rocky steps to the hillside above the mill.

She needed to be alone. She wanted to think and decide whether she could really go through with her daring plan. As she climbed, she stopped in surprise. A broad, flat pathway was being carved out of the hillside and it looked as if they were digging a tunnel through the hills. Whatever for? Hannah wondered. 'I'll ask Ted,' she murmured. 'He'll know.'

Just below the workings, Hannah sat down on the grass and looked down on the mill. Her gaze travelled to the line of houses set above the mill and the former apprentice house where she had lived for several years. Then higher still to the rows of houses, teetering on the hillside. Most of their residents gained their livelihood from the mill. Then further along still, above the path along which she had walked yesterday with Adam and set high on the cliff, stood the Critchlow mansion. Presumably, Adam lived there with his father. Before his death, Mr Nathaniel had lived there too. A house of men, with no women, except servants, within its walls. Then her gaze swivelled and travelled in the opposite direction down the dale until she saw the roof of the Grundys' farmhouse.

She sighed. She was not a conceited girl, but she knew that certain look that came into a young man's eyes when he looked at a girl who attracted him. She'd seen it first in Luke's eyes. And that had grown into love: a first love, an innocent love, pure and unsullied. She'd seen that sort of look in Edmund's eyes, yet his was tinged with selfish lust and depravity. He cared nothing for the object of his desire, only for his own gratification.

And now she was seeing that look again in Adam's

eyes. But which did his resemble? Luke's or Edmund Critchlow's? And then there was Ted. His was a teasing, flirting kind of look, but still, there was no doubting the admiration in his eyes.

Hannah sighed. Could she go through with it? Was her first love still so strong that she could give up all hope of future happiness to bring about her revenge on the man who'd robbed Luke of his life?

She pulled herself up and her gaze came roaming over the mill and then swivelled to the Critchlows' house. The answer was yes. Yes, she could devote the whole of her life, if needs be, to avenging the cruelty of the Critchlows, their deception, their callous treatment of others. It was not only Luke she was doing this for, but her mother and Nell and all the countless others who'd suffered at their hands. Maybe, she mused, even the girl whose machine she now worked.

Hannah looked about her again. It was such a beautiful setting. Who would guess that such inhumanity went on in such an idyllic place? But it wasn't the place, she reminded herself, it was the people. And most of the people who lived in this place were good, decent people. People like the Grundys and the Scarsfields and all the ordinary villagers who worked in the mill. People like the Bramwells – oh, she wished she knew what had happened to the Bramwells. It was only a few – a very few – whose powerful position and greed had corrupted them that spoilt this place. As the sun reached its zenith, casting its golden light over the hillsides and shining deep into the dale, Hannah hurried down the hillside. Ted would be waiting and, if no one else, she owed him an explanation.

*

'I thought you liked me,' Ted said dolefully, hurt in his eyes.

'Oh, Ted, I do.' Hannah touched his hand. 'That's why I'm being honest with you now. I – I don't want to hurt you.'

'You already have,' he muttered, avoiding her glance as they sat together on the wall at the very top of the hill on the road leading out of the dale. The proposed trip into Bakewell had been postponed as, once again, rain clouds threatened.

'You'll get soaked and catch yer death,' Lily had warned. 'Just go for a little walk, the pair of you, and you can come back here for your tea.'

But tea was the last thing on their minds at present.

'It's so difficult, Ted. Maybe I'm presuming, being conceited, reading too much into you asking me out . . .'

'No,' he sighed. 'No, you're not. I want you to be my girl. There, that's putting it straight. But you're saying "no".'

'Yes, no – I mean yes, I'm saying no. But, Ted, can't we be friends?'

'Huh!'

'Does that mean we can't be?'

The young man sighed heavily. 'Oh, Hannah, Anna – or whatever you want to be called now – I'd never do anything to hurt you and . . . and if you were in trouble, I'd always help you, but . . . but I can't think of you as just a friend. I love you, Hannah,' he ended simply, and the hangdog look on his face tore at her heart.

'I'm sorry, Ted, truly I am, but I've made up my mind. I came back here for one reason and one reason only. And I intend to carry it out – however much it costs me.'

Ted regarded her steadily as he said softly, 'And you don't care who you hurt in the process, eh?'

'I don't want to hurt you, Ted. You of all people, but I've been honest with you from the day I came back.'

'Yes, you have,' Ted acknowledged, 'but I didn't realize it would stop us . . . well, walking out together.'

Hannah bit her lip, embarrassed to tell him the whole truth.

They were both silent as they walked back down the hill, each deep in their own thoughts, so deep that they didn't notice the clip-clop of a horse's hooves behind them until it was almost upon them. Ted grabbed Hannah and pulled her to the side of the road, his arms about her to steady her. The rider reined his mount in and sat looking down at them.

Hannah drew in a startled breath and whispered, 'Oh no,' as she found herself looking up into Adam's face, his expression a mixture of anger and hurt. His eyes bore into hers and then turned cold. His glance swivelled away from her and met Ted's belligerent gaze.

Though not a word passed between them, a kind of war was silently declared between the two young men. And she was the cause.

Then Adam kicked his horse and urged it down the steep hill at a dangerous pace.

Ted released his hold and stared after him. 'What on earth was all that about?'

Hannah sighed, straightened her skirt. 'I went walking with him yesterday evening.'

Ted stared at her and then at the place where the cantering horse had disappeared round the bend in the road. They could still hear the beat of its hooves. He was thoughtful for a moment before he said quietly, 'And does Master Adam figure in this . . . this plan of yours?'

'Yes,' she said simply. 'I think he does.'

'Then I'd be very careful, Hannah, because even if you think you can take *him* for a fool, you certainly can't make one of his father.'

Forty

Tea at the Grundys' was strained, the two young ones hardly speaking to each other and avoiding each other's eyes. Lily, sensitive to the atmosphere, tried to make cheerful conversation, but when Ted left to go home, she confronted Hannah.

'What's going on between you two? Had a row, have yer?'

Hannah sighed. There was nothing else for it but to tell the truth. 'Ted wanted me to be his girl—'

'So?' Lily interrupted. 'He's a nice lad. A good lad. You could do far worse.'

'I know. He *is* a nice lad. That's why . . . that's why I can't. He shouldn't have anything to do with me.'

'Eh?' Lily was perplexed. 'Aw lass, don't put yourself down. Ted's not the sort to bother about your past. Who you are or where you came from or . . . or the fact that – well – you've got no dad. All families have got something.'

'It's not that,' Hannah put in hastily. 'Like I told him – I had to be honest with him, Mrs Grundy, and I'm being honest with you. If – when I've told you – you want me to leave, then I'll go. Find other lodgings, only, please, hear me out.'

'Go on.' Lily's tone was not encouraging.

'You know why I've come back. I've told you. I can't even think about . . . about Ted, not in that way, not until I've done what I came back to do. And . . . and he doesn't like what it involves.'

'What do you mean "what it involves"?'

Hannah lifted her chin determinedly and her blue eyes were as cold as steel. 'Being friendly – very friendly – with Master Adam.'

Lily's mouth dropped open and her eyes had the very same anxious look that Ted'd had. 'Aw, Hannah, mind what you're doing. You'll be the one ending up getting hurt, if you don't watch out.'

Hannah didn't see Adam for three days. She was sure that where before he'd sought her out, now he was deliberately avoiding her. On the fourth day, as she was leaving work in the evening, he was crossing the yard towards the mill.

'Adam,' she began, but he gave her a curt nod and carried on walking swiftly past her.

She ran after him and caught hold of his sleeve. 'Please – let me explain.'

Angrily, he shook her off. 'I have nothing to say to you, *Miss Morgan*.'

'Oh, have it your own way,' she cried, close to tears. 'There's nothing between Ted and me. I just wanted you to know that. He's the Grundys' nephew and they'd invited him to tea.' It was not quite the truth, but it was near enough. 'But if you don't *want* to believe me . . .'

Now it was she who turned away and, picking up her skirts, began to run across the yard.

'Anna – Anna. Wait. Don't go.' He caught up with her. 'I'm sorry.' He took her hands in his, not caring now who might see them together. 'Do you mean it? Is he nothing to you?'

'He's the Grundy's nephew. I can hardly ignore him, can I? He's a friend. That's all.'

Adam shook his head and his smile held disbelief. 'You really think that any young man in their right mind can look upon you as a friend?'

Keeping her expression innocent, she looked up at him with her wide, appealing blue eyes. 'Why ever not?' she said huskily.

'Oh, Anna – if only you knew.' She felt his grasp, warm and firm, holding her cold hands. She felt him squeeze them and knew what he was trying to say.

Pretending shyness, she dropped her gaze. 'Oh!' she breathed.

'We can't talk here. Not properly.' His eyes burned with desire. 'Meet me tonight. Please, Anna. Come back to the mill – no one will be here then. I have a key. We can go into the office.'

'All right,' she agreed, putting just the right amount of maidenly hesitancy into her tone. Her heart was beating fast, not with love or desire for him but with excitement that her devious and dangerous plan seemed to be working even better than she'd dared to hope. He was like one of the fish in the river and she was playing him on the end of her hook.

He raised her hands to his lips and kissed them both. Then he released her and continued his way across the yard. She stood, watching him, like any young girl would on the brink of falling in love with a handsome young man. At the door into the building, he turned, smiled and waved before disappearing inside. With a smile of satisfaction, Hannah skipped down the road towards the farm. And now, with only the sheep in the nearby field to hear her, she sang at the top of her voice.

It was almost dark when she slipped along the lane back to the mill. She'd had to steal out of the house without Mrs Grundy being aware of her going. If they'd gone to bed by the time she returned she knew where the spare key for the back door was hidden.

It was eerie walking into the mill at night-time: no one hurrying across the yard, no sound of the huge water-wheel, no clatter of machinery from several floors. Hannah, pulling her shawl closely about her, hurried across the yard and in through the door. The stairs were dimly lit and she felt her way up to the offices. Passing through the one occupied by Mr Roper during the daytime, she tapped on the inner door. It flew open at once, and Adam reached out for her and pulled her into his arms. Pushing the door shut with his foot, he began to kiss her. 'Sweet, adorable Anna . . .'

She returned his kisses. It was not difficult; he was a handsome young man. She liked him, but he was not Luke. And Luke had been the love of her life.

'Oh, Anna, Anna, I want you so. Let me love you. Please, let me love you . . .' With trembling fingers he began to fumble at the buttons of her blouse.

She stiffened and pulled back, smacking his hands away. 'No!'

He stared down at her, a mixture of anger and longing in his eyes. 'I won't hurt you. I promise. I'll be careful, I'll . . .'

Hannah shook her head firmly. 'No, I'm not that sort of girl.'

'Oh, Anna, I'd never think that about you. But I love you so much.'

'You hardly know me. You don't know anything about me.'

'I know enough to know I love you.'

'And what would your . . . your mother and father say? You consorting with a mill girl?'

His face was bleak for a moment. 'My mother's dead.' His tone became bitter. 'And my father is in no position to find fault.'

Hannah widened her eyes, feigning ignorance. 'Whatever do you mean?'

Adam looked uncomfortable. 'He . . . he "consorts" with the mill girls, as you so delicately put it.'

'Oh! I see.'

'No, no, you don't,' he burst out angrily. 'I'm not like him. I wouldn't tire of you and cast you off.'

Daringly, Hannah murmured, 'And if I were to get with child? What then?'

'Then . . . then I'd marry you. Of course, I would.'

'Then,' she whispered, 'marry me now.'

With a groan, he pulled her to him and buried his face against her neck. 'I would. You know I would. I'd give anything to marry you, but I can't. I daren't.'

'Daren't? Why "daren't"?'

'My father. He'd disown me. I'd lose my inheritance – the mill – everything.'

'But we'd be together. We'd have each other. We could work.'

Adam gave a wry laugh. 'Work? What do you suppose I could do? I've never lifted a finger to work in my life.'

381

'But you work here. You help run the mill. Surely you could get a job as a manager or an overlooker in another mill.'

'My father and Roper run the mill. I just put the time in. And not even that sometimes, if I'm honest.'

'But you must know something about what goes on? You come round the mill. You talk to the workers.'

'Even if I did what you say – even if I applied for a job somewhere else – how long do you suppose it'd be before my father found out where I was and got in touch with the owners? They'd sack me as soon as look at me, if my father asked them to. Perhaps you don't realize just how powerful my father is in the district. And beyond, if the truth be known.'

I think I do, Hannah wanted to say bitterly. If a man can be the cause of a boy's death and get away with it just because he has friends in high places, then anything is possible. Instead, she murmured, 'I hadn't realized,' adding sadly, 'then there's nothing to be done.'

'But I must see you. I must hold you. Please, Anna. I think about you all the time. I can't sleep at night for thinking about you.'

'We can see each other. We can meet.'

'But I want so much more. I want you.'

Was this how his father seduced the young girls? How he'd seduced Nell? With flattery and empty promises of love?

Hannah was resolute. 'Then put a ring on my finger.'

Adam's only answer was a deep groan. He buried his fingers in her hair and rained kisses on her forehead, her eyes, and lastly, her mouth.

*

It was as dark as pitch in the lane from the mill to the farm with no moon to light her way. She crept into the yard, closed the gate quietly and tiptoed across the yard. Near the back door, the Grundys' collie came out of his kennel.

'Shh, boy. It's only me,' she whispered, and the animal wagged his tail and licked her hand. The back door key was kept hidden just inside the dog's kennel and Hannah felt around until her fingers found it. With one last pat on the dog's head, she inserted the key in the lock, turned it and opened the door. To her horror, it only opened a few inches and then rattled against a chain.

Hannah had forgotten that last thing at night Ollie looped a chain across the inside of the back door.

'Serves you right if you was locked out,' was all Lily Grundy had to say next morning as Hannah appeared sheepishly through the back door, heavy eyed and with bits of straw in her hair from a night spent in the hayloft. Lily clicked her tongue in irritation and disapproval. 'I don't know what you think you're up to, lass, but you'll come to a bad end if you don't mind. Oh, go on with you. Into the scullery and get washed and come and get your breakfast.'

As she sat down at the table moments later, Ollie winked at her. 'I heard the chain rattle and I was coming down to let yer in, but 'er,' he gestured towards his wife with a nod, 'wouldn't let me.'

'I should think not an' all,' Lily said, banging a dish of thick porridge in front of Hannah. 'Coming home when decent folks are all in their beds. My Ollie works long, hard hours, m'girl. He doesn't want his sleep broken by you traipsing in at all hours.'

'No, Mrs Grundy. I'll mind it doesn't happen again.'

Lily sniffed and disappeared to the scullery. Ollie leaned over. 'Don't worry, lass. When I know you're out, I won't put the chain on. You know where key is?'

Hannah nodded. Ollie winked and tapped the side of his nose. 'What the eye doesn't see, eh? But just take care of yourself. I wouldn't want you getting hurt.'

'I won't, Mr Grundy, I promise you that. And I'm sorry for disturbing you.'

'That's all right. We'll say no more about it.'

And no more was said, but Lily was not quite so forgiving, and Hannah had the uncomfortable feeling that it was more to do with her rejection of Ted than with her late homecoming.

'You're wanted in the office.' One of the young girls approached Hannah at her machine. 'I'll take over here.'

'Who sent for me?'

The girl shrugged. 'Dunno.' She eyed Hannah, who was smiling. 'Don't know what you're looking so pleased about. We only get called up to the office if we've done summat wrong. What have you been up to?'

'Nothing,' Hannah said airily. But of course she had been up to plenty and with the young master. He was becoming more possessive, more ardent in his demands with each passing day, and she knew that her refusal to let him make love to her was driving him insane with desire.

As she hurried down the length of the workroom, she saw Daniel glowering at her. 'Can't wait till night, eh?' he mouthed at her. Folks who worked in the mills became expert at lip-reading, and whilst she couldn't hear his words, she knew exactly what he had said. She stopped and moved closer. 'What do you mean?'

'What I say. We all know about you and the young master. You can't keep secrets round here, Hannah, you should know that.'

'Don't call me that, my name's—'

'I'll call you whatever I like.' His eyes narrowed. 'I could think of one or two names that would fit you nicely.'

'How dare you?'

'Oh, I dare. D'you know something, Hannah – and I never thought I'd hear meself say such a thing – but I'm glad that my brother isn't alive to see it. To see how you're behaving. It'd've broken his heart.'

Tears sprang to Hannah's eyes as she blurted out, 'If Luke was still alive, I wouldn't be doing it.'

Then she whirled around and ran, and did not stop until she opened the door to the outer office and, breathless, almost fell into the room. Without taking any notice of Mr Roper, bent as always over his books, she ran towards the inner door. Her hand was on the doorknob when he spoke.

'There's no one in there,' came Josiah Roper's silky voice.

Hannah turned to face him, the tears of anger at Daniel's words still brimming in her eyes. 'What . . . what d'you mean? I was sent for. Adam—'

'Oho, Adam, is it?'

Too late, she realized her mistake. 'I mean Master Adam,' she stammered, but the damage was done.

Slowly, Josiah put down his pen, slipped off his high stool and regarded her for a moment over the top of his small oval spectacles perched on his beak-like nose.

'You needn't worry. Everyone here knows about you and Master Adam. Including me. Especially me.' He paused. 'But what no one else knows – except me – is . . .' He paused and then added with an ominous threat in his tone, 'Exactly – who *you* are.'

Forty-One

Standing in the office facing Josiah Roper, Hannah gasped, the colour fleeing from her face. 'What . . . what do you mean? My name's Anna Morgan.'

'Don't play your devious games with me, girl. You're Hannah Francis. I knew you the minute you walked through that door.' He flung his arm out to indicate the office door. 'Think dying your hair that ridiculous colour is going to hide your identity? It's not quite as easy as that. Oh, I've no doubt you've fooled a few here. The ones who didn't know you that well. Master Adam, for one,' he added pointedly. 'But wait till Mr Edmund decides to come home. He'll know you. Oh yes, he'll know you all right.'

Hannah's shoulders slumped. 'So you're going to tell Adam?'

A sly look came over Josiah's face. 'No, actually, I'm not.'

Now Anna was surprised. 'You're not?'

He shook his head. 'I don't quite know yet what devious game it is you're playing or why – and I don't expect you're going to tell me.' He paused a moment as if giving her time to do just that. When she remained silent he gave a little shrug and went on. 'I assume you're setting your cap at Master Adam. And,' he raised his eyebrows, 'by all accounts, it seems to be working. Trying to get him to marry you, are you?'

'I . . .'

Josiah nodded. 'I thought so. Well, the master won't like that. He won't like that at all.'

'So,' Hannah asked carefully. 'Why aren't you going to tell Master Adam who I really am?'

'Because,' another pause whilst Hannah waited, holding her breath, 'it suits my purpose not to.'

'*Your* purpose? Whatever d'you mean?'

His thin smile did not reach his eyes as he said silkily, 'Because anything that *dis*pleases Mr Edmund *pleases* me.'

Hannah's eyes widened as she stared at him. 'But . . . but I thought . . . I mean you're Mr Edmund's lackey,' she blurted out. 'You're forever toadying up to him.'

Josiah's features twisted nastily. 'You know nothing, girl. Nothing about me.'

'But you told on me when you thought I was running away. Dragged me back here to be thrown in the punishment room. Why? If you're not bothered about Mr Edmund, why didn't you just let me go then?'

'Because it was my duty. Because it was what he expected me to do. What he pays me to do. Just as now I shall have to write and report to him that, in his absence, his son is keeping – er – undesirable company.'

Hannah was still puzzled. 'So this time you're giving me time to get away before he comes back?'

Josiah shook his head. 'Not at all. I'm giving you time to bring whatever it is you have to do to fruition. That's if you can manage it.'

Hannah shook her head wonderingly. 'Why? I just don't understand.'

'Why is my business,' he snapped. 'I'm just giving you fair warning what I'm going to do, that's all. I needn't write immediately,' he said. Now he was thinking aloud, laying out his plans. 'He's abroad, so the letter will take quite a while to reach him. Then it'll take him a few days to get back here. I reckon you've got about a month all told.'

Why, she wanted to demand again, but knew he was not going to tell her. 'Are you going to tell him in your letter who . . . who I am?' There was no point in her trying to carry on the deception further. At least, not with Josiah Roper.

Josiah didn't answer immediately. He turned and perched himself back on his high stool and picked up his pen. He twirled it between his fingers and than glanced back at her over his shoulder. 'No. I think it would be . . . amusing – see if he recognizes you for himself. Don't you?'

Then he turned back to the open ledger on his desk and calmly began checking a long column of figures.

Hannah stood staring at him in bewilderment for a few moments before she turned and went quietly out of the office without another word.

A month. For some devious, twisted reason of his own, Josiah Roper had given her a month to get Adam to marry her.

Hannah pondered how much to tell Adam. She didn't want him to know her true identity, and whilst she couldn't understand why he was doing it, she was grateful that Josiah Roper was for the moment keeping her secret. But there was another way she could put the pressure on Adam. Hannah smiled as she ran back across the yard to the workroom, another devious twist to her plan beginning to take shape.

'Darling,' she said, winding her arms about his waist as they stood together beneath the cliff on the narrow path beside the river. 'Everyone knows about us.'

Adam sighed. 'You can't keep secrets in a place like this.'

How true that was, Hannah thought ruefully. Even she had been unmasked by two people already and it was surely only a matter of time before either Daniel or Mr Roper told someone. Or someone else recognized her as a face from the past. She was surprised that Ernest Scarsfield hadn't realized who she was. He'd always been kind to her – as he still was, even though he thought she was a totally different person. And yes, she was a very different person to the innocent, naive child she'd been then. She shuddered, realizing with searing clarity that she did not like the new person she'd become.

Aloud, she said, 'What will happen when your father comes home? Because someone will tell him about us.'

'I don't know,' Adam said worriedly. 'I've been thinking about that. Roper will tell him for sure, if no one else does.' He was thoughtful for a moment before murmuring, 'I suppose I could sack Roper before Father gets back.'

'No,' Hannah said at once, afraid that if he did, the vindictive Josiah Roper would reveal her true identity. 'If Mr Roper doesn't tell him, someone else will.' She tried to be light-hearted. 'You can't sack everybody.'

She bit her lip and sighed dramatically. 'Your father will no doubt throw me out.'

'Then he'll have to throw me out too.'

'No . . . no, he wouldn't do that to you. Not his own son. Not if . . . not if you promise to give me up?'

'Give you up?' His arms tightened about her. 'I'll never do that. How can you even think it?'

Hannah pulled a wry face. 'You'll have to if you don't want to lose your inheritance.'

Adam groaned. 'I'd rather lose that than lose you.'

'You don't think he'd really do that, do you? Cut you off, I mean.'

Adam was thoughtful. 'He'd probably use it as a threat more than . . . than actually do it. You see, I'm the only heir there is. I've no cousins nor even more distant relatives that I know of.'

You have a little half-brother, Hannah wanted to say. Maybe more than one if the truth be known. But she held her tongue.

'And Father's very proud of the Critchlow family and its traditions. He wouldn't want to see the mill that my great-grandfather started pass into other hands. He'd do anything to stop that happening.'

'Well, I'm going to have to go when he comes back. I don't fancy ending up in the punishment room like—' She stopped, appalled that she had dropped her guard. Flustered she added, 'Like they say used to happen.'

Despite the seriousness of their conversation, Adam laughed. 'I can't imagine anyone being able to put a fiery redhead like you into the punishment room. Besides, it was only used when we had the pauper apprentices. And all that stopped a few years ago.'

Here was her chance to ask questions that had been puzzling her. 'The pauper apprentices? What do you mean? Who were they?'

'Oh, it was an old system whereby we took orphan children from the workhouse and gave them an apprenticeship here.'

He made it sound so philanthropic, as if the Critchlow family had been doing these poor, unfortunate children a favour. As he went on, Hannah realized that Adam thought that was exactly what they had done.

'We gave them a home and there was even a nice couple who ran the apprentice house. It was like one big, happy family for those poor kids. The kind of home that a lot of them had never known. I don't suppose being born and brought up in a workhouse could be much fun.'

No, Hannah could have answered. And it wasn't much fun being indentured to your family either. But in fairness, she thought, he was right about one thing. The Bramwells had been a nice couple. Carefully, she asked, 'So, where was this – what did you call it – the house?'

'The apprentice house. It's the one near the old schoolroom on the end of the row of houses directly behind the mill.'

'And do the couple who ran it still live there?' she asked deliberately, wondering if he knew any more than the Grundys.

'Oh no, the house is empty now. The Bramwells left. Went away somewhere. I'm not sure what they're doing now.' And he sounded as if he didn't really care either. The Bramwells had been thrown out of their job and their home and he didn't even know for sure what had become of them.

Hannah felt a cold chill run through her. Was Adam more like his father than she'd thought?

'Why did it finish? This . . . this apprentice system?'

'Laws were passed for shorter working hours for children, more schooling and such like. All very praiseworthy, but uneconomical from our point of view.'

Hannah had to bite down hard on her lower lip to stop the words bursting out. He sounded almost regretful at the ending of a system that had enslaved young children to fill the coffers of the already rich and powerful. She wondered if he'd ever realized just what the lives of the children had been like: the long hours of gruelling work, the punishments for any kind of misdemeanour, however trivial. The fines, the beatings and the punishment room. She said no more, relieved that her slip in mentioning the punishment room had not resulted in him asking awkward questions.

There was a long silence between them. They stood with their arms about each other watching the ducks swimming serenely on the river, the fish jumping . . .

As they walked home, hand in hand, Adam still had not said the words Hannah wanted to hear.

Three weeks later, Adam came into the workroom and, not caring now who saw them together, he walked straight up to Hannah at her machine.

'He's coming home. He'll be back here next week. I've had a letter. Roper's written to tell him about us. He's so angry, threatening, well, all sorts.'

'To throw us both out, you mean?'

Adam avoided her gaze. 'Well, sort of, but worse.'

'Worse? What do you mean – worse?'

'Look, we can't talk here. Come up to the office as soon as you can. I'll wait for you there. We'll have to decide what to do.'

Without waiting for her reply, he turned and walked away, his shoulders hunched, a look of desperation on his face.

As soon as she could, Hannah left her work and hurried after him. As she moved through the long room Daniel stepped out in front of her. 'Trouble in paradise, is there? He went out of here looking as if the world was going to end.'

'Maybe it is,' Hannah said tartly. '*His* world anyway.'

She side-stepped around him and would have hurried away, but Daniel caught hold of her arm. 'Be careful, Hannah. I mean it. Just be very careful what you're doing.' For the first time, there was genuine anxiety in his eyes. 'They're powerful people. They'll stop at nothing.'

Hannah nodded. 'I know,' she said huskily, touched by his concern. 'But you see, Daniel, there's nothing they can do to hurt me. Not now. Not any more.'

Roper was not in the outer office, and as Hannah opened the door to the inner room, she saw Adam sitting at the desk, his head in his hands.

At the sound of her entrance he looked up. 'Oh, Anna, what are we to do? What *are* we to do?'

Hannah bit her lip. She didn't want to be the one

to suggest it. She wanted the words to come from him.

He rose and came round the desk to her, taking her in his arms and burying his face against her neck. 'I love you, Hannah. I love you so much. I can't bear to lose you. And once my father comes home, that's what will happen. He . . . he's threatening to have you arrested.'

'Arrested? Whatever for? On what charge?'

'I . . . I don't know. But he'll think of something. He always does. And . . . and he has friends who'll help him.'

I could have told you that, she thought bitterly, but aloud she said, 'Then I must leave, straight away.'

'No,' he clasped her to him as if he would prevent her physically from walking away from him. 'I won't let you go. We . . . we'll get married. Now. Right away. Before he comes home. Then there won't be a thing he can do about it.'

Hannah was triumphant. She put her arms about him and pressed herself to his chest, hiding her face so that he should not read her feelings showing clearly on her face. 'Are you sure?' she whispered, injecting into her tone all the trembling delight and yet at the same time uncertainty that she could muster. 'You said yourself he's a powerful man.'

'When he's got used to the idea, when he's had time to meet you, to get to know you, he'll love you too. I know he will.'

Hannah said nothing.

'If only my grandfather was still alive,' Adam went on. 'He'd've been on my side. In his eyes, I could do no wrong.'

Hannah said nothing. Though Nathaniel had not

been quite so bad as his son, Edmund, she had vowed to hate all Critchlows. With a vengeance.

It was all arranged with such speed that Hannah wondered inwardly at the legality of it all.

'We've to go to a place in Yorkshire.' Adam grinned boyishly. 'It's like a local Gretna Green. No questions asked. It'll be quite a journey and we'll have to stay there for a while. In separate rooms until we're married,' he added hastily, in case she was thinking he meant to seduce her and then not go through with the marriage. 'Can you be ready tomorrow morning? We'll leave early.'

Hannah's eyes shone, not with the happiness as Adam saw it, but with victory. 'Oh yes,' she said. 'I can be ready.'

'I'll be leaving tomorrow, Mrs Grundy. I just want to thank you so much for everything you've done for me. I know it hasn't been easy for you especially . . . especially because you think I've been unfair to Ted.'

'I do,' Lily said shortly. 'Anyway, that's as maybe. Least said, soonest mended, I suppose.' She eyed Hannah. 'So your fancy plans didn't work out then? You're going back home, are yer? Back to Macclesfield?'

Hannah shook her head. 'No,' she said quietly. 'I'm going away with Adam Critchlow. We're going to be married.'

Forty-Two

They returned to Millersbrook Manor hand in hand to face Adam's father like two naughty school children caught stealing apples. But their sin was far greater than taking fruit from a neighbour's orchard.

'He'll be home by now,' Adam said as they walked down the hill and through the dale. 'He'll know.'

'Know what?'

'That we're married.'

Hannah's eyes widened. She had achieved what she'd schemed for, yet now that the moment had come to face Mr Edmund, her resolve almost failed her. She was still afraid, deep down, that he had the power to hurt her.

And her fear was mirrored in Adam's face.

It was almost dusk as they passed the Grundys' farm. Hannah was thankful that there was no one about; the last people she wanted to see at that moment were either of the Grundys or, worse still, Ted.

They climbed the steep hill through the village until they came to the driveway leading to the big house perched on top of the cliff overlooking the river flowing through the dale below.

'Well, here we are.' Adam turned to her and, forcing a lightness into his tone that she knew he wasn't feeling, he said, 'I suppose I ought to carry you over the threshold.'

Hannah laughed weakly. 'I don't think you'd better.'

'Oh, what the hell . . . ?' He dropped their bags to the ground and swung her into his arms. 'You pull the bell.'

They waited for what seemed an age, feeling rather foolish, until the heavy front door swung open and the Critchlows' butler stood there. For once, even the straight-faced manservant couldn't hide his surprise.

'Master Adam and . . . and . . .' he faltered not knowing how to refer to the girl being carried by the young master.

'And Mrs Anna Critchlow,' Adam said as he walked into the house and deposited Hannah on the floor. Ignoring the manservant's presence, Adam bent and kissed her. 'Welcome home, Mrs Critchlow.'

The butler coughed discreetly. 'The master is in the library, Master Adam. I . . . er . . . think he would want to see you straight away.'

Adam took hold of Hannah's hand. 'Come on, let's get it over with then.' He crossed the hall, pulling her along with him. Her heart was thumping painfully as he opened the door and they entered the room.

Edmund Critchlow was standing in front of the fireplace. Tall and broad, just as she remembered him. Yet, as she drew closer, she could see that there were noticeable differences even in the three and a half years since she'd last seen him. His dark hair was now flecked with white. His undeniably handsome face was florid, his skin blotchy. The excesses of the life he lived were beginning to take their toll and show on his features. But his eyes were just the same: hard and cruel and vindictive.

He scarcely glanced at Hannah and she kept her head lowered in submissive meekness. She left the talking – such as he was given chance to do – to Adam.

'You can pack your bags and be gone from this house.'

'Father—'

'You are a disgrace to the name of Critchlow. I never want to see you or this . . . this slut again.'

'She's no slut, she's—'

'Then pray tell me – who is she? Where does she come from and who are her family?'

The questions were genuine. He didn't know who she was – not yet. Hannah thought fleetingly of Josiah Roper. Whatever game of his own he was playing was certainly working to her advantage at the moment. He had not revealed her identity.

Adam faced his father squarely. 'She's the girl I love. She's my wife.'

Edmund stared for a moment, then threw back his head and laughed a loud, cruel sound. 'Ha! You silly young cub, you don't have to marry 'em just because you get 'em with child. If I'd married every one of them, I'd have a veritable harem.' He eyed Adam keenly. 'You mean you've actually been through a ceremony with her?'

Adam ran his tongue around his dry lips. 'Yes, a week ago. And – since you brought the subject up – she is not expecting my child. We . . . we didn't lie together until after the marriage.'

Now Edmund stared at his son in disbelief. 'Then,

boy, you are more of a milksop and a fool than even I thought you. Love 'em and leave 'em. That should be your motto. Far safer.'

Listening, Hannah was seething. She could scarcely contain her rage. All the years of bitterness and resentment, the years of hatred, welled up inside her. But now was not the time. She must wait. Whatever it cost her not to speak up right this minute, she must hold her tongue. This was only the beginning.

Edmund was pacing the hearth in front of the roaring fire in the huge grate. 'What am I to do with you, boy? Thank God your grandfather is not alive to see this day. It would have broken his heart. He lived only to see the mill pass down the generations. How could you do this to his memory, Adam? How could you do it to me? Everything I hold dear is wrapped up in this mill and in you. I have worked and schemed to pass on a great inheritance to you. And this!' He flung his arm out towards Hannah. 'This is how you repay me.'

'Father, I—'

Edmund held up his hand, palm outwards. 'Not another word, boy. Go to your room. I'll talk to you later – when I have decided what to do.'

Adam stood his ground. 'There's nothing to decide. I've thought it all out. I know exactly what I'm doing.'

'I don't think so—' Edmund began nastily, but Adam interrupted with surprising calm.

'I am your only *legitimate* son and heir.' The accent on the word legitimate startled Hannah. So, Adam knew about his father's philandering. A spark of anger ignited against her new husband. But then, she realized, what could a young man do against his own father? At least, Adam appeared determined not to follow in his sire's footsteps. That was a point in his favour. She listened now as he went on. 'If you wish us to leave, then so be it. But I hope you will reconsider. If you don't want us to live here – in this house – then we can move into the apprentice house. We can no doubt take in lodgers as well as work at the mill. That is – if we still have jobs at the mill.'

Edmund's only answer was a grunt as he still paced up and down the hearth. At last he said, 'Go. Get out of my sight. Leave me to think.'

'But if you'd only talk to Anna – get to know her.'

'I have no wish to get to know her. Go, Adam, just go.'

They went up to Adam's room to wait whilst their fate was decided.

'He'll come around,' Adam said confidently as he closed the bedroom door behind them and took her in his arms. 'It's just a shock for him, that's all.'

Hannah hugged him in return and buried her head against his shoulder. She was experiencing a strange, unexpected tumult of emotions. She'd achieved her goal – or almost. Edmund was beside himself with rage, and he'd be devastated when, to cap everything, he found out who she really was. She'd have achieved it all then. But revenge didn't taste as sweet as she'd anticipated.

She'd reckoned without Adam. He'd been but a pawn in her dangerous game. She'd not spared a thought for him. And she'd believed herself immune to any feelings of sympathy for him.

But as she'd watched him stand up to his formidable father, she realized that he was indeed prepared to give up everything for his love for her. The realization humbled her. And suddenly, without warning, she felt an overwhelming affection for him. She hugged him harder. He chuckled softly. 'Hey, what's this?' he asked, surprised but delighted.

She raised her face to look up at him and there were tears in her eyes.

'Oh, Anna, don't cry.' Gently, he smoothed away her tears with his forefinger. 'Please don't cry. It'll be all right.'

'Oh, Adam, I'm sorry – I'm so sorry if I've hurt you, I didn't mean that to happen. Please – believe me . . .' He couldn't know the full meaning behind her gabbled words as he kissed her gently. His kisses became more urgent and he had begun to draw her towards the bed when a knock came at the door.

With a click of impatience he released her and opened the door. The manservant stood there. 'Mrs Childs wonders if you'd like something to eat, master Adam. You and . . . er . . . Mrs Critchlow.'

Adam beamed at him – more because of the butler's acknowledgement of Anna as his wife than for the food he was offering. 'Thank you, Beamish, that'd be wonderful.'

The man, though always conscious of his position, leaned forward and smiled conspiratorially. 'I expect you'd prefer a tray up here, sir?'

'Thank you, Beamish. That's most thoughtful of you.'

The hours passed. They ate, made love and slept wrapped in each other's arms in the bed that had been Adam's since boyhood.

It was only now that she was here in his home that Hannah realized just how little she knew of the man she'd married. Apart from the fact that he had been away at school when she had lived here before, she knew nothing about his life. She had believed he would be another Critchlow: selfish, self-centred and with a cruel steak.

She was beginning to see that the truth might be very different.

Night came and there was still no summons from Edmund. A light supper was brought to them on a tray and a maid brought hot water to their room. At midnight they climbed into bed but now sleep eluded them and they both lay awake staring into the darkness and listening to the creaking of the old house. They fell into a restless sleep in the early hours and woke late to a knock on the door.

'Breakfast is served in the dining room, sir, and the master asks that you both should join him.'

'Right, Beamish, thank you.'

'Very good, sir. The maid will bring hot water for you both in a moment.' The butler gave a little bow and Adam closed the door and turned towards Hannah, who was still lying in the bed.

'There! You see? I was right. He wants us to join him for breakfast. He's coming round. I said he would. Come on, darling. Let's get dressed quickly and go down.'

'Oh, Adam, you go. I . . . I can't face him.'

Her reluctance was genuine, though Adam couldn't know the real reason. He thought she was just afraid of his father's temper, whilst the truth was that she was feeling the first stirrings of regret that she'd ever entered upon such a game of revenge. She certainly wished she'd not involved Adam. She wished now that she'd found some other way.

'Oh, please come down, Anna. We must face him together. I'll be with you. I won't leave you alone with him, I promise.' His face was so boyishly appealing that she couldn't hold out against him any longer. All her resolve, all her single-minded desire for revenge was melting away beneath Adam's charm and his genuine love for her.

What have I done? she asked herself silently. *Oh, what have I done?* But it was too late now – she had to carry on. As they descended the stairs hand in hand a few minutes later, she found herself praying the very opposite to what she had planned and schemed for weeks and months.

She was now hoping that Edmund Critchlow would not recognize her.

Forty-Three

He was sitting at the end of the long table. When they entered the dining room, he waved them to their places, one on either side of him. There was no welcoming smile. He didn't speak, not even to wish them good morning.

For him, Hannah knew, it was anything but a good morning.

The three of them ate in silence, though Hannah could hardly be said to be eating. She picked at the food set before her by a solicitous Beamish and kept her eyes downcast.

As the meal came to an end, Edmund rose and spoke for the first time. 'Adam, you will oblige me by joining me in my study.' As they both made to rise from the table and follow him, Edmund barked, 'Not you. I wish to speak to my son alone.'

Hannah sank back into her chair as Edmund marched from the room. Adam came around the table to kiss her. 'Don't worry. I'll stand up to him.'

She touched his hand and smiled weakly at him. 'Good luck,' she whispered, and was surprised to find that she really meant it.

When the study door across the hall closed, Hannah went back upstairs to Adam's bedroom. She couldn't think of it as 'theirs' for she doubted it ever would be. Sitting on the window seat overlooking the steep drop down the cliff to the river below, Hannah leaned her forehead against the cool pane and sighed. They'd all tried to warn her: Auntie Bessie, Nell, the Grundys, Ted – even Daniel. But she hadn't listened. She'd been hell-bent on avenging the innocent life that Edmund had taken. She lifted her eyes and looked up above the river to the hillside opposite. She could see the narrow path that she and Luke had walked. And in her fanciful imagination, she could see herself and Luke – two youngsters walking along the path on a bright, sunlit day, hand in hand. So young, so innocent, so in love. A cloud hid the sun and the vision faded. She could no longer recall Luke's face clearly nor hear his voice in her head. Her memories of him were no longer so vivid. A tiny corner of her heart would always belong to him – her first love. But now, there was someone else who was pushing his way into her heart and her mind. Adam.

She chewed on her lip, wondering what was happening in the study. Had Edmund recognized her? Was he, at this very minute, telling Adam just who she was? And if so, what would Adam's reaction be? Would he love her still – or hate her?

It seemed an age before she heard footsteps in the passageway outside. Slowly, Hannah rose to her feet. Her heart was doing painful somersaults inside her chest as the bedroom door opened and Adam came in. He looked pale and drawn, but he was smiling.

He opened his arms to her and she ran across the room to him. She hardly dared to ask, yet she had to know. 'What happened?'

Adam took a deep shuddering breath and his voice was unsteady. 'He's disowning me. He's going to change his will and cut me out. I can work in the mill but I'm no longer to regard myself as his son. I'm to be an ordinary worker.'

Hannah gasped. It was not what she had expected at all. She couldn't believe that Edmund would cast his one and only legitimate son aside in such a callous manner, no matter what he'd done. She'd fully expected that he'd get rid of her. Have the marriage annulled, have her sent back to the workhouse – anything to break them up. But he'd keep his son. Oh yes, he'd keep his son close.

Her mind was working quickly. No, she didn't believe what Adam was telling her. Edmund was doing this only to teach Adam a lesson. It was his way of bringing his young pup to heel.

'And what about me? Am I to work in the mill?'

'He . . . he didn't mention you.'

'Not at all? Didn't he tell you to . . . to end it? To send me away?'

Adam looked uncomfortable. 'Well, yes, but I refused. That was when he came up with the alternative. I can work here, but that's all.'

Hannah shook her head slowly. 'I don't think it's all by any means,' she said quietly. 'He'll have other plans. He . . . he'll be up to something to get rid of me.'

Adam held her close. 'Oh, darling, don't think that. You make him sound an ogre. He's stern and strict with his employees – I know that – but he's not so bad. He'll come around. I know he will.' His eyes sparkled as he looked down at her. 'And if we give him a grandson – you'll see. I'll be restored to the family fold – and you along with me.'

Hannah stared at him, amazed at his naivety. He didn't know his father at all.

Edmund Critchlow would stop at nothing to rid himself of an unwanted daughter-in-law.

There was only one thing she could do that might yet save Adam. The very thing that she'd planned all along, but now it was with a very different purpose in mind. It was not only to exact her revenge upon Edmund, but now it was to save Adam too. She'd have to reveal her true identity herself. She'd do nothing yet, she decided. She'd bide her time and wait and see what happened. *But*, she thought, *I still have a trump card to play – if I have to.*

Her mind was spinning and she heard Adam's plans with only half an ear. 'We'll live in the apprentice house and take in lodgers. I know we don't have the orphans any more but we still get single young men and women coming to work at the mill and needing lodgings. You could do that, darling. Run it as a lodging house, couldn't you? There'd be no need for you to work in the mill any more. And when the family comes along . . .'

Adam was full of ideas, happily planning their future and confident that, in time, his father would come around.

Oh, how little you know of him, Hannah thought.

It was eerie to walk back into the apprentice house. So many ghosts lingered in the rooms. She could almost hear their voices: the Bramwells, Nell – and now Luke too. She fancied she could hear his laughter, teasing her. Calling up to her from below the window of the punishment room. Hannah shivered.

'I know it's cold and damp,' Adam said, throwing open all the doors and going from room to room, dragging Hannah in his wake. 'But we'll soon have it cleaned and warmed through. Perhaps some of the girls from the mill would help ... Oh!' He stopped and his face fell. 'I was forgetting,' he murmured. 'I'm no longer the owner's son. I can't ask for help.'

'You could still ask,' Hannah said.

'I could, I suppose,' Adam said doubtfully, 'but I couldn't arrange for them to be paid, could I?'

'No,' Hannah said. 'No, I suppose not, unless ...'

'Unless what?'

'How do you get on with Mr Roper?'

'Roper?' Adam was puzzled. 'Well, all right, but ...' His face cleared. 'Oh, I see what you're getting at. Roper could arrange their pay.'

'Mmm.'

Adam shook his head. 'He wouldn't do it. He wouldn't do anything that would go directly against my father's wishes.'

Hannah said nothing. She was not so sure.

It was high time she had a word with Mr Roper herself. There were one or two matters that needed to be sorted out.

A week later, when Hannah heard that Edmund would be away on business for a few days, she crossed the yard and climbed the stone steps to the offices. She'd not been inside the mill since her marriage, but she knew the news would have travelled through the mill like a raging fire.

Josiah Roper was, as ever, sitting at his desk. As she opened the door and marched in, he looked up and smiled his thin, humourless smile as he saw who it was.

'Ah, the new Mrs Critchlow,' he said sarcastically. He laid down his pen and turned to face her. 'And to what do I owe this honour?'

Hannah smiled brightly at him. 'I've come to ask a favour, Mr Roper.'

'A favour? From me?'

'If Adam were to ask one or two of the girls to help clean out the apprentice house, would you arrange for them to be paid?'

For the first time that she could remember, Hannah saw surprise on Josiah's face. 'Arrange for them . . . to be paid?' he spluttered. 'For . . . for helping you?'

'Yes, Mr Roper.'

He stared at her and shook his head wonderingly. 'You've got some nerve, I'll say that for you. I always did admire your spirit. Grudgingly, of course.'

Hannah's smile widened. 'Of course.'

There was silence as they stared at each other. 'And how would you suggest that I justify such an action to Mr Edmund?'

Hannah put her head on one side. 'He's going away, isn't he?'

'Yes,' Josiah said slowly.

'And whilst he's away, you'll be in charge?'

'Mm.'

'Have you been told – officially, for I'm sure you will have heard the gossip – that Master Adam is no longer to be treated as son and heir?'

Josiah raised his eyebrows. 'Mr Edmund told me that his son's allowance was to be stopped. That he is to become an ordinary worker in the mill and treated as such.' He paused and then his beady eyes gleamed. 'But he said nothing about disinheriting him.' He was thoughtful for a moment before saying slowly, 'He didn't tell me that I was no longer to take instructions from his son – especially,' he added with emphasis, 'in his absence.'

'You're not afraid it'll cause trouble for you on Mr Edmund's return?'

His smile twisted wryly. 'I've never been afraid of Edmund Critchlow. Oh, I pander to him. To his every whim,' he added bitterly. 'And I expect I'm a laughing stock amongst the workers, but you see, Mrs Critchlow,' for some strange reason he seemed to delight in repeating her new-found title, 'I know exactly what I'm doing and why I'm doing it. And Mr Edmund trusts me. Trusts me implicitly. I'm the keeper of his secrets, you see.' He nodded meaningfully at her. 'I'm a very good keeper of secrets, Mrs Critchlow.'

'So – you'll do it?'

He turned back to his desk, dismissing her. 'Tell Master Adam to let me know the details of the young women involved and how much he wishes them to be paid.'

For a moment, Hannah stared at his hunched back. He was a complex, devious and mysterious character. She couldn't pretend to understand him.

When she told Adam what she had done, he put his arms about her. 'We'll make a great team, you and I. It's going to be all right. We're going to be so happy and everything will work out. I know it will.'

If only I could be as sure, Hannah thought.

Forty-Four

'So you've managed to hook him, then. What do you intend to do now?'

Crossing the yard after another meeting with Josiah Roper, to present him with the list of the names of the girls who were at this very moment scrubbing floors and flinging open the windows in the apprentice house, Hannah was met by Daniel, stepping out of the shadows to bar her way. She wondered if he'd seen her on her way in and had been waiting to waylay her.

'Daniel!'

'Ma'am,' he said sarcastically and doffed his cap to her.

How she wished now that she hadn't confided in Daniel! Her feelings had undergone a radical change. Whilst she still wanted to bring Edmund to justice in some way for causing Luke's death – that desire would never die – she wished she could do it without harming Adam. But it was seeming impossible now. Adam still respected his father, loved him, she supposed. Whatever she did to Edmund was bound to hurt Adam.

Now she faced Daniel. 'We're going to open up the apprentice house. Live there – take in young people working at the mill who need somewhere to live.'

'Starting up the pauper apprentice scheme again, are you?' His lip curled. 'Talk about poacher turned gamekeeper.'

'No, we're not. We're just going to offer a nice home to single folk.'

'Huh! I'll believe that when I see it. Well, I wish you joy.' He turned on his heel, pulled his cap back on and disappeared into the mill. Hannah stared after him. He wished her anything but joy. She could hear it in his tone: Daniel wished her nothing but ill.

She sighed and carried on out of the yard. In the lane she hesitated. There was one other person she ought to see. It had been praying on her mind and she'd better get it over with.

She would do it now. She would go and see Mrs Grundy.

'Oh, it's you.'

Lily Grundy's greeting was far from welcoming. She turned and went back into her kitchen without inviting Hannah in, but she left the door open as if expecting Hannah to follow. Hannah stepped inside and closed the back door.

'So, you're married to young Critchlow then?'

'That's right.'

'All part of the grand plan, was it?'

Hannah licked her lips, unsure how much to confide in Lily. But there was no one else. No Auntie Bessie, no Nell. Yet in many ways Lily reminded her so much of Auntie Bessie that almost before she realized what she was doing, she was sobbing out the truth.

'Oh, Mrs Grundy, I don't know what to do. I'm so confused . . . so mixed up. I . . . I wanted to get revenge on Mr Edmund – for everything he'd done. For the cruelty he inflicted on the child workers who were supposed to be in his care. For all the suffering and

413

the deaths he caused. I didn't care how I did it or who I hurt in the process. Not Ted or Adam or anyone. I . . . I just wanted to make him pay.'

Lily stared at her for a moment and then, seeing that the girl's distress was genuine, she set her hot iron in the hearth and pulled a chair up close to Hannah. Putting her arm around the girl's shoulders, she said gently, 'Now, why don't you tell me all about it and then we'll see what can be done.'

So Hannah confided everything to her, how she'd made Adam fall in love with her but how the tables had now turned and she was finding herself falling in love with him.

'I don't think it's as simple as that, Hannah,' Lily said. 'You think you've made Master Adam fall for you. But you haven't. It either happens or it doesn't. He was going to fall for you anyway – once he'd set eyes on you, whether you wanted it or not. You can't make someone love you, lass, unless they want to.' She sighed. 'And I was wrong to go on at you about our Ted. I'm fond of the lad and I'm fond of you and I'd've liked nothing better than to see the two of you happy together. I thought you weren't giving him a chance, giving yourself a chance to like him, but I see now that if you were going to fall for Ted, then you would've done and you wouldn't have been able to help yourself. Besides,' she added, laughing a little sheepishly, 'I have to admit our Ted's a bit of a one for the girls. He's got his eye on a lass from the village already, so I don't think his heart is broken after all.'

Hannah smiled through her tears. 'I'm glad. I didn't want to hurt Ted and I hated you being angry with me. It was just that . . . that . . . well . . . even if I hadn't been bent on setting my cap at Adam, I still wouldn't have been right for Ted. I . . . I was believing myself still in love with Luke then.'

'You can't live in the past, love,' Lily said. She sighed. 'I s'pose I've been guilty of that. Never forgiving and never forgetting. Always bearing a grudge against them Critchlows because of our Lucy. But now, we'd best move on. All of us. Them days is gone. The apprenticing of young children has stopped – and a good thing too. I s'pect things is better up at the mill now, are they?'

'Not so's you'd notice,' Hannah said bitterly, thinking of the long working hours, the dusty, unhealthy atmosphere and the pitiful wage that most of the workers received. The punishment room might be gone, but workers were still fined for breaking the rules.

'If only—' She stopped, appalled to realize another consequence of her unremitting desire for revenge. 'If only Adam were in charge, things would be a lot better. He's kind and considerate and . . . and . . . oh, but I've put an end to all that, haven't I? He'll never have the chance to inherit the mill now. Oh, Mrs Grundy, what have I done?'

Lily squeezed the girl's shoulders but she could think of nothing to say that would bring any comfort.

By the time Edmund returned from his business trip, the apprentice house was looking much as it had done when Hannah had lived there before. Better, in fact, for most of the walls were freshly whitewashed and the whole house scrubbed from top to bottom. Two of the carpenters from the mills had put up partitions in the dormitories, dividing the space up into single rooms. And best of all, the dreaded punishment room had been turned into a cosy bedroom.

If only Hannah didn't feel such dreadful guilt hanging over her, she could have counted herself as happy.

'Roper. Roper! Come in here at once.'

Josiah laid down his pen, slid from his perch and ambled into his master's office. 'Sir?'

Edmund prodded the page in the open ledger lying on the desk in front of him. 'What is the meaning of this? These extra payments to some of the girls. And two of the men too. What was it for and who authorized it? Scarsfield? Because if so, he's exceeded his authority.'

Josiah went around the desk, pretending to look over Edmund's shoulder at the offending entries. 'Oh those, sir.'

'Yes, Roper. Those. Explain, if you would be so good?'

'It was work authorized by Master Adam, sir. On the apprentice house.'

'The apprentice house?' Edmund was growing steadily more purple by the minute. 'What on earth is he doing with the apprentice house?'

'Restoring it, sir, to it's – a-hem – former glory.' Edmund eyed Josiah, but decided to let the man's sarcasm pass. 'Master Adam and his good lady wife are living there, sir. But of course, you knew all that.'

'No, I didn't know all that,' Edmund roared, but Josiah didn't even flinch. Years of working for Edmund had immured him to his master's bursts of temper. In fact, Josiah revelled in bringing one about.

'Oh dear, have I done wrong, sir?'

'Done wrong? Done wrong? Of course you've bloody well done wrong.' Edmund thumped the desk. 'I've disowned my son, Roper. You know that full well.'

Josiah calmly shook his head. 'No, sir, on the contrary, I knew nothing of the sort.'

'But I told you – I *told* you that he was to work in the factory and treated as an ordinary worker.'

Josiah smiled obsequiously. 'Well, yes, sir, but I thought that was all part of the young man's training, so that when he takes over one day, he will have a true understanding of the workings of the mill. If I remember correctly, sir, you worked in the mill for a while – at your father's insistence.'

Edmund glowered. 'But I didn't marry a slut of a girl and try to bring her into our home.'

'No, sir. You didn't *marry* them, did you? But God alone knows how many bastards you have residing in various workhouses up and down the country.'

'Roper,' Edmund said menacingly. 'Watch your tongue.' But Josiah only smiled. Turning back to the matter in hand, Edmund frowned again. 'Nor did I give permission for them to live in the apprentice house.'

'I understand they are turning it into a lodging house for mill workers.' With measured mildness, he added, 'They're making a very good job of it, too, by all accounts. But then, I'm not surprised. Your son's bride is a very enterprising young woman.' He paused and licked his lips before saying with deliberate mildness. '*She always was.*'

Edmund stared at him. 'What do you mean? "She always was"?'

Josiah raised his eyebrows. 'Well, sir, you know who she is, don't you?'

Feeling a sudden, inexplicable fear sweep through him, Edmund shook his head. 'Tell me.'

'She's Hannah Francis. The girl you were chasing when that young lad fell in the wheel and was killed. I'm so sorry, sir. I could've told you weeks ago. I recognized her the moment I saw her. And I thought you were sure to have done so too. Oh, she's dyed her hair, tried to make herself look different. But she couldn't alter the colour of those magnificent eyes, could she?' As he saw the veins standing out on Edmund's forehead, saw his eyes take on a peculiar glazed look, Josiah thrust home his final barb. Edmund was now slumped in his chair, his hands shaking. 'She's come back and married your son. She's got her revenge all right, hasn't she?'

When Edmund had recovered a little from the shock, though his hands were still trembling uncontrollably, he gasped out, 'Get them. Fetch them here. Both . . . both of them. I want to see for myself. I know you, Roper. You're a lying toad . . .'

But Josiah only smiled at the insult and left the office. He sent one of the mill boys running to the apprentice house to summon Adam and Hannah.

When the message came, Adam was jubilant. 'You see, I told you, he's come around. He's been away and had time to think. Maybe all this work's been for nothing and he wants us to live at the Manor.'

'I'd rather live here anyway, Adam,' Hannah said swiftly.

'Yes, you're right. Time we stood on our own feet.'

Hand in hand they hurried to the mill, but as they

stepped into Edmund's office they were shocked by his appearance.

'Father!' Adam hurried round the desk to him. The man looked dreadful. His face was purple, his eyes bulged and his whole body seemed to be shaking. But he waved his son aside. His glare was fixed on Hannah standing helplessly in front of him. She was suddenly very afraid.

Mr Roper, she thought. *He's told him. I wondered why he never looked up as we came through his office.*

Edmund was levering himself unsteadily to his feet.

'No, Father, sit down. You're ill. I'll send for the doctor . . .'

With a surprising sudden surge of strength, Edmund swung his arm, striking Adam in the chest. 'Out of my way,' he said, his speech slurred. 'I want to see . . . her.'

He staggered round the desk like a drunkard and lurched towards Hannah. He stood before her, swaying slightly, but his gaze was intent upon her, boring into her soul.

'Look at me.'

Slowly, Anna raised her head and met his eyes. Suddenly, he raised both his hands and grasped her hair, pulling the pins from it. Then he pulled hanks of it apart so that the tell-tale line of recently grown blonde hair near her scalp was plainly visible.

'Father – you're hurting her. Stop it. Whatever's got into you?'

'Hurt her! I'll hurt the little trollop,' he spat. Saliva trickled down his chin and he swayed again. Hannah thought he was going to wrench the hair from her head and winced in pain.

'Father!' Adam shouted. 'Let her go.' Now, he tried to prise his father's hands open. 'Let her go!'

At last, Edmund loosened his grip. He stood swaying and if Adam had not been supporting him, he might have fallen.

'Sit down,' Adam said, and helped him back into his chair behind the desk. 'Now, what is all this about?'

Edmund jabbed a shaking finger at Hannah. 'Ask her. Ask your . . . your bride.'

Adam turned puzzled eyes on her. 'Anna?'

'She's not Anna,' Edmund spluttered. 'She's Hannah. Hannah Francis.'

Adam glanced from one to the other, still puzzled.

'She's been here before,' Edmund dragged out the words. 'She was here when . . . she was that . . . that boy's girl. Luke Hammond's girl.'

Forty-Five

Adam paled as he stared at her. 'Is it true?'

He had no need to ask for further explanation. He knew only too well who Luke Hammond was.

There was no point in further denial. Hannah nodded. Adam shook his head slowly. 'Why? Why did you come back, and why did you pretend to be someone else?'

Before she could think what to say, Edmund said, 'Revenge. That's what it is. Revenge on me – on us all. On all the Critchlow family.'

'No, I don't believe it,' Adam whispered, the colour draining from his face. 'Oh, Anna.' He still couldn't think of her by any other name. 'Say it's not true. Please, say it's not true.'

She opened her mouth to say the words he wanted to hear, but she couldn't speak. She could no longer lie to him. Whatever it cost her, Adam deserved better than that. He was the innocent in all this and he deserved the truth.

'I . . . I'll explain it all to you – everything. But not now. Not,' she nodded towards Edmund, 'not here.'

She saw the anguish darken Adam's eyes. He'd wanted an immediate denial and she hadn't been able to give him that. So now he thought the worst. He stared at her for a moment longer before saying flatly, 'I'd better get him home.'

Hannah moved forward, as if to help, but Adam said harshly, 'We'll manage. Go ...' he hesitated, reluctant to use the word 'home' until he knew the truth, knew whether they had a future together – or not.

Hannah went back to the apprentice house to wait for Adam. He was a long time before he came back – a long time in which she had time to think how to explain it to him. But there was no easy way. There was no way around the shameful truth. And she was now deeply ashamed.

When he came at last it was growing dusk outside. She was sitting at the kitchen table – the same table where she had sat with Luke, Daniel, Nell and all the others whose ghosts still seem to haunt the rooms. A fire burned in the grate casting eerie dancing shadows around the room. She didn't move as he came and sat down opposite. She didn't even look up at him, not at first, though she could feel his gaze upon her.

'So,' he said in a tone that was not encouraging. 'Are you going to tell me?'

Slowly, Hannah raised her head and met his gaze. His eyes were wary and full of hurt.

'I'm going to tell you everything – right from the beginning. If you will hear me out.'

'Oh yes,' he said, and already there was a note of bitterness in his tone. She wondered what more his father had said. Had he already poisoned Adam's mind against her? 'I'll hear you out.'

'How is your father? Is he all right?'

Adam raised his eyebrows. 'Do you care?'

She stared at him. How swift and sudden was the

change in his tone. It was cold, devoid of love. She sighed and looked down at her hands lying limply on the table. 'I care – for your sake.'

'Really?'

There was a long silence before Hannah began to speak. She began at the very beginning – the beginning as far as she knew it. She told him how her mother had fallen in love with a married man, who, even when he became free to marry her, hadn't done so. She recounted her childhood memories living with her mother and her grandmother in the terraced house – her happiest time. But then, as she'd grown older, the cruel taunts about her bastardy. It all came spilling out – the workhouse and then the circumstances of her arrival at the mill.

'The Critchlows and Mr Goodbody, the master of the workhouse, had some scheme going. I think money changed hands for the supply of pauper apprentices. Children of twelve and younger who had to sign a paper binding them here for years until they were eighteen.' She looked up then and met Adam's gaze. 'How could a child of that age know what they are doing? They just did as they were told. They'd no choice. They weren't given a choice.'

Adam was silent, just staring at her as she went on, telling him about her life and the lives of the pauper children in the Critchlows' so-called care. She told him about their working conditions, the dangers, the accidents. She told him what had happened to Jane. Even though she knew he'd heard about the accident, now she spared him none of the gruesome details. And then, taking a deep breath she began to tell him about his father.

'There was this girl called Nell. She was so kind to

us all when we arrived. She showed us what to do, warned us about what not to do. If it hadn't been for Nell I might have spent half my life in the punishment room. I spent many an hour in there as it was. Most of us did at some time or another. There was one time when they thought I'd run away – I was only trying to go to see my mother because I'd heard nothing from her from the time I left the workhouse. I found out later that your father and the Goodbodys had hatched a plot to keep me happy. Mrs Goodbody wrote letters as if from my mother to make me believe she was still alive. But when I tried to go and see her for myself, Mr Roper caught me and dragged me back. No one would believe that I wasn't trying to run away, so I ended up in the punishment room for days after a cruel beating from your father. If it hadn't been for Luke sending me up food through the window, I might've starved. And he'd've earned himself a beating if he'd been caught.'

'I knew about the punishment room at the apprentice house. But beating? I didn't know about that. They . . . they beat the children? Girls too? You . . . you were beaten?'

'Oh yes.' She paused before continuing. 'Things were reasonable for a few years after that. We grew up, and Luke and I . . .' She ran her tongue over her lips. 'We liked each other. More than . . . more than liked. On Sundays, we'd go out for walks. We roamed the hills. We were happy together.'

'Were you lovers?' Adam asked bluntly.

Hannah shook her head. 'No. Not physically, if that's what you mean. It was all very innocent.' She raised her head and met his gaze. 'But I did love him with that first very special love. The love two children

424

have for each other that as they grow can either blossom into adult love or can wither and die. But we . . . we never got the chance, did we? We never got the chance to find out.'

Adam said nothing. If he knew little about the running of the mill when he had been away at school, he at least knew about Luke's death.

Hannah took a deep breath and said, 'Your father was a womanizer. He'd have his way with any of the girls from the mill – especially the pauper girls who had no one to turn to for protection. And they daren't refuse. How could they? The Critchlows ruled their lives. Even the Bramwells. I believe they did their best to protect the children in their charge, but even they couldn't do anything to prevent the cruelty. Not really.'

She glanced briefly at Adam, and now his face wore a disbelieving expression. It was going to be tough to convince him of his father's true nature. But Hannah told him all about Nell, ending, 'So, living in Macclesfield you have a three-year-old half-brother.'

'Really?' Adam said sarcastically. 'And I suppose once you'd hooked me and wormed your way into the family, they'll be along to claim his inheritance?'

Hannah shook her head. 'No. Nell is happily married now, to a policeman, and he plans to adopt Tommy legally. I shouldn't think she ever wants to hear the name Critchlow again.'

'We shall no doubt see,' he said tightly. There was a pause before Adam asked, 'And is that it? Is that all you've got to say?'

'No. I haven't told you what happened the day of the accident.'

'I know what happened—'

'No. No, you don't. And you promised to hear me out.'

'Go on, then.' His tone was not encouraging, but Hannah was determined that he should hear it all.

So, haltingly, painfully, she described the events of that terrible day which ended in Luke's death. 'After his funeral, I ran away. I just went.' She said nothing of the Grundys' involvement. She wanted to keep them out of it. Details of her escape were not important. 'I went back to Macclesfield. I daren't go back to the workhouse because Goodbody would have informed your father.' She went on, telling him how she had found Auntie Bessie and then Nell. 'She'd been sent back to the workhouse by your father when he found out she was carrying his child. But we got her out. She came to live with us. And then she met Jim and she's happy now.'

'So why weren't you happy too? Why couldn't you put it all behind you – like Nell?'

'Forget the lies and deceit? Forget that your father caused Luke's death and got away with it?'

'So you never forgive, you never forget, eh?' he murmured.

Now Hannah buried her face in her hands, her voice muffled as she said, 'That's how I felt then. Not now. Not any more.' Slowly she raised her head and looked directly at him. 'I don't expect you to believe me,' she whispered, 'but I love you. Oh yes, I admit I started out with the sole intention of wreaking revenge on your father – on the whole Critchlow family, including you. But . . . but you're so kind and good and . . . and you do love me, don't you, Adam?' He was silent, just staring at her as she finished simply, 'That I've fallen in love with you.'

There was a long silence before Adam spoke. His voice was hoarse with pain. 'You're right. I don't believe you. And as for loving you – well, I did. Very much. But at this moment, I loathe the very sight of you. I can't bear to be anywhere near you. I—'

What he might have gone on to say, tearing her to shreds, was never said. There was a knock at the door. An urgent knock. Without even waiting for an answer, the door opened and a boy stood there.

'Sir, they've sent word from the Manor. It's your father. They reckon he's had a seizure. You'd best come at once, sir.'

As Adam ran from the room, Hannah dropped her head into her hands. 'Oh no. No!' she whispered.

Now she had her revenge upon Edmund Critchlow. A more cruel and lasting revenge than even she had planned. But now it left a bitter taste. She'd hurt him just as she'd schemed, but she'd hurt Adam too. Adam, whom she now loved.

Forty-Six

Edmund Critchlow recovered slowly. The seizure had been a severe one. It had robbed him of his speech for a while. That returned slowly but left him slurring his words, like a drunkard. He was partially paralysed down his left side and had to be helped to dress, to walk, even to eat. Adam employed a nurse who moved into the Manor and cared for his father day and night.

Staying alone at the apprentice house, Hannah fretted, feeling sick with worry and remorse. She dared not go up to the Manor where Adam was now staying – not after the way in which they'd parted.

Her sickness got worse until she reached the stage where she didn't want to get out of bed in the morning. If only Adam would come home and talk to her. At least she would know what to do then. It was this waiting that was making her ill. Not knowing if he was ever going to forgive her. Not knowing if they had any kind of future together.

At last, she could bear it no longer. She rose, dressed and forced herself to eat a little Then she set off down the road to the farm

Lily Grundy would tell her what to do.

'So, I hear you got your way then? Edmund Critchlow's in a bad way I hear.'

Hannah nodded. 'I just wanted to make him angry – to give him a taste of his own medicine. Show him that he can't always have his own way. I . . . I didn't mean to make him ill.'

'Huh! It almost killed him, by what they say.' Lily laughed wryly. 'But I shouldn't waste your pity on him, lass.' Despite her earlier words, Lily Grundy was still unforgiving. 'It's no more than he deserves.'

'But it's Adam,' Hannah said, her eyes filling with tears. 'He hates me now. Oh, Mrs Grundy, what shall I do? It's making me ill. I feel sick all the time. Sick with worry.'

Lily regarded her steadily. 'Sick? When exactly?'

'All the time. 'Specially in a morning when I first get up.'

'When did you last have your monthly visitor?'

'Eh?' Startled Hannah looked up at her. Lily nodded, smiling grimly. 'You're expecting, Hannah. That's what. You're carrying a Critchlow.'

When she returned to the apprentice house, her head in a whirl, she found Adam in their bedroom collecting his belongings.

'Adam – please? Can we talk?'

'I've nothing to say to you.' He carried on pushing his clothes into a bag.

For a moment, biting her lip, she watched him, 'Are you . . . are you moving back to the Manor for good?'

'No.'

'No? Then . . . then what are you doing? Where are you going?'

He swung round to face her. 'I'm leaving.'

'Leaving?'

'Must you repeat everything I say? Yes, I'm leaving. I can't bear to look at you. I can't bear to be anywhere near you.'

She gasped and fell against the wall. She was trembling from head to foot and felt as if she was going to be violently sick any minute. She reached out a trembling hand to him, pleading, 'Oh, Adam, please don't go. If . . . if you don't want to stay here, then go back to the Manor.'

Bitterly he said, 'I'm not wanted there. Every time my father sees me he becomes agitated again. The nurse has advised me to keep away. So, I'm going. Right away.'

'What about the mill? You'll have to run the mill now.'

'Damn and blast the mill,' Adam shouted. 'I don't care what happens to the mill.'

'But it's your inheritance.'

'Not any more it isn't. Thanks to you.'

Instinctively, she put her hand protectively over her belly. 'But it's your child's inheritance, Adam.'

He stared at her. 'What child? I haven't any children. And now . . .' He stopped and stared at her as she nodded slowly.

'I'm expecting a child, Adam.'

She saw the conflict raging within him show clearly on his face. Then his features twisted. 'Another of your lies, Anna?'

'No, no, I swear.'

He picked up his bag and made to push past her. In the doorway, he paused. Close to her, he looked down at her as if taking in every feature of her face. 'Oh, Anna, you'll never know how very much I loved you. But I didn't *know* you at all, did I? I didn't know what a scheming evil bitch you really are. I don't care if I never set eyes on you again as long as I live.'

As he pushed past her, she caught hold of his arm. 'No, don't go, Adam. You stay. I . . . I'll go. I should be the one to leave. You should stay here and run the mill.'

His lip curled. 'Oh no, Anna. You stay. You run the mill. It's what you wanted, isn't it?'

He pulled himself free and ran down the stairs, out of the house and out of her life.

With heart-wrenching sobs, Hannah staggered to the bed. She lay down, curling herself into a ball, shivering and weeping uncontrollably. 'What have I done? Oh, what have I done?'

She stayed in the house for two days, drinking water, but eating very little. She had no appetite and felt sick all day long.

On the morning of the third day, there was a knock at the door. When she opened it Ernest Scarsfield was standing there.

'Morning, Mrs Critchlow,' he said politely, though a little awkwardly. He pulled off his cap and seemed about to speak again, when he stopped and stared at her. All thoughts of the difference in their positions now fled as he said, his voice full of concern, 'Aw lass, what a state you're in. Are you ill? Shall I send for the doctor?'

Hannah shook her head, pulled open the door wider. 'Come in,' she said hoarsely. As she moved back to sit down near the cold range, he followed her. In the mirror above the mantelpiece, she saw herself. No wonder Ernest had been startled. She looked a mess. Her eyes were swollen, her face blotchy. Her hair hung down in dirty, bedraggled lengths, the blonde at its roots showing clearly now that it was not fastened up. Her dress was crumpled and stained for she had not taken it off even to sleep at night.

'I . . . er . . .' Ernest began awkwardly. 'I came to ask where Mr Adam is? I need to ask him—'

'He's gone,' she blurted out. 'He . . . he's left.'

'Left?' For a moment Ernest was puzzled, then his face cleared. 'Oh, gone away on business, you mean? In place of his father?'

Hannah shook her head. 'No, he's gone away. For good. He won't be coming back.'

'Won't be—?' Now Ernest truly was shocked. 'But the mill? What'll happen to the mill? His father's in no fit state to run it. At least, not at the moment, so they say. It'll be a long time before he's fit enough.' His voice dropped as he muttered, 'If he ever is.'

'I don't know,' Hannah whispered, 'what's going to happen. Can . . . can you and Mr Roper keep things going, just for the moment and I . . . I'll . . . ?'

Without warning, a spark of her old spirit ignited. This was not like her. This was not Hannah Francis who fought whatever life threw at her, who sang no matter what. Whatever was she doing shutting herself away like this, moping and starving herself and her child?

Her child! She must think of her child. He – or she – was heir to the mill. Her child was a Critchlow, but it was Adam's child. It had a chance – a good chance – not to be like the old order of Critchlows. She could bring it up to be different, and one day it would own and run the mill. But in the meantime . . .

Hannah squared her shoulders.

'Mr Scarsfield, will you do something for me?'

The man was still dazed by the news that Adam had gone. He couldn't take it in. He couldn't believe that young master Adam would leave. Not now. Not of all times now when his father was incapable of running the mill. Surely . . . He dragged his attention back to what the new Mrs Critchlow was saying.

'Of course – anything, ma'am.'

She smiled at him. 'First thing, please call me Hannah.'

'Hannah? But I thought your name was Anna?'

She sighed. 'I can't explain it all now. I will soon, I promise. I'll tell you everything. I'd sooner you heard it from me than from anyone else. But there's no time now. Would you send word to the Grundys to have some provisions brought here? I've no food in the house. And then this afternoon, I'll come to the mill.'

'Very well.' He rose and then stood looking down at her for a long moment, then he murmured, 'You know, I thought there was summat familiar about you. You're that young lass that was here years ago, aren't you?'

Hannah nodded and held her breath, wondering what was coming next. But Ernest pulled on his cap and smiled. 'Well, I always did like that little lass. Loved to hear her singing about the place. I hope we'll hear you singing again, Hannah.'

With that, he gave a brief nod and left her. For a long moment, she sat staring after him. Then she too rose, squared her shoulders and lifted her chin. She put her hand on her belly and smiled softly. 'Come along, my little one. We've a mill to run.'

433

As she went to fetch paper and kindling and coal to light the fire in the range, Hannah was humming softly to herself.

About mid-afternoon, Hannah marched across the yard to the mill, her head held high and determination in every stride. She had washed, pinned up her hair and changed her clothes, and now she climbed the stairs and went straight to the offices. Without knocking, she strode into the outer office.

'Mr Roper.' She beamed at him. 'It's time you and I had a little chat.' She gestured with her hand towards the inner door. 'Please would you come into *my* office.'

There was no mistaking the emphasis on her appropriation of Mr Edmund's office. Josiah stared at her for a moment and then shrugged, put down his pen, slid off his stool and followed her.

'Please,' Hannah said as she moved around the desk and sat down in the well-worn chair behind it. 'Do sit down.'

Josiah sat in the chair placed for visitors in front of the desk. It was slightly lower than the chair in which Hannah was now sitting and she had the advantage of looking down upon him. It gave her confidence.

'Mr Roper, as you know, Mr Edmund is very ill and unable to undertake his normal work of running the mill. As you may not know – though I expect the gossip grapevine has already been busy – Adam has gone away. His father informed him who I really am.' She paused for a moment, looking Josiah straight in the eyes, leaving him in no doubt that she was well aware just how Mr Edmund had found out. Josiah dropped his gaze, but said nothing. 'He – Mr Edmund that is – has disowned Adam,' Hannah went on. 'It seems – even though he cannot run the mill himself for the time being – that he would sooner see the mill ruined than have his son in charge.' Hannah leaned towards Josiah. 'But, Mr Roper, we are not going to let that happen. We – and by that I mean you, Mr Scarsfield and me – are going to keep this place going.'

Josiah, for once, looked surprised. 'I'd've thought that was exactly what you wanted to see happen? The Critchlows ruined?'

Hannah sighed, rested her elbows on the desk and her chin in her hands. 'Yes. Once I did. Once upon a time I would have been singing with joy at the thought. But things have changed.' She hesitated briefly. It was difficult to talk to a man like Josiah Roper about affairs of the heart. She couldn't believe he would understand. She couldn't believe he had ever been in love. But he had to be told.

'You see, what started out as revenge against the Critchlows has rather rebounded on me. I . . . I fell in love with Adam.'

Josiah stared at her and then he smirked, 'Well, I might have known. Women can't keep up their desire for revenge. Not like a man. It takes years. It takes patience and single-mindedness. Women haven't got the stomach for it. They're too soft, too forgiving. Never forgive and never forget. That's my motto and I live by it.' His eyes gleamed with such relish that Hannah shivered. She couldn't understand Josiah Roper and probably never would, but she needed him. She needed his knowledge and his expertise if she were to run the mill – if she were to save it for her unborn child. Adam's child and Mr Edmund's grandchild.

'I haven't exactly forgiven and certainly not forgotten

what Mr Edmund did. But Adam was not to blame for any of it.'

'He's a Critchlow.'

Hannah regarded him steadily as she said, 'So's the child I'm carrying.'

For a moment, Josiah looked as if he too might have a seizure. He turned purple with rage. 'Another Critchlow bastard!' he spat.

'No, Mr Roper. Adam and I are legally married, if you remember. The child—'

'It might not be born a bastard legally, but it'll be one by nature. It'll have Critchlow blood in it.'

'Yes, but Adam's blood. He's a good man. Even you must agree with that.'

Josiah gave a non-committal grunt. 'But what,' he asked nastily, 'if it takes after its grandfather?'

Hannah grinned suddenly. 'Then I'll probably drown it.'

Of course she was not serious and Josiah knew it, but her statement relieved the tension. Even Josiah allowed himself a small smile. There was a long silence before he said, 'So, how do you intend to run this mill?' His tone was scathing. 'What do you know of business? Of dealing with suppliers and buyers?'

'Absolutely nothing. But, Mr Roper, you do, don't you?'

'Me?' He looked startled now. 'I've never been allowed to meet with buyers and such.'

'But you know what's done, don't you? There must've been times when meetings have taken place in this very office.' She leaned forward again. 'I'm sure that door is not so thick that you haven't been able to hear what's been going on.'

He wriggled his shoulders. 'Well, yes, Mr Edmund had me in sometimes to make notes for him. Figures and such like.'

'So you do know how Mr Edmund conducted his business meetings?'

'Well, yes.'

'Then I suggest you and I – and Mr Scarsfield too, if he's willing – should meet such people together.'

Josiah's eyes gleamed. 'You're as crafty as a cart-load of monkeys. I expect you'll pile on the charm and make out you're a weak and naive woman, whilst we drive home the bargains. That it, eh?'

Hannah smiled and her eyes twinkled merrily. 'Something like that, Mr Roper.'

'What about travelling abroad? Mr Edmund did quite a bit of that?'

Hannah put her head on one side. 'Was it always strictly business? Was it always really necessary?'

Josiah gave a bark of wry laughter. 'See straight through the old bugger, don't you? To answer your questions: no, it wasn't, but there were times when it was. Occasional trips abroad are very necessary.' He sighed. 'Especially now.'

Hannah frowned. 'What do you mean? Especially now?'

'You've heard about the war in America?'

'Vaguely.'

'There's a civil war going on in America. It started about three or four months ago. The north versus the south.' He reached for a newspaper lying on the desk, placed there every day for his master. 'There was an item in the paper. I kept it,' he murmured, scanning the small print. 'Ah yes, here it is.'

He came around the desk and spread the paper in front of her, jabbing at a paragraph with his bony finger. 'Read it for yourself.'

Hannah stared down at the tiny, close print. Whilst she was bright and had been a quick learner, her schooling had been spasmodic. She could read simple texts, write a neat hand and do arithmetic quickly in her head, but the tiny print and the long, complicated words baffled her.

'Er, you tell me what it says, Mr Roper.' She looked up at him and pulled a wry face. 'My learning doesn't go as far as the fancy words in *The Times*.'

For once, Josiah did not smirk derisively. He merely nodded briefly, picked up the paper to read the item again to refresh his memory whilst Hannah waited with impatient anxiety.

'The gist of it,' he began, 'is this. The majority of raw cotton that comes to this country comes from the Southern States of America. The people who do most of the work connected with the growing of cotton are black slaves belonging to the plantation owners. There's been a movement to abolish slavery, but of course the south don't want it because they want to keep their slaves – their cheap labour. But the people in the north believe it's wrong to snatch people from their homeland – that's Africa,' he added by way of explanation, 'and transport them to a far-off land and sell them to the highest bidder who'll probably work them to death . . .'

Hannah's face was grim. To her, there were echoes from her own life. Hadn't she been torn away from her mother and brought here to work at the mill for a pittance, made to sign a piece of paper she scarcely understood and been bound to the Critchlows for years?

As if reading her thoughts, Josiah Roper said softly, 'But there's no escape for them, Mrs Critchlow. Not ever. They're owned, body and soul, by the plantation owners. They even have to forget their own African names and live by whatever slave name their master chooses, taking his surname as their own.'

Hannah shuddered. She'd taken her master's name now, but the choice, for whatever devious reason, had at least been her own to make.

Josiah went on, warming to his tale now that he had such a willing listener. It was the one thing he missed since his aged mother had died – having someone to talk to about world affairs and political matters. Once – in the early days – Edmund had treated him almost as an equal and had occasionally indulged in such discussion. But of late, Mr Edmund had treated Josiah with the contempt he showed all his workers. Josiah Roper was now no more to Edmund that the lowliest floor sweeper in his mill. 'Now, the north and south are fighting each other over giving the slaves their freedom. It's called a civil war and it sets friend against friend, even brother against brother.'

Hannah gasped. 'Oh, how terrible!'

For a brief moment even the hard-hearted Josiah Roper spared a thought for the internal strife that must be tearing that great nation apart.

'So,' Josiah finished, 'we need to find other suppliers.'

'Could you do that?'

Josiah wrinkled his brow. 'Manchester's the place to go – or Liverpool. I could find out what's going on. It might even be necessary for me to go abroad. Rumour has it that we'll need to get Indian cotton, though some of that is inferior quality. It would need someone who knew what they were doing to make sure the brokers don't cheat us.'

'Would you be willing to go abroad? To seek out other supplies? All expenses paid, of course.'

For the first time a genuine look of pleasure crossed Josiah's face. 'I . . . I've always wanted to travel. See a bit of the world. Do . . . do you mean it?'

Hannah nodded, knowing instinctively that she'd won him over. 'I wouldn't be able to go – not with the child coming. And besides . . .' She put her head on one side, resorting to a little flattery to win him over. 'I wouldn't know where to start or what to do.'

'I'm sure you wouldn't be long in learning,' Josiah murmured with a wry smile. It was the nearest he would come to paying her a compliment. He was still looking thoughtful, but now there was a hint of admiration for her in his eyes. 'Do you know,' he said slowly, 'I think we could do it. The three of us together – you, me and Scarsfield. I really think we could keep this place going.'

'I'm sure all the workers will help.'

Now Josiah pulled a face. 'They'll be glad enough to keep their jobs, but as for actually helping, well, their hatred for the Critchlows goes deep.'

'But it won't be the Critchlows running it, will it? Not for a while, anyway.'

'You're a Critchlow now, don't forget,' he reminded her, though this time there was no malice in his tone.

Hannah pulled a wry face but then she laughed. 'Ah, but not by birth. That's the difference. And things are going to be very different, let me tell you. There are going to be a few changes around here, Mr Roper. Oh yes, in fact quite a lot of changes.'

Forty-Seven

Ernest Scarsfield sat with a bemused expression on his face as Hannah explained all that had happened and detailed her plans. 'Finally, you should know that I am expecting Adam's child. Whatever happens with Mr Edmund and . . . and . . .' her voice trembled a little, 'Adam, there's going to be an heir.' She glanced at both Ernest and Josiah now. 'So – will you both help me? Can we work together to save the mill?'

The two men glanced at each other.

'If you think we can do it, lass, well, yes, of course,' Ernest said.

'I'm sure we can. There's just one more thing,' she said as she stood up. 'I'll have to go and see Mr Edmund.'

'Well, I wish you luck,' Josiah said.

And almost beneath his breath, Ernest muttered, 'You're going to need it.'

'I'll go now,' Hannah said firmly, before her nerve failed. 'Get it over with.'

If the coming meeting with Mr Edmund hadn't been so nerve-racking, Hannah would have enjoyed the walk up the hill, through the village and into the grounds of the Manor. It was a hot, still day with only the sound of birdsong and the distant weir to disturb the peace.

Edmund was in his bedroom, sitting near the window so that he could look out, down the river valley. As she approached him, Hannah could see that the upper part of the mill was plainly visible. He was slouched to one side of his chair, a rug over his knee. The left side of his face was drawn down, giving him a lopsided appearance. But he recognized her at once, for he began to splutter. He raised his right arm and, with a trembling hand, waved her away, making strange, unintelligible sounds. Saliva dribbled from the side of his mouth.

He was a pitiful sight, yet Hannah hardened her heart. He'd been a cruel, ruthless man and even now, when he was helpless, he was still trying to turn her away.

Ignoring his feeble protests, she sat down in a chair opposite him.

'Adam's gone,' she said bluntly, sparing him nothing. 'You've driven him away.'

He made a noise and prodded his forefinger at her.

'Yes, I've no doubt you blame me. And you're right. I have much to answer for.' Another grunt from Edmund, but Hannah went on. She leaned towards him. 'But it's me you should have sent away – not Adam. You could have done. You were good at it once. Remember Nell Hudson?'

He dropped his gaze and let his hand fall back into his lap.

'Yes,' she whispered. 'I see that you do.' She paused and then added softly, 'I wonder just how many bastards you've sired.'

Now Edmund brought forth a growl of anger, but Hannah only laughed. 'You probably don't even know how many might come banging on your door one day to demand a share of their birthright.'

'Huh!'

'They'd get short shrift from you, I've no doubt. But Adam is your legitimate heir – and I am his wife and I intend to keep the mill running until he comes back to claim his rightful inheritance.'

Edmund shook his head and made angry noises, but Hannah went on, relentlessly, 'And here's something else for you to think about. I am carrying his child – his legitimate child – and your grandchild.'

With a great effort, Edmund reached out towards the small table placed beside him. A glass of water stood there and, thinking he wanted a drink, Hannah half rose from her chair to help him. But Edmund grasped the glass with his one good hand, picked it up and flung it at her. It struck her on the left-hand side of her forehead, just below her hairline, leaving an inch-long cut and spilling the water down her blouse and skirt. The glass fell to the floor and smashed as blood began to trickle down Hannah's face.

She did not move, did not raise her hand to touch her forehead. She stood there, quite still, staring at him for several moments, then slowly she turned and walked from the room, her resolve more steadfast than ever.

Hannah did not visit Edmund again, though she heard that he was improving slowly. She had plenty to occupy her at the mill.

For the first few months, the mill ran smoothly. There was still plenty of cotton in the storeroom and another delivery arrived, but the man who brought it was gloomy.

'Don't know when I'll bring you any more,' he told Josiah, who checked the paperwork assiduously. 'There's a mill in Lancashire threatening to close.

We're going to go through some hard times. You mark my words . . .'

Josiah did mark his words and passed on the man's dire predictions to both Hannah and Ernest, but Hannah refused to be downhearted.

Things were so much better. She'd arranged for the local doctor to visit the mill twice a month. Any worker who wished to consult him could do so. From the moment she'd suggested such a notion, Ernest had been all for the idea, but Josiah had shaken his head. 'It will cost too much. If we're facing hard times, we didn't ought to be letting ourselves in for extra expense.'

It was strange how quickly the three of them had assumed ownership of the mill and full responsibility for its running and the people who worked there. Hannah had even thought about releasing all the apprentices who were still tied to the Critchlow name – just like she hoped the poor slaves in America would win their freedom, so she wanted to set the bound apprentices free.

'Tell you what,' Ernest suggested, unwilling to see such a good idea quashed by the careful clerk. 'Why don't we ask all the workers to contribute a penny a week towards the scheme?'

Hannah stared at him. 'What – every week whether they need a doctor or not?'

Ernest nodded. 'I've heard of it being done in other places. It's not much, yet folk feel reassured that if they really need a doctor, they're not going to be faced with a huge bill to pay. And there's one mill I've heard of that has a visiting dentist as well. There's a room set aside with all the equipment in. A chair and everything.'

'Oh, now you are taking it too far,' Josiah said, but Hannah laughed.

'Now *I'll* tell *you* what,' she said. 'We'll sound out all the workers. See what they think, and if they agree we'll certainly have the doctor come regularly, and if the money will run to it, we can have the dentist come if anyone needs him.'

Ernest beamed and Josiah shrugged philosophically. As long as his books balanced, he didn't mind what the new mistress of the mill did.

And as for Hannah, she was happier than she had thought it possible to be. The mill was still working. As yet, they hadn't even had to put any of the workers on short time and now she was looking forward to the birth of her child in a few months' time.

Every month she wrote diligently to Auntie Bessie and Nell, and in return she received letters written by Jim – dictated to him, of course, by Bessie and Nell. Whilst they hadn't approved of what she had done, they nevertheless still assured her of their love and wished her well.

'Don't forget you've a home here with us if you ever need it. You and your little one,' Jim wrote in every letter.

Despite the threat of hard times to come hanging over them all, Hannah thrived and bloomed. There was only one thing that caused her deep sadness.

Not one word had come from Adam.

Sunday afternoon was the only time Hannah allowed herself some free time; the rest of the week was fully occupied with running the mill. On a surprisingly warm October afternoon, she walked along the narrow path across the footbridge over the waterfall and pulled herself up the steep, precarious path on the hillside opposite Millersbrook village and the Manor. Panting a little, she realized there would be not many more weeks when she would be able to tackle the climb. Smiling gently to herself, she ran her hand lightly over the swelling mound of her belly. 'You're growing fast, my little one.' And she felt a flutter of movement and believed the child she carried beneath her heart already understood. She walked on until she rounded the curve of the hill directly opposite the impressive manor house that stood on the edge of the cliff above the deep valley where the River Wye meandered. Sitting on the grass to catch her breath, she eyed the long windows glinting in the sunlight and wondered if Edmund was behind one of them, watching her.

Then her thoughts turned, as they always did when she came up here, to Luke. Her gaze roamed the hillside. She could almost see herself and Luke running up the hill, fancied she heard the echo of their young and innocent laughter. Tears filled her eyes and she pulled at the grass at the side of her. A lump came to her throat and a sob escaped her lips.

'Oh, Luke, if only you hadn't died,' she whispered. 'If only —'

'Hannah? You all right?'

Hannah jumped at the sudden sound of a voice. For one fleeting, foolish moment, she thought it was Luke.

Taking a deep breath, she lifted her head and squinted up against the sun to see Ted standing a few feet away, grinning down at her.

'Ted!'

He came and sat down beside her. 'Should you be up here?' he asked, genuine concern in his tone. 'Auntie Lily says you're . . . well, you know.' All of a sudden, the young man was embarrassed.

Hannah smiled and said, 'I'm fine. I'm only five months gone.' She pulled a wry face. 'But you're right. I won't be able to come up here many more times. It was a bit of an effort today, I must admit.'

'Well then, you're not to come up again,' Ted said firmly, but his bossiness was tempered by an affectionate grin. 'At least, not without me.'

'And what would your girlfriend say to that, eh?'

Ted laughed. 'Which one?'

'Oh, you!' Hannah laughed and punched his shoulder lightly.

'If you ever want any help, Hannah, you've only to say the word.' Now Ted was being serious.

'Thanks, Ted.'

She felt his gaze on her. 'There is something, isn't there?'

'Well . . .' She plucked at the grass again self-consciously.

'Come on, out with it.'

'It's just that there's two rooms at the apprentice house that we – that I – haven't got cleaned out and whitewashed. I can't really take in lodgers till I get them done. And I need to. Adam—' Her voice broke as she spoke his name, but she pulled in a deep breath and struggled on, 'was doing all that, but . . .'

'But he didn't get it finished before he went away,' Ted said gently.

Unable to speak, Hannah nodded.

'Consider it done.' Ted grinned. 'I'll—'

447

Whatever Ted had been going to say was cut off abruptly by an angry voice. 'Another poor sod in tow, eh?'

Startled, Hannah and Ted turned towards Daniel standing a few feet away, his hands clenched angrily by his side, his face thunderous. Ted rose to his feet and held out his hand to help Hannah up too. He knew who Daniel was, knew he was the twin of the boy who'd died years earlier, but that was all. He was unaware of the young man's bitterness, much of which was directed at Hannah. Knowing nothing of this, Ted thought that Daniel's interest in the pretty young woman was what any red-blooded young man's would be.

He grinned at Daniel. 'Jealous, a' ya?'

Daniel's frown only deepened and he spat crudely on the ground. 'I wouldn't want her if she was the last woman on this earth. You're welcome to her. But I'll warn you, she's bad news. She's trouble. And you,' he shook his fist at Hannah, 'you're no better than a whore.'

He turned and began to run along the narrow, precarious path.

'Daniel . . . !' Hannah cried, frightened that he would stumble and pitch headlong down the steep hillside.

Ted caught hold of her arm, fearful that she was going to go after Daniel. 'Let him go, Hannah.' He paused as they both stood watching until Daniel had disappeared around the curve of the hillside. 'What's eating him, then? Fancies you himself, I bet.'

If it hadn't been so serious, Ted's remark would have been funny. As it was, Hannah smiled but it was a sad smile. 'He hates me. He blames me for Luke's death.'

Ted was puzzled. 'How can he do that?'

'Mr Edmund was ... was ... well, Luke came to my rescue, if you know what I mean.'

Ted's face was grim. He knew all about Edmund Critchlow and his reputation with girls, especially the young girls at the mill.

Hannah sighed. 'That's when they fought and Luke fell in the wheel. I suppose ... I suppose Daniel's right in a way. If it hadn't been for me, there wouldn't have been a fight and Luke would still be alive.'

'And you're still blaming yourself, aren't you, Hannah?'

Hannah sank to the ground and covered her face. 'Oh, Ted, I've been so stupid and ... and wicked.' Tears flowed down her face.

'Oh, now come on, Hannah, love.' Ted squatted down on his haunches beside her. 'I can't bear to see you cry.'

She could see she was embarrassing him, so she sniffed and brushed away the tears with the back of her hand. She forced a tremulous smile.

Now she was calmer, Ted took hold of her hand and held it between his own. His touch was warm and comforting. 'Come on, tell Uncle Ted all about it.'

'I ... I thought you'd've known. I told Mrs Grundy.'

'Oh, Auntie Lily wouldn't say a word to a soul. She knows how to keep a confidence. And so do I, Hannah.'

'I set my cap at Adam Critchlow – deliberately – to get revenge on his father.'

'Well, yes, I'd sort of guessed that, but I don't quite know why you had to go as far as marrying him. That did surprise me a bit.'

'Well, I had to. How else would it've really hurt Mr Edmund? He'd've just sent me away and that'd've been the end of it. But now, I've ended up hurting myself and . . . and the man I now love.'

'You mean, you *love* Adam Critchlow?'

Hannah nodded.

'Oh.'

There was a long silence between them until Hannah could bear it no more. 'So now you see why Daniel hates me, why Adam hates me and . . . and now I suppose you will too.'

'No,' Ted said at once. 'No, Hannah, because I can understand now how it's all come about. My family felt very bitter about our Lucy's death so if anyone can understand why you've acted the way you have, then it's me.' He gave a rueful laugh. 'When Lucy died I reckon me dad wanted to kill Edmund Critchlow with his bare hands. But he'd only have hurt all the family even more if he'd've faced the hangman for it, wouldn't he?'

Hannah nodded.

'And, like you say, it's you that's hurting now because you fell in love with Adam.'

Again, Hannah nodded silently.

'See.' Ted nudged her and winked, deliberately trying to lighten her mood. 'I said you should have married me.'

'Oh, Ted . . .' she was crying and laughing too now.

'Come on,' he said getting up and hauling her to her feet. 'It's time you were getting home, and next Sunday I'll come and whitewash those two rooms for you. Sunday's the only time I get. A right couple of slave drivers, me auntie and uncle are.'

It wasn't true about the Grundys, of course, but Ted's words reminded Hannah of the difficulties to come. Difficulties that arose because of the struggle half a world away to free those bound to real slavery. Despite all the hardship that might result because of it, she couldn't help but be sympathetic to the cause. And now, having unburdened herself to Ted and knowing that she still had his friendship, she returned home with a light heart and her resolve to save the mill and all its workers strengthened.

By the time Hannah gave birth, her hair had returned to its natural golden colour. She had cut it short and all trace of the dyed hair was now gone. But her baby son was born with wisps of black hair, and eyes that would soon become the dark brown of his father and his grandfather.

'What're you going to call him?' Lily demanded, the first of a surprisingly long line of visitors to the bedroom in the apprentice house where Hannah lay with her son in her arms.

Smiling down at the sleeping child, Hannah traced a gentle finger around the shape of his face. The baby slept on. 'I don't know. I . . . I'd like to call him Luke, but . . .'

'Best not. If Adam comes back one day, it's hardly fair, is it?'

'No,' Hannah murmured. 'No, it isn't.' She sighed. 'But I don't want to call him after any of the Critchlows, nor,' she added with an edge to her tone, 'my own father.'

'Well, just choose a name that doesn't mean anything. Just a name – the little chap's own name.'

'Well,' she said tentatively. 'I was wondering if . . . if Ted would mind if I called him after him. He's been a good friend – a real friend to me – these past weeks and . . . and he doesn't seem to have any hard feelings about . . . well, about what happened. And I . . . I'd like him to be one of the godfathers.'

Lily laughed. 'He'll be thrilled.'

'Then will you tell him?'

'You should ask him yourself, but I'll tell him you want to see him.'

Two days later, Ted stood at the end of her bed, twirling his cap through his fingers in nervous embarrassment, but beaming. 'I don't know what to say, Hannah. I've never been asked to be a godfather before. What do I have to do? I mean –' his face clouded for an instant – 'are you sure you want me? I'm only an ordinary chap.'

'You're just the sort of chap I want.' Hannah laughed. 'You're a good friend, Ted. I won't forget what you've done for me. All you have to do is come to the christening and make some promises and then see that I bring him up properly.' Her eyes became sad. 'If Adam doesn't come back, then you're just the sort of man I'd like my son to have in his life.' Huskily, she added, 'I can't think of anyone better.'

Ted puffed out his chest. 'Then I'd be honoured.'

'And we'll call him Edward?'

Ted nodded enthusiastically, but now he was unable to speak for the lump in his throat.

As soon as Hannah was well enough, she wrapped the baby in warm clothes and a copious shawl and set off up the hill to the Manor.

It was time that Edmund Critchlow met his grandson.

452

Forty-Eight

He was sitting in the huge window of his study over-looking the river. Like his bedroom, from here he could see the mill. The butler showed her in and as Edmund turned in his chair to look at her, she could see a vast improvement in him since the last time she had visited. The side of his face was no longer dragged down, and even in the simple act of turning in his chair, she could see that he had so much more move-ment in his limbs. And he no longer sat with a rug over his knees like an invalid.

His gaze was fixed upon her and the child in her arms as she crossed the room towards him. She stood before him and then bent down and placed the baby in the crook of his arm.

'I thought it time that you saw your grandson. His name is Edward. Edward Critchlow.' Deliberately, she emphasized the surname.

Edmund looked down at the child and Hannah was sure that his features softened.

'He's only three weeks old. So he's very tiny still,' she went on, 'but he's healthy and strong and he eats.' She laughed wryly. Her breasts were sore from her demanding son, but she didn't mind. She would put up with any discomfort for his wellbeing.

Edmund looked up and stared at her for a long moment. 'Please – sit – down.' He had fought hard to regain his speech, and though his words came out haltingly and a little slurred, he could at last make himself understood.

'Thank you,' Hannah murmured, drawing her chair close. Though she was determined to introduce Edward to his grandfather, adamant that Edmund should accept the child, she was still unsure of the man's reaction. But Edmund was holding the baby quite easily and tenderly. A slow smile spread across his face and he parted the shawl with a gentle finger to take a better look.

'He's – got – dark – hair.'

'Yes, just like you and Adam,' Hannah said.

'Sleeps well?'

Hannah grimaced. 'In between his feeds, every four hours round the clock.'

'You must – be tired. Have you – help? A nurse-maid?'

Hannah shook her head and said softly, 'No. I want to care for my son myself.'

'Then a – maid – to do housework?'

Again, Hannah shook her head.

'Take – Sarah – for a while. Just – just to help you.'

Hannah stared at him. He was making a gesture – she knew that – a gesture towards some kind of reconciliation.

'Thank you,' she said graciously. 'I would appreciate that.'

He nodded, but his eyes were still on the child.

They sat together for almost an hour, not speaking much, but there was no tension between them, no anger now. At last, the child began to stir and whimper, and Hannah rose and reached out for him.

'He's getting hungry. I'd better go.'

He let her lift the child out of his arms, but Hannah could read the disappointment on his face. As she settled the baby in her arms, she looked down at Edmund. 'Would you like me to bring him to see you again?'

'Please.'

'Very well then. In a few days.'

'Tomorrow?' His tone was pleading, no longer demanding.

She smiled. 'Very well. Tomorrow afternoon.'

As she turned to go, he said, 'The mill . . .'

She glanced back and waited, her heart beating a little faster, expecting the worst. But to her surprise and delight, he said, 'A good job – you've done a – good job.'

'Thank you.' She smiled.

'Roper – comes. Tells me – what's happening.'

'Yes, I know. I arranged that he should come up every week, show you the books and keep you informed.'

He nodded. 'Thank you – Hannah.'

They stared at each other and between them there passed a kind of truce. As she left the house, Hannah kissed her baby's forehead and murmured, 'You're a little miracle worker, my darling little Eddie, that's what you are.'

Life settled down to a comfortable routine. Hannah recovered quickly from the birth of her child; she was young and strong and healthy. Sarah came as her housemaid for a few weeks, but when Hannah told her she could return to the Manor, the girl burst into tears. 'I don't want to go back there. Cook's a tartar and Beamish, the butler, he's never a kind word for anyone. And if I have to see the master, I shake from head to foot. Oh, madam, can't I stay here? I'll look after little Eddie. I love little ones and . . . and I am good with him, aren't I, madam?'

'You are,' Hannah agreed. She'd left the child in Sarah's care a few times whilst she went to the mill. She was quite happy that he was in safe hands.

Hannah was thoughtful. It would be a boon to have the girl work for her permanently. It would enable Hannah to resume her place at the mill. Since Eddie's birth, Josiah Roper had come to the house every Friday afternoon on his way back from his visit to the Manor, to lay his books before her and report on the week's activities at the mill. Ernest Scarsfield, too, came often, but he did not visit Mr Edmund.

'I'll leave that to old Roper, if you don't mind, Hannah. He's Mr Edmund's right-hand man.' He chuckled wickedly. 'I could think of other names to call him, but I won't be vulgar. Not in front of the little chap.'

Hannah laughed. 'I don't think he's quite ready to pick up bad language yet, Ernest.'

Ernest moved to the crib and tickled Eddie under the chin. 'By, he's like Master Adam, Hannah. Spitting image of him at the same age, he is. I remember his mother bringing him to the mill when he wasn't much older than this little feller.'

'Ernest – what happened to Adam's mother?'

'She died. About two years after Adam was born, I think it was. In childbirth. Little girl, but the poor little mite died too. Nice woman she was.' He glanced at Hannah. 'Too good for the likes of Edmund Critchlow,' he added in a low voice.

'He's changed. This illness seems to have – I don't know, what's the word? – cowed him.'

'Huh!' Ernest gave a wry laugh. 'Don't you believe it, lass. That one'll never change. Oh, he might not be able to shout and storm about the place like he used to.' His face was grim as he added, 'At least the girls at the mill are getting a bit of peace just now, but mark me, Hannah, he'll not have changed. Not in here, he won't.' He smote his own chest.

'But he seems to have taken to Eddie. He's quite upset if I miss a day taking him up there.'

'Oh aye, he will be. Eddie's his grandson. His eventual heir. He'll want him all right. And whilst the child's very young, he'll need you. But you watch out, Hannah. If ever he regains his health and strength, he'll be just like he always was. He'll want the child – oh yes, he'll want the child. But as for you – well, like I say Hannah, watch out.'

After Ernest had left, Hannah was thoughtful. She had thought that Edmund had mellowed, but like Ernest said, it could just be the debilitating illness that had curbed his ways. But he was recovering now. Hannah could see improvement almost daily.

And once Edmund Critchlow got his strength back, well, who knew what might happen then?

'Looks like he really has deserted you, then? That husband of yours?' Daniel was waiting to waylay her in the yard as she left the mill one evening, hurrying home to her baby.

'So it seems,' she said tartly.

'Luke wouldn't have done that.' He stood in front of her, barring her way. She was not afraid of him –

not physically – but every time she met him, she was reminded so sharply of Luke.

She swallowed hard, gritted her teeth and said, almost haughtily, 'If you'll excuse me, I have a baby to feed.'

'Oh yes, your son.' His face darkened. 'The child that should've been my nephew.'

She lifted her head and met his resentful eyes. 'Yes, Daniel,' she said, softening. 'He should've been. He should've been Luke's child. And I promise you, he would have been if . . . if . . .'

'If your husband's father hadn't killed him.'

'Oh, Daniel. Let the past go. Don't live your life with bitterness.'

'I'll never forgive and I'll never forget. And I thought better of you. I admired you, the way you were planning revenge on the Critchlows, but now, you're giving in to them.' His lip curled. 'Just like everyone else. Well, I won't. The only reason I've stayed here all these years is because of Luke. I can't leave him. He won't rest until he's been avenged.'

Suddenly, there was a strange look of madness in his eyes as he vowed never to forgive and forget. Hannah shuddered. They were the same words that Josiah Roper had used. They made a good pair, she thought.

'I must go,' she muttered, side-stepped around him and hurried away. But the conversation had left her feeling unsettled and strangely afraid.

Hannah did not forget either Ernest's dire warnings nor Daniel's continuing resentment, but there was one person who, surprisingly, did seem to have changed.

Josiah Roper was in his element. It was what he'd always dreamed of: holding a position of authority, his talents recognized at last. He, in turn, was courteous and mindful of Hannah's position, silently grateful to her that she was treating him with the credit he believed he deserved. And between Josiah and Ernest, who'd always disliked each other, there grew a mutual respect.

One Friday afternoon in March when they met in the inner office, both Josiah and Ernest entered to greet Hannah with glum faces.

'What is it?' she said at once. 'What's happened?'

They sat down and glanced at each other solemnly. 'Things are getting worse, Hannah,' Josiah began. 'As you know I was in Manchester yesterday. They say that the mills there are on short time.'

'Several have had to close,' Ernest put in, 'and workers are seeking public relief.'

'We've been lucky until now. We had a fair stock of raw cotton, but that's running low now and the price is rocketing,' Josiah went on. 'Since last October the brokers have been demanding one shilling and more a pound for the type we used to buy for eight pence. And prices are still rising. We can't absorb all of it and still make a profit.'

'Profit be hanged, Mr Roper. All we need to do is break even.'

Josiah raised his eyebrows and smirked, but Ernest laughed out loud. 'Well said, Hannah. Well said.'

'Mr Edmund won't like that.'

'Mr Edmund will have to lump it, if we're to save the mill,' Hannah said, grimly determined.

'We could ask the workers to take a cut in wages,' Josiah suggested, but Ernest snorted derisively.

'You'll have a strike on your hands if you do.'

'Was there *any* cotton to be had?' Hannah asked. 'What about Indian cotton?'

Josiah shrugged. 'Some, but only very inferior quality to what we normally use and the price of that has risen too.'

'But these aren't normal times,' Hannah said, trying to hold on to her patience. It seemed as if Josiah was loath to accept change. But change there would have to be if they were to survive. She turned to Ernest. 'Could we use inferior cotton?'

'We'll have to.'

Hannah smiled. At least Ernest was of the same mind as she was.

By April, Wyedale Mill had only very poor quality yarn to work with and the quantity Josiah could acquire for an acceptable price was not enough to keep the whole mill running. There was no alternative but to put the workers on short time.

Hannah called a meeting of all the workers. The warm, balmy evening mocked the grim faces. Some of the women were in tears. It was no more than Hannah had expected. The news from the cities and the mills in Lancashire was desperate. Families were facing starvation. They had burned every stick of furniture they had in an effort to keep warm. New-born babies were dying for lack of nourishment and children cried for food. And soon such hardship would reach Wyedale Mill.

Earlier in the day she'd walked down the lane to the Grundys' farm. Sitting in Lily Grundy's warm kitchen and sipping hot tea gratefully, she said, 'This is what I'm going to miss the most. Tea.'

'Bad as that, is it, lass?'

Ollie and Lily sat opposite, their solemn faces turned towards her, as Hannah nodded. 'I'm afraid it is and it's going to get worse. I've called all the workers together for a meeting tonight at the mill. We're going to have to put them on short time, even lay a few off. I thought I should come and tell you, because it'll likely affect you. You've always supplied the village folk and . . .'

She saw Ollie and Lily glance at each other. Then Ollie cleared his throat. 'Look, lass, me an' the missis've been talking things over. The mill and the villagers've given us our living for years. And a good living it's been too. Oh, it's not easy, farming. It's hard work and – ' he smiled a little – 'not many days off in a year, I can tell you. But it's a good life, a satisfying life. And now, we want to give a bit back.'

Hannah glanced from one to the other. 'I don't understand.'

'Well,' Ollie began, 'for a start I can take some of the fellers on to work on the land. If they're willing to do a few hours each, it'd help several families, wouldn't it. What I mean is, rather than take on one or two full time, they could sort of – sort of share the jobs out.'

'But do you need any more help? You and Ted have always managed.'

Ollie laughed. 'Mebbe we have, but that doesn't mean we wouldn't be glad of a bit more help.'

Tears sprang to Hannah's eyes. Ollie, Lily – and Ted must be in on it too – were creating jobs for the out-of-work millhands.

'With more help,' Ollie went on, 'we can grow more food for everyone.'

Hannah reached out and clasped their hands as the tears now flooded down her face unchecked. 'Oh, how good you are.'

Now, as Hannah stood on a box before a sea of worried faces, with Josiah and Ernest on either side of her, she began to explain the situation. 'We're all in this together.'

'You mean we'll all be in the workhouse together,' a voice from the back cried out.

Anger flashed in Hannah's blue eyes and she shook her fist in the air. 'Don't let anyone mention the word "workhouse" in my hearing. No one – *no one* – from this village will ever go into the workhouse.'

There was muttering amongst the crowd and shaking of heads. They couldn't believe her, however much they wanted to.

One of the men, Bill Ryan, who'd worked at the mill all his life pushed his way to the front to stand before her. He was tall, broad shouldered and strong. With a note of deference, he pulled off his cap, but he still addressed her as 'Hannah'. Now, they all knew exactly who she was, and whilst they were always courteous towards her, she herself had insisted that everyone should call her by the name they always had. She didn't want to be called 'Mrs Critchlow'.

'Hannah,' Bill began, 'we all know that you – and Mr Roper and Ernest here – have kept us going so far and we're grateful. And we also 'preciate you always being honest with us.' A low murmuring confirmed his words, 'But times is hard and they're going to get worse. Whole families work at the mill – you know that. Most of us have no other income except what we earn here, and soon we'll not have bread to feed our wives and families.' The proud man glanced around at his workmates and friends. 'And we're not going to sit idle about the house watching our families starve. If you've got to put us on short time or reduce our wages, then . . . then we'll have to look for other work or go on the parish, lass. I'm sorry, but there it is. And we can't even afford the penny a week for the doc no more.'

Hannah nodded. 'I know and I understand, but first, let me tell you what we have planned. For one thing, Dr Barnes has agreed to keep coming even if he doesn't get paid. "We must all pull together," he said.'

There was another murmuring, louder this time, at the doctor's kind sacrifice.

Hannah went on, raising her voice to be heard. 'I'm going to open up the schoolroom again. We'll start reading classes and—'

Before she could say more, a shout came from the back and a fist was raised in the air. 'That won't put food in our bellies. Reading! Pah!'

'*And,*' Hannah went on as if uninterrupted, 'there are to be sewing classes and shoemaking.'

The murmuring grew to excited chatter. Now they could begin to see the usefulness of the idea. Hannah stamped on the box for quiet. 'The Grundys at the farm are willing to take on hands to work on the land to help grow more food for all of us. And some of you might be able to find work on the hillside.'

The workings that Hannah had seen were for a railway that was to run through the dale all the way to Buxton. When she'd heard about it, Hannah had thought wryly, *It's come a few years too late for me. If there'd been a train then, Josiah might not have caught me.* Work on the track had been going on for months and it was rumoured that the line was due to open in the summer. At her suggestion, she saw several men turn to one another and nod their heads.

'And,' she went on, and now she was smiling broadly for she knew her last piece of news would be the best of all, 'whilst we are facing such difficulties, none of you will pay a penny in rent.'

A gasp of surprise rippled through the throng and Hannah heard Bill Ryan's deep laughter. 'I dare bet Mr Edmund hasn't approved that, Hannah.'

She smiled down at him. 'No, Mr Ryan, he hasn't, but we three have.'

She dared not look down at Josiah, for she knew he would be frowning. He hadn't agreed to the scheme, but he'd been overruled by herself and Ernest.

'We all have to make sacrifices,' Hannah had told him determinedly. 'Even the Critchlows.'

'I daren't think what Mr Edmund will say,' Josiah had muttered, but then a sly smile had appeared on his face that, for the moment, Hannah hadn't understood.

Forty-Nine

Late that evening, as Hannah was settling Eddie down for the night, she heard a knock at the back door.

'Sarah, see who that is, will you?' she called. 'There, there, my little man,' she crooned, her attention returning to her son. Distantly, she heard voices and then Sarah's footsteps running up the stairs.

'Oh, ma'am.' Her eyes were shining. 'They're back, they've come back.'

For a moment, Hannah's heart lurched with hope. Adam! He'd come home. But then she realized that the girl had said 'they' not 'he'. Her heart plummeted.

Levelly, she asked, 'Who is it, Sarah?'

'The Bramwells, ma'am. They've come home. You go down, ma'am, I'll stay with master Eddie.'

Hannah picked up her skirts and hurried downstairs and into the kitchen. They were standing awkwardly just inside the doorway, each carrying a bundle of belongings. Hannah gasped and covered her mouth with her hand, staring at them with wide eyes.

If Sarah hadn't told her who it was, Hannah doubted she would have recognized them. Although she hadn't seen them for several years, she was shocked by the change in them. Arthur was thinner and stooped. He looked an old man, his grey hair straggling almost to his shoulders, unkempt and unwashed. A grizzled, untidy beard covered the lower

465

part of his face and his eyes were desperate. But it was the change in Ethel Bramwell that shocked Hannah the most. She was thin and gaunt, her cheeks hollowed, her skin sallow. Her eyes, sunk into dark shadows, were lifeless and defeated. Her shabby clothes were little more than filthy rags. To see the once neat and particular woman reduced to such poverty tore at Hannah's heart.

A sob escaped Hannah's throat as she stretched out her arms and rushed across the room to them, trying to embrace them both at once. 'Oh, Mrs Bramwell, Mr Bramwell. Come in, come in, do. Sit down. Here, let me take your things. Sarah,' the girl had followed her downstairs and was standing near the door, eyes wide with curiosity, 'Sarah make tea for us all.'

'Tea, ma'am?' Sarah hesitated. Tea was an even more precious commodity in these hard times. 'Yes, yes, tea. You, too. We shall all have a cup to celebrate Mr and Mrs Bramwell's return. Oh, how good it is to see you both. Come and sit down by the fire.' She urged them to sit close to the warmth, deeply anxious. They looked ill, both of them, but old habits die hard and she couldn't bring herself – not yet – to fire at them the questions that were whirling around her mind. To her, they were still Mr and Mrs Bramwell, superintendents of the apprentice house.

As they sat together, sipping the tea, Hannah began tentatively, willing them to tell her themselves how they came to be in such straitened circumstances.

'I heard you'd gone to Manchester after leaving here. Mrs Grundy told me.'

She saw them glance at each other, an awkward, embarrassed glance. Arthur cleared his throat. 'It's . . .

it's because of Lily Grundy that . . . that we've dared to come back.'

Hannah raised her eyebrows. 'Dared?' She was surprised by his choice of word. Then her face cleared, thinking she understood. 'Oh, there's nothing to fear from Mr Edmund, he's . . .' She stopped. Arthur was shaking his head.

'It's not him. It's, well, you can see for yourself how we are.' He gestured sadly towards his wife and himself and his voice broke as he said, 'Little more than beggars, Hannah.'

With shaking hands, Ethel placed her cup down and took up their sorry tale. 'Mr Edmund dismissed us when he stopped taking the apprentices. There were only a few with their indentures still running and he found lodgings for them in the village. Said there was no longer any need for the expense of the apprentice house. We begged to be allowed to stay, to turn it into a lodging house, that we could run and pay him rent. But no, he wanted us out, Hannah. Said we'd been a thorn in his side for years with our soft ways towards the children.' She faltered, her eyes filling with tears.

'Soft ways, he said,' Arthur put in. 'When I had to beat little lads for nothing except being normal, spirited youngsters and shut girls in the punishment room.' He shook his head. 'Whatever's happened to us, at least I'm glad I don't have to do that any more.'

Ethel sniffed and took up the story once more. 'We went to Manchester to try and get work in the mills there. We both used to work in the mills when we were young, so we weren't entirely without experience. We've been fine until . . . until this last year. They started by putting us on short time and then the mill closed and we were out of work.'

'There's no work to be had, Hannah. Not in Manchester. I tried road sweeping for a time – anything I could lay me hands to, but . . .' His voice faded away, defeated and hopeless.

'We wrote to Lily, asking what was happening here. Whether it had affected the mill here. And she told us about you coming back and marrying Master Adam and then about Mr Edmund being ill and all the wonderful things you've done here at the mill. We thought . . . we thought . . .' Her voice trailed away.

Hannah put down her cup and reached out to them both. Her voice was husky as she said, 'I'm so glad you've come back. I hadn't realized it, but I need someone just like you to help me. Oh, this is wonderful. Wonderful.'

The Bramwells glanced at each other, relief and thankfulness on their faces. Yet, their worries were not quite over.

'We . . . we've nowhere to live.'

'You'll live here, of course,' Hannah said at once and turned to Sarah. 'Make up a bed for Mr and Mrs Bramwell.' She laughed. 'You'll see some changes in the house. We've made the dormitories into smaller, separate rooms now. We'd hoped to run it as a lodging house for workers at the mill, but, of course, with all the trouble, we haven't anyone yet.'

'We . . . we can't pay you,' Arthur said hesitantly.

'No need,' Hannah said cheerfully. 'You'll be working for your keep.' She laughed as she added impishly, 'I'm not offering you charity, Arthur Bramwell. You'll earn your keep, believe you me.'

And with these few words she restored both hope and pride in the despairing couple.

'But first, you need some rest. Sarah—' She stopped as she turned to see the girl sobbing, the corner of her white apron lifted to cover her face. She put her arm about the young girl's shoulders. 'Whatever's the matter?'

'You'll not want me now. You'll send me back, won't you?'

'Oh, you silly goose. Of course I'm not going to send you back. I couldn't do without you, you know I couldn't. And Eddie certainly couldn't. You might have to look after him more, but you wouldn't mind that, would you?'

Sarah uncovered her wet face, but now her eyes were shining. 'Oh, I'd love it, ma'am. do . . . do you really mean it? You won't send me back to work for Mr Edmund?'

'I give you my solemn promise that whatever happens, I will never send you back there.'

The girl laughed and flung her arms around Hannah. 'Oh, thank you, thank you. I'll work ever so hard for you, ma'am. And I'll look after Master Eddie like he was me own.'

'I know you will,' Hannah said, giving the girl a quick hug and then saying briskly, 'Come along now, there's work to be done.'

At once, there was a stillness in the kitchen. Time seemed to tilt and it was Ethel's voice saying those very same words, exhorting the little apprentices to go about their chores.

Hannah broke the silence and, laughing, turned towards Ethel. 'You see, all your teaching did stick.'

And, suddenly, they were all laughing.

*

'Soup, that's what we need,' Ethel Bramwell said firmly. 'We can make enough soup to feed the whole village.'

The railway line had been finished and opened in the summer of 1862, but it didn't help the people of Wyedale unless they wanted a trip to Buxton, and now few had the money for the fare. But it was fascinating to see the engines steaming through the dale and hear the shrill whistle as they disappeared into the tunnel. The months passed and now another year on they were facing winter again. There was little work at the mill now but the whole community had pulled together with remarkable spirit. Even those who were not directly connected with the mill willingly became involved. The surrounding farming community, led by the Grundys, supplied food and took on workers whenever they could.

'Can't see folks starving,' one burly farmer delivering a cart load of potatoes to Hannah's door said gruffly. 'Can't sleep in me bed at night with a full belly whilst other folks is going hungry.'

'You're a good man, Mr Earnshaw,' Hannah said simply. 'Thank you.'

The big man's face reddened. 'Aye well, that's as may be, but as I hear it you're the real heroine in all this. But for you, folks'd be turned out of their homes to die on the streets.'

Now it was Hannah's turn to blush. 'Oh, I don't know about that. We're all pulling together.'

And indeed they were. The Bramwells' return had been like a talisman, a lucky charm. Once they had rested, eaten some good, wholesome food and washed themselves and their clothes, it was like they'd never been away. Arthur sought out Ernest, to be greeted like the old friend he was, and Ethel took over the running of the house once again whilst Hannah dealt with the pressing problems of the decreasing workload at the mill.

'I've heard all about what you're doing here, lass,' Farmer Earnshaw went on. 'Set up sewing classes for the women to turn old clothes into whatever's needed. And the fellers are learning cobbling,' he laughed, a great loud guffaw that made Hannah smile, despite her ever-present worries. 'I'll know where to come now when I wants me boots mending, won't I? Oh, I nearly forgot. There's a bundle of clothes in the front of the cart. The missis has been collecting 'em up from all round the district.'

'Oh, how good of her. These are wonderful – wonderful! Please, do thank your wife for all of us won't you?'

'Aye, lass, I will. Keep up the good work,' he called, climbing back onto the front of his cart. 'I'll see you again – soon as I can.'

Hannah stood with her arms full of the clothes and watched him trundle away. His shape became indistinct through the blur of her tears.

How good people were.

'So, how do we make this soup, Mrs Bramwell?' Despite their closeness, Hannah could still not bring herself to call the woman Ethel or her husband Arthur, but gradually the names got shortened to an affectionate Mr B and Mrs B.

Ethel picked up a piece of paper on which she had been writing. 'Whatever meat we can lay our hands on. Beef is the best, if we can get it. Barley, split peas, onions and salt.'

'My mouth's watering already.' Hannah laughed,

but behind her laughter the constant worry gnawed at her. How was she to keep the whole village fed through the winter?

The war in America had been going now for over two and a half years, and hard times had come to the mill towns of Lancashire during the first year of the war. Yet Wyedale Mill had struggled on, thanks to Josiah's clever dealings and Ernest's fair distribution amongst the workers of what work there was to be had. But now, the work had all but dried up and any meagre savings the workers had were gone. Already, folks were burning whatever they could to try to keep warm. As yet there had been no deaths in the village that could be directly contributed to the hardship.

That winter of 1863 was tough for the people of Wyedale, but they struggled through it together, and with the spring of the new year came more available work on the land. Every spare piece of garden or land was given over to growing vegetables. Every scrap of cloth that came from the generous donations of old clothes was carefully utilized. The wooded hillsides had been stripped of every dead tree. Anything that could be burned to give warmth was carried home in triumph by the village youngsters.

'You know, one thing surprises me,' Ernest mused, stroking his moustache as he sat in the kitchen with the Bramwells and Hannah on one of his frequent visits. 'We haven't had any thieving. I'd've laid money on it, if I had any, mind,' he added with wry humour, 'that we'd've had kids stealing from the orchards and fields roundabout. But no, far as I know, nothing.'

'There'd better not be,' Hannah declared, 'else they'll have me to reckon with.' She laughed out loud. 'I'd have to think about reopening up the punishment room.'

They all laughed, but more seriously Arthur said, 'Well, I reckon if there is a bit going on, folks aren't doing anything about it. Turning a blind eye, you might say.'

There was silence amongst them.

'I hope no one has got as low as that, though,' Hannah murmured, and to herself silently added, *not yet*.

Fifty

'I miss hearing you singing about the place,' Ethel remarked one morning as she stirred a huge pan of soup. 'It used to raise everyone's spirits to hear you, no matter how bad things got.'

Hannah sighed. 'To tell you the truth, Mrs B, I haven't felt like singing much lately. Not since Adam left, if I'm honest.'

'No word from him, then?' Ethel asked softly. She'd heard a little from Lily Grundy and surmised the rest for herself from the few words Hannah herself had said about him. But they were few. It seemed as if the girl had locked away the sadness in her heart, buried her misery deep whilst she filled her days with helping others. 'Hasn't his father heard anything?'

'I never ask him,' Hannah said shortly. 'I don't talk to him much if I can help it and then only about Eddie.'

Hannah still took her growing son up the hill to the Manor to visit his grandfather, though she never spoke of other matters to Edmund Critchlow – never discussed what was happening at the mill. That she left to Josiah Roper.

Eddie was two years old now, a sturdy, bright youngster who climbed on his grandfather's knee and chattered to him without inhibition or fear.

It amazed Hannah to see Edmund with his grandson. There was genuine love for the child in his face, she was sure of it. But the thought gave Hannah no comfort.

Instead it brought a chill of fear to her heart.

The day that Edmund Critchlow came back to the mill and took his rightful place behind his desk once more should have been an occasion for great rejoicing. But it wasn't.

They'd got through another spring and summer but now they all faced another hard winter, and how would Edmund Critchlow react to his silent mill and idle workers who were still living in his houses but paying him no rent?

They were not long in finding out.

He sat in his chair with Josiah's carefully written ledgers spread out on the desk before him.

On the opposite side of the desk, Hannah, Josiah and Ernest stood facing him. Ernest's brow was creased with worry and he tugged self-consciously at his moustache. Hannah bit her lip anxiously, but Josiah's face was an expressionless mask.

'So, I see that you three have all but ruined me . . .'

'That's not true,' Hannah burst out. 'We've saved the villagers from starvation—'

'Pah!' Edmund thumped the desk with his fist. 'The villagers! Idle wastrels, living on my charity. Charity be damned! It stops here. You –' he prodded his forefinger towards Josiah – 'you can go this very day and start collecting the rents again. And you'd better tell them I'll be collecting every back penny they owe me.'

Hannah gasped. 'How d'you think they can pay?

They're not earning. Only a few shillings here and there when the farmers employ them.'

Edmund leaned forward. 'They'll pay or leave. The choice is up to them.'

'And where do you suggest they go? To starve on the streets?'

Edmund laughed cruelly. 'I couldn't care less about what happens to the idle good-for-nothings. They've lived off me for years whilst I've been laid up. But I'm back now. And you two,' he pointed at Josiah and Ernest, 'had better watch out. I'm well aware that you've been aiding and abetting this strumpet.' He turned back to glare at Hannah. 'Well, what are you waiting for? You can go now. I'm back. You can go home and attend to your child.'

Hannah lifted her chin. 'I see your thanks didn't last long. You've no right to treat any of us in this way. We've worked well together. We kept this place running as long as we could. Longer than a lot of places. But for us, you wouldn't have a mill at all by now.'

Edmund's grim smile was still a little lopsided. 'I expect I've come back only just in time to save it from going under completely. What work is there, Scarsfield?'

'Very little, sir. We've some Indian cotton—'

'Indian cotton? Pah! That rubbish.'

'There's nothing else to be had sir and the prices of that are extortionate,' Josiah put in.

'Allow me to be the judge of that. You always were useless, Roper.'

'That's not true and you know it isn't,' Hannah cried heatedly. 'It's only thanks to Mr Roper's clever negotiations with the brokers. He's been to Manchester and Liverpool and even abroad—'

'Abroad? At my expense?' Edmund was growing red in the face. 'Is this true?'

'Well, yes, sir. I was trying to find new suppliers, open up new markets. America is closed to us. The blockades—'

Edmund leaned back in his chair. It was as if he'd never been out of it. 'So, I have you to thank, have I, for saving my mill? According to *her*,' he jabbed his finger at Hannah, 'it's all down to you and your wonderful negotiating skills.' His tone was heavy with sarcasm and Hannah winced. She wasn't bothered for herself, but Josiah and Ernest deserved his gratitude for the way they had pulled together to save his mill.

Hannah glanced at Josiah. His eyes were wary. Smoothly, he said, 'That's kind of her to say so, sir, but it's been the three of us. Scarsfield, myself and Mrs Critchlow. We – Scarsfield and I – couldn't have done it without her. She's taken all the decisions, led the way in the improvements.'

'Improvements? What improvements?' Edmund gripped the sides of his chair and leaned forward.

'We have a doctor visit regularly to look after the health of the workers and—'

'A doctor!' His face was growing purple. 'How much is that costing?'

'Well, before the work began to dry up, the workers contributed a penny each a week and we – I mean the company – doubled it. It covers the doctor's visits and any medicines he prescribes.'

'You mean to tell me that we're paying for their medicines?'

477

'In a way, but like I said, the workers are all contributing too. Well, they were. Since the American war, the doctor has given his services for free. But presumably he'll be hoping that we'll revert to that system again once the war is over.'

'Well, that won't happen, I can assure you. And I'll tell him so myself. You can't be soft with workers. They'll take advantage. Any kindness and they'll see it as weakness. Oh no,' he shook his head. 'This has to stop.' He thumped the arm of his chair. 'Now! Roper – see to it. And you, Scarsfield. You can tell the workers.'

'You're wrong,' Hannah spoke up. 'They appreciate it. They—'

'Appreciate it? Are you soft in the head, girl? They appreciate nothing. Employees need a firm hand. And, like I said, your presence here is no longer required. See to your child. You can keep that girl – what's her name? – Sarah. Ugly little thing, she is. Not the sort of girl I want around me. You're welcome to her. I'll make you an allowance and you can live in the apprentice house. Take in lodgers – do what you like – but I don't want to see you in the mill again. Clear?'

'Very,' Hannah said tightly. 'But I'm afraid you won't get rid of me as easily as that. Goodness knows why, but I care about the mill. Apart from the fact that it's my son's inheritance, I enjoy being involved, I—'

'I don't want you here,' Edmund interrupted. 'And you can send those parasites, the Bramwells, packing, too, and if you're not careful, you'll not be far behind them, though –' he smiled maliciously – 'your son would not be going with you.'

The blood drained from Hannah's face and she swayed, but Edmund took no notice. 'And you, Scarsfield, had better attend to the business of the mill. I'll soon have the wheel turning again, now I'm back. And as for you, Roper, you can go back to your pen pushing. No more fancy trips abroad for you at my expense.'

Josiah's eyes narrowed and his thin lips pursed. But he said nothing. No word of protest or pleading passed his lips. But Hannah could see that the bitterness and resentment from the old days were back in his eyes, one thousand fold.

Edmund Critchlow was making a mistake. A very serious mistake. He had revived all the enmity in Josiah Roper. And, when the news got around the mill, he wouldn't be the only enemy Edmund would make this day.

Banished to her home, Hannah paced the length of her sitting room waiting for Josiah and Ernest to arrive. It had been three days since Edmund's rash ultimatum and, hearing nothing, Hannah was fretting what was happening at the mill. So one evening after she'd seen Edmund leave to return home, she sent Sarah with a message asking Josiah and Ernest to come and see her.

'Please, come and sit down,' she said as they came in. 'Sarah, bring the gentlemen a tankard of ale each and a glass of milk for me, please. Now, tell me,' she said turning to the two men. 'What's happening?'

'Chaos, Hannah,' Ernest said, sitting down, placing his cap on his knee. 'He'll have a strike on his hands, if he doesn't watch out.'

'He's stopped the doctor coming, even though the man is demanding no payment until the troubles are over. He's ordered everyone to go back to work at once,' Josiah began.

'But he's reduced their hourly rate,' Ernest said.

'But . . . but there's no cotton. What are they going to work with?'

She saw Ernest and Josiah exchange a glance then Josiah shrugged. 'He's found some, Hannah. I don't know how or where from but he says he's got enough coming to start the mill up again.'

'He's demanding rent from all his tenants in the village,' Ernest said. 'And back payments.'

'Is he mad?' Hannah was still pacing the floor distractedly. 'How can they pay?' She stopped suddenly and turned to face them. 'Is that his way of getting rid of them? If they can't pay their rent, he's going to turn them out?'

The two men lifted their shoulders helplessly.

'Don't you upset yourself, Hannah. You've your little one to think of.'

'That's exactly who I am thinking of, Ernest. The mill is Eddie's future. If only . . .' She bit her lip. 'Tell me – and be honest with me – has anyone heard anything of Adam? Does anyone know where he is?'

Josiah and Ernest glanced at each other again. 'Well, we didn't know whether to tell you.'

Hannah felt as if her heart stopped. 'What? What is it?'

'We heard he's blockade running.'

Hannah drew in a frightened breath and her eyes were wide with fear. 'That's dangerous, isn't it? He . . . he could get arrested or . . . or even killed, couldn't he?'

480

'Aye, he could,' Ernest said bluntly. 'And if he does, it'll be greedy men like his own father who've sent him to his death in their demand for cotton by whatever means.'

Fifty-One

The mill was deathly silent once more. No wheel turning, no clatter of spinning mules and weaving looms, no sound of voices. The workrooms were deserted. But not now because of a lack of supply of raw material. Somehow, from somewhere, Edmund had obtained some cotton. Inferior quality though it was, it could have kept the water-wheel turning even if only for a little while. But there were no spinners, no weavers, no piecers or doffers. The great mill was empty, its workers on strike against the tyrannical owner. After the months of working together, of helping each other, joining together to fight the hardship that was none of their making, Edmund Critchlow's harsh demands had finally tipped the villagers over the edge. They had seen how the mill could be operated, glimpsed a promising future. Once the war was over and the raw cotton available again, life could be so much better. If they could just hold out, hang on until the war ended. But Edmund's return had dashed all their hopes and dreams. And worst of all, he'd taken revenge on the one person they all acknowledged had been the saviour of them all, of the mill and all its workers.

Hannah.

'They don't like the way he's treated you. Not after all you've done. And as for threatening you over little

Eddie, well, that's the last straw. Folks round here love the little chap. They see him as their hope for the future,' Ernest told her soberly. 'They're calling a strike, Hannah.'

'Oh no, Ernest. They mustn't. Not on my account, please.'

'It's not all about you, love, but even if it was, I wouldn't try to stop them even if I could. I'm with them all the way. I'm one of 'em.'

'But how did they find out. I mean, about me. About him threatening to send me away and keep Eddie here?'

Ernest grinned without a trace of embarrassment. 'I told 'em, lass. I told 'em.' He began to turn away, but hesitated to ask, 'What about the Bramwells?'

'Oh, they're not going anywhere. If we have to go, we're all going together. The Bramwells, Sarah, me – *and* Eddie.' She laughed suddenly. 'Don't forget, I'm the expert at running away from this place.'

'Aye, well, I hope it won't come to that, lass, 'cos it'll be a sad day if we all lose you again.' He turned away abruptly. A bluff, kindly man though he was, he wasn't one to hand out the compliments very often. It embarrassed him, yet he had to let this girl know exactly what she'd come to mean to him and all the villagers. If she went again, he believed there'd be a stream of folk following her up the hill.

By the time the chilly days of November were upon them with a vengeance, the only people at the mill now were a few men gathered near the gate, guarding the entrance to stop anyone going in to work. They stamped their feet against the cold and lit a brazier.

Yet they needn't have stood there in the snow and the biting wind; there were no strike breakers. Their action against Edmund was unanimous – at least amongst the spinners and weavers.

Only two people passed through the gate. Edmund Critchlow and Josiah Roper.

The first was greeted with morose silence, the second ran the gauntlet of questions and threats.

'We thought you was on our side, Roper.'

'You helped keep things going. Why're you siding with him now?'

'Reckons he'll fare better buttering up to the master.'

'We'll remember you, Roper. We won't forget.'

Josiah walked on, head lowered against the taunts. *No*, he thought, *and neither will I. I don't forget. If only you knew!*

On the evening of the third day of the strike, just as Josiah was about to leave for home, Edmund flung open his office door. 'I blame you for all this, Roper. You and Scarsfield and that blasted girl. Look where your pampering has got us. Kindness? To workers? They don't understand it. The whip hand, that's what they understand. That's what they fear and that's what keeps them in line.'

Josiah said nothing. He raised not one word of protest. His silence seemed to enrage Edmund even more. He jabbed his forefinger towards Josiah. 'You're sacked, Roper.'

Josiah didn't move, didn't turn round. He carried on writing slowly and clearly in the ledger. The only betrayal of emotion was a slight tremor in his hand and a line of uncharacteristic shaky handwriting.

'Make your own pay up. Leave tonight. I don't

want to see your face in this office again.' With that parting shot, Edmund slammed the door with such force that it shuddered on its hinges.

Josiah carried on writing for a few moments longer. Then slowly he closed the book, knowing it was for the last time. He put his head on one side, listening for any sound from beyond the door. No doubt Edmund was leaning back in his chair, indulging in his usual early evening tot of whisky, which he kept in his desk drawer.

Josiah put on his coat and stood listening again for a moment. Then he bent and from the very back of a cupboard he took out a slim ledger, which he slipped quickly into the copious pocket of his coat. With one last glance around the room where he'd spent the greater part of his adult life, he was about to snuff out the candle that burned on his desk, when he hesitated. His eyes gleamed as an idea began to form in his mind. He left the office closing the door soundlessly behind him and carrying the candle carefully, shading the flickering light with his hand so that the flame did not blow out.

He began to descend the stairs, then halfway down he stopped. The whole building was silent, yet drifting through the open door at the bottom of the stairs he could hear the voices of the men standing guard at the gate. Slowly, he descended the rest of the way, but instead of going outside, he went into the storeroom on the ground floor that was directly below the offices. No longer was it stuffed to overflowing with bales of raw cotton, but there was enough there for Josiah's purpose.

As he closed the door of the room moments later, the flames were beginning to lick at the few bales of cotton. Josiah hurried out into the yard. He hadn't long. It wouldn't take many minutes for the fire to spread through the whole room, and when that happened someone would be bound to notice, yet perhaps not as quickly as if the mill was still running.

'Here comes the scab,' Daniel sneered as Josiah pushed his way between them. For the first time he was physically jostled, as the five men congregated there surrounded him. He felt a moment's alarm, but he glared at them, betraying nothing of his fear in his eyes.

'Good day, gentlemen,' he said smoothly. 'I'd be obliged if you'd let me pass.'

'Aye, we'll let you pass this time, Roper. But no more. You'll not pass through this gate again. Not until this business is settled.'

Josiah gave a brief nod and they parted to let him through. As he hurried up the hill towards his lodgings on Prentice Row, Josiah was smiling. How prophetic! He had no intention of ever returning to the mill again.

Within twenty minutes, Josiah had flung his few belongings into a bag, collected his money and personal papers from a hiding place beneath the floorboards of his room, and was hurrying along the pathway behind the mill to the bridge over the waterfall and up the steep slope. It was growing colder as he emerged from beneath the trees and gained the narrow path leading up to the railway line. He slipped and slithered on the frosty ground as he climbed.

He glanced back just once at the building below. Already he could see the flames in the window two storeys directly below Edmund's office. With an evil smile he turned away and clambered up to the railway line. He glanced both ways, but it was silent. He peered down in the darkness and stepped onto the track. He trod heavily on an icy, uneven sleeper, and his foot slipped and twisted over. He felt a jab of pain in his ankle and dropped his bag. It fell open, scattering his possessions. Josiah cried out as he fell to his knees, the pain making him feel sick and faint. In the darkness, he scrabbled around for his belongings strewn around him, unaware of the train appearing out of the tunnel and bearing down upon him.

'Fire! There's a fire at the back of the mill.' Hannah had seen it from her windows at the apprentice house and now she came running pell-mell down the hill towards the men at the gate.

'Fire? Where?' Ernest Scarsfield demanded.

'I think it's in the storeroom where the bales are kept.' Breathless, she put her hand on her chest. Her heart was hammering painfully. Distantly, they heard a train, heard its whistle, but none of them was consciously aware of it.

'Is anyone in there?' Hannah demanded. 'Josiah – is he still working?'

'No, he left about half an hour ago.'

There was a brief silence. They all seemed frozen, unable to move.

'But Mr Edmund hasn't come out, has he?' Daniel muttered.

'Oh no!' Hannah gasped. Before anyone could stop her, she had picked up her skirts and was running to the door into the mill.

'Hannah, no!' Daniel cried and began to run after her.

Galvanized into action, Ernest began to issue orders. 'You – get to the village. Fetch all the workers – as many as you can round up. You – find as many buckets as you can. When more get here form a chain . . .'

Hannah had entered the building. But she didn't go to where the fire was, but up the stairs to the office. Already smoke was drifting up the stairwell and into the rooms on the first and second storeys.

'Mr Edmund,' she called, as she felt her way through the smoke, 'Mr Edmund – are you there?'

She almost fell into the outer office. The smoke hadn't reached here yet. Mr Edmund was probably sitting in his office, serenely unaware of the tragedy unfolding two floors below. She rushed across the room and opened the inner door. 'Mr Edmund—'

She stopped, aghast. Edmund was certainly still there, sitting in his chair with a half-empty whisky bottle on the desk. On the floor to one side lay a shattered glass and liquid spilt around it. Edmund was slumped awkwardly in his chair, the side of his face pulled down, his eyes glazed, his arms hanging down limply on either side of him.

She ran to him, lifted his arm and felt for his pulse. It was there, but erratic.

'Hannah, Hannah, where are you?'

'Daniel,' she cried out thankfully. 'In here. In the office. Quick. We must get him out.'

Daniel appeared the doorway.

'I think he's had another seizure. You must help me. We must get him out of here.'

Daniel stood transfixed in the doorway, staring at the helpless man.

'Daniel – come *on*.'

He half turned away, mumbling, 'I'll fetch help.'

'No, there's no time. You'll have to help me lift him. You get on one side.'

Reluctantly, Daniel moved forward. The paralysed man was a dead weight, but they managed to get him upright between them, looping his useless arms around their shoulders and grasping him from each side around his torso.

'We'll never manage him. He's a ton weight,' Daniel protested, but nevertheless he helped Hannah drag Edmund to the door, through the outer office and to the top of the stairs. The smoke was thicker here now and they began to cough. Slowly, they stumbled down the stairs, not daring to stop though their lungs were bursting with the effort and the smoke.

'We'll never make it. Leave him,' Daniel said. 'Why should we save this bastard?'

Hannah didn't answer – she hadn't the breath or the strength.

'Hannah? Daniel? Where are you?' A voice called through the smoke.

'Ernest,' Hannah gasped. 'We're here – on the stairs. Help us.'

In a moment, he was with them, steadying and guiding them to the bottom of the stairs and out into the blissful fresh air. 'Here, Hannah, let me take him.'

Gratefully, Hannah relinquished her hold and Ernest shouldered the weight. Two more men hurried forward, carrying a door on which to lay Edmund.

'Take him home and mind his man calls the doctor,' Ernest instructed. 'Now we'd best get this fire out.'

Hannah glanced around her. Figures were running everywhere, but already they were organized into a working team, though it took a while to get the flames under control. The storeroom was ruined, what little stock there was spoiled. The fire had only spread into the neighbouring rooms, but the smoke had permeated through most of the building.

When the fire itself was out, the exhausted workers stood around the yard in small groups, talking in low voices, glancing at Hannah, who leaned against the wall, breathing hard. Her dress was drenched with sweat, her hair hanging in bedraggled hanks.

'You look all in, lass. Get yourself home and—' Ernest began, but Hannah shook her head.

'No, I must get things organized, Ernest. I'm sure Mr Edmund has had another seizure. And if that's so,' she stood up, squaring her shoulders, 'then I – we – are in charge again. This foolishness has gone on long enough. Get word around all the workers.'

Ernest waved his hands towards the men and women standing about the yard. 'Most of 'em are here.'

Hannah nodded. 'Then call them together. I have something to say.'

In a few moments, Hannah was standing on a crate, the workers gathered around her.

'Thank you for saving the mill.' She glanced around. No one spoke and most of them looked as if they couldn't have cared less whether the mill was saved or not. Yet some inner instinct had driven them to come running when their place of work was endangered. They muttered morosely amongst themselves. Hannah raised her voice. 'I'm going up to the Manor to see how Mr Edmund is. Please – may I ask you all to come back here in the morning, when I shall have some news for you?'

Ernest held out his hand and she stepped down

from the box. 'I was going to tell them to go back to work – that everything would be all right – but I changed my mind. If Mr Edmund is not as bad as he looked and likely to return to work, then it's no good me making them promises that won't be kept, is it?'

'No, lass, it ain't,' he said soberly. 'I won't send a message to him, Hannah, because right at this moment I don't quite know what to think – or say.'

Hannah sighed and glanced around her. The workers were all drifting away now towards their homes, their futures hanging in the balance.

'It's a bad situation, Ernest,' Hannah murmured. 'How can you wish a man harm, and yet—?'

'I know, lass. I know just what you mean.'

There was a pause and then she said, 'I'll see you back here in the morning then.'

'Right you are.'

Fifty-Two

At home, Hannah washed and changed her clothes and then hurried to the Manor. Her breathing was laboured from the effects of the smoke and she would've liked nothing better than to lie down and rest. But she had to find out what had happened to Edmund.

As the butler ushered her into the hall, the doctor was coming down the stairs. His face was grave.

'A word with you, Hannah, if I may?' By now, Dr Barnes was a friend. He'd given generously to the villagers through their time of hardship and was beloved by them all.

'Of course.'

'If you would come this way, sir, madam.' The butler led them towards the morning room.

'How is he?' Hannah asked, as soon as the door closed and the doctor and she were alone.

Dr Barnes shook his head. 'It's a very bad one. It's touch and go if he'll even survive it. And if he does, I doubt he'll make any kind of reasonable recovery. I fear he will be paralysed and speechless this time.'

'I see.'

The doctor glanced at her keenly. 'I'm sorry to hear about the fire at the mill. Has it done much damage?'

'A fair amount, but with a lot of work I think we

can be up and running inside a week.' She pulled a wry face. 'That's if we can get any raw cotton.'

'But the workers are on strike, aren't they?'

'Not for much longer, I hope. I've asked them to meet me at the mill in the morning, but I needed to know how Mr Edmund is before . . . before . . .' She took a deep breath, but the doctor finished her sentence for her. 'Before you could tell them that the strike is over and that they can come back to work.'

She nodded.

'Good,' he said, picking up his bag. 'Some of the families are in a poor way. Their health would've suffered before long and then it's a downward spiral, isn't it? And all your efforts to keep things going through these hard times would've been for nothing.'

Hannah nodded. 'Talking of their health, would you be prepared to come to the mill again? Like you did before?'

'Gladly.' Dr Barnes smiled. 'By the way, it's rumoured that the war in America is coming to an end.'

Hannah clasped her hands together. 'Oh, is it true? Is it really true?'

'I think so,' he began, but as he opened the door for her and they moved into the hall, the butler was opening the front door to two men.

'Is the doctor here?' One began, but then, catching sight of Dr Barnes, he pulled his cap off. 'Ah, there you are, Doctor. Can you come? There's been a terrible accident on the railway track. Some poor devil got hit by a train. It's a nasty mess, Doctor.'

'He's dead?'

'Oh aye. It must have hit him a glancing blow and

493

knocked him flying. He wouldn't've known much about it. I shouldn't think the train driver even realized he'd hit anything. He didn't stop.'

'Did you find the body?'

'Yeah. We work on the line, see?'

'I'll come at once. Have you called the police?'

The two men looked at each other. 'No – we didn't think of that.'

'Then could one of you go and find Constable Jacques and ask him to meet me up there?'

'We found these scattered around him.' The man held out a ledger and a wad of paper money.

'You really ought to have left it for the police,' Dr Barnes murmured.

'We never thought of that, sir, I have to admit. But it was blowing all over the place. We thought we ought to pick it up.'

Hannah gasped and moved forward. 'That's a fortune.' She glanced at the two railway workers. They'd been very honest in handing over the money.

'We couldn't think why anyone should be carrying all that, but we thought – well . . .' The two men glanced at each other. 'We thought he might have family that'd be glad of it.'

Hannah's glance was now on the book they were holding out. 'That . . . that looks like one of our ledgers.' She took it and opened it up.

The lines of figures, all in Josiah Roper's neat handwriting, danced before her eyes. 'Oh,' she gasped and swayed a little.

'And we found this too.' Now one of the men held out a smaller item. 'Maybe it's his.'

Hannah's hand trembled as she reached out to take

the battered wallet the man held. She opened it up, and in a flat voice said, 'It's Josiah Roper's.'

As Hannah had predicted, the mill was running again in under a week, though the supply of cotton – any cotton – was spasmodic. Once they knew that their jobs were safe for the foreseeable future and that Hannah and Ernest Scarsfield were once more in charge, all the workforce had worked around the clock to clean up the damage and get the huge water-wheel turning and the machinery running again.

There was only one mystery that remained: what had Josiah Roper been doing on the railway track with a large amount of cash and a bag containing clothing and personal belongings? Hannah, seated once more behind Edmund's desk, puzzled over the ledger.

'I don't understand it, Ernest. It's just a list of dates and figures. It starts years ago and it's all small amounts. Sometimes just a few shillings, even pence. I can't think what it can be.'

Ernest moved around the desk to stand beside her.

'That first date – there . . .' He pointed. 'That's the year he started here. I remember it, because he came just a month or two after I did.'

'Really?' Hannah turned page after page noting how the figures mounted up in the running total column. She came to the more recent pages. 'Look, he's deducted an amount here and here and – Ernest, those dates coincide with when he went abroad. I know they do, because he was away just before I had Eddie and . . . and I was worried he might not be back in time.'

Ernest leaned on the desk. 'You know what, Hannah,

I reckon he's been thieving from the Critchlows all these years – stashing it away. And then, when he got the chance, he's taken it abroad. I bet somewhere there's a bank with Roper's nice little nest egg.'

Hannah gasped. 'You're right.' She remembered Josiah's reaction when Edmund had put a stop to his trips abroad. 'And I bet this time he was going for good. Ernest, d'you think he started the fire?' She'd be relieved to be able to believe it was the embittered clerk. For a few dreadful moments she'd suspected Daniel, though she hadn't voiced her fears to anyone else.

'It's possible. In fact, I'd say it was probable.' Ernest stroked his moustache thoughtfully. 'But that's something we'll never know. Thank goodness you saw it in time before it got a real hold.'

'Yes,' Hannah murmured absently, her mind still on the book in front of her. She could hardly believe the evidence before her, and yet now the little remarks that Josiah had made over the years all seemed to fall into place. His bitterness and resentment against the Critchlows had festered for years and he'd taken revenge, only to have Fate deal him a final blow.

'I wonder if there's any way of finding out if he has got a bank account abroad somewhere?' Ernest murmured.

'There are some numbers at the back of the ledger. Perhaps there's a clue there, but it doesn't make any sense to me. I'm going to hand it all over to the police, Ernest. Let them sort it out – if they can.'

'Right,' he said, standing up. 'Then I'll be getting on. Oh, by the way, Daniel wants to see you. Shall I tell him to come up?'

Hannah nodded.

A few moments later, Daniel came into the office.

'Hello.' Hannah smiled. 'Are you all right? Have you recovered from the smoke?'

'Yes, thanks. You?'

'I'm fine.'

There was an awkward pause before Daniel cleared his throat and the words came tumbling out, as if he had been rehearsing them and now wanted to get them out before he forgot what he wanted to say. 'Hannah – I've been doing a lot of thinking and I ... I've decided to leave. It's time I put the past behind me. Got on with my own life, but ... but I can't do it here. There's too many memories. Too many ghosts.'

'What about Luke?' Hannah asked gently.

Daniel's chin quivered for a moment then he said hoarsely, 'I shall go to his grave – say "goodbye". I think he'll understand.'

'I'm sure he will,' Hannah whispered.

They gazed at each other. 'Would you ... mind if I came with you?' she asked hesitantly, and then added swiftly, 'Say if you'd rather I didn't. I'll understand.'

He smiled. For the first time in years it was a real smile that lit up his eyes. In that instant he looked a young boy again, so like Luke that Hannah's heart turned over. 'I'd like you to come.'

'Sunday then? After the service?'

Daniel nodded.

Fifty-Three

Sunday was frosty but bright, and after the family service in the schoolroom, they walked to the cemetery, Eddie riding piggy-back style on Daniel's shoulders, and Hannah carrying a small posy of flowers. When they reached Luke's unmarked grave they stood together looking down at the place where the boy they'd both loved lay. Hannah knelt down and placed the posy on the grave.

'I'd've loved to have put a headstone up, but I couldn't afford it,' Daniel murmured. 'Maybe one day.'

'Would you . . . let me have one put up, Daniel?' Hannah asked tentatively, not wanting to destroy the growing understanding between them. 'If . . . if you tell me what wording you'd like, I'll see it's done.'

'Pay for it with Critchlow money, you mean?'

'Well – yes, I suppose it would be.'

Daniel was thoughtful for a moment before he nodded slowly and said, 'I reckon that's the least they could do.'

They were silent for a few moments before Daniel said haltingly, 'I'm letting go of it, Hannah. Like you said. Harbouring bitterness all these years, well, I've only hurt myself – not the man I wanted to. But I reckon Fate's taken a hand and done it for me. He's got his just deserts now.'

'Yes, Daniel, I think he has.'

'What about you? Are you staying here? Running the mill?'

She nodded. 'If I can.'

'Oh, you can, Hannah. I've seen that. It's as if you were born to do it.' He ruffled Eddie's hair. 'Look after yourself – and him. He's a grand little chap.'

'Thank you, Daniel,' she said huskily, taking her son's hand.

'Do you mind if . . . if I just have a few moments alone with . . . with Luke?'

'Of course not. Shall I see you again before you leave?'

Daniel shook his head. 'No, I'm off first thing tomorrow morning on the early train.'

'So . . . so this is goodbye then.'

They stared at each other, and then awkwardly, Daniel bent and kissed her cheek. 'God be with you, Hannah,' he whispered. 'And come and see Luke sometimes for me, won't you?'

'Of course I will. And don't forget to let me have the wording for the headstone. I'll see it's done. I promise.'

He nodded now, unable to speak.

She squeezed his hand and turned and walked away. At the gate, she glanced back, but he was kneeling on the ground, his head bowed, bidding his twin a final farewell.

Hannah set off steadily down the hill towards the apprentice house, slowing her walk to the little boy's pace. She was about to turn into the narrow path that ran behind the houses, when she saw a man standing near the big gate leading into the mill yard. He was tall with dark hair blowing in the wind, and the lower half of his face was covered with a dark, bushy beard. He was half-turned away from her, looking through the gate into the yard, but there was something about the way he was standing, the set of his shoulders . . .

Her heart missed a beat as she continued slowly down the hill towards him, hardly daring to breathe, hardly daring to hope . . .

Eddie pointed at the man, and in his clear, piping voice called, 'Hello.'

Hearing him, the man turned and looked up towards them. He stared for a moment, then wiped the back of his hand across his forehead, as if shaken by the sight of her. She stopped, her eyes wide, her mouth agape.

'Adam,' she whispered. 'Oh, Adam.'

Slowly, he came towards her until they were standing only a couple of paces apart. His gaze was on her face and he reached out and traced the line of her cheek with his finger.

He's safe, she was thinking, *he's safe and he has come back*. Her thoughts were a prayer of thanks.

'I thought you . . . I mean,' his deep voice was husky with emotion, 'we docked in Liverpool and I heard about the fire – that someone was hurt. I was so afraid that you . . .' His voice trailed away and his gaze shifted to the child, quiet now, staring in turn at the man who was a stranger to him. With a sad little smile, Adam squatted down in front of his son. His voice shook as he murmured, 'I should have believed you, Anna. Can you ever forgive me?'

'There's nothing to forgive. It's me who should ask forgiveness . . .' she began, but his attention was wholly on his son now. The little boy reached out his chubby hand and stroked the man's beard. It tickled his hand and Eddie chortled with delight.

'And what's your name, young man?'

'Ed-ward,' the little boy answered with careful deliberation.

Adam nodded and murmured, 'Edward Critchlow of Wyedale Mill. Yes, it has a good sound to it. And you're going to make a fine master one day, aren't you?'

She hardly dared to ask, but she had to know. 'Are you . . . are you back to stay? Have you come home, Adam?'

He straightened up and held out both his hands to her, palms upwards in supplication. 'If you'll both have me . . . ?'

And then she was in his arms and they were kissing and laughing and hugging, with Eddie clutching at their legs and laughing too. There was so much to say and yet there was no need now for anything to be said at all.

Adam was home.

Fairfield Hall
Margaret Dickinson

A matter of honour. A sense of duty. A time for courage.

Ruthlessly ambitious Ambrose Constantine is determined that his daughter, Annabel, shall marry into the nobility. A self-made trawler owner and fish merchant, he has only his wealth to buy his way into Society.

When Annabel's secret meetings with a young man employed at her father's offices stop suddenly, she finds that Gilbert has mysteriously disappeared. Heartbroken, she finds solace with her grandparents on their Lincoln-shire farm, but her father will not allow her to bury herself in the countryside and enlists the help of a business connection to launch his daughter into Society.

During the London Season, Annabel is courted by James Lyndon, the Earl of Fairfield, whose country estate is only a few miles from her grandfather's farm. Believing herself truly loved at last, Annabel accepts his offer of marriage. It is only when she arrives at Fairfield Hall that she realises the true reason behind James's proposal and the part her scheming father has played.

Through the years that follow, Annabel will know both heartache and joy, but the birth of her son should secure the future of the Fairfield Estate. Yet there are others who lay claim to the inheritance in a feud that will not be resolved until the trenches of a bitter world war.

ISBN: 978-1-4472-3724-2

_mm_

FOR MORE ON

MARGARET DICKINSON

sign up to receive our

SAGA NEWSLETTER

Packed with **features, competitions, authors'
and readers' letters** and **news of exclusive events,**
it's a must-read for every Margaret Dickinson fan!

Simply fill in your details below and tick to confirm that you would
like to receive saga-related news and promotions and return to us at
Pan Macmillan, Saga Newsletter, 20 New Wharf Road, London, N1 9RR.

NAME _____

ADDRESS _____

_____

_____ POSTCODE _____

EMAIL _____

☐ *I would like to receive saga-related news and promotions (please tick)*

*You can unsubscribe at any time in writing or through our website where you can also see
our privacy policy which explains how we will store and use your data.*